OXFORD WORLD'S CLASSICS

YOUNG GOODMAN BROWN
AND OTHER TALES

NATHANIEL HAWTHORNE was born in 1804 in Salem, Massachusetts, a descendant of the William Hathorne who had emigrated to New England with the first generation of Puritan settlers in 1630. Hawthorne's interest in the history and legend of his region was revealed in his early stories, which began to appear in print in the 1830s. New England Puritanism and its legacy provided Hawthorne with the means of exploring many of the themes that concerned him deeply, among them the conflict between patriarchal authority and the impulse to a variety of freedoms, including the freedom of the artist. Though he immersed himself in the early literature of New England, Hawthorne's own writings are peculiarly modern in some of their leading characteristics. One is the self-reflexiveness of narratives which make the telling a part of the tale. Another is the concern with signifying practices, with the relationships between objects (a Red Cross, a Black Veil, a Scarlet Letter) and what they come to signify.

Never willing to submit to the conventions of the realist novel, when he abandoned the short story and the sketch for longer works, Hawthorne claimed the imaginative freedom of the romance. His first—*The Scarlet Letter*—was published in 1850 and brought him immediate critical recognition, if not financial success. In quick succession he completed two more romances—*The House of the Seven Gables* (1851) and *The Blithedale Romance* (1852)—and consolidated his position as a major writer of his day. After his appointment as consul at Liverpool and Manchester in 1853 Hawthorne produced no more fiction until 1860, when *The Marble Faun* was published. Returning to Massachusetts in that year after travels in France and Italy, he struggled to finish other romances but left them uncompleted at his death in 1864.

BRIAN HARDING is a Senior Lecturer in the English Department of the University of Birmingham. He is the author of *American Literature in Context II, 1830–1865* (1982).

OXFORD WORLD'S CLASSICS

For over 100 years Oxford World's Classics have brought
readers closer to the world's great literature. Now with over 700
titles—from the 4,000-year-old myths of Mesopotamia to the
twentieth century's greatest novels—the series makes available
lesser-known as well as celebrated writing.

The pocket-sized hardbacks of the early years contained
introductions by Virginia Woolf, T. S. Eliot, Graham Greene,
and other literary figures which enriched the experience of reading.
Today the series is recognized for its fine scholarship and
reliability in texts that span world literature, drama and poetry,
religion, philosophy and politics. Each edition includes perceptive
commentary and essential background information to meet the
changing needs of readers.

OXFORD WORLD'S CLASSICS

NATHANIEL HAWTHORNE

Young Goodman Brown
and Other Tales

Edited with an Introduction and Notes by
BRIAN HARDING

OXFORD
UNIVERSITY PRESS

OXFORD
UNIVERSITY PRESS

Great Clarendon Street, Oxford OX2 6DP

Oxford University Press is a department of the University of Oxford.
It furthers the University's objective of excellence in research, scholarship,
and education by publishing worldwide in

Oxford New York

Athens Auckland Bangkok Bogotá Buenos Aires Calcutta
Cape Town Chennai Dar es Salaam Delhi Florence Hong Kong Istanbul
Karachi Kuala Lumpur Madrid Melbourne Mexico City Mumbai
Nairobi Paris São Paulo Shanghai Singapore Taipei Tokyo Toronto Warsaw

with associated companies in Berlin Ibadan

Oxford is a registered trade mark of Oxford University Press
in the UK and in certain other countries

Published in the United States
by Oxford University Press Inc., New York

Introduction, Note on the Texts, Select Bibliography,
and Explanatory Notes © Brian Harding 1987

The moral rights of the author have been asserted

Database right Oxford University Press (maker)

This selection first published 1987 as a World's Classics paperback
Reissued as an Oxford World's Classics paperback 1998

British Library Cataloguing in Publication Data

Data available

Library of Congress Cataloging in Publication Data

Hawthorne, Nathaniel, 1804–1864.
Young Goodman Brown and other tales.
(Oxford world's classics)
Bibliography: p.
I. Harding, Brian.   II. Title.
PS1852.H37   1987   813'.3   87–11119

ISBN 0–19–283600–5

5 7 9 10 8 6 4

Printed in Great Britain by
Cox & Wyman Ltd.
Reading, Berkshire

CONTENTS

Introduction   vii

Note on the Text   xxxi

A Chronology of Nathaniel Hawthorne   xxxii

THE GENTLE BOY (1832)   3

MY KINSMAN, MAJOR MOLINEUX (1832)   37

ROGER MALVIN'S BURIAL (1832)   56

THE CANTERBURY PILGRIMS (1833)   76

THE SEVEN VAGABONDS (1833)   86

THE GREY CHAMPION (1835)   103

YOUNG GOODMAN BROWN (1835)   111

WAKEFIELD (1835)   124

THE MAYPOLE OF MERRY MOUNT (1836)   133

THE MINISTER'S BLACK VEIL (1836)   144

DR HEIDEGGER'S EXPERIMENT (1837)   158

ENDICOTT AND THE RED CROSS (1838)   168

THE BIRTHMARK (1843)   175

THE CELESTIAL RAILROAD (1843)   192

THE CHRISTMAS BANQUET (1844)   209

EARTH'S HOLOCAUST (1844)   228

THE ARTIST OF THE BEAUTIFUL (1844)   248

DROWNE'S WOODEN IMAGE (1844)   272

RAPPACCINI'S DAUGHTER (1844)   285

ETHAN BRAND (1850)   316

Explanatory Notes   333

Select Bibiography   382

Textual Notes   392

INTRODUCTION

IN November 1835, over the ascription 'Ashley A. Royce', the *New-England Magazine* carried a story about a tormented young writer who burned all his manuscripts in a fit of revulsion against his own literary productions. As the title—'The Devil in Manuscript'—suggests, the writer has convinced himself that the fiend has become involved—or is present—in his works. In a declamatory and extravagant style worthy of an Edgar Allan Poe protagonist confessing his guilt-laden madness, Hawthorne's writer, who has 'taken the name of Oberon', cries: 'Oh! I have a horror of what was created in my own brain, and shudder at the manuscripts.'[1] His self-loathing is such that he resolves, 'Not a scorched syllable shall escape!' He therefore sets fire to the manuscripts, only to discover that when 'the fiend has gone forth by night' (via the blazing chimney) the whole town has caught fire. In the words of the narrator—who describes himself as Oberon's friend, yet is given to deflationary irony in his account of the artist's suffering—'His frenzy took the hue of joy, and with a wild gesture of exultation, he leaped almost to the ceiling of the chamber.' Oberon's joy, it seems, was caused by the literal application of a commonplace metaphor. The tale depends for its point on the working of a fairly obvious figure of speech as Oberon exclaims: 'Huzza! Huzza! My brain has set the town on fire!'

Ashley A. Royce was a pen-name adopted by Nathaniel Hawthorne. Oberon was a nickname he had used in letters to his friend Horatio Bridge after they had left Bowdoin College in 1825. This tale, though its tone flickers from the melodramatic to the bathetic, has an obvious autobiographical reference, for Hawthorne repeatedly told the story of his own burned manuscripts. He told it in a personal letter to two

---

[1] *The Snow-Image and Uncollected Tales, The Centenary Edition of the Works of Nathaniel Hawthorne*, ed. William Charvat *et al.* (Columbus: Ohio State University Press, 1962–), xi (1974), 171. All subsequent references to the *Works* will be to this edition and will be abbreviated to *CE*.

literary friends in December 1841, when he said that he had burned 'whole quires of manuscript stories, in past times'.[2] Later, he told it publicly and made it part of his own legend, in the Preface to the 1851 edition of *Twice-told Tales*, when he made claims—with wry, self-deprecatory humour—for the superiority of the immolated tales over his other works in terms of brilliance. Fact and fiction are hard to disentangle here, not just in the matter of the destruction of the manuscripts, but also in the more significant matter of the diabolic possession. In 'The Devil in Manuscript' Oberon explains that he believes, or—oddly—'would believe, if I chose', that 'there is a devil in this pile of blotted papers'. The devil is present, according to Oberon, in 'that conception, in which I endeavoured to embody the character of a fiend, as represented in our traditions and the written records of witchcraft'. For the writer, then, to put the fiend in his works by *imagining* him may be to give that devil some sort of reality and power. Oberon sees an analogy between the way in which the devil of tradition sucked away the happiness of those who subjected themselves to his power and the way in which his own ambitions as a writer have destroyed his pleasure in life. In his words:

I am surrounding myself with shadows, which bewilder me, by aping the realities of life. They have drawn me aside from the beaten path of the world, and led me into a strange sort of solitude—a solitude in the midst of men.[3]

Thus the writer's subjection to the devil takes the form of his entrapment in the world of his own imagination and his exclusion from the 'real' world.

When Hawthorne wrote to Longfellow to explain the obscurity of his life in the years between leaving college and the publication of his first collection of tales in 1837, he used the metaphor that he had used in 'The Devil in Manuscript', and he used it without any ironic detachment: 'By some witchcraft or other—for I really cannot assign any reasonable why and wherefore—I have been carried apart from the main

---

[2] *CE*, xv, 600.
[3] *CE*, xi, 172.

current of life, and find it impossible to get back again.'[4] He went on to say that he had not lived 'but only dreamed about living'. Witchcraft, dreaming, the enchantment that separates from life, diabolic possession and potentially dangerous (inflammatory) writing: this concatenation of ideas is at the heart of Hawthorne's thought about the meaning of fiction and its creation.[5]

Witchcraft was, literally, a theme of Hawthorne's first projected collection of stories, which was to have had the title 'Seven Tales of My Native Land', according to the recollection of his sister Elizabeth,[6] who believed that the tales were complete as early as 1825. Certainly, the only tale definitely intended for the volume that survived the conflagration in its original form—'The Hollow of the Three Hills'—bears out Elizabeth's statement, while 'Alice Doane's Appeal', a revised version of the 'Alice Doane' intended for 'Seven Tales',[7] not only includes a Gothic story of wizardry and its evil effects but also evokes the Salem witch trials in its frame narrative, which takes the listeners and the reader to Gallows Hill. Hawthorne's personal sense of his family's guilt in the matter of the witch trials would be given a very public, even histrionic, expression in the 'Custom-House' sketch that prefaced *The Scarlet Letter* in 1850. There the speaker takes on himself the inherited shame from that ancestor John Hathorne who had held pre-trial hearings at Salem Village and had committed several of the accused for trial. A more covert acknowledgement of his family's involvement was made some fifteen years earlier in 'Young Goodman Brown', another tale that dealt with the infamous episode in New England history.

[4] *CE*, xv, 251.

[5] Numerous scholars have discussed Hawthorne's concern with the relationship between witchcraft and the imagination, among them Stein (1953), Millicent Bell (1962), Baym (1976), Turner (1980). On the dream in relation to Hawthorne's art, see Pattison (1967) and Gollin (1978; 1979). Dryden (1977) has made the most elaborate investigation of the meaning of enchantment in Hawthorne's works.

[6] See Julian Hawthorne, *Nathaniel Hawthorne and His Wife* (1884), i, 124.

[7] The most useful study of the projected but unpublished early collections is still Adkins (1945). For a fuller treatment see Weber (1973), and for a succinct statement on the probable contents of each volume see Baym (1976).

There is no uncertainty of tone in 'Young Goodman Brown'. Whereas in 'The Devil in Manuscript' the diabolism was qualified by a bantering tone,[8] 'Young Goodman Brown' is sombre throughout. Yet there is in this tale an uncertainty of a more disturbing kind for the reader; uncertainty about the status of the events described in the narrative. The story begins definitely enough, with a simplicity and clarity of style that might well have appealed to the young Ernest Hemingway when he was seeking the 'simple declarative sentence'. The verbs are unequivocal; they tell us what happened in the (here trivial) action. Young Brown 'came forth' into the village street and 'put his head back . . . to exchange a parting kiss with his young wife'. The wife 'thrust her own pretty head into the street' and called her husband. Nothing could be plainer, or more banal, than this domestic incident in the Puritan Salem Village. But the light of common day soon gives way to obscurity and the unknown. Faith has obviously experienced the sort of disquieting dream to which—she says—a lone woman is vulnerable. Her husband, for all his trite confidence ('Say thy prayers . . . go to bed at dusk . . . and no harm will come to thee'), is clearly no stranger to the realm of dreams, for he suspects that Faith's anxiety springs from a premonitory dream in which his own evil purpose has been revealed to her.

In the domain of the dark forest at least the initial verbs of action seem unambiguous. Brown 'beheld' a decently dressed man who 'arose' and 'walked' at the young man's side. But the noun 'figure' in the phrase 'figure of a man', though apparently harmless and neutral, will prove to be one of the words in which the problem of perception is focused, for 'figure'[9] will turn out to be a synonym of 'shape' and—by implication—both will be distinguished from 'substance'. The problematic status of Brown's perceptions will be indistinguishable to the reader from the problem of the status

---

[8] On the tone of the Oberon pieces see Turner (1980, p. 75) and Colacurcio (1984, p. 492).

[9] See below, note to p. 121. The terms used in Salem witchcraft trials, as Hawthorne knew from his sources, were 'apparition', 'spectre', 'appearance', 'likeness'.

of the events narrated, for both relate to the role of the narrator. As Brown and his companion journey into the heart of darkness, the verbs of perception are qualified. The second traveller was about fifty years old, 'as nearly as could be discerned': discerned by Brown, we assume, but when we are told that they 'might have been taken for father and son', we might well ask 'by whom?' since there were, of course, no witnesses, unless the narrator was lurking in the bushes, uncertain of what he saw, or imagining the uncertainty of any possible witnesses. The old gentleman's staff 'might almost be seen' (by Brown, presumably) to twist and wriggle like a living serpent, but this 'must have been an ocular deception'. Is this Brown's scepticism, or the narrator's? Is the narrator distancing himself from Brown's credulousness, or expressing Brown's doubts? The question of the narrator's distance takes on greater urgency when we are told that Brown 'recognized' Goody Cloyse, far in the wilderness at nightfall. The historical Goody Cloyse was accused of witchcraft in 1692 on evidence no different in kind from Brown's vision of her. Her dialogue with the devil, implicating 'that unhanged witch, Goody Cory', must have taken place before 22 September 1692, for the historical Martha Cory *was* hanged as a witch on that day. The conversation is recorded by a narrator whose word we must surely trust, unless it should prove that he is merely reporting what Brown thought he overheard. The narrator does not commit himself on the other voices Brown hears. One voice is 'like the deacon's', while the reply comes in the 'solemn old tones of the minister'. However, our narrator seems to throw the weight of his authority behind Brown when he says—of the figures gathered for the witches' sabbath—'in truth' they were, as Goodman Brown said, 'a grave and dark-clad company'. Though he is merely reporting rumour about the governor's lady ('some affirm' that she was there, but how could they, unless 'some' were present?), he concedes that 'at least there were high dames well known to her'. More shocking, even, is the narrator's unqualified statement that the veiled female was led forward to be initiated into diabolic rites by Goody Cloyse and Martha Carrier, who had 'the Devil's promise to be queen of hell'. The unfortunate

Martha Carrier was hanged for a witch in 1692. The devil's promise to her is recorded by Cotton Mather in his *Wonders of the Invisible World*, a thoroughly credulous account of the witchcraft episode written by a ruthless persecutor of 'witches', and our narrator speaks in *his* words.

Having also spoken in Mather's words when he refers to Martha Carrier as a 'rampant hag', the narrator seems to throw off earlier doubts and to record the events of the witches' sabbath as facts. What the dark figure 'said' is reported verbatim, and the responses of his audience of sinners are noted unequivocally: they 'turned, and when commanded to look at each other, they did so'. When welcomed to the communion of evil, they—'the fiend worshippers'—actually repeated the devil's word 'welcome . . . in one cry of despair and triumph'. Yet this definiteness, too, is undermined by the narrator's reference to the 'dark *figure*' and 'sable *form*' who speaks, and his statement that the worshippers were seen 'flashing forth, *as it were*, in a sheet of flame'. Small wonder, then, that one careful reader of the tale has come to the conclusion that the narrator does not seem to fully understand what he sees.[10]

A final return to the simple declarative statement is more convincing, for there is no doubt at all in anyone's mind that when Brown 'came slowly into the street of Salem village' he was a changed man. He undoubtedly 'shrank' from the minister, who passed for a 'venerable saint' and plainly did snatch a child from the grasp of Goody Cloyse. Even more definitely, he 'passed on without a greeting', having 'looked sternly and sadly' into his wife's face when she came, bursting with joy at the sight of him. But this clarity is followed by a notable example of what Ivor Winters called Hawthorne's formula of alternative possibilities.[11] Addressing the reader, the narrator asks: 'Had Goodman Brown fallen asleep in the forest, and only dreamed a wild dream of a witch-meeting?' The reply—'Be it so, if you will'—throws responsibility for deciding the status of the events on to the reader, yet, in the

---

[10] The reader in question is Doubleday in his excellent *Hawthorne's Early Tales* (1972), p. 205.

[11] Winters (1937, repr. 1947), p. 170.

words of one of the most astute commentators on the tale, Hawthorne seems to have 'purposely led his readers astray or . . . at least allowed them to go astray'.[12] Sheldon Liebman's analysis of the 'dissimulated point of view' in this story (and, by extension, in many of the short stories) offers us a means of understanding Hawthorne's technique. The point of view (he argues) shifts imperceptibly from narrator to character, so that the reader sees through the eyes of the character, even when he thinks he is seeing through the narrator's. Consequently, the story forces the reader to undergo the very temptations (of believing the 'evidence' so dubiously presented) that Brown himself has to endure. The focus of the art of the story thus becomes the reader's response, for if the reader does decide that Brown *really* saw the people of Salem Village at the ceremony in the forest, then the reader has listened to the devil's voice, and has been welcomed to the communion of lost souls. Putting it another way, Taylor Stoehr has suggested that 'Young Goodman Brown', with its obvious concern about the nature of belief in imagined realities and the status of such realities, is about itself. That is to say, since the reader has constantly to bear in mind that it is only a fiction he is engrossed in, he may not lose sight of the fact that the mode of the story is 'supposing', not 'believing'.[13] Not only in this tale, but generally in his fictions, according to this account of Hawthorne's theory of mimesis, the reader is required to distinguish between the products of the imagination and natural or 'real' truths. Fictions, in Hawthorne's works, are then the equivalents of dreams and visions.

'Young Goodman Brown' is now undoubtedly among the best known of Hawthorne's tales. It is included in all selections from his short stories and in the major anthologies of nineteenth-century American literature. By common consent, it is one of Hawthorne's most powerful tales, perhaps even the most impressive of his short works. Yet when he came to make his own selection from his already-published

[12] Liebman (1975), p. 157.
[13] Stoehr (1969), p. 403.

pieces for the first collection of his writings—the *Twice-told Tales* of 1837—Hawthorne passed over this story. Even more surprising is the fact that he again rejected the tale when he was invited to prepare a new collection in 1845, even though Evert Duyckinck, who had suggested the idea of a new volume, had listed 'Young Goodman Brown' among the stories he thought suitable.[14] Only when it became clear that *Mosses from an Old Manse* (1846) would run to two volumes did Hawthorne allow the story to be included. When we consider that he selected such lightweight pieces as 'Little Annie's Ramble' and 'The Vision of the Fountain' for the first edition of *Twice-told Tales*, and further that he told Longfellow (to whom he sent a copy) that the volume contained 'such articles as seemed best worth offering to the public a second time',[15] we may well draw the conclusion that Hawthorne's notion of his achievement as a writer and his valuation of his own works were very different from that which is now current.

An alternative explanation is that when he made his début as an author (his magazine pieces had regularly been published anonymously or pseudonymously) Hawthorne wanted above all to avoid the possibility of alienating his readers by presenting them with puzzling or difficult stories. In the view of one eminent Hawthorne scholar, *Twice-told Tales* was intended to provide a variety of theme and mood and, thus, to offer something for everyone. Hawthorne, so J. Donald Crowley believes,[16] wanted to become a genuinely popular writer in an age that had inherited (from the eighteenth-century Scottish Common Sense philosophers) a widespread suspicion of the imagination and (from the seventeenth-century Puritans) a hostility towards the arts. If Hawthorne's preface to the 1851 edition of *Twice-told Tales* can be believed, in 1837 he felt that he had no public to address. When, in that preface, he spoke of opening an intercourse with the world, he can be taken to have meant

[14] See *CE*, xvi, 88, n. 4 to Hawthorne's letter to Duyckinck dated 7 April 1845.

[15] *CE*, xv, 249.

[16] Crowley, 1973, pp. 50, 43; and 1968, p. 86.

establishing a bond of sympathy between himself and his readers. If—as Professor Crowley believes—the need to create an audience for his works was a matter of urgency throughout Hawthorne's career, then the autobiographical essays and personal introductions to his volumes, from 'The Old Manse' on, can be seen as devices by means of which he 'sought to guarantee the reliability of his fiction through the presentation of a reliable narrator—himself'. It follows, in this interpretation, that a leading characteristic of Hawthorne's fiction is a 'consistent narrative voice or presence', since the narrator 'mediates' between the author and his audience.[17] Certainly, the persona Hawthorne created or developed in his prefaces performs such a mediatory role in the sense that he addresses the reader as a friend and assumes (within strict limits) a sort of intimacy with that reader. But the narrative presence in the tales—and the narrative voice— may be more elusive than this formula suggests.

Had the early tales been published in collections, as Hawthorne planned, rather than separately, as the harsh realities of the market determined, the narrative presence would have been easier to establish. Before Horatio Bridge's financial guarantee to the publishers made the publication of *Twice-told Tales* possible in 1837, Hawthorne had planned two collections of his short stories to follow the abortive 'Seven Tales of My Native Land'. The first of these projected volumes was to have been called 'Provincial Tales'. Though the full list of contents is now a matter for speculation, it seems certain that 'The Gentle Boy', 'Roger Malvin's Burial', and 'My Kinsman, Major Molineux' were to have been included, for each was mentioned in the acknowledgement that Samuel Goodrich, the intended publisher, sent to Hawthorne when he received the material for the volume in December 1829. When it became clear that the project would not come to fruition, Goodrich used each of these tales in *The Token*, an annual published in Boston, an appropriate place for New England tales.[18]

---

[17] Crowley, 1970, p. 1; 1968, p. 86; 1971, p. 87.

[18] Goodrich's reply to Hawthorne is dated 19 January 1830. See *CE*, xv, 200, n. 1. Goodrich also mentions 'Alice Doane', the early version of 'Alice Doane's Appeal'. On the fate of the 'Provincial Tales' collection, see Adkins (1945), pp. 127–31.

Since three of the stories that were clearly intended for the collection began with an historical introduction, this may have been a characteristic of all the 'Provincial Tales'. In 'The Gentle Boy', before the story of Ilbrahim begins 'on the evening of the autumn day' in 1659 on which the first executions of the Quakers took place in Massachusetts, the narrator outlines the history of the Quaker attempt to preach their faith in Puritan New England. A reference to 'our pious forefathers' in the second paragraph of the tale obviously assumes that narrator and reader share a New England heritage, but since the piety of the forefathers manifested itself in the 'fines, imprisonments, and stripes, liberally distributed' among the Quakers, any sense of a common heritage that might be felt by story-teller and his audience must be troubled. In the first published version of the tale, the narrator follows his mention of the martyrdom of the Quakers with a paragraph extenuating the bigotry of his (and his readers') forefathers. Though conceding that 'an indelible stain of blood' was on the hands of all those who were responsible for the executions, the narrator explains that the Puritans who settled in New England had left their homes, and the relative comfort and safety of England, in order to establish a community where they would be free to exercise their own mode of worship. They had no intention of encouraging universal liberty of conscience and, moreover, the threat to their religion was conceived by them as a threat to the very survival of their government. Assuming the role of an unbiased, equitable commentator who nevertheless understands the Puritans, the narrator decides that 'it would be hard to say whether justice did not authorize' their determination to keep their refuge in the New World safe from those who lacked 'the prescribed title to admittance'.

When Hawthorne revised this story for inclusion in *Twice-told Tales* he omitted his second paragraph with its lengthy extenuation of Puritan bigotry. He also omitted the concluding sentence of the tale in which the narrator pronounced himself glad of the triumph of the Puritans' better nature in their tolerance and indulgence of the Quaker woman Catharine—years after the events that brought about the death of her son Ilbrahim. In its first version, the tale closed with the narrator's 'kindlier feeling for the fathers' of his 'native land'; yet since he had just stated that the Puritan kindness gave cheaply bought self-esteem, even this affirmation was not without irony. Earlier in the tale, when telling of Catharine's intrusion into the Puritan meeting house and her trespass into the pulpit, the narrator accuses her—in the 1832 version of the text—of usurping 'a station to which she had no title'. Here, as in the earlier allusion to the Quakers' lack of 'title', the narrator seems to speak for the Puritan forefathers and to voice their legalistic conception of religious rights, as well as their sexual prejudices. Even more striking is his opening reference to the 'mystic and pernicious principles' of the Quakers, for the word 'pernicious'[19] is exactly the term used by the Puritan leaders. If the narrator is merely reporting the reputation of the Quakers, he nevertheless seems to stand close indeed to his forefathers, but the teller is elusive in this tale. In the first version he offers extenuation of the forefathers' bigotry, yet tells a story which clearly shows that both Puritan bigots and Quaker fanatics are incapable of responding to the divine in man—to Ilbrahim, 'sweet infant of the skies'. Even when the narrative seems neutral, there are ambiguities that bring alive the problem of the narrator's stance. Preaching on the subject of the Quakers, the Puritan minister 'gave a history of that sect, and a description of their tenets, in which error predominated, and prejudice distorted the aspect of what was true'. The syntactical ambiguity is entirely appropriate for a narrative that finds error and prejudice both in the Quakers and in the Puritan view of their behaviour.

Hawthorne's revision of 'The Gentle Boy' has been interpreted as a clarification of the terms of the tragedy. To Seymour Gross, the changes made in the *Twice-told Tales* version seem to achieve a firmer point of view and a better balance between Puritan and Quaker.[20] Certainly the revised tale is more balanced, but the omissions have the apparent

[19] For Hawthorne's source, see below, note to p. 3.
[20] Gross (1954), p. 196.

effect of disengaging the narrator from the tale, since the openly evaluative and judgemental statements are removed, to be replaced by implication, and this hardly produces a 'firmer' point of view. 'The Gentle Boy' is the story of a Quaker mother, Catharine, who sacrifices her love for her own son, Ilbrahim, to her sense of her divine calling. When he doubled the examples of such fanaticism, introducing the figure of an elderly Quaker who leaves his daughter on her death-bed to answer the call of the voice of his Lord, Hawthorne put in the foreground of his tale the question of the authority of those voices by which men feel themselves inspired. To balance the Quaker triumph over humanity (or over the divine in man) we are shown the diabolic cruelty of the Puritan infants whose Devil is that of their authoritarian fathers. A story about voices and authority is told by a narrator who sometimes speaks in voices not his own, and who speaks in an implied context of histories (Sewel's Quaker and Mather's Puritan stories)[21] that are—in their contrasting biases—as prejudiced as the sermon of the Puritan minister within the tale. In inviting his readers to ponder all authorities, the implied author is also compelling his audience to ponder the status of all stories (histories, scriptures, fictions). Yet when Hawthorne added a preface to the 1851 edition of *Twice-told Tales*, he claimed that his stories and sketches had 'none of the abstruseness of idea, or obscurity of expression, which mark the communication of a solitary mind with itself'. In arguing that the style of the volume was that of 'man of society', he went so far as to state that 'Every sentence, so far as it embodies thought or sensibility, may be understood and felt by anybody, who will give himself the trouble to read it, and will take up the book in a proper mood'.[22] Since the collection included 'The Gentle Boy' as well as 'Little Annie's Ramble', Hawthorne's retrospective comment can hardly have been ingenuous.

'Roger Malvin's Burial' was not collected in 1837; like 'Young Goodman Brown' it was passed over until the 1846 *Mosses from an Old Manse*, though it was reprinted in the

[21] For details, see below, notes to pp. 5, 106.
[22] *CE*, ix, 6.

Democratic Review in 1843. The other undoubted 'Provincial Tales' story, 'My Kinsman, Major Molineux', had to wait until *The Snow-Image* (1852) before it took its place in a collection of tales. Both stories begin with brief sketches in New England history and both have an obvious appropriateness for a New England audience. To establish the 'proper mood' in which either story can be understood by anybody who takes the trouble to read it is, however, difficult. The narrator in the former tale begins by explaining that 'certain circumstances' concerning the frontier story of Lovewell's Fight must be cast 'judicially' into the shade[23] if the imagination is to see much to admire in 'the heroism of a little band' of New Englanders who helped drive back the Indians from the frontier. In the latter story, the narrator asks the reader to 'dispense with' the account of the train of circumstances that produced the events (intrigue and riot) with which the tale will deal. Both stories begin, then, with the suppression of relevant information, yet both allow themselves to be read as patriotic tales of development towards nationhood, in extending the frontier and in resisting the tyranny of British rule. Yet if Robin Molineux's bewilderment in moonlit Boston can be taken as a stage in his growth towards an independence emblematic of that about to be achieved by his country, 'Roger Malvin's Burial' is a story about the disastrous personal consequences of casting certain circumstances in the shade, for that is precisely what Reuben Bourne does when he tells his story of the burial of Dorcas's father.

Another New England story that may have been intended for 'Provincial Tales' is 'The Grey Champion', which was first published in the *New-England Magazine* in 1835. This story, too, begins with a historical sketch. In it, the narrator discusses the threat posed by James II to 'our liberties' and 'our religion'. In the opinion of one critic, the repeated use of 'our' suggests that Hawthorne was desperate to establish a bond with his readers.[24] In writing of 'our free soil' under

---

[23] In *The Token* and editions of *Twice-told Tales* before 1854 the word was 'judiciously'.

[24] Becker (1971), p. 32.

threat from invading mercenaries, Hawthorne—in this view—
was assuming the role of the public poet who celebrated the
traditional liberties of New England. Other commentators
have noted that the tale's peroration, in which the revolt
in 1689 against Governor Andros and the 'Popish Monarch'
is linked to Lexington and Bunker Hill, is in the mode
of celebratory oratory that derived the eighteenth-century
spirit of political independence from the seventeenth-
century Puritan spirit of religious freedom.[25] Yet
though Hawthorne's narrator sees the New England patriots
of Revolutionary times as the inheritors of the 'strong and
sombre features' of their Puritan forefathers, and though the
reader is clearly supposed to have descended from the Puritan
fathers who settled in Massachusetts, the tale is not an
unambiguous celebration of the great tradition of American
liberty. Here, as in 'The Gentle Boy', the 'pious fierceness' of
the first generations of New England Puritans is remembered.
The narrator alludes to the slaughter of the Narragansett
Indians in King Philip's War, though that reference can
hardly flatter the reader's sense of his ancestral past. What is
more, there is a marked discrepancy between the rhetoric of
the concluding paragraph and the discourse of the tale, for the
invocation of the legend of the 'Angel of Hadley' is not only
a 'lapse in historical logic',[26] but also a clear indication that
the 'Champion'—and the spirit—of New England will not
stop short of killing. The Champion's words in the tale—'I
have stayed the march of a king'—and the narrator's allusion
to the Court's sentence—'too mighty for the age, but glorious
in all after times'—are euphemisms for an act which, if
justified by the beliefs of the judges, was nevertheless bloody.
Here, as in the later but no less ambiguous 'Endicott and the
Red Cross', it is clear that the narrator speaks in more than
one voice. In both of these 'celebrations' of New England
heroes, the complexity of the story is at odds with the
narrator's interpretation of it. If there is a consistent narrative
presence in these early tales, it is consistently problematic.

[25] See, for example, Doubleday (1972), p. 88 and McWilliams (1984),
p. 55.
[26] The phrase is McWilliams's.

Had the projected 'Provincial Tales' volume materialized, the New England past would surely have provided thematic coherence for the collection. The individual tales would have reinforced each other in what Michael Colacurcio has called the 'significant temporality of their own local settings'.[27] It is even possible that Hawthorne intended to present the tales in chronological order so that, if 'The Maypole of Merry Mount' was intended for the volume, they would have moved from 1628, the date of the Mount Wollaston incident, to 1765, the date of the Boston Stamp Act riots which feature in 'My Kinsman, Major Molineux'. But Hawthorne's 'intractably historical'[28] stories are—some of them—also intractably resistant to holistic interpretation; they are, in Barthes' sense of the term, '*writerly*'[29], which is to say that they oblige the reader to become a co-producer rather than a consumer of the text. Indeed, in one of the tales intended for 'The Story Teller' (Hawthorne's next projected volume), the reader is invited to accompany the writer through the life of the protagonist while 'we . . . shape out our idea' of the character and thus of the fiction, for in 'Wakefield' story and character are one. The 'we' may, of course, merely be an example of the authorial plural, but the implication surely is that the process of creation is collaborative. If the reader goes to 'Wakefield' expecting what Thomas Walsh Jr. has called a 'tale to enjoy',[30] then he will have to agree that this piece fits into the category of the 'illustrated idea' rather than the story, for—as Walsh says—the element of suspense has been sacrificed to the moral question. Such categories are, however, hardly appropriate to Hawthorne's fictions, which clearly do not offer the readers the pleasures of the text subsumed in the class of 'tales to enjoy'. As Emerson noted in 1846, it was characteristic of Hawthorne's art that he invited his readers into his study and then opened the process of invention before them. Emerson disapproved, believing—presumably—that such self-reflexiveness robbed the reader of enjoyment, but

---

[27] Colacurcio (1984), pp. 520–1.
[28] Ibid.
[29] Roland Barthes, *S/Z*, tr. Richard Miller (1975), p. 4.
[30] Walsh (1961), pp. 31–3.

his comment was astute. It was, he said, 'as if the confectioner should say to his customers, "Now let us make the cake." '[31] When he made this observation, Emerson was probably responding to *Mosses from an Old Manse*, but the remark would apply with equal fitness to *Twice-told Tales*, for that contained, in addition to 'Wakefield', the 'Morality' called 'Fancy's Show Box' in which Fancy visits a certain Mr Smith to provide an imaginary example of guilt. 'Alice Doane's Appeal' was not collected in any of the short-story volumes in Hawthorne's lifetime. Had it been, it would have offered one of the most fascinating examples of his metafictional techniques, for in it the narrator discusses with his reader the responses of his listeners to a Gothic story of witchcraft he has told, making his narrative strategies and his success (or lack of it) the subject of the frame narrative. Thus 'Alice Doane's Appeal' brings together Hawthorne's concern with witchcraft and his concern with the status of fictions in a story about two stories (one the Gothic story of the Doanes; the other the story of the historic executions of the Salem witches) *and* about the listener-reader's response.

Hawthorne was planning 'The Story Teller' as early as the summer of 1832. The manuscript of the tales for the intended volume reached the publisher in 1834. Each of the tales was to have been told by an itinerant story-teller who would have described his travels, through New England, upstate New York, and parts of Canada, thus giving a geographical continuity to the collection. A more obvious unifying principle would clearly have been the attention to the art of fiction, since the particular tales would have been framed by an ongoing account of the career—and the narrative skills—of the man who told them. When book publication proved impossible, the opening sections of the frame narrative and the first story were published in the *New-England Magazine*, in 1834. In them, the narrator accounts for his choice of career as a wandering story-teller partly as a result of a chance encounter with some roving entertainers (an episode described

---

[31] *The Journals and Miscellaneous Notebooks of Ralph Waldo Emerson*, ed. William H. Gilman *et al.* (Cambridge, Mass.: Harvard University Press, 1960–), ix, 405.

in 'The Seven Vagabonds'), but gives as a deeper reason his rebellion against the moral tyranny of his Calvinistic guardian Parson Thumpcushion, under whose 'stern old Pilgrim spirit' and inflexible mind the narrator endured a miserable childhood. In rebelling against the parson, the would-be artist is making his protest against the iron Puritanism evoked in many of Hawthorne's tales. In choosing a profession that combines the roles of novelist and actor, the young man offers the maximum outrage to his guardian's moral system, since— to the Thumpcushion mentality—a writer of stories has no kind of business in life and is a mere idler, while an actor is the sort of vagabond who could only find a home at Merry Mount. However, in a flat refutation of the Puritan view of fiction-mongering, the narrator discovers that story-telling demands everything from its practitioners:

No talent or attainment could come amiss; every thing, indeed, was requisite; wide observation, varied knowledge, deep thoughts, and sparkling ones; pathos and levity, and a mixture of both . . . lofty imagination, veiling itself in the garb of common life; and the practised art which alone could render these gifts, and more than these, available. (*CE*, x, 416.)

Since he so emphatically rejects the pious (and trivializing) view of his art, it is all the more remarkable that, having met (accidentally, or providentially) a young theological student, whom he supposes to belong to Andover College, that bastion of Congregationalist orthodoxy, the story-teller makes a travelling companion of the pious Eliakim Abbott. Abbott intends to devote himself to itinerant preaching, and so the two young pilgrims (or vagabonds) complement each other. Examining his own playbills, which appear 'sacrilegiously' on the door of the meeting house, the narrator notices small slips of paper fixed beneath his own 'flaming' (with hell fire?) posters, announcing that Eliakim will address sinners on the welfare of their immortal souls. It is not necessary to believe, with George Parsons Lathrop,[32] that the stories would regularly have illustrated the texts used by the preacher to see

[32] Lathrop advances this theory in his 'Introductory Note' to the Riverside Edition of *Twice-told Tales*.

that Hawthorne's story-teller would tell his profane tales in the context of sacred discourse. Similarly, in the 'Old Manse' introduction to *Mosses*, the author invites his readers into his study and devotes some pages to an account of the theological library of his predecessor at the Manse, thus providing (literally and figuratively) a scriptural context for his fictions.

The first story told by the aspiring story-teller is 'Mr Higginbotham's Catastrophe', a sacrilegious tale of the 'death' and 'resurrection' of the title character which can be read as a parody of the argument between the Humean sceptics and the Christian believers on the subject of miracles.[33] The tale is told to an audience composed of the devotees of Mirth who respond so enthusiastically to the teller's buffoonery that the theatre benches break and throw to the ground these jolly folk who would never frequent the mourning benches. In contrast to the uproarious success of the story-teller, Eliakim meets with dismal failure. His tiny congregation melts away, uninspired by his unconfident prayers. But at the instant of the triumph of the profane story-teller, a letter arrives from Parson Thumpcushion reminding him of the austere duty of life which he has neglected for the company of the theatrical people. That was the moment, says the narrator, looking back on a wasted life, when he made his choice between a good and evil fate. Like the Oberon of 'Fragments from the Journal of a Solitary Man', this nameless story-teller regards his artistic career as a disaster. The narrative present of the tale is a later phase of his life from which he reviews his career, admits that the mass of his stories have 'vanished like cloud-shapes', and acknowledges that the remaining tales are 'cold'. This would-be artist, then, admits defeat and submits to the Calvinist Thumpcushion's verdict on his art. To identify him with Hawthorne is, however, to confuse the teller with the 'teller' and to confuse both with the tale.

When 'Mr Higginbotham's Catastrophe' was included in the 1837 *Twice-told Tales* it was detached from its context in 'The Story Teller'. Consequently, it lost all reference to the Puritan values represented by Parson Thumpcushion. It also

---

[33] See Duban (1979) and Colacurcio (1984), p. 503.

lost much of its self-reflexive quality, for the story of
Dominicus Pike's story of Mr Higginbotham was no longer
presented as an example of the Story Teller's art. Even
without its narrative frame, however, 'Mr Higginbotham's
Catastrophe' is a story about narration, for Dominicus, the
travelling tobacco peddler, is a man who is governed by an
inner need to turn a brief item of news (or rumour) into a
'respectable narrative'. He finds the good people of Parker's
Falls as avid to consume such tales as he is eager to produce
them; but when they find that his story is 'quite unfounded'
and that Mr Higginbotham has not been murdered, they are
ready almost to murder the man who entertained them with
the story. He escapes tarring and feathering but is pelted with
mud, which is emblematic—so the narrator tells us—of undeserved opprobrium. It is undeserved, presumably, because
Dominicus invented his story in good faith, and because the
inhabitants of Parker's Falls responded to his narrative,
delivered with a voice like a field-preacher, as if they were
members of a camp-meeting. In a sense, then, Dominicus is
like the Seven Vagabonds who intended to do their duty by
the 'poor souls' at the Stamford camp meeting. Their art, and
that of Dominicus, might seem debased when measured by the
'iron gravity' of the Methodist minister or the Calvinist
parson, but the poor soul needs its fictions.

The souls of the original settlers of New England had
needed only one story to sustain them and had accepted
only one authority in the telling. By the 1830s, the 'lower
and narrower'[34] souls of the descendants of those original
Puritans had established what has been aptly termed a
'bourgeois-Calvinist'[35] set of orthodoxies that constituted an
iron cage for the artist. The fictions that Hawthorne offered
his readers in the first published collection of his works—the
Twice-told Tales of 1837—may have been selected to present
an implied author who would endorse rather than challenge
those orthodoxies. If the narrators of the stories were assumed
to speak for the author, then that author's stance might even

[34] *CE*, xi, 68. In 'Main Street' Hawthorne describes the sons and
grandsons of the first settlers thus.
[35] Colacurcio (1984), 505.

be considered one of appeasement towards an audience suspicious of the claims of art and of the imagination.[36] However, the problematic relationship between narrator and tale that has been noted above could, of course, occur in stories whose official moral would appear to be thoroughly unsubversive, as was the case in 'The Grey Champion', so that—to adapt a phrase of Professor Crowley's[37]—the narrator would act as mediator between the story and the public, but the significance of the tale would lie in the unsettling of the conventional relationships between the teller, the tale, and the listener.

Clearly, the items selected for the first *Twice-told Tales* were not randomly chosen and assembled. The polarities of past and present, community and isolation, action and perception, reality and illusion that provided a structure for the whole volume were dramatized in the juxtaposition of the first two pieces in the collection: 'The Grey Champion' and 'Sunday at Home'.[38] Hawthorne's retrospective judgement—in the Preface to the 1851 edition—constitutes an intervention on behalf of the real, the active and the communal, for in it he deprecates the earlier dependence of his art on the shadowy world of seclusion and meditation. As early as 1841, in the letter to Duyckinck and Mathews in which he spoke of having burned quires of his own manuscripts, he had stated that he would write no more stories or, if he did continue to write, would produce tales unlike those which had grown out of the 'quietude and seclusion' of his life before 1837. In that year, or just after, the world, so he said, had sucked him into its vortex, so that he could not have returned to his former solitude even had he wanted to.[39] In terms of his art, Hawthorne left no doubt that contact with 'the world' seemed to him beneficial—a means of escape from a twilight atmosphere into the sunshine.

In 1837, the world into which Hawthorne found himself drawn was, to a considerable extent, the world of John L.

---

[36] See Baym (1976), 54.
[37] See Crowley (1968): 'The Artist as Mediator'.
[38] Crowley (1973), 43–4.
[39] *CE*, xv, 600.

O'Sullivan's *United States Magazine and Democratic Review*. In that year, the enterprising O'Sullivan persuaded Hawthorne to contribute regularly to his magazine, which had been launched in Washington, DC with support from leading Democratic Party members and which would carry articles on such public issues as the Texas Question as well as stories and sketches by the hitherto-retiring New England author.[40] Of course, Hawthorne's new horizons after 1837 were not limited to those opened up by O'Sullivan; he exchanged the retirement of his room in Salem not only for the life of the Boston customs house and the communitarian society of Brook Farm but also for the cultural world of Concord that he celebrated in the 'Old Manse' introduction to *Mosses*, and the society of Sophia, who joined him in the 'Eden' to which he moved in 1842. The shift in emphasis towards the contemporary in his fictions was already evident in the 1842 edition of *Twice-told Tales*, with the addition of thirteen recent pieces, as well as five earlier ones.[41] In the 1846 *Mosses*, though not all the tales are given specific settings in time or place, the materials with which the major part are concerned are connected with the author's own time and show his concern to deal with external reality in its immediacy.[42] The critique of the mechanistic spirit of the times in 'The Celestial Railroad' is Carlylean in its engagement, as well as in its controlling symbolism, while the satirical power of 'Earth's Holocaust' depends on its author's considerable knowledge of contemporary movements of thought and insight into them. Of the twenty-one pieces he wrote between July 1842 and October 1845, none used the historical sources of the kind he had relied on for his earlier fictions, and only one looked back to the colonial past, yet if there was a deliberate attempt on Hawthorne's part to move towards a Trollopean conception of reality in his fictions of the Old Manse period, that was balanced, as John J. McDonald has noted, by his continued use of the distancing devices of allegory.[43]

[40] See *CE*, xv, 52–9 for a useful summary of Hawthorne's relationship with O'Sullivan.

[41] Crowley (1973), 51.

[42] See McDonald (1972), 15.

[43] McDonald (1974), 77–8.

The continuity between the *Mosses* volume and the earlier tales is also striking in the problematic relationship between narrator and narrative in the three major stories of the 1846 collection. In 'The Birthmark' the reader is denied an authoritative evaluation of the idealism of the scientist Aylmer and may even be deliberately misled by Georgiana's estimate of her husband's nobility. In 'The Artist of the Beautiful', the narrator's final account of Owen Warland's achievement seems flatly to contradict a narrative in which the artist has been shown to be a petulant child-man, incapable of adult passion and ironically dedicated to an ideal of art that is both mechanical and trivialized. 'Rappaccini's Daughter', which followed 'Young Goodman Brown' in the 1846 *Mosses*, not only repeats the themes of the earlier story, but also presents its narrative problems in an intensified form. Just as Brown saw, or thought he saw, his wife Faith at the witches' sabbath, so Giovanni sees, or thinks he sees, evidence of the corrupt or poisonous nature of Beatrice. Since we are told that the young man's senses are inflamed by the beauty of the young Beatrice and since his voyeuristic delight renders him feverish, the reader may scrupulously distance himself from Giovanni's judgements, but, at a certain point in the narrative, the narrator informs us that Beatrice really is poisonous. In the view of one commentator, there are two tales co-present in 'Rappaccini's Daughter', each complete from the start: the story of an innocent girl destroyed by faithless love and the story of a dangerous woman who entices an innocent boy. The narrative seems as if it were possessed now by one and now by another pre-existing structure. In this view, by authorially affirming two antithetical interpretations of the same fiction, Hawthorne has solved the problem of the unreality of his works by making the fantastic itself real.[44] Yet it may be that the author affirms neither interpretation, and in refusing to do so subverts the conventions of story-telling with which he began to work. The story then becomes one in which the reader's entanglement in the enigmas of the hermeneutic and pro-airetic codes leads to a challenge to the reader's judgement

---

[44] Dauber (1977), 25–34.

on a metafictional level: she/he must judge which of the sources of information to trust.[45] Putting it another way, the story becomes a sort of anti-story in which the reader is required, or invited, to assume responsibility for the fiction.

Hawthorne's explicit comments on his own art, both in the evaluation of Aubépine's work in the introduction to 'Rappaccini's Daughter' and in his letter to Duyckinck dated 24 January 1846, show his dissatisfaction with his achievement in the short-story form and his reluctance to continue as a writer of tales.[46] One story in *Mosses*, however, was untypically confident on the subject of the artist's powers and uncharacteristically straightforward in its narrative techniques. 'Drowne's Wooden Image' tells the story of the prosaic woodcarver Drowne whose love for the beautiful woman he is commissioned to portray inspires him so that his 'magic touch' brings to life the wooden image he makes of her. Drowne lives in eighteenth-century Boston, where he is safe from the 'bigots of the day' who at once suspect that the spirits which have entered the beautiful form he has created must be evil. But the presence of a Puritan of the old stamp, who assumes that Drowne has sold his soul to the devil, and the reference to witch-times, when 'our forefathers' would have piously consigned such an image or apparition to the flames, reminds us that what to the artist Copley seems 'the divine, the life-giving touch' would have led to Gallows Hill in the Salem of 1692. By 1837 Hawthorne had read in Sir Walter Scott's *Letters on Demonology* that the witch of Christian Europe (hex) derived from the priestess (haxa) of the Germanic tribes who was credited with prophetic powers and thought to speak with divine inspiration.[47] Hawthorne did not need Scott to alert him to the fact that the imagination was the realm in which bigotry could have deadly effects, nor, of course, was he the indiscriminate champion of all who claimed

---

[45] Mailloux (1982), 78 ff.

[46] *CE*, xvi, 140.

[47] Sir Walter Scott, *Letters on Demonology and Witchcraft Addressed to J. G. Lockhart* (1830), 101. Hawthorne borrowed this volume from the Salem Athenaeum in 1837. See Kesselring (1949).

to speak with the divine authority of the antinomian, but in Scott he found confirmation of his early intuition that the shapes and figures *he* would create as an artist would be apprehended—like witchcraft and like prophecy—as negations of the 'real'.

In an account of William Gilmore Simms's *Views and Reviews* that Hawthorne wrote for the *Salem Advertiser* in 1846, he asserted that the 'prophet of art' needed a magic touch that would enable him to cause 'new intellectual and moral shapes to spring up in the reader's mind'. When that mind had previously been a barren waste, the prophet of art could make it fertile with varied life. Though Hawthorne's habit of self-deprecation would not allow him to claim those prophetic powers, there can be no doubting his power to bewitch the reader's mind and enliven it with shapes or apparitions.

[48] Quoted in Randall Stewart, 'Hawthorne's Contributions to the *Salem Advertiser*', *American Literature*, 5 (1934), 332.

NOTE ON THE TEXT

WITH the exception of 'The Gentle Boy', the texts of the tales in this selection are those of the World's Classics *Tales by Nathaniel Hawthorne*, edited by Carl Van Doren (1928). This was essentially an anglicized version of the text of the Riverside Edition of the works of Nathaniel Hawthorne, edited by George Parsons Lathrop.

All Hawthorne's tales were published in newspapers, periodicals, or annuals before they were republished in the three collections of his short works published in his lifetime: *Twice-told Tales*, *Mosses from an Old Manse*, and *The Snow-Image*. In the now-standard Ohio State University Press Centenary Edition of the works of Nathaniel Hawthorne, editorial policy has been to take the first-published texts of the tales as copy-texts (where there is no extant manuscript) in accidentals, and to judge later substantive emendations on the authority of their sources. Hawthorne marked proposed emendations in his copies of clippings from the periodical texts of some tales, but these were not all followed, and many emendations lack authority; some are demonstrably compositor's errors. Earlier editors, including Lathrop, took the texts of the various collected editions as copy-texts, ignoring variations in the earlier published versions. In the textual notes to this edition, substantive variations between the 1928 World's Classics text and the texts in their first published forms are noted only where the earlier text has some authority or interest. Variations between the World's Classics and the Centenary texts are also noted. Errors in the World's Classics text have been silently corrected.

The text of 'The Gentle Boy', here included in the World's Classics selection for the first time, is that of *The Token* for 1832, though the spelling has been anglicized. Hawthorne's major revisions in this tale for the 1837 *Twice-told Tales* were omissions. These are marked in the explanatory or textual notes.

A CHRONOLOGY OF
NATHANIEL HAWTHORNE

1804   4 July: born in Salem, Massachusetts, second of three children of Elizabeth (*née* Manning) and Nathaniel Hathorne.

1808   Father, a ship's captain, dies of yellow fever at Surinam (Dutch Guiana). The Hathornes move to the Manning family home in Salem.

1813   November: a foot injury causes lameness and keeps Nathaniel from school for fourteen months.

1818   October: the Hathorne family moves to Raymond, Maine, which is still a wilderness area. Nathaniel hunts, fishes, and runs wild.

1819   July: Nathaniel returns to Salem to live with his mother's family, under the guardianship of his uncle Robert Manning. His mother stays in Maine.

1820   Prepares for college under Benjamin L. Oliver in Salem.

1821   October: enters Bowdoin College, Brunswick, Maine. College friendships with Horatio Bridge, Franklin Pierce, Jonathan Cilley.

1822   H. W. Longfellow enters Bowdoin. He and Hawthorne meet.

1825   September: graduates from Bowdoin. Returns to live with family in Salem. According to his sister Elizabeth, Nathaniel has completed 'Seven Tales of My Native Land' by the time he graduates from Bowdoin.

1828   October: *Fanshawe* published anonymously and at the author's expense. By now Nathaniel has added the 'w' to his family name.

1829   Plans a second collection of stories, to be called 'Provincial Tales', and submits manuscript to S. G. Goodrich, editor of *The Token*, an annual.

1830   12 November and 21 December: 'The Hollow of the Three Hills' and 'An Old Woman's Tale'—Hawthorne's first known tales to appear in print—published in *Salem Gazette*.

1831   Releases some tales intended for 'Provincial Tales' for publication in *The Token*, dated 1832: 'The Gentle Boy', 'The Wives of the Dead', 'Roger Malvin's Burial', 'My Kinsman, Major Molineux'.

1832   Plans a third collection, to be called 'The Story Teller'. September–October: makes extensive journeys in Vermont and New York State, gathering literary materials.

1834   November and December: 'The Story Teller, Nos I and II' published in *New-England Magazine*.

1835   'The Minister's Black Veil', 'The Maypole of Merry Mount', and 'The Wedding-Knell' published in *The Token* for 1836.

1836   January: moves to Boston to edit *American Magazine of Useful and Entertaining Knowledge*. March: first issue with Nathaniel Hawthorne as editor. His salary is not paid. Magazine goes bankrupt in May. May to September: writes—with the help of Elizabeth—*Peter Parley's Universal History, on the Basis of Geography*.

1837   March: *Twice-told Tales* published. Unknown to Hawthorne, Horatio Bridge has given financial guarantee to publisher. July: Longfellow's highly favourable review of *Twice-told Tales* appears in the *North American Review*. November: meets Sophia Amelia Peabody. October: begins his association with John L. O'Sullivan's *Democratic Review*. Eight Hawthorne pieces appear there in fifteen months.

1838   July–September: begins three months of seclusion in North Adams, Massachusetts, with trips to the Berkshires, upstate New York, Vermont, Connecticut.

1839   January: takes up appointment as measurer in the Boston Custom House. 6 March: writes first surviving love-letter to Sophia Peabody.

1840   November: resigns from Custom House with effect from 1 January 1841. December: *Grandfather's Chair* published, dated 1841, a children's history of New England.

1841   January: returns to Salem. *Famous Old People* published. March: *The Liberty Tree* published. April: joins the Brook Farm Associationist experiment at West Roxbury, near Boston, as working member. Becomes a paying boarder at the Farm, with no work commitments, in the autumn.

September: buys two shares in the Brook Farm project, planning to bring Sophia to live there when they are married. October: leaves the Farm for Boston.

1842   January: second edition of *Twice-told Tales* published, with additional volume containing sixteen recent tales and sketches together with five that antedate the 1837 collection. 9 July: Hawthorne and Sophia Peabody married. They move to Concord, Mass., where they rent the Old Manse. October: withdraws from the Brook Farm project and requests return of his stock.

1844   3 March: daughter (Una) born.

1845   January–April: edits Horatio Bridge's *Journal of an African Cruiser*. October: the Hawthornes move to Herbert Street, Salem, as the owner wants Old Manse.

1846   9 April: sworn in as surveyor at Salem Custom House, having been nominated by President Polk, the new Democratic President. June: *Mosses from an Old Manse* published in two volumes. A critical, but not a financial, success. 22 June: Julian Hawthorne born. August: Hawthornes move to Salem.

1848   November: becomes manager and corresponding secretary of Salem Lyceum. Invites Emerson, Thoreau, Theodore Parker, Horace Mann, Louis Agassiz to lecture.

1849   7 June: removed from office in Custom House, following election of Whig President, Zachary Taylor, in 1848. 31 July: Mother dies. September: begins writing *The Scarlet Letter* and 'The Custom-House'.

1850   16 March: *The Scarlet Letter* published in edition of 2,500 copies. April: second edition published. May: Hawthornes move to 'Red Cottage', Lenox, Massachusetts. 5 August: Hawthorne meets Melville at a literary picnic. August: begins *The House of the Seven Gables*. 17 and 24 August: Melville's 'Hawthorne and His Mosses' appears anonymously in *The Literary World*. November: *True Stories* (reissue of *Grandfather's Chair* and *Biographical Stories*) published, dated 1851.

1851   April: *The House of the Seven Gables* published. March: third edition of *Twice-told Tales* published, with preface. 20 May: Rose Hawthorne born. November: *A Wonder Book for Girls and Boys* published, dated 1852. December: *The Snow-Image* published, dated 1852.

1852   April: buys the Alcott House in Concord, naming it 'The Wayside'. July: *The Blithedale Romance* published. September: *Life of Franklin Pierce*—a campaign biography of the Presidential candidate—published.

1853   March: nominated to consulship at Liverpool and Manchester by President Pierce. Appointment confirmed by US Senate. July: sails for England with family. September: *Tanglewood Tales* published.

1853–7   While working as consul, Hawthorne keeps notebooks in which he records his English experiences and impressions.

1854   Revised edition of *Mosses* published.

1856   November: Melville visits Hawthorne in Liverpool on way to the Holy Land. He also meets Hawthorne briefly on return journey in May 1857.

1857   October: gives up consulship.

1858   January: travels to Italy by way of France. Takes up residence in Rome. Keeps notebooks on his Italian experiences and begins work on an English romance, never to be completed, but published posthumously as *The Ancestral Footstep*. May to October: the Hawthornes live in Florence. He begins work on romance with an Italian theme.

1859   June: returns to England, where he rewrites the Italian romance.

1860   February: *The Transformation* published in England; in March the romance is published in America with the title *The Marble Faun*. June: returns to America and settles at 'The Wayside', Concord, where he begins work on a second version of his English romance.

1861   Abandons the romance, after making seven studies for the story. The fragment is published posthumously as *Dr Grimshawe's Secret*. Autumn: begins work on series of English essays. Begins a new romance on theme of the elixir of life but abandons this in 1862. Set at the time of the Revolution, the fragment is published posthumously as *Septimius Felton*.

1863   September: *Our Old Home* published—the collected essays on England—most of which had appeared separately in the *Atlantic Monthly*.

1864   19 May: dies at Plymouth, New Hampshire, having written three chapters of another romance about the elixir of life, which is posthumously published as *The Dolliver Romance*.

Young Goodman Brown
and Other Tales

THE GENTLE BOY

IN the course of the year 1656,* several of the people called
Quakers, led, as they professed, by the inward movement of
the spirit, made their appearance in New England. Their
reputation, as holders of mystic and pernicious* principles,
having spread before them, the Puritans early endeavoured to
banish, and to prevent the further intrusion of the rising sect.
But the measures by which it was intended to purge the land
of heresy, though more than sufficiently vigorous, were
entirely unsuccessful. The Quakers, esteeming persecution as
a divine call to the post of danger, laid claim to a holy courage,
unknown to the Puritans themselves, who had shunned the
cross, by providing for the peaceable exercise of their religion
in a distant wilderness. Though it was the singular fact, that
every nation of the earth rejected the wandering enthusiasts
who practised peace towards all men, the place of greatest
uneasiness and peril, and therefore in their eyes the most
eligible, was the province of Massachusetts Bay. The fines,
imprisonments, and stripes, liberally distributed by our pious
forefathers;* the popular antipathy, so strong that it endured
nearly a hundred years after actual persecution had ceased,
were attractions as powerful for the Quakers, as peace,
honour, and reward, would have been for the worldly-minded.
Every European vessel brought new cargoes of the sect, eager
to testify against the oppression which they hoped to share;
and, when shipmasters were restrained by heavy fines from
affording them passage, they made long and circuitous
journeys through the Indian country, and appeared in the
province as if conveyed by a supernatural power. Their
enthusiasm, heightened almost to madness by the treatment
which they received, produced actions contrary to the rules of
decency, as well as of rational religion, and presented a
singular contrast to the calm and staid deportment of their
sectual* successors of the present day. The command of the
spirit, inaudible except to the soul, and not to be con-
troverted on grounds of human wisdom, was made a plea

for most indecorous exhibitions, which, abstractly considered, well deserved the moderate chastisement of the rod. These extravagances, and the persecution which was at once their cause and consequence, continued to increase, till, in the year 1659, the government of Massachusetts Bay indulged two members of the Quaker sect with the crown of martyrdom.*

That those who* were active in, or consenting to, this measure, made themselves responsible for innocent blood, is not to be denied: yet the extenuating circumstances of their conduct are more numerous than can generally be pleaded by persecutors. The inhabitants of New England were a people, whose original bond of union was their peculiar religious principles. For the peaceful exercise of their own mode of worship, an object, the very reverse of universal liberty of conscience, they had hewn themselves a home in the wilderness; they had made vast sacrifices of whatever is dear to man; they had exposed themselves to the peril of death, and to a life which rendered the accomplishment of that peril almost a blessing. They had found no city of refuge prepared for them, but, with Heaven's assistance, they had created one; and it would be hard to say whether justice did not authorize their determination, to guard its gate against all who were destitute of the prescribed title to admittance. The principle of their foundation was such, that to destroy the unity of religion, might have been to subvert the government, and break up the colony, especially at a period when the state of affairs in England had stopped the tide of emigration, and drawn back many of the pilgrims to their native homes. The magistrates of Massachusetts Bay were, moreover, most imperfectly informed respecting the real tenets and character of the Quaker sect. They had heard of them, from various parts of the earth, as opposers of every known opinion, and enemies of all established governments; they had beheld extravagances which seemed to justify these accusations; and the idea suggested by their own wisdom may be gathered from the fact, that the persons of many individuals were searched, in the expectation of discovering witch-marks. But after all allowances, it is to be feared that the death of the Quakers was principally owing to the polemic fierceness, that distinct passion of human nature, which has so often produced frightful guilt in the most sincere and zealous advocates of virtue and religion. An indelible stain of blood is upon the hands of all who consented to this act, but a large share of the awful responsibility must rest upon the person then at the head of the government.* He was a man of narrow mind and imperfect education, and his uncompromising bigotry was made hot and mischievous by violent and hasty passions; he exerted his influence indecorously and unjustifiably to compass the death of the enthusiasts; and his whole conduct, in respect to them, was marked by brutal cruelty. The Quakers, whose revengeful feelings were not less deep because they were inactive, remembered this man and his associates, in after times. The historian of the sect* affirms that, by the wrath of Heaven, a blight fell upon the land in the vicinity of the 'bloody town' of Boston, so that no wheat would grow there; and he takes his stand, as it were, among the graves of the ancient persecutors, and triumphantly recounts the judgments that overtook them, in old age or at the parting hour. He tells us that they died suddenly, and violently, and in madness; but nothing can exceed the bitter mockery with which he records the loathsome disease, and 'death by rottenness,'* of the fierce and cruel governor.

*   *   *   *   *

On the evening of the autumn day, that had witnessed the martyrdom of two men of the Quaker persuasion, a Puritan settler was returning from the metropolis to the neighbouring country town in which he resided. The air was cool, the sky clear, and the lingering twilight was made brighter by the rays of a young moon, which had now nearly reached the verge of the horizon. The traveller, a man of middle age, wrapped in a grey frieze cloak, quickened his pace when he had reached the outskirts of the town, for a gloomy extent of nearly four miles lay between him and his house.* The low, straw-thatched houses were scattered at considerable intervals along the road, and the country having been settled but about thirty years, the tracts of original forest still bore no small proportion to the cultivated ground. The autumn wind wandered among the branches, whirling away the leaves from all except the pine-trees, and moaning as if it lamented the desolation of which it was the instrument. The road had penetrated the mass of woods that lay nearest to the town, and was just emerging into an open space, when the traveller's ears were saluted by a sound more mournful than even that of the wind. It was like the wailing of someone in distress, and it seemed to proceed from beneath a tall and lonely fir-tree, in the centre of a cleared, but unenclosed and uncultivated field. The Puritan could not but remember that this was the very spot, which had been made accursed a few hours before, by the execution of the Quakers, whose bodies had been thrown together into one hasty grave, beneath the tree on which they suffered. He struggled, however, against the superstitious fears which belonged to the age, and compelled himself to pause and listen.

'The voice is most likely mortal, nor have I cause to tremble if it be otherwise,' thought he, straining his eyes through the dim moonlight. 'Methinks it is like the wailing of a child; some infant, it may be, which has strayed from its mother, and chanced upon this place of death. For the ease of mine own conscience, I must search this matter out.'

He therefore left the path, and continued somewhat fearfully across the field. Though now so desolate, its soil was pressed down and trampled by the thousand footsteps of those who had witnessed the spectacle of that day, all of whom had now retired, leaving the dead to their loneliness. The traveller at length reached the fir-tree, which from the middle upward was covered with living branches, although a scaffold had been erected beneath, and other preparations made for the work of death. Under this unhappy tree, which in after times was believed to drop poison with its dew, sat the one solitary mourner for innocent blood. It was a slender and light-clad little boy, who leaned his face upon a hillock of fresh-turned and half-frozen earth, and wailed bitterly, yet in a suppressed tone, as if his grief might receive the punishment of crime. The Puritan, whose approach had been unperceived, laid his hand upon the child's shoulder, and addressed him compassionately.

'You have chosen a dreary lodging, my poor boy, and no

wonder that you weep,' said he. 'But dry your eyes, and tell me where your mother dwells. I promise you, if the journey be not too far, I will leave you in her arms tonight.'

The boy had hushed his wailing at once, and turned his face upward to the stranger. It was a pale, bright-eyed countenance, certainly not more than six years old, but sorrow, fear, and want, had destroyed much of its infantile expression. The Puritan, seeing the boy's frightened gaze, and feeling that he trembled under his hand, endeavoured to reassure him.

'Nay, if I intended to do you harm, little lad, the readiest way were to leave you here. What! you do not fear to sit beneath the gallows on a new-made grave, and yet you tremble at a friend's touch. Take heart, child, and tell me what is your name, and where is your home?'

'Friend,' replied the little boy, in a sweet, though faltering voice, 'they call me Ilbrahim, and my home is here.'

The pale, spirited face, the eyes that seemed to mingle with the moonlight, the sweet, airy voice, and the outlandish name, almost made the Puritan believe, that the boy was in truth a being which had sprung up out of the grave on which he sat. But perceiving that the apparition stood the test of a short mental prayer, and remembering that the arm which he had touched was life-like, he adopted a more rational supposition. 'The poor child is stricken in his intellect,' thought he, 'but verily his words are fearful, in a place like this.' He then spoke soothingly, intending to humour the boy's fantasy.

'Your home will scarce be comfortable, Ilbrahim, this cold autumn night, and I fear you are ill provided with food. I am hastening to a warm supper and bed, and if you will go with me, you shall share them!'

'I thank thee, friend, but though I be hungry and shivering with cold, thou wilt not give me food nor lodging,' replied the boy, in the quiet tone which despair had taught him, even so young. 'My father was of the people whom all men hate. They have laid him under this heap of earth, and here is my home.'

The Puritan, who had laid hold of little Ilbrahim's hand, relinquished it as if he were touching a loathsome reptile. But he possessed a compassionate heart, which not even religious prejudice could harden into stone.

'God forbid that I should leave this child to perish, though he comes of the accursed sect,' said he to himself. 'Do we not all spring from an evil root? Are we not all in darkness till the light doth shine upon us? He shall not perish, neither in body, nor, if prayer and instruction may avail for him, in soul.' He then spoke aloud and kindly to Ilbrahim, who had again hid his face in the cold earth of the grave. 'Was every door in the land shut against you, my child, that you have wandered to this unhallowed spot?'

'They drove me forth from the prison when they took my father thence,' said the boy, 'and I stood afar off, watching the crowd of people, and when they were gone, I came hither, and found only this grave. I knew that my father was sleeping here, and I said, this shall be my home.'

'No, child, no; not while I have a roof over my head, or a morsel to share with you!' exclaimed the Puritan, whose sympathies were now fully excited. 'Rise up and come with me, and fear not any harm.'

The boy wept afresh, and clung to the heap of earth, as if the cold heart beneath it were warmer to him than any in a living breast. The traveller, however, continued to entreat him tenderly, and seeming to acquire some degree of confidence, he at length arose. But his slender limbs tottered with weakness, his little head grew dizzy, and he leaned against the tree of death for support.

'My poor boy, are you so feeble?' said the Puritan. 'When did you taste food last?'

'I ate of bread and water with my father in the prison,' replied Ilbrahim, 'but they brought him none neither yesterday nor today, saying that he had eaten enough to bear him to his journey's end. Trouble not thyself for my hunger, kind friend, for I have lacked food many times ere now.'

The traveller took the child in his arms and wrapped his cloak about him, while his heart stirred with shame and anger against the gratuitous cruelty of the instruments in this persecution. In the awakened warmth of his feelings, he resolved that, at whatever risk, he would not forsake the poor little defenceless being whom Heaven had confided to his care. With this determination, he left the accursed field, and resumed the homeward path from which the wailing of the boy had called him. The light and motionless burthen scarcely impeded his progress, and he soon beheld the fire-rays from the windows of the cottage which he, a native of a distant clime, had built in the western wilderness. It was surrounded by a considerable extent of cultivated ground, and the dwelling was situated in the nook of a wood-covered hill, whither it seemed to have crept for protection.

'Look up, child,' said the Puritan to Ilbrahim, whose faint head had sunk upon his shoulder; 'there is our home.'

At the word 'home,' a thrill passed through the child's frame, but he continued silent. A few moments brought them to the cottage-door, at which the owner knocked; for at that early period, when savages were wandering everywhere among the settlers, bolt and bar were indispensable to the security of a dwelling. The summons was answered by a bond-servant, a coarse-clad and dull-featured piece of humanity, who, after ascertaining that his master was the applicant, undid the door, and held a flaring pine-knot torch to light him in. Farther back in the passage-way, the red blaze discovered a matronly woman, but no little crowd of children came bounding forth to greet their father's return. As the Puritan entered, he thrust aside his cloak, and displayed Ilbrahim's face to the female.

'Dorothy, here is a little outcast whom Providence hath put into our hands,' observed he. 'Be kind to him, even as if he were of those dear ones who have departed from us.'

The wife's eyes* filled with tears; she inquired neither who little Ilbrahim was, nor whence he came, but kissed his cheek and led the way into the dwelling. The sitting-room, which was also the kitchen, was lighted by a cheerful fire upon the large stone-laid hearth, and a confused variety of objects shone out and disappeared in the unsteady blaze. There were the household articles, the many wooden trenchers, the one large pewter dish, and the copper kettle whose inner surface was glittering like gold. There were the lighter implements of husbandry, the spade, the sickle, and the scythe, all hanging by the door, and the axe before which a thousand trees had bowed themselves. On another part of the wall were the steel cap and iron breast-plate, the sword and the matchlock gun. There, in a corner, was a little chair, the memorial of a brood of children whose place by the fire-side was vacant forever. And there, on a table near the window, among all those tokens of labour, war, and mourning, was the Holy Bible, the book of life, an emblem of the blessed comforts which it offers, to those who can receive them, amidst the toil, the strife, and sorrow of this world. Dorothy hastened to bring the little chair from its corner; she placed it on the hearth, and, seating the poor orphan there, addressed him in words of tenderness, such as only a mother's experience could have taught her. At length, when he had timidly begun to taste his warm bread and milk, she drew her husband apart.

'What pale and bright-eyed little boy is this, Tobias?' she inquired. 'Is he one whom the wilderness folk have ravished from some Christian mother?'

'No, Dorothy, this poor child is no captive from the wilderness,' he replied. 'The heathen savage would have given him to eat of his scanty morsel, and to drink of his birchen cup; but Christian men, alas! had cast him out to die.'

Then he told her how he had found him beneath the gallows, upon his father's grave; and how his heart had prompted him, like the speaking of an inward voice, to take the little outcast home, and be kind unto him. He acknowledged his resolution to feed and clothe him, as if he were his own child, and to afford him the instruction which should counteract the pernicious errors hitherto instilled into his infant mind. Dorothy was gifted with even a quicker tenderness than her husband, and she approved of all his doings and intentions. She drew near* to Ilbrahim, who, having finished his repast, sat with the tears hanging upon his long eye-lashes, but with a singular and unchildlike composure on his little face.

'Have you a mother, dear child?' she inquired.

The tears burst forth from his full heart, as he attempted to reply; but Dorothy at length understood that he had a mother, who, like the rest of her sect, was a persecuted wanderer. She had been taken from the prison a short time before, carried into the uninhabited wilderness, and left to perish there by hunger or wild beasts. This was no uncommon method of disposing of the Quakers, and they were accustomed to boast, that the inhabitants of the desert were more hospitable to them than civilized man.

'Fear not, little boy, you shall not need a mother, and a kind one,' said Dorothy, when she had gathered this information. 'Dry your tears, Ilbrahim, and be my child, as I will be your mother.'

The good woman prepared the little bed, from which her own children had successively been borne to another resting place. Before Ilbrahim would consent to occupy it, he knelt down, and as Dorothy listened to his simple and affecting prayer, she marvelled how the parents that had taught it to him could have been judged worthy of death. When the boy had fallen asleep, she bent over his pale and spiritual countenance, pressed a kiss upon his white brow, drew the bed-clothes up about his neck, and went away with a pensive gladness in her heart.

Tobias Pearson* was not among the earliest emigrants from the old country. He had remained in England during the first years of the civil war, in which he had borne some share as a coronet* of dragoons, under Cromwell. But when the ambitious designs of his leader began to develop themselves, he quitted the army of the parliament, and sought a refuge from the strife, which was no longer holy among the people of his persuasion, in the colony of Massachusetts. A more worldly consideration had perhaps an influence in drawing him thither; for New England offered advantages to men of unprosperous fortunes, as well as to dissatisfied religionists, and Pearson had hitherto found it difficult to provide for a wife and increasing family. To this supposed impurity of motive, the more bigoted Puritans were inclined to impute the removal by death of all the children, for whose earthly good the father had been over-thoughtful. They had left their native country blooming like roses, and like roses they had perished in a foreign soil. Those expounders of the ways of Providence, who had thus judged their brother, and attributed his domestic sorrows to his sin, were not more charitable when they saw him and Dorothy endeavouring to fill up the void in their hearts, by the adoption of an infant of the accursed sect. Nor did they fail to communicate their disapprobation to Tobias; but the latter, in reply, merely pointed at the little quiet, lovely boy, whose appearance and deportment were indeed as powerful arguments as could possibly have been adduced in his own favour. Even his beauty, however, and his winning manners, sometimes produced an effect ultimately unfavourable; for the bigots, when the outer surfaces of their iron hearts had been softened and again grew hard, affirmed that no merely natural cause could have so worked upon them. Their antipathy to the poor infant was also increased by the ill success of divers theological discussions, in which it was attempted to convince him of the errors of his sect. Ilbrahim, it is true, was not a skilful controversialist; but the feeling of his religion was strong as instinct in him, and he could neither be enticed nor driven from the faith which his father had died for. The odium of this stubbornness was shared in a great measure by the child's protectors, insomuch that Tobias and Dorothy very shortly began to experience a most bitter species of persecution, in the cold regards of many a friend whom they had valued. The common people manifested their opinions more openly. Pearson was a man of some consideration, being a Representative to the General Court, and an approved Lieutenant in the train-bands, yet, within a week after his adoption of Ilbrahim, he had been both hissed and hooted. Once, also, when walking through a solitary piece of woods, he heard a loud voice from some invisible speaker; and it cried, 'What shall be done to the backslider? Lo! the scourge is knotted for him, even the whip of nine cords, and every cord three knots!' These insults irritated Pearson's temper for the moment; they entered also into his heart, and became imperceptible but powerful workers towards an end, which his most secret thought had not yet whispered.

* * * * *

On the second Sabbath after Ilbrahim became a member of their family, Pearson and his wife deemed it proper that he should appear with them at public worship. They had anticipated some opposition to this measure from the boy, but he prepared himself in silence, and at the appointed hour was clad in the new mourning suit which Dorothy had wrought for him. As the parish was then, and during many subsequent years, unprovided with a bell, the signal for the commencement of religious exercises was the beat of a drum; in connexion* with which peculiarity it may be mentioned, that an apartment of the meetinghouse served the purposes of a powder-magazine and armory. At the first sound of that martial call to the place of holy and quiet thoughts, Tobias and Dorothy set forth, each holding a hand of little Ilbrahim, like two parents linked together by the infant of their love. On their path through the leafless woods, they were overtaken by many persons of their acquaintance, all of whom avoided them, and passed by on the other side; but a severer trial awaited their constancy when they had descended the hill, and drew near the pine-built and undecorated house of prayer. Around the door, from which the drummer still sent forth his thundering summons, was drawn up a formidable phalanx, including several of the oldest members of the congregation, many of the middle-aged, and nearly all the younger males. Pearson found it difficult to sustain their united and disapproving gaze, but Dorothy, whose mind was differently circumstanced, merely drew the boy closer to her, and faltered not in her approach. As they entered the door, they overheard the muttered sentiments of the assemblage, and when the reviling voices of the little children smote Ilbrahim's ear, he wept.

The interior aspect of the meetinghouse was rude. The low ceiling, the unplastered walls, the naked woodwork, and the undraperied pulpit, offered nothing to excite the devotion, which, without such external aids, often remains latent in the heart. The floor of the building was occupied by rows of long, cushionless benches, supplying the place of pews, and the broad-aisle formed a sexual division, impassable except by children beneath a certain age. On one side* of the house sat the women, generally in sad-coloured and most unfanciful apparel, although there were a few high head-dresses, on which the 'Cobler of Agawam'* would have lavished his empty wit of words. There was no veil to be seen among them all, and it must be allowed that the November sun, shining brightly through the windows, fell upon many a demure but pretty set of features, which no barbarity of art could spoil. The masculine department of the house presented somewhat more variety than that of the women. Most of the men, it is true, were clad in black or dark-grey broadcloth, and all coincided in the short, ungraceful, and ear-displaying cut of their hair. But those who were in martial authority, having arrayed themselves in their embroidered buffcoats, contrasted strikingly with the remainder of the congregation, and attracted many youthful thoughts which should have been otherwise employed. Pearson and Dorothy separated at the door of the meetinghouse, and Ilbrahim, being within the years of infancy, was retained under the care of the latter. The wrinkled beldams involved themselves in their rusty cloaks as he passed by; even the mild-featured maidens seemed to dread contamination; and many a stern old man arose, and turned his repulsive and unheavenly countenance upon the gentle boy, as if the sanctuary were polluted by his presence. He was a sweet infant of the skies, that had strayed away from his home, and all the inhabitants of this miserable world closed up their impure hearts against him, drew back their earth-soiled garments from his touch, and said, 'We are holier than thou.'

Ilbrahim, seated by the side of his adopted mother, and retaining fast hold of her hand, assumed a grave and decorous demeanour, such as might befit a person of matured taste and understanding, who should find himself in a temple dedicated to some worship which he did not recognize, but felt himself bound to respect. The exercises had not yet commenced, however, when the boy's attention was arrested by an event, apparently of trifling interest. A woman, having her face muffled in a hood, and a cloak drawn completely about her form, advanced slowly up the broad-aisle and took place upon the foremost bench. Ilbrahim's faint colour varied, his nerves fluttered, he was unable to turn his eyes from the muffled female.

When the preliminary prayer and hymn were over, the minister arose, and having turned the hour-glass which stood by the great bible, commenced his discourse. He was now well-stricken in years, a man of pale, thin, yet not intellectual countenance,* and his grey hairs were closely covered by a black velvet scull-cap. In his younger days he had practically learned the meaning of persecution, from Archbishop Laud,* and he was not now disposed to forget the lesson against which he had murmured them. Introducing the often discussed subject of the Quakers, he gave a history of that sect, and a description of their tenets, in which error predominated, and prejudice distorted the aspect of what was true. He adverted to the recent measures in the province, and cautioned his hearers of weaker parts against calling in question the just severity, which God-fearing magistrates had at length been compelled to exercise. He spoke of the danger of pity, in some cases a commendable and Christian virtue, but inapplicable to this pernicious sect. He observed that such was their devilish obstinacy in error, that even the little children, the sucking babes, were hardened and desperate heretics. He affirmed that no man, without Heaven's especial warrant, should attempt their conversion, lest while he bent his hand to draw them from the slough, he should himself be precipitated into its lowest depths. Into this discourse* was worked much learning, both sacred and profane, which, however, came forth not digested into its original elements, but in short quotations, as if the preacher were unable to amalgamate his own mind with that of the author. His own language was generally plain, even to affectation, but there were frequent specimens of a dull man's efforts to be witty—little ripples fretting the surface of a stagnant pool.

The sands of the second hour were principally in the lower half of the glass, when the sermon concluded. An approving murmur followed, and the clergyman, having given out a hymn, took his seat with much self-congratulation, and endeavoured to read the effect of his eloquence in the visages of the people. But while voices from all parts of the house were tuning themselves to sing, a scene occurred, which, though not very unusual at that period in the province, happened to be without precedent in this parish.

The muffled female, who had hitherto sat motionless in the front rank of the audience, now arose, and with slow, stately, and unwavering step, ascended the pulpit stairs. The quaverings of incipient harmony were hushed, and the divine sat in speechless and almost terrified astonishment, while she undid the door, and stood up in the sacred desk from which his maledictions had just been thundered. Having thus* usurped a station to which her sex can plead no title, she divested herself of the cloak and hood, and appeared in a most singular array. A shapeless robe of sackcloth* was girded about her waist with a knotted cord; her raven hair fell down upon her shoulders, and its blackness was defiled by pale streaks of ashes, which she had strewn upon her head. Her eyebrows, dark and strongly defined, added to the deathly whiteness of a countenance which, emaciated with want, and wild with enthusiasm and strange sorrows, retained no trace of earlier beauty. This figure stood gazing earnestly on the audience, and there was no sound, nor any movement, except a faint shuddering which every man observed in his neighbour, but was scarcely conscious of in himself. At length, when her fit of inspiration came, she spoke, for the first few moments, in a low voice, and not invariably distinct utterance. Her discourse gave evidence of an imagination hopelessly entangled with her reason; it was a vague and incomprehensible rhapsody, which, however, seemed to spread its own atmosphere round the hearer's soul, and to move his feelings by some influence unconnected with the words. As she proceeded, beautiful but shadowy images would sometimes be seen, like bright things moving in a turbid river; or a strong and singularly shaped idea leapt forth, and seized at once on the understanding or the heart. But the course of her unearthly eloquence soon led her to the persecutions of her sect, and from thence the step was short to her own peculiar sorrows. She was naturally a woman of mighty passions, and hatred and revenge now wrapped themselves in the garb of piety; the character of her speech was changed, her images became distinct though wild, and her denunciations had an almost hellish bitterness.

'The Governor and his mighty men,' she said, 'have gathered together, taking counsel among themselves and saying, "What shall we do unto this people—even unto the people that have come into this land to put our iniquity to the blush?" And lo! the devil entereth into the council-chamber, like a lame man of low stature and gravely apparelled, with a dark and twisted countenance, and a bright, downcast eye. And he standeth up among the rulers; yea, he goeth to and fro, whispering to each; and every man lends his ear, for his word is "slay, slay!" But I say unto ye, Woe to them that slay! Woe to them that shed the blood of saints! Woe to them that have slain the husband, and cast forth the child, the tender infant, to wander homeless, and hungry, and cold, till he die; and have saved the mother alive, in the cruelty of their tender mercies! Woe to them in their life-time, cursed are they in the delight and pleasure of their hearts! Woe to them in their death hour, whether it come swiftly with blood and violence, or after long and lingering pain! Woe, in the dark house, in the rottenness of the grave, when the children's children shall revile the ashes of the fathers! Woe, woe, woe, at the judgement, when all the persecuted and all the slain in this bloody land, and the father, the mother, and the child, shall await them in a day that they cannot escape! Seed of the faith, seed of the faith, ye whose hearts are moving with a power that ye know not, arise, wash your hands of this innocent blood! Lift your voices, chosen ones, cry aloud, and call down a woe and a judgement with me!'

Having thus given vent to the flood of malignity which she mistook for inspiration,* the speaker was silent. Her voice was succeeded by the hysteric shrieks of several women, but the feelings of the audience generally had not been drawn onward in the current with her own. They remained stupefied, stranded as it were, in the midst of a torrent, which deafened them by its roaring, but might not move them by its violence. The clergyman, who could not hitherto have ejected the usurper of his pulpit otherwise than by bodily force, now addressed her in the tone of just indignation and legitimate authority.

'Get you down, woman, from the holy place which you profane,' he said. 'Is it to the Lord's house that you come to pour forth the foulness of your heart, and the inspiration of the devil? Get you down, and remember that the sentence of death is on you; yea, and shall be executed, were it but for this day's work.'

'I go, friend, I go, for the voice* hath had its utterance,' replied she, in a depressed and even mild tone. 'I have done my mission unto thee and to thy people. Reward me with stripes, imprisonment, or death, as ye shall be permitted.'

The weakness of exhausted passion caused her steps to totter as she descended the pulpit stairs. The people, in the meanwhile, were stirring to and fro on the floor of the house, whispering among themselves, and glancing towards the intruder. Many of them now recognized her as a woman who had assaulted the Governor with frightful language,* as he passed by the window of her prison; they knew, also, that she was adjudged to suffer death, and had been preserved only by an involuntary banishment into the wilderness. The new outrage, by which she had provoked her fate, seemed to render further lenity impossible; and a gentleman in military dress, with a stout man of inferior rank, drew towards the door of the meetinghouse, and awaited her approach. Scarcely did her feet press the floor, however, when an unexpected scene occurred. In that moment of her peril, when every eye frowned with death, a little timid boy pressed forth, and threw his arms round his mother.

'I am here, mother, it is I, and I will go with thee to prison,' he exclaimed.

She gazed at him with a doubtful and almost frightened expression, for she knew that the boy had been cast out to perish, and she had not hoped to see his face again. She feared, perhaps, that it was but one of the happy visions, with which her excited fancy had often deceived her, in the solitude of the desert, or in prison. But when she felt his hand warm within her own, and heard his little eloquence of childish love, she began to know that she was yet a mother.

'Blessed art thou, my son,' she sobbed. 'My heart was withered; yea, dead with thee and with thy father; and now it leaps as in the first moment when I pressed thee to my bosom.'

She knelt down, and embraced him again and again, while the joy that could find no words, expressed itself in broken accents, like the bubbles gushing up to vanish at the surface of a deep fountain. The sorrows of past years, and the darker peril that was nigh, cast not a shadow on the brightness of that fleeting moment. Soon, however, the spectators saw a change upon her face, as the consciousness of her sad estate returned, and grief supplied the fount of tears which joy had opened. By the words she uttered, it would seem that the indulgence of natural love had given her mind a momentary sense of its errors, and made her know how far she had strayed from duty, in following the dictates of a wild fanaticism.

'In a doleful hour art thou returned to me, poor boy,' she said, 'for thy mother's path has gone darkening onward, till now the end is death. Son, son, I have borne thee in my arms when my limbs were tottering, and I have fed thee with the food that I was fainting for; yet I have ill performed a mother's part by thee in life, and now I leave thee no inheritance but woe and shame. Thou wilt go seeking through the world, and find all hearts closed against thee, and their sweet affections turned to bitterness for my sake. My child, my child, how many a pang awaits thy gentle spirit, and I the cause of all!'

She hid her face on Ilbrahim's head, and her long, raven hair, discoloured with the ashes of her mourning, fell down about him like a veil. A low and interrupted moan was the voice of her heart's anguish, and it did not fail to move the sympathies of many who mistook their involuntary virtue for a sin. Sobs were audible in the female section of the house, and every man who was a father, drew his hand across his eyes. Tobias Pearson was agitated and uneasy, but a certain feeling like the consciousness of guilt oppressed him, so that he could not go forth and offer himself as the protector of the child. Dorothy, however, had watched her husband's eye. Her mind was free from the influence that had begun to work on his, and she drew near the Quaker woman, and addressed her in the hearing of all the congregation.

'Stranger, trust this boy to me, and I will be his mother,' she said, taking Ilbrahim's hand. 'Providence has signally marked out my husband to protect him, and he has fed at our table and lodged under our roof, now many days, till our hearts have grown very strongly unto him. Leave the tender child with us, and be at ease concerning his welfare.'

The Quaker rose from the ground, but drew the boy closer

to her, while she gazed earnestly in Dorothy's face. Her mild, but saddened features, and neat, matronly attire, harmonized together, and were like a verse of fireside poetry. Her very aspect proved that she was blameless, so far as mortal could be so, in respect to God and man; while the enthusiast, in her robe of sackcloth and girdle of knotted cord, had as evidently violated the duties of the present life and the future, by fixing her attention wholly on the latter. The two females, as they held each a hand of Ilbrahim, formed a practical allegory; it was rational piety* and unbridled fanaticism, contending for the empire of a young heart.

'Thou art not of our people,' said the Quaker, mournfully.

'No, we are not of your people,' replied Dorothy, with mildness, 'but we are Christians, looking upward to the same Heaven with you. Doubt not that your boy shall meet you there, if there be a blessing on our tender and prayerful guidance of him. Thither, I trust, my own children have gone before me, for I also have been a mother; I am no longer so,' she added, in a faltering tone, 'and your son will have all my care.'

'But will ye lead him in the path which his parents have trodden?' demanded the Quaker. 'Can ye teach him the enlightened faith which his father has died for, and for which I, even I, am soon to become an unworthy martyr? The boy has been baptized in blood; will ye keep the mark fresh and ruddy upon his forehead?'

'I will not deceive you,' answered Dorothy. 'If your child become our child, we must breed him up in the instruction which Heaven has imparted to us; we must pray for him the prayers of our own faith; we must do towards him according to the dictates of our own consciences, and not of yours. Were we to act otherwise, we should abuse your trust, even in complying with your wishes.'

The mother looked down upon her boy with a troubled countenance, and then turned her eyes upward to heaven. She seemed to pray internally, and the contention of her soul was evident.

'Friend,' she said at length to Dorothy, 'I doubt not that my son shall receive all earthly tenderness at thy hands. Nay, I will believe that thy imperfect lights may guide him to a better world; for surely thou art on the path thither. But thou hast spoken of a husband. Doth he stand here among this multitude of people? Let him come forth; for I must know to whom I commit this most precious trust.'

She turned her face upon the male auditors, and after a momentary delay, Tobias Pearson came forth from among them. The Quaker saw the dress which marked his military rank, and shook her head; but then she noted the hesitating air, the eyes that struggled with her own, and were vanquished; the colour that went and came, and could find no resting place. As she gazed, an unmirthful smile spread over her features, like sunshine that grows melancholy in some desolate spot. Her lips moved inaudibly, but at length she spake.

'I hear it, I hear it. The voice speaketh within me and saith, "Leave thy child, Catharine, for his place is here, and go hence, for I have other work for thee. Break the bonds of natural affection, martyr thy love, and know that in all these things eternal wisdom hath its ends." I go, friends, I go. Take ye my boy, my precious jewel. I go hence, trusting that all shall be well, and that even for his infant hands there is a labour in the vineyard.'

She knelt down and whispered to Ilbrahim, who at first struggled and clung to his mother, with sobs and tears, but remained passive when she had kissed his cheek and arisen from the ground. Having held her hands over his head in mental prayer, she was ready to depart.

'Farewell, friends, in mine extremity,' she said to Pearson and his wife; 'the good deed ye have done me is a treasure laid up in heaven, to be returned a thousand fold hereafter. And farewell ye, mine enemies, to whom it is not permitted to harm so much as a hair of my head, nor to stay my footsteps even for a moment. The day is coming, when ye shall call upon me to witness for ye to this one sin committed,* and I will rise up and answer.'

She turned her steps towards the door, and the men, who had stationed themselves to guard it, withdrew, and suffered her to pass. A general sentiment of pity overcame the virulence of religious hatred. Sanctified by her love, and her affliction, she went forth, and all the people gazed after her till she had journeyed up the hill, and was lost behind its brow. She went, the apostle of her own unquiet heart, to renew the wanderings of past years. For her voice had been already heard in many lands of Christendom; and she had pined in the cells of a Catholic Inquisition, before she felt the lash, and ate the bread,* of the Puritans. Her mission had extended also to the followers of the Prophet, and from them she had received the courtesy and kindness, which all the contending sects of our purer religion united to deny her. Her husband and herself had resided many months in Turkey,* where even the Sultan's countenance was gracious to them; in that pagan land, too, was Ilbrahim's birthplace, and his oriental name was a mark of gratitude for the good deeds of an unbeliever.

*   *   *   *   *

When Pearson and his wife had thus acquired all the rights over Ilbrahim that could be delegated, their affection for him became, like the memory of their native land, or their mild sorrow for the dead, a piece of the immovable furniture of their hearts. The boy, also, after a week or two of mental disquiet, began to gratify his protectors, by many inadvertent proofs that he considered them as parents, and their house as home. Before the winter snows were melted, the persecuted infant, the little wanderer from a remote and heathen country, seemed native in the New England cottage, and inseparable from the warmth and security of its hearth. Under the influence of kind treatment, and in the consciousness that he was loved, Ilbrahim's demeanour lost a premature manliness, which had resulted from his earlier situation; he became more childlike, and his natural character displayed itself with freedom. It was in many respects a beautiful one, yet the disordered imaginations of both his father and mother had perhaps propagated a certain unhealthiness in the mind of the boy. In his general state, Ilbrahim would derive enjoyment from the most trifling events, and from every object about him; he seemed to discover precious views of happiness, by a faculty analogous to that of the witch-hazle, which points to hidden treasure where all is barren to the eye. His airy gaiety, coming to him from a thousand sources, communicated itself to the family, and Ilbrahim was like a domesticated sun-beam, brightening moody countenances, and chasing away the gloom from the dark corners of the cottage. On the other hand, as the susceptibility of pleasure is also that of pain, the exuberant cheerfulness of the boy's prevailing temper sometimes yielded to moments of deep depression. His sorrows could not always be followed up to their original source, but most frequently they appeared to flow, though Ilbrahim was young to be sad for such a cause, from wounded love. The flightiness of his mirth rendered him often guilty of offences against the decorum of a Puritan household, and on these occasions he did not invariably escape rebuke. But the slightest word of real bitterness, which he was infallible in distinguishing from pretended anger, seemed to sink into his heart and poison all his enjoyments, till he became sensible that he was entirely forgiven. Of the malice, which generally accompanies a superfluity of sensitiveness, Ilbrahim was altogether destitute; when trodden upon, he would not turn; when wounded, he could but die. His mind was wanting in the stamina for self-support; it was a plant that would twine beautifully round something stronger than itself, but if repulsed, or torn away, it had no choice but to wither on the ground. Dorothy's acuteness taught her that severity would crush the spirit of the child, and she nurtured him with the gentle care of one who handles a butterfly. Her husband manifested an equal affection, although it grew daily less productive of familiar caresses.

The feelings of the neighbouring people, in regard to the Quaker infant and his protectors, had not undergone a favourable change, in spite of the momentary triumph which the desolate mother had obtained over their sympathies. The scorn and bitterness, of which he was the object, were very grievous to Ilbrahim, especially when any circumstance made him sensible that the children, his equals in age, partook of the enmity of their parents. His tender and social nature had already overflowed in attachments to everything about him, and still there was a residue of unappropriate* love, which he yearned to bestow upon the little ones who were taught to hate him. As the warm days of spring came on, Ilbrahim was accustomed to remain for hours, silent and inactive, within hearing of the children's voices at their play; yet, with his usual delicacy of feeling, he avoided their notice, and would flee and hide himself from the smallest individual among them. Chance, however, at length seemed to open a medium of communication between his heart and theirs; it was by means of a boy about two years older than Ilbrahim, who was injured by a fall from a tree in the vicinity of Pearson's habitation. As the sufferer's own home was at some distance, Dorothy willingly received him under her roof, and became his tender and careful nurse.

Ilbrahim was the unconscious possessor of much skill in physiognomy, and it would have deterred him, in other circumstances, from attempting to make a friend of this boy. The countenance of the latter immediately impressed a beholder disagreeably, but it required some examination to discover that the cause was a very slight distortion of the mouth, and the irregular, broken line, and near approach of the eye-brows. Analogous, perhaps, to these trifling deformities, was an almost imperceptible twist of every joint, and the uneven prominence of the breast; forming a body, regular in its general outline, but faulty in almost all its details. The disposition of the boy was sullen and reserved, and the village schoolmaster stigmatized him as obtuse in intellect; although, at a later period of life, he evinced ambition and very peculiar talents. But whatever might be his personal or moral irregularities, Ilbrahim's heart seized upon, and clung to him, from the moment that he was brought wounded into the cottage; the child of persecution seemed to compare his own fate with that of the sufferer, and to feel that even different modes of misfortune had created a sort of relationship between them. Food, rest, and the fresh air, for which he languished, were neglected; he nestled continually by the bed-side of the little stranger, and, with a fond jealousy, endeavoured to be the medium of all the cares that were bestowed upon him. As the boy became convalescent, Ilbrahim contrived games suitable to his situation, or amused him by a faculty which he had perhaps breathed in with the air of his barbaric birthplace. It was that of reciting imaginary adventures, on the spur of the moment, and apparently in inexhaustible succession. His tales were of course monstrous, disjointed, and without aim; but they were curious on account of a vein of human tenderness, which ran through them all, and was like a sweet, familiar face, encountered in the midst of wild and unearthly scenery. The auditor paid much attention to these romances, and sometimes interrupted them by brief remarks upon the incidents, displaying shrewdness above his years, mingled with a moral obliquity which grated very harshly against Ilbrahim's instinctive rectitude. Nothing, however, could arrest the progress of the latter's affection, and there were many proofs that it met with a response from the dark and stubborn nature on which it was lavished. The boy's parents at length removed him, to complete his cure under their own roof.

Ilbrahim did not visit his new friend after his departure; but he made anxious and continual inquiries respecting him, and informed himself of the day when he was to reappear among his playmates. On a pleasant summer afternoon, the children of the neighbourhood had assembled in the little forest-crowned amphitheatre behind the meetinghouse, and the recovering invalid was there, leaning on a staff. The glee of a score of untainted bosoms was heard in light and airy voices, which danced among the trees like sunshine become audible; the grown men of this weary world, as they journeyed by the spot, marvelled why life, beginning in such brightness, should proceed in gloom; and their hearts, or their imaginations, answered them and said, that the bliss of childhood gushes from its innocence. But it happened that an unexpected addition was made to the heavenly little band. It was Ilbrahim, who came towards the children, with a look of sweet confidence on his fair and spiritual face, as if, having manifested his love to one of them, he had no longer to fear a repulse from their society. A hush came over their mirth, the moment they beheld him, and they stood whispering to each other while he drew nigh; but, all at once, the devil of their fathers* entered into the unbreeched fanatics, and, sending up a fierce, shrill cry, they rushed upon the poor Quaker child. In an instant, he was the centre of a brood of baby-fiends, who lifted sticks against him, pelted him with stones, and displayed an instinct of destruction, far more loathsome than the bloodthirstiness of manhood. The invalid, in the meanwhile, stood apart from the tumult, crying out with a loud voice, 'Fear not, Ilbrahim, come hither and take my hand;' and his unhappy friend endeavoured to obey him. Having watched the victim's struggling approach, with a calm smile and unabashed eye, the foul-hearted little villain lifted his staff, and struck Ilbrahim on the mouth, so forcibly that the blood issued in a stream. The poor child's arms had been raised to guard his head from the storm of blows; but now he dropped them at once, for he was stricken in a tender part.* His persecutors beat him down, trampled upon him, dragged him by his long, fair locks, and Ilbrahim was on the point of becoming as veritable a martyr as ever entered bleeding into heaven. The uproar, however, attracted the notice of a few neighbours, who put themselves to the trouble of rescuing the little heretic, and of conveying him to Pearson's door.

Ilbrahim's bodily harm was severe, but long and careful nursing accomplished his recovery; the injury done to his sensitive spirit was more serious, though not so visible. Its signs were principally of a negative character, and to be discovered only by those who had previously known him. His gait was thenceforth slow, even, and unvaried by the sudden bursts of sprightlier motion, which had once corresponded to his overflowing gladness; his countenance was heavier, and its former play of expression, the dance of sunshine reflected from moving water, was destroyed by the cloud over his existence; his notice was attracted in a far less degree by passing events, and he appeared to find greater difficulty in comprehending what was new to him, than at a happier period. A stranger, founding his judgement upon these circumstances, would have said that the dullness of the child's intellect widely contradicted the promise of his features; but the secret was in the direction of Ilbrahim's thoughts, which were brooding within him when they should naturally have been wandering abroad. An attempt of Dorothy to revive his former sportiveness was the single occasion, on which his quiet demeanour yielded to a violent display of grief; he burst into passionate weeping, and ran and hid himself, for his heart had become so miserably sore, that even the hand of kindness tortured it like fire. Sometimes, at night and probably in his dreams, he was heard to cry, 'Mother! Mother!' as if her place, which a stranger had supplied while Ilbrahim was happy, admitted of no substitute in his extreme affliction. Perhaps, among the many life-weary wretches then upon the earth, there was not one who combined innocence and misery like this poor, broken-hearted infant, so soon the victim of his own heavenly nature.

While this melancholy change had taken place in Ilbrahim, one of an earlier origin and of different character had come to its perfection in his adopted father. The incident with which this tale commences found Pearson in a state of religious dullness, yet mentally disquieted, and longing for a more fervid faith than he possessed. The first effect of his kindness to Ilbrahim was to produce a softened feeling, an incipient love for the child's whole sect; but joined to this, and resulting perhaps from self-suspicion, was a proud and ostentatious contempt of their tenets and practical extravagances. In the course of much thought, however, for the subject struggled irresistibly into his mind, the foolishness of the doctrine began to be less evident, and the points which had particularly offended his reason assumed another aspect, or vanished entirely away. The work within him appeared to go on even while he slept, and that which had been a doubt, when he laid down to rest, would often hold the place of a truth, confirmed by some forgotten demonstration, when he recalled his thoughts in the morning. But while he was thus becoming assimilated to the enthusiasts, his contempt, in nowise decreasing towards them, grew very fierce against himself; he imagined, also, that every face of his acquaintance wore a sneer, and that every word addressed to him was a gibe. At length,* when the change in his belief was fully accomplished, the contest grew very terrible between the love of the world, in its thousand shapes, and the power which moved him to sacrifice all for the one pure faith; to quote his own words, subsequently uttered at a meeting of Friends, it was as if 'Earth and Hell had garrisoned the fortress of his miserable

soul, and Heaven came battering against it to storm the walls.'
Such was* his state of warfare at the period of Ilbrahim's
misfortune; and the emotions consequent upon that event
enlisted with the besieging army, and decided the victory.
There was* a triumphant shout within him, and from that
moment all was peace. Dorothy had not been the subject of
a similar process, for her reason was as clear as her heart was
tender.

In the mean time neither the fierceness of the persecutors,
nor the infatuation of their victims, had decreased. The
dungeons were never empty; the streets of almost every village
echoed daily with the lash; the life of a woman, whose mild
and christian spirit no cruelty could embitter, had been
sacrificed; and more innocent blood was yet to pollute the
hands, that were so often raised in prayer. Early after the
Restoration, the English Quakers represented to Charles II
that a 'vein of blood was opened in his dominions';* but
though the displeasure of the voluptuous king was roused, his
interference was not prompt.* And now the tale must stride
forward over many months, leaving Pearson to exult in*
the midst of ignominy and misfortune; his wife to a firm
endurance of a thousand sorrows; poor Ilbrahim to pine and
droop like a cankered rose-bud; his mother to wander on a
mistaken errand, neglectful of the holiest trust which can be
committed to a woman.

*　*　*　*　*

A winter evening, a night of storm, had darkened over
Pearson's habitation, and there were no cheerful faces to drive
the gloom from his broad hearth. The fire, it is true, sent forth
a glowing heat and a ruddy light, and large logs, dripping with
half-melted snow, lay ready to be cast upon the embers. But
the apartment was saddened in its aspect by the absence of
much of the homely wealth which had once adorned it; for the
exaction of repeated fines, and his own neglect of temporal
affairs, had greatly impoverished the owner. And with the
furniture of peace, the implements of war had likewise
disappeared; the sword was broken, the helm and cuirass were
cast away forever; the soldier had done with battles, and might
not lift so much as his naked hand to guard his head. But the

Holy Book remained, and the table on which it rested was drawn before the fire, while two of the persecuted sect sought comfort from its pages. He who listened, while the other read, was the master of the house, now emaciated in form, and altered as to the expression and healthiness of his countenance; for his mind had dwelt too long among visionary thoughts, and his body had been worn by imprisonment and stripes. The hale and weather-beaten old man, who sat beside him, had sustained less injury from a far longer course of the same mode of life. His features* were strong and well connected, and seemed to express firmness of purpose and sober understanding, although his actions had frequently been at variance with this last attribute. In person he was tall and dignified, and, which alone would have made him hateful to the Puritans, his grey locks fell from beneath the broad-brimmed hat, and rested on his shoulders. As the old man read the sacred page, the snow drifted against the windows, or eddied in at the crevices of the door, while a blast kept laughing in the chimney, and the blaze leaped fiercely up to seek it. And sometimes, when the wind struck the hill at a certain angle, and swept down by the cottage across the wintry plain, its voice was the most doleful that can be conceived; it came as if the Past were speaking, as if the Dead had contributed each a whisper, as if the Desolation of Ages were breathed in that one lamenting sound.

The Quaker at length closed the book, retaining however his hand between the pages which he had been reading, while he looked steadfastly at Pearson. The attitude and features of the latter might have indicated the endurance of bodily pain; he leaned his forehead on his hands, his teeth were firmly closed, and his frame was tremulous at intervals with a nervous agitation.

'Friend Tobias,' inquired the old man, compassionately, 'hast thou found no comfort in these many blessed passages of scripture?'

'Thy voice has fallen on my ear like a sound afar off and indistinct,' replied Pearson, without lifting his eyes. 'Yea, and when I have hearkened carefully, the words seemed cold and lifeless, and intended for another and a lesser grief than mine.

Remove the book,' he added, in a tone of sullen bitterness. 'I have no part in its consolations, and they do but fret my sorrow the more.'

'Nay, feeble brother, be not as one who hath never known the light,' said the elder Quaker, earnestly, but with mildness. 'Art thou he that wouldst be content to give all, and endure all, for conscience sake; desiring even peculiar trials, that thy faith might be purified, and thy heart weaned from worldly desires? And wilt thou sink beneath an affliction which happens alike to them that have their portion here below, and to them that lay up treasure in heaven? Faint not, for thy burthen is yet light.'

'It is heavy! It is heavier than I can bear!' exclaimed Pearson, with the impatience of a variable spirit. 'From my youth upward I have been a man marked out for wrath; and year by year, yea, day after day, I have endured sorrows such as others know not in their lifetime. And now I speak not of the love that has been turned to hatred, the honour to ignominy, the ease and plentifulness of all things to danger, want, and nakedness. All this I could have borne, and counted myself blessed. But when my heart was desolate with many losses, I fixed it upon the child of a stranger, and he became dearer to me than all my buried ones; and now he too must die, as if my love were poison. Verily, I am an accursed man, and I will lay me down in the dust, and lift up my head no more.'

'Thou sinnest, brother, but it is not for me to rebuke thee; for I also have had my hours of darkness, wherein I have murmured against the cross,' said the old Quaker. He continued, perhaps in the hope of distracting his companion's thoughts from his own sorrows. 'Even of late was the light obscured within me, when the men of blood had banished me on pain of death, and the constables led me onward from village to village, towards the wilderness. A strong and cruel hand was wielding the knotted cords; they sunk deep into the flesh, and thou might have tracked every reel and totter of my footsteps by the blood that followed. As we went on'—

'Have I not borne all this; and have I murmured?' interrupted Pearson, impatiently.

'Nay, friend, but hear me,' continued the other. 'As we journeyed on, night darkened on our path, so that no man could see the rage of the persecutors, or the constancy of my endurance, though Heaven forbid that I should glory therein. The lights began to glimmer in the cottage windows, and I could discern the inmates as they gathered, in comfort and security, every man with his wife and children by their own evening hearth. At length we came to a tract of fertile land; in the dim light, the forest was not visible around it; and behold! there was a straw-thatched dwelling, which bore the very aspect of my home, far over the wild ocean, far in our own England. Then came bitter thoughts upon me; yea, remembrances that were like death to my soul. The happiness of my early days was painted to me; the disquiet of my manhood, the altered faith of my declining years. I remembered how I had been moved to go forth a wanderer, when my daughter, the youngest, the dearest of my flock, lay on her dying bed,* and'—

'Couldst thou obey the command at such a moment?' exclaimed Pearson, shuddering.

'Yea, yea,' replied the old man, hurriedly. 'I was kneeling by her bed-side when the voice spoke loud within me; but immediately I rose, and took my staff, and gat me gone. Oh! that it were permitted me to forget her woful look, when I thus withdrew my arm, and left her journeying through the dark valley alone! for her soul was faint, and she had leaned upon my prayers. Now in that night of horror I was assailed by the thought that I had been an erring Christian, and a cruel parent; yea, even my daughter, with her pale, dying features, seemed to stand by me and whisper, "Father, you are deceived; go home and shelter your grey head." Oh! thou, to whom I have looked in my farthest wanderings,' continued the Quaker, raising his agitated eyes to heaven, 'inflict not upon the bloodiest of our persecutors the unmitigated agony of my soul, when I believed that all I had done and suffered for Thee was at the instigation of a mocking fiend! But I yielded not; I knelt down and wrestled with the tempter, while the scourge bit more fiercely into the flesh. My prayer was heard, and I went on in peace and joy towards the wilderness.'

The old man, though his fanaticism had generally all the calmness of reason, was deeply moved while reciting this tale; and his unwonted emotion seemed to rebuke and keep down that of his companion. They sat in silence, with their faces to the fire, imaging, perhaps, in its red embers, new scenes of persecution yet to be encountered. The snow still drifted hard against the windows, and sometimes, as the blaze of the logs had gradually sunk, came down the spacious chimney and hissed upon the hearth. A cautious footstep might now and then be heard in a neighbouring apartment, and the sound invariably drew the eyes of both Quakers to the door which led thither. When a fierce and riotous gust of wind had led his thoughts, by a natural association, to homeless travellers on such a night, Pearson resumed the conversation.

'I have well nigh sunk under my own share of this trial,' observed he, sighing heavily; 'yet I would that it might be doubled to me, if so the child's mother could be spared. Her wounds have been deep and many, but this will be the sorest of all.'

'Fear not for Catherine,'* replied the old Quaker; 'for I know that valiant woman, and have seen how she can bear the cross. A mother's heart, indeed, is strong in her, and may seem to contend mightily with her faith; but soon she will stand up and give thanks that her son has been thus early an accepted sacrifice. The boy hath done his work, and she will feel that he is taken hence in kindness both to him and her. Blessed, blessed are they, that with so little suffering can enter into peace!'

The fitful rush of the wind was now disturbed by a portentous sound; it was a quick and heavy knocking at the outer door. Pearson's wan countenance grew paler, for many a visit of persecution had taught him what to dread; the old man, on the other hand, stood up erect, and his glance was firm as that of the tried soldier who awaits his enemy.

'The men of blood have come to seek me,' he observed, with calmness. 'They have heard how I was moved to return from banishment; and now am I to be led to prison, and thence to death. It is an end I have long looked for. I will open unto them, lest they say, "Lo, he feareth!" '

'Nay, I will present myself before them,' said Pearson, with recovered fortitude. 'It may be that they seek me alone, and know not that thou abidest with me.'

'Let us go boldly, both one and the other,' rejoined his companion. 'It is not fitting that thou or I should shrink.'

They therefore proceeded through the entry to the door, which they opened, bidding the applicant 'Come in, in God's name!' A furious blast of wind drove the storm into their faces, and extinguished the lamp; they had barely time to discern a figure, so white from head to foot with the drifted snow that it seemed like Winter's self, come in human shape to seek refuge from its own desolation.

'Enter, friend, and do thy errand, be it what it may,' said Pearson. 'It must needs be pressing, since thou comest on such a bitter night.'

'Peace be with this household,' said the stranger, when they stood on the floor of the inner apartment.

Pearson started; the elder Quaker stirred the slumbering embers of the fire, till they sent up a clear and lofty blaze; it was a female voice that had spoken; it was a female form that shone out, cold and wintry, in that comfortable light.

'Catherine, blessed woman,' exclaimed the old man, 'art thou come to this darkened land again! art thou come to bear a valiant testimony as in former years? The scourge hath not prevailed against thee, and from the dungeon hast thou come forth triumphant; but strengthen, strengthen now thy heart, Catherine, for Heaven will prove thee yet this once, ere thou go to thy reward.'

'Rejoice, friends!' she replied. 'Thou who hast long been of our people, and thou whom a little child hath led to us, rejoice! Lo! I come, the messenger of glad tidings, for the day of persecution is overpast. The heart of the king, even Charles, hath been moved in gentleness towards us, and he hath sent forth his letters to stay the hands of the men of blood. A ship's company of our friends hath arrived at yonder town, and I also sailed joyfully among them.'

As Catherine spoke, her eyes were roaming about the room, in search of him for whose sake security was dear to her. Pearson made a silent appeal to the old man, nor did the latter shrink from the painful task assigned him.

'Sister,' he began, in a softened yet perfectly calm tone, 'thou tellest us of His Love, manifested in temporal good; and now must we speak to thee of that self-same love, displayed in chastenings. Hitherto, Catherine, thou hast been as one journeying in a darksome and difficult path, and leading an infant by the hand; fain wouldst thou have looked heavenward continually, but still the cares of that little child have drawn thine eyes, and thy affections, to the earth. Favourite sister! go on rejoicing, for his tottering footsteps shall impede thine own no more.'

But the unhappy mother was not thus to be consoled; she shook like a leaf, she turned white as the very snow that hung drifted into her hair. The firm old man extended his hand and held her up, keeping his eye upon hers, as if to repress any outbreak of passion.

'I am a woman, I am but a woman; will He try me above my strength?' said Catherine, very quickly, and almost in a whisper. 'I have been wounded sore; I have suffered much; many things in the body; many in the mind; crucified in myself, and in them that were dearest to me. Surely,' added she, with a long shudder, 'He hath spared me in this one thing.' She broke forth with sudden and irrepressible violence. 'Tell me, man of cold heart, what has God done to me? Hath He cast me down never to rise again? Hath He crushed my very heart in his hand? And thou, to whom I committed my child, how hast thou fulfilled thy trust? Give me back the boy, well, sound, alive, alive; or earth and heaven shall avenge me!'

The agonized shriek of Catherine was answered by the faint, the very faint voice of a child.

On this day it had become evident to Pearson, to his aged guest, and to Dorothy, that Ilbrahim's brief and troubled pilgrimage drew near its close. The two former would willingly have remained by him, to make use of the prayers and pious discourses which they deemed appropriate to the time, and which, if they be impotent as to the departing traveller's reception in the world whither he goes, may at least sustain him in bidding adieu to earth. But though Ilbrahim uttered no complaint, he was disturbed by the faces that looked upon him; so that Dorothy's entreaties, and their own conviction that the child's feet might tread heaven's pavement and not soil it, had induced the two Quakers to remove. Ilbrahim then closed his eyes and grew calm, and, except for now and then, a kind and low word to his nurse, might have been thought to slumber. As night-fall came on, however, and the storm began to rise, something seemed to trouble the repose of the boy's mind, and to render his sense of hearing active and acute. If a passing wind lingered to shake the casement, he strove to turn his head towards it; if the door jarred to and fro upon its hinges, he looked long and anxiously thitherward; if the heavy voice of the old man, as he read the scriptures, rose but a little higher, the child almost held his dying breath to listen; if a snow-drift swept by the cottage, with a sound like the trailing of a garment, Ilbrahim seemed to watch that some visitant should enter. But, after a little time, he relinquished whatever secret hope had agitated him, and, with one low, complaining whisper, turned his cheek upon the pillow. He then addressed Dorothy with his usual sweetness, and besought her to draw near him; she did so, and Ilbrahim took her hand in both of his, grasping it with a gentle pressure, as if to assure himself that he retained it. At intervals, and without disturbing the repose of his countenance, a very faint trembling passed over him from head to foot, as if a mild but somewhat cool wind had breathed upon him, and made him shiver. As the boy thus led her by the hand, in his quiet progress over the borders of eternity, Dorothy almost imagined that she could discern the near, though dim delightfulness, of the home he was about to reach; she would not have enticed the little wanderer back, though she bemoaned herself that she must leave him and return. But just when Ilbrahim's feet were pressing on the soil of Paradise, he heard a voice behind him, and it recalled him a few, few paces of the weary path which he had travelled. As Dorothy looked upon his features, she perceived that their placid expression was again disturbed; her own thoughts had been so wrapt in him, that all sounds of the storm, and of human speech, were lost to her; but when Catherine's shriek pierced through the room, the boy strove to raise himself.

'Friend, she is come! Open unto her!' cried he.

In a moment, his mother was kneeling by the bed-side; she drew Ilbrahim to her bosom, and he nestled there, with no violence of joy, but contentedly as if he were hushing himself to sleep. He looked into her face, and reading its agony, said, with feeble earnestness;

'Mourn not, dearest mother. I am happy now.' And with these words, the gentle boy was dead.

*   *   *   *   *

The king's mandate to stay the New England persecutors was effectual in preventing further martyrdoms; but the colonial authorities, trusting in the remoteness of their situation, and perhaps in the supposed instability of the royal government, shortly renewed their severities in all other respects. Catherine's fanaticism had become wilder by the sundering of all human ties; and wherever a scourge was lifted, there was she to receive the blow; and whenever a dungeon was unbarred, thither she came, to cast herself upon the floor. But in process of time, a more christian spirit—a spirit of forbearance, though not of cordiality or approbation, began to pervade the land in regard to the persecuted sect. And then, when the rigid old Pilgrims eyed her rather in pity than in wrath; when the matrons fed her with the fragments of their children's food, and offered her a lodging on a hard and lowly bed; when no little crowd of school-boys left their sports to cast stones after the roving enthusiast; then did Catherine return to Pearson's dwelling, and made that her home. As if Ilbrahim's sweetness yet lingered round his ashes; as if his gentle spirit came down from heaven to teach his parent a true religion, her fierce and vindictive nature was softened by the same griefs which had once irritated it. When the course of years had made the features of the unobtrusive mourner familiar in the settlement, she became a subject of not deep, but general interest; a being on whom the otherwise superfluous sympathies of all might be bestowed. Every one spoke of her with that degree of pity which it is pleasant to experience; every one was ready to do her the little kindnesses, which are not costly, yet manifest good will; and when at last she died, a long train of her once bitter persecutors followed her, with decent sadness and tears that were not painful, to her place by Ilbrahim's green and sunken grave. My heart* is glad of this triumph of our better nature; it gives me a kindlier feeling for the fathers of my native land; and with it I will close the tale.

MY KINSMAN, MAJOR MOLINEUX

AFTER the kings of Great Britain had assumed the right of appointing the colonial governors*, the measures of the latter seldom met with the ready and general approbation which had been paid to those of their predecessors, under the original charters. The people looked with most jealous scrutiny to the exercise of power which did not emanate from themselves, and they usually rewarded their rulers with slender gratitude for the compliances by which, in softening their instructions from beyond the sea, they had incurred the reprehension of those who gave them. The annals of Massachusetts Bay* will inform us, that of six governors* in the space of about forty years from the surrender of the old charter, under James II, two were imprisoned by a popular insurrection; a third, as Hutchinson inclines to believe, was driven from the province by the whizzing of a musket-ball; a fourth, in the opinion of the same historian, was hastened to his grave by continual bickerings with the House of Representatives; and the remaining two, as well as their successors, till the Revolution, were favoured with few and brief intervals of peaceful sway. The inferior members of the court party, in times of high political excitement, led scarcely a more desirable life. These remarks may serve as a preface to the following adventures, which chanced upon a summer night, not far from a hundred years ago.* The reader, in order to avoid a long and dry detail of colonial affairs, is requested to dispense with an account of the train of circumstances that had caused much temporary inflammation of the popular mind.*

It was near nine o'clock of a moonlight evening, when a boat crossed the ferry* with a single passenger, who had obtained his conveyance at that unusual hour by the promise of an extra fare. While he stood on the landing-place, searching in either pocket for the means of fulfilling his agreement, the ferryman lifted a lantern, by the aid of which, and the newly risen moon, he took a very accurate survey of the stranger's figure. He was a youth of barely eighteen years, evidently country-bred, and now, as it should seem, upon his first visit to town. He was clad in a coarse grey coat, well worn, but in excellent repair; his under garments were durably constructed of leather, and fitted tight to a pair of serviceable and well-shaped limbs; his stockings of blue yarn were the incontrovertible work of a mother or a sister; and on his head was a three-cornered hat, which in its better days had perhaps sheltered the graver brow of the lad's father. Under his left arm was a heavy cudgel, formed of an oak sapling, and retaining a part of the hardened root; and his equipment was completed by a wallet, not so abundantly stocked as to incommode the vigorous shoulders on which it hung. Brown, curly hair, well-shaped features, and bright, cheerful eyes were nature's gifts, and worth all that art could have done for his adornment.

The youth, one of whose names was Robin, finally drew from his pocket the half of a little province bill of five shillings, which, in the depreciation of that sort of currency, did but satisfy the ferryman's demand, with the surplus of a sexangular piece of parchment, valued at three pence. He then walked forward into the town, with as light a step as if his day's journey had not already exceeded thirty miles, and with as eager an eye as if he were entering London city, instead of the little metropolis of a New England colony. Before Robin had proceeded far, however, it occurred to him that he knew not whither to direct his steps; so he paused, and looked up and down the narrow street, scrutinizing the small and mean wooden buildings that were scattered on either side.

'This low hovel cannot be my kinsman's dwelling,' thought he, 'nor yonder old house, where the moonlight enters at the broken casement; and truly I see none hereabouts that might be worthy of him. It would have been wise to enquire my way of the ferryman, and doubtless he would have gone with me, and earned a shilling from the Major for his pains. But the next man I meet will do as well.'

He resumed his walk, and was glad to perceive that the street now became wider, and the houses more respectable in their appearance. He soon discerned a figure moving on moderately in advance, and hastened his steps to overtake it. As Robin drew nigh, he saw that the passenger was a man in years, with a full periwig of grey hair, a wide-skirted coat of dark cloth, and silk stockings rolled above his knees. He carried a long and polished cane, which he struck down perpendicularly before him, at every step; and at regular intervals he uttered two successive hems, of a peculiarly solemn and sepulchral intonation. Having made these observations, Robin laid hold of the skirt of the old man's coat, just when the light from the open door and windows of a barber's shop fell upon both their figures.

'Good evening to you, honoured sir,' said he, making a low bow, and still retaining his hold of the skirt. 'I pray you tell me whereabouts is the dwelling of my kinsman, Major Molineux.'*

The youth's question was uttered very loudly; and one of the barbers, whose razor was descending on a well-soaped chin, and another who was dressing a Ramillies wig,* left their occupations, and came to the door. The citizen, in the meantime, turned a long-favoured countenance upon Robin, and answered him in a tone of excessive anger and annoyance. His two sepulchral hems, however, broke into the very centre of his rebuke, with most singular effect, like a thought of the cold grave obtruding among wrathful passions.

'Let go my garment, fellow! I tell you, I know not the man you speak of. What! I have authority,* I have—hem, hem—authority; and if this be the respect you show for your betters, your feet shall be brought acquainted with the stocks by daylight, tomorrow morning!'

Robin released the old man's skirt, and hastened away, pursued by an ill-mannered roar of laughter* from the barber's shop. He was at first considerably suprised by the result of his question, but, being a shrewd youth,* soon thought himself able to account for the mystery.

'This is some country representative,' was his conclusion, 'who has never seen the inside of my kinsman's door, and lacks the breeding to answer a stranger civilly. The man is old, or verily—I might be tempted to turn back and smite him on the nose. Ah, Robin, Robin! even the barber's boys laugh at you for choosing such a guide! You will be wiser in time, friend Robin.'

He now became entangled in a succession of crooked and narrow streets, which crossed each other, and meandered at no great distance from the waterside. The smell of tar was obvious to his nostrils, the masts of vessels pierced the moonlight above the tops of the buildings, and the numerous signs, which Robin paused to read, informed him that he was near the centre of business.* But the streets were empty, the shops were closed, and lights were visible only in the second stories of a few dwelling-houses. At length, on the corner of a narrow lane, through which he was passing, he beheld the broad countenance of a British hero swinging before the door of an inn, whence proceeded the voices of many guests. The casement of one of the lower windows was thrown back, and a very thin curtain permitted Robin to distinguish a party at supper, round a well-furnished table. The fragrance of the good cheer steamed forth into the outer air, and the youth could not fail to recollect that the last remnant of his travelling stock of provision had yielded to his morning appetite, and that noon had found and left him dinnerless.

'O, that a parchment three-penny might give me a right to sit at yonder table!' said Robin, with a sigh. 'But the Major will make me welcome to the best of his victuals; so I will even step boldly in, and inquire my way to his dwelling.'

He entered the tavern, and was guided by the murmur of voices and the fumes of tobacco to the public room. It was a along and low apartment, with oaken walls, grown dark in the continual smoke, and a floor which was thickly sanded, but of no immaculate purity. A number of persons—the larger part of whom appeared to be mariners, or in some way connected with the sea—occupied the wooden benches, or leather-bottomed chairs, conversing on various matters, and occasionally lending their attention to some topic of general interest. Three or four little groups were draining as many bowls of punch, which the West India trade had long since made a familiar drink in the colony. Others, who had the appearance of men who lived by regular and laborious handicraft, preferred the insulated bliss of an unshared potation, and became more taciturn under its influence. Nearly all, in short, evinced a predilection for the Good Creature in some of its various shapes, for this is a vice to which, as Fast-day sermons* of a hundred years ago will testify, we have a long hereditary claim. The only guests to whom Robin's sympathies inclined him were two or three sheepish countrymen, who were using the inn somewhat after the fashion of a Turkish caravansary;* they had gotten themselves into the darkest corner of the room, and, heedless of the Nicotian atmosphere, were supping on the bread of their own ovens, and the bacon cured in their own chimney-smoke. But though Robin felt a sort of brotherhood with these strangers, his eyes were attracted from them to a person who stood near the door, holding whispered conversation with a group of ill-dressed associates. His features were separately striking almost to grotesqueness, and the whole face left a deep impression on the memory. The forehead bulged out into a double prominence, with a vale between; the nose came boldly forth in an irregular curve, and its bridge was of more than a finger's breadth; the eyebrows were deep and shaggy, and the eyes glowed beneath them like fire in a cave.

While Robin deliberated of whom to inquire respecting his kinsman's dwelling, he was accosted by the innkeeper, a little man in a stained white apron, who had come to pay his professional welcome to the stranger. Being in the second generation from a French Protestant, he seemed to have inherited the courtesy of his parent nation; but no variety of circumstances was ever known to change his voice from the one shrill note in which he now addressed Robin.

'From the country, I presume, sir?' said he, with a profound bow. 'Beg leave to congratulate you on your arrival, and trust you intend a long stay with us. Fine town here, sir, beautiful buildings, and much that may interest a stranger. May I hope for the honour of your commands in respect to supper?'

'The man sees a family likeness! the rogue has guessed that I am related to the Major!' thought Robin, who had hitherto experienced little superfluous civility.

All eyes were now turned on the country lad, standing at the door, in his worn three-cornered hat, grey coat, leather breeches, and blue yarn stockings, leaning on an oaken cudgel, and bearing a wallet on his back.

Robin replied to the courteous innkeeper, with such an assumption of confidence as befitted the Major's relative. 'My honest friend,' he said, 'I shall make it a point to patronize your house on some occasion, when'—here he could not help lowering his voice—'when I may have more than a parchment threepence in my pocket. My present business,' continued he, speaking with lofty confidence, 'is merely to inquire my way to the dwelling of my kinsman, Major Molineux.'

There was a sudden and general movement in the room, which Robin interpreted as expressing the eagerness of each individual to become his guide. But the innkeeper turned his eyes to a written paper on the wall, which he read, or seemed to read, with occasional recurrences to the young man's figure.

'What have we here?' said he, breaking his speech into little dry fragments. ' "Left the house of the subscriber, bounden servant, Hezekiah Mudge,—had on, when he went away, grey coat, leather breeches, master's third-best hat. One pound currency reward to whosoever shall lodge him in any jail of the province." Better trudge, boy, better trudge!'

Robin had begun to draw his hand towards the lighter end of the oak cudgel, but a strange hostility in every countenance induced him to relinquish his purpose of breaking the courteous innkeeper's head. As he turned to leave the room, he encountered a sneering glance from the bold-featured personage whom he had before noticed; and no sooner was he beyond the door, than he heard a general laugh, in which the innkeeper's voice might be distinguished, like the dropping of small stones into a kettle.

'Now, is it not strange,' thought Robin, with his usual shrewdness,—'is it not strange that the confession of an empty pocket should outweigh the name of my kinsman, Major

Molineux? Oh, if I had one of those grinning rascals in the woods, where I and my oak sapling grew up together, I would teach him that my arm is heavy, though my purse be light!'

On turning the corner of the narrow lane, Robin found himself in a spacious street, with an unbroken line of lofty houses on each side, and a steepled building at the upper end, whence the ringing of a bell announced the hour of nine. The light of the moon, and the lamps from the numerous shop-windows, discovered people promenading on the pavement, and amongst them Robin hoped to recognize his hitherto inscrutable relative. The result of his former inquiries made him unwilling to hazard another, in a scene of such publicity, and he determined to walk slowly and silently up the street, thrusting his face close to that of every elderly gentleman, in search of the Major's lineaments. In his progress, Robin encountered many gay and gallant figures. Embroidered garments of showy colours, enormous periwigs, gold-laced hats, and silver-hilted swords glided past him and dazzled his optics. Travelled youths, imitators of the European fine gentlemen of the period, trod jauntily along, half dancing to the fashionable tunes which they hummed, and making poor Robin ashamed of his quiet and natural gait. At length, after many pauses to examine the gorgeous display of goods in the shop-windows, and after suffering some rebukes for the impertinence of his scrutiny into people's faces, the Major's kinsman found himself near the steepled building, still unsuccessful in his search. As yet, however he had seen only one side of the thronged street; so Robin crossed, and continued the same sort of inquisition down the opposite pavement, with stronger hopes than the philosopher seeking an honest man, but with no better fortune. He had arrived about midway towards the lower end, from which his course began, when he overheard the approach of some one who struck down a cane on the flagstones at every step, uttering, at regular intervals, two sepulchral hems.

'Mercy on us!' quoth Robin, recognizing the sound.

Turning a corner, which chanced to be close at his right hand, he hastened to pursue his researches in some other part of the town. His patience now was wearing low, and he seemed to feel more fatigue from his rambles since he crossed the ferry, than from his journey of several days on the other side. Hunger also pleaded loudly within him, and Robin began to balance the propriety of demanding violently, and with lifted cudgel, the necessary guidance from the first solitary passenger whom he should meet. While a resolution to this effect was gaining strength, he entered a street of mean appearance, on either side of which a row of ill-built houses was straggling towards the harbour. The moonlight fell upon no passenger along the whole extent, but in the third domicile which Robin passed there was a half-opened door, and his keen glance detected a woman's garment within.

'My luck may be better here,' said he to himself.

Accordingly, he approached the door, and beheld it shut closer as he did so; yet an open space remained, sufficing for the fair occupant to observe the stranger, without a corresponding display on her part. All that Robin could discern was a strip of scarlet petticoat, and the occasional sparkle of an eye, as if the moonbeams were trembling on some bright thing.

'Pretty mistress,' for I may call her so with a good conscience, thought the shrewd youth, since I know nothing to the contrary,—'my sweet pretty mistress, will you be kind enough to tell me whereabouts I must seek the dwelling of my kinsman, Major Molineux?'

Robin's voice was plaintive and winning, and the female, seeing nothing to be shunned in the handsome country youth, thrust open the door, and came forth into the moonlight. She was a dainty little figure, with a white neck, round arms, and a slender waist, at the extremity of which her scarlet petticoat jutted out over a hoop, as if she were standing in a balloon. Moreover, her face was oval and pretty, her hair dark beneath the little cap, and her bright eyes possessed a sly freedom, which triumphed over those of Robin.

'Major Molineux dwells here,' said this fair woman.

Now, her voice was the sweetest Robin had heard that night, the airy counterpart of a stream of melted silver; yet he could not help doubting whether that sweet voice spoke Gospel truth. He looked up and down the mean street, and then surveyed the house before which they stood. It was a small, dark edifice of two stories, the second of which projected over the lower floor; and the front apartment had the aspect of a shop for petty commodities.

'Now, truly, I am in luck,' replied Robin, cunningly,* 'and so indeed is my kinsman, the Major, in having so pretty a housekeeper. But I prithee trouble him to step to the door; I will deliver him a message from his friends in the country, and then go back to my lodgings at the inn.'

'Nay, the Major has been abed this hour or more,' said the lady of the scarlet petticoat; 'and it would be to little purpose to disturb him tonight, seeing his evening draught was of the strongest. But he is a kind-hearted man, and it would be as much as my life's worth to let a kinsman of his turn away from the door. You are the good old gentleman's very picture, and I could swear that was his rainy-weather hat. Also he has garments very much resembling those leather small-clothes. But come in, I pray, for I bid you hearty welcome in his name.'

So saying, the fair and hospitable dame took our hero by the hand; and the touch was light, and the force was gentleness, and though Robin read in her eyes what he did not hear in her words, yet the slender waisted woman in the scarlet petticoat proved stronger than the athletic country youth. She had drawn his half-willing footsteps nearly to the threshold, when the opening of a door in the neighbourhood startled the Major's housekeeper, and, leaving the Major's kinsman, she vanished speedily into her own domicile. A heavy yawn preceded the appearance of a man, who, like the Moonshine of Pyramus and Thisbe,* carried a lantern, needlessly aiding his sister luminary in the heavens. As he walked sleepily up the street, he turned his broad, dull face on Robin, and displayed a long staff, spiked at the end.

'Home, vagabond, home!' said the watchman, in accents that seemed to fall asleep as soon as they were uttered. 'Home, or we'll set you in the stocks, by peep of day!'

'This is the second hint of the kind,' thought Robin. 'I wish they would end my difficulties, by setting me there to-night.'

Nevertheless, the youth felt an instinctive antipathy towards the guardian of midnight order, which at first prevented him from asking his usual question. But just when the man was about to vanish behind the corner, Robin resolved not to lose the opportunity, and shouted lustily after him,—

'I say, friend! will you guide me to the house of my kinsman, Major Molineux?'

The watchman made no reply, but turned the corner and was gone; yet Robin seemed to hear the sound of drowsy laughter stealing along the solitary street. At that moment, also, a pleasant titter saluted him from the open window above his head; he looked up, and caught the sparkle of a saucy eye; a round arm beckoned to him, and next he heard light footsteps descending the staircase within. But Robin, being of the household of a New England clergyman, was a good youth, as well as a shrewd one; so he resisted temptation, and fled away.

He now roamed desperately, and at random, through the town, almost ready to believe that a spell was on him, like that by which a wizard of his country had once kept three pursuers wandering, a whole winter night, within twenty paces of the cottage which they sought. The streets lay before him, strange and desolate, and the lights were extinguished in almost every house. Twice, however, little parties of men, among whom Robin distinguished individuals in outlandish attire, came hurrying along; but though on both occasions they paused to address him, such intercourse did not at all enlighten his perplexity. They did but utter a few words in some language of which Robin knew nothing, and perceiving his inability to answer, bestowed a curse upon him in plain English, and hastened away. Finally, the lad determined to knock at the door of every mansion that might appear worthy to be occupied by his kinsman, trusting that perseverance would overcome the fatality that had hitherto thwarted him. Firm in this resolve, he was passing beneath the walls of a church, which formed the corner of two streets, when, as he turned into the shade of its steeple, he encountered a bulky stranger, muffled in a cloak. The man was proceeding with the speed of earnest business, but Robin planted himself full before him, holding the oak cudgel with both hands across his body as a bar to further passage.

'Halt, honest man, and answer me a question,' said he, very resolutely. 'Tell me, this instant, whereabouts is the dwelling of my kinsman, Major Molineux!'

'Keep your tongue between your teeth, fool, and let me pass!' said a deep, gruff voice, which Robin partly remembered. 'Let me pass, I say, or I'll strike you to the earth!'

'No, no, neighbour!' cried Robin, flourishing his cudgel, and then thrusting its larger end close to the man's muffled face. 'No, no, I'm not the fool you take me for, nor do you pass till I have an answer to my question. Whereabouts is the dwelling of my kinsman, Major Molineux?'

The stranger, instead of attempting to force his passage, stepped back into the moonlight, unmuffled his face, and stared full into that of Robin.

'Watch here an hour, and Major Molineux will pass by,' said he.

Robin gazed with dismay and astonishment on the unprecedented physiognomy of the speaker. The forehead with its double prominence, the broad hooked nose, the shaggy eyebrows, and fiery eyes were those which he had noticed at the inn, but the man's complexion had undergone a singular, or, more properly, a twofold change. One side of the face blazed an intense red, while the other was black as midnight, the division line being in the broad bridge of the nose: and a mouth which seemed to extend from ear to ear was black or red, in contrast to the colour of the cheek. The effect was as if two individual devils, a fiend of fire and a fiend of darkness, had united themselves to form this infernal visage.* The stranger grinned in Robin's face, muffled his party-coloured features, and was out of sight in a moment.

'Strange things we travellers see!' ejaculated Robin.

He seated himself, however, upon the steps of the church-door, resolving to wait the appointed time for his kinsman. A few moments were consumed in philosophical speculations upon the species of man who had just left him; but having settled this point shrewdly, rationally, and satisfactorily, he was compelled to look elsewhere for his amusement. And first he threw his eyes along the street. It was of more respectable appearance than most of those into which he had wandered, and the moon, creating, like the imaginative power, a beautiful strangeness in familiar objects, gave something of romance to a scene that might not have possessed it in the light of day. The irregular and often quaint architecture of the houses, some of whose roofs were broken into numerous little peaks, while others ascended, steep and narrow, into a single point, and others again were square; the pure snow-white of some of their complexions, the aged darkness of others, and the thousand sparklings, reflected from bright substances in the walls of many; these matters engaged Robin's attention for a while, and then began to grow wearisome. Next he endeavoured to define the forms of distant objects, starting away, with almost ghostly indistinctness, just as his eye appeared to grasp them; and finally he took a minute survey of an edifice which stood on the opposite side of the street, directly in front of the church-door, where he was stationed. It was a large, square mansion,* distinguished from its neighbours by a balcony, which rested on tall pillars, and by an elaborate Gothic window, communicating therewith.

Perhaps this is the very house I have been seeking,' thought Robin.

Then he strove to speed away the time, by listening to a murmur which swept continually along the street, yet was scarcely audible, except to an unaccustomed ear like his; it was a low, dull, dreamy sound, compounded of many noises, each of which was at too great a distance to be separately heard. Robin marvelled at this snore of a sleeping town, and marvelled more whenever its continuity was broken by now and then a distant shout, apparently loud where it originated. But altogether it was a sleep-inspiring sound, and, to shake off its drowsy influence, Robin arose, and climbed a window-frame, that he might view the interior of the church. There the moonbeams came trembling in, and fell down upon the deserted pews, and extended along the quiet aisles. A fainter yet more awful radiance was hovering around the pulpit, and one solitary ray had dared to rest upon the open page of the great Bible. Had nature, in that deep hour, become a worshipper in the house which man had built? Or was that heavenly light the visible sanctity of the place—visible because no earthly and impure feet were within the walls? The scene made Robin's heart shiver with a sensation of loneliness stronger than he had ever felt in the remotest depths of his native woods; so he turned away and sat down again before the door. There were graves around the church, and now an uneasy thought obtruded into Robin's breast. What if the object of his search, which had been so often and so strangely thwarted, were all the time mouldering in his shroud?* What if his kinsman should glide through yonder gate, and nod and smile to him in dimly passing by?

'Oh, that any breathing thing were here with me!' said Robin.

Recalling his thoughts from this uncomfortable track, he sent them over forest, hill, and stream, and attempted to imagine how that evening of ambiguity and weariness had been spent by his father's household. He pictured them assembled at the door, beneath the tree, the great old tree, which had been spared for its huge twisted trunk, and venerable shade, when a thousand leafy brethren fell. There, at the going down of the summer sun, it was his father's custom to perform domestic worship, that the neighbours might come and join with him like brothers of the family, and that the wayfaring man might pause to drink at that fountain, and keep his heart pure by freshening the memory of home. Robin distinguished the seat of every individual of the little audience; he saw the good man in the midst, holding the Scriptures in the golden light that fell from the western clouds; he beheld him close the book and all rise up to pray. He heard the old thanksgivings for daily mercies, the old supplications for their continuance, to which he had so often listened in weariness, but which were now among his dear remembrances. He perceived the slight inequality of his father's voice when he came to speak of the absent one; he noted how his mother turned her face to the broad and knotted trunk; how his elder brother scorned, because the beard was rough upon his upper lip, to permit his features to be moved; how the younger sister drew down a low hanging branch before her eyes; and how the little one of all, whose sports had hitherto broken the decorum of the scene, understood the prayer for her playmate, and burst into clamorous grief. Then he saw them go in at the door; and when Robin would have entered also, the latch tinkled into its place, and he was excluded* from his home.

'Am I here, or there?' cried Robin, starting; for all at once, when his thoughts had become visible and audible in a dream, the long, wide, solitary street shone out before him.

He aroused himself, and endeavoured to fix his attention steadily upon the large edifice which he had surveyed before. But still his mind kept vibrating between fancy and reality; by turns, the pillars of the balcony lengthened into the tall, bare stems of pines, dwindled down to human figures, settled again into their true shape and size, and then commenced a new succession of changes. For a single moment, when he deemed himself awake, he could have sworn that a visage—one which he seemed to remember, yet could not absolutely name as his kinsman's—was looking towards him from the Gothic window. A deeper sleep wrestled with and nearly overcame him, but fled at the sound of footsteps along the opposite pavement. Robin rubbed his eyes, discerned a man passing at the foot of the balcony, and addressed him in a loud, peevish, and lamentable cry.

'Hallo, friend! must I wait here all night for my kinsman, Major Molineux?'

The sleeping echoes awoke, and answered the voice; and the passenger, barely able to discern a figure sitting in the oblique shade of the steeple, traversed the street to obtain a nearer view. He was himself a gentleman in his prime, of open, intelligent, cheerful, and altogether prepossessing countenance. Perceiving a country youth, apparently homeless and without friends, he accosted him in a tone of real kindness,* which had become strange to Robin's ears.

'Well, my good lad, why are you sitting here?' inquired he. 'Can I be of service to you in any way?'

'I am afraid not, sir,' replied Robin, despondingly; 'yet I shall take it kindly if you'll answer me a single question. I've been searching, half the night, for one Major Molineux; now, sir, is there really such a person in these parts, or am I dreaming?'

'Major Molineux! The name is not altogether strange to me,' said the gentleman, smiling. 'Have you any objection to telling me the nature of your business with him?'

Then Robin briefly related that his father was a clergyman, settled on a small salary, at a long distance back in the country, and that he and Major Molineux were brothers' children. The Major, having inherited riches, and acquired civil and military rank, had visited his cousin, in great pomp, a year or two before; had manifested much interest in Robin and an elder brother, and, being childless himself, had thrown out hints respecting the future establishment of one of them in life. The elder brother was destined to succeed to the farm which his father cultivated in the interval of sacred duties; it was therefore determined that Robin should profit by his kinsman's generous intentions, especially as he seemed to be rather the favourite, and was thought to possess other necessary endowments.

'For I have the name of being a shrewd youth,' observed Robin, in this part of his story.

'I doubt not you deserve it,' replied his new friend, good-naturedly; 'but pray proceed.'

'Well, sir, being nearly eighteen years old, and well grown, as you see,' continued Robin, drawing himself up to his full height, 'I thought it high time to begin the world. So my mother and sister put me in handsome trim, and my father gave me half the remnant of his last year's salary, and five days ago I started for this place, to pay the Major a visit. But, would you believe it, sir! I crossed the ferry a little after dark, and have yet found nobody that would show me the way to his dwelling; only, an hour or two since, I was told to wait here, and Major Molineux would pass by.'

'Can you describe the man who told you this?' inquired the gentleman.

'Oh, he was a very ill-favoured fellow, sir,' replied Robin, 'with two great bumps on his forehead, a hook nose, fiery eyes; and, what struck me as the strangest, his face was of two different colours. Do you happen to know such a man, sir?'

'Not intimately,' answered the stranger, 'but I chanced to meet him a little time previous to your stopping me. I believe you may trust his word, and that the Major will very shortly pass through this street. In the meantime, as I have a singular curiosity to witness your meeting, I will sit down here upon the steps, and bear you company.'

He seated himself accordingly, and soon engaged his companion in animated discourse. It was but of brief continuance, however, for a noise of shouting, which had long been remotely audible, drew so much nearer that Robin inquired its cause.

'What may be the meaning of this uproar?' asked he. 'Truly, if your town be always as noisy, I shall find little sleep while I am an inhabitant.'

'Why, indeed, friend Robin, there do appear to be three or four riotous fellows abroad to-night,' replied the gentleman. 'You must not expect all the stillness of your native woods, here in our streets. But the watch will shortly be at the heels of these lads, and—'

'Aye, and set them in the stocks by peep of day,' interrupted Robin, recollecting his own encounter with the drowsy lantern-bearer. 'But, dear sir, if I may trust my ears, an army of watchmen would never make head against such a multitude of rioters. There were at least a thousand voices went up to make that one shout.'

'May not a man have several voices, Robin, as well as two complexions?'* said his friend.

'Perhaps a man may; but Heaven forbid that a woman should!' responded the shrewd youth, thinking of the seductive tones of the Major's housekeeper.

The sounds of a trumpet in some neighbouring street now became so evident and continual, that Robin's curiosity was strongly excited. In addition to the shouts, he heard frequent bursts from many instruments of discord, and a wild and confused laughter filled up the intervals. Robin rose from the steps, and looked wistfully towards a point whither several people seemed to be hastening.

'Surely some prodigious merry-making is going on,' exclaimed he. 'I have laughed very little since I left home, sir, and should be sorry to lose an opportunity. Shall we step round the corner by that darkish house, and take our share of the fun?'

'Sit down again, sit down, good Robin,' replied the gentleman, laying his hand on the skirt of the grey coat. 'You forget that we must wait here for your kinsman; and there is reason to believe that he will pass by, in the course of a very few moments.'

The near approach of the uproar had now disturbed the neighbourhood; windows flew open on all sides; and many heads, in the attire of the pillow, and confused by sleep suddenly broken, were protruded to the gaze of whoever had leisure to observe them. Eager voices hailed each other from house to house, all demanding the explanation, which not a soul could give. Half-dressed men hurried towards the unknown commotion, stumbling as they went over the stone steps that thrust themselves into the narrow foot-walk. The shouts, the laughter, and the tuneless bray, the antipodes of music, came onwards with increasing din, till scattered individuals, and then denser bodies, began to appear round a corner at the distance of a hundred yards.

'Will you recognize your kinsman, if he passes in this crowd?' inquired the gentleman.

'Indeed, I can't warrant it, sir; but I'll take my stand here, and keep a bright lookout,' answered Robin, descending to the outer edge of the pavement.

A mighty stream of people now emptied into the street, and came rolling slowly towards the church. A single horseman wheeled the corner in the midst of them, and close behind him came a band of fearful wind-instruments, sending forth a fresher discord, now that no intervening buildings kept it from the ear. Then a redder light disturbed the moonbeams, and a dense multitude of torches shone along the street, concealing, by their glare, whatever object they illuminated. The single horseman, clad in a military dress, and bearing a drawn sword, rode onward as the leader, and, by his fierce and variegated countenance, appeared like war personified; the red of one cheek was an emblem of fire and sword; the blackness of the other betokened the mourning that attends them. In his train were wild figures in the Indian dress, and many fantastic shapes without a model, giving the whole march a visionary air, as if a dream had broken forth from some feverish brain, and were sweeping visibly through the midnight streets. A mass of people, inactive, except as applauding spectators, hemmed the procession in; and several women ran along the sidewalk, piercing the confusion of heavier sounds with their shrill voices of mirth or terror.

'The double-faced fellow has his eye upon me,' muttered Robin, with an indefinite but an uncomfortable idea that he was himself to bear a part in the pageantry.

The leader turned himself in the saddle, and fixed his glance full upon the country youth, as the steed went slowly by. When Robin had freed his eyes from those fiery ones, the musicians were passing before him, and the torches were close at hand; but the unsteady brightness of the latter formed a veil which he could not penetrate. The rattling of wheels over the stones sometimes found its way to his ears, and confused traces of a human form appeared at intervals, and then melted into the vivid light. A moment more, and the leader thundered a command to halt: the trumpets vomited a horrid breath, and then held their peace; the shouts and laughter of the people died away, and there remained only a universal hum, allied to silence. Right before Robin's eyes was an uncovered cart. There the torches blazed the brightest, there the moon shone out like day, and there, in tar-and-feathery dignity, sat his kinsman, Major Molineux!

He was an elderly man, of large and majestic person, and strong, square features, betokening a steady soul; but steady as it was, his enemies had found means to shake it. His face was pale as death, and far more ghastly; the broad forehead was contracted in his agony, so that his eyebrows formed one grizzled line; his eyes were red and wild, and the foam hung white upon his quivering lip. His whole frame was agitated by a quick and continual tremor, which his pride strove to quell, even in those circumstances of overwhelming humiliation. But perhaps the bitterest pang of all was when his eyes met those of Robin; for he evidently knew him on the instant, as the youth stood witnessing the foul disgrace of a head grown grey in honour. They stared at each other in silence, and Robin's knees shook, and his hair bristled, with a mixture of pity and terror. Soon, however, a bewildering excitement began to seize upon his mind; the preceding adventures of the night, the unexpected appearance of the crowd, the torches, the confused din and the hush that followed, the spectre of his kinsman reviled by that great multitude, all this, and, more than all, a perception of tremendous ridicule in the whole scene, affected him with a sort of mental inebriety. At that moment a voice of sluggish merriment saluted Robin's ears; he turned instinctively, and just behind the corner of the church stood the lantern-bearer, rubbing his eyes, and drowsily enjoying the lad's amazement. Then he heard a peal of laughter like the ringing of silvery bells; a woman twitched his arm, a saucy eye met his, and he saw the lady of the scarlet petticoat. A sharp, dry cachinnation appealed to his memory, and, standing on tiptoe in the crowd, with his white apron over his head, he beheld the courteous little innkeeper. And lastly, there sailed over the heads of the multitude a great, broad laugh, broken in the midst by two sepulchral hems; thus, 'Haw, haw, haw,—hem, hem,—haw, haw, haw, haw!'

The sound proceeded from the balcony of the opposite edifice, and thither Robin turned his eyes. In front of the Gothic window stood the old citizen, wrapped in a wide gown, his grey periwig exchanged for a nightcap, which was thrust back from his forehead, and his silk stockings hanging about his legs. He supported himself on his polished cane in a fit of convulsive merriment, which manifested itself on his solemn old features like a funny inscription on a tombstone. Then Robin seemed to hear the voices of the barbers, of the guests of the inn, and of all who had made sport of him that night. The contagion was spreading among the multitude, when, all at once, it seized upon Robin, and he sent forth a shout of laughter that echoed through the street;—every man shook his sides, every man emptied his lungs, but Robin's shout was the loudest there. The cloud-spirits peeped from their silvery islands, as the congregated mirth went roaring up the sky! The Man in the Moon heard the far bellow. 'Oho,' quoth he, 'the old earth is frolicsome to-night!'

When there was a momentary calm in that tempestuous sea of sound, the leader gave the sign, the procession resumed its march. On they went, like fiends that throng in mockery around some dead potentate,* mighty no more, but majestic still in his agony. On they went, in counterfeited pomp, in senseless uproar, in frenzied merriment, trampling all on an old man's heart. On swept the tumult and left a silent street behind.

* * * * *

'Well, Robin, are you dreaming?' inquired the gentleman, laying his hand on the youth's shoulder.

Robin started, and withdrew his arm from the stone post to which he had instinctively clung, as the living stream rolled by him. His cheek was somewhat pale, and his eye not quite as lively as in the earlier part of the evening.

'Will you be kind enough to show me the way to the ferry?' said he, after a moment's pause.

'You have, then, adopted a new subject of inquiry?' observed his companion, with a smile.

'Why, yes, sir,' replied Robin, rather dryly. 'Thanks to you, and to my other friends, I have at last met my kinsman, and he will scarce desire to see my face again. I begin to grow weary of a town life, sir. Will you show me the way to the ferry?'

'No, my good friend Robin,—not to-night, at least,' said the gentleman. 'Some few days hence, if you wish it, I will speed you on your journey. Or, if you prefer to remain with us, perhaps, as you are a shrewd youth, you may rise in the world without the help of your kinsman, Major Molineux.'

ROGER MALVIN'S BURIAL

ONE of the few incidents of Indian warfare naturally susceptible of the moonlight of romance was that expedition undertaken for the defence of the frontiers in the year 1725, which resulted in the well-remembered 'Lovell's Fight'. Imagination, by casting certain circumstances judicially into the shade,* may see much to admire in the heroism of a little band who gave battle to twice their number in the heart of the enemy's country. The open bravery displayed by both parties was in accordance with civilized ideas of valour; and Chivalry itself might not blush to record the deeds of one or two individuals. The battle, though so fatal to those who fought, was not unfortunate in its consequences to the country; for it broke the strength of a tribe and conduced to the peace which subsisted during several ensuing years. History and tradition are unusually minute in their memorials of this affair; and the captain of a scouting party of frontier men has acquired as actual a military renown as many a victorious leader of thousands. Some of the incidents contained in the following pages will be recognized, notwithstanding the substitution of fictitious names, by such as have heard, from old men's lips, the fate of the few combatants who were in a condition to retreat after 'Lovell's Fight'.

*   *   *   *   *

The early sunbeams hovered cheerfully upon the tree-tops, beneath which two weary and wounded men had stretched their limbs the night before. Their bed of withered oak leaves was strewn upon the small level space, at the foot of a rock, situated near the summit of one of the gentle swells by which the face of the country is there diversified. The mass of granite, rearing its smooth flat surface fifteen or twenty feet above their heads, was not unlike a gigantic gravestone, upon which the veins seemed to form an inscription in forgotten characters. On a tract of several acres around this rock, oaks and other hard wood trees had supplied the place of the pines, which were the usual growth of the land; and a young and vigorous sapling stood close beside the travellers.

The severe wound of the elder man had probably deprived him of sleep; for, as soon as the first ray of sunshine rested on the top of the highest tree, he reared himself painfully from his recumbent posture and sat erect. The deep lines of his countenance and the scattered grey of his hair marked him as past the middle age; but his muscular frame would, but for the effects of his wound, have been as capable of sustaining fatigue as in the early vigour of life. Languor and exhaustion now sat upon his haggard features; and the despairing glance which he sent forward through the depths of the forest proved his own conviction that his pilgrimage was at an end. He next turned his eyes to the companion who reclined by his side.

The youth—for he had scarcely attained the years of manhood—lay, with his head upon his arm, in the embrace of an unquiet sleep, which a thrill of pain from his wounds seemed each moment on the point of breaking. His right hand grasped a musket; and, to judge from the violent action of his features, his slumbers were bringing back a vision of the conflict of which he was one of the few survivors. A shout— deep and loud in his dreaming fancy—found its way in an imperfect murmur to his lips; and, starting even at the slight sound of his own voice, he suddenly awoke. The first act of reviving recollection was to make anxious inquiries respecting the condition of his wounded fellow traveller. The latter shook his head.

'Reuben,* my boy,' said he, 'this rock beneath which we sit will serve for an old hunter's gravestone. There is many and many a long mile of howling wilderness* before us yet; nor would it avail me anything if the smoke of my own chimney were but on the other side of that swell of land. The Indian bullet was deadlier than I thought.'

'You are weary with our three days' travel,' replied the youth, 'and a little longer rest will recruit you. Sit you here while I search the woods for the herbs and roots that must be our sustenance; and, having eaten, you shall lean on me, and we will turn our faces homeward. I doubt not that, with my help, you can attain to some one of the frontier garrisons.'

'There is not two days' life in me, Reuben,' said the other, calmly, 'and I will no longer burden you with my useless body, when you can scarcely support your own. Your wounds are deep and your strength is failing fast; yet, if you hasten onward alone, you may be preserved. For me there is no hope, and I will await death here.'

'If it must be so, I will remain and watch by you,' said Reuben, resolutely.

'No, my son, no,' rejoined his companion. 'Let the wish of a dying man have weight with you; give me one grasp of your hand, and get you hence. Think you that my last moments will be eased by the thought that I leave you to die a more lingering death? I have loved you like a father, Reuben; and at a time like this I should have something of a father's authority. I charge you to be gone, that I may die in peace.'

'And because you have been a father to me, should I therefore leave you to perish and to lie unburied in the wilderness?' exclaimed the youth. 'No; if your end be in truth approaching, I will watch by you and receive your parting words. I will dig a grave here by the rock, in which, if my weakness overcome me, we will rest together or, if Heaven gives me strength, I will seek my way home.'

'In the cities and wherever men dwell,' replied the other, 'they bury their dead in the earth; they hide them from the sight of the living; but here, where no step may pass perhaps for a hundred years, wherefore should I not rest beneath the open sky, covered only by the oak-leaves when the autumn winds shall strew them? And for a monument, here is this grey rock, on which my dying hand shall carve the name of Roger Malvin; and the traveller in days to come will know that here sleeps a hunter and a warrior. Tarry not, then, for a folly like this, but hasten away, if not for your own sake, for hers who will else be desolate.'

Malvin spoke the last few words in a faltering voice, and their effect upon his companion was strongly visible. They reminded him that there were other and less questionable duties than that of sharing the fate of a man whom his death could not benefit. Nor can it be affirmed that no selfish feeling strove to enter Reuben's heart, though the consciousness made him more earnestly resist his companion's entreaties.

'How terrible to wait the slow approach of death in this solitude!' exclaimed he. 'A brave man does not shrink in the battle; and, when friends stand round the bed, even women may die composedly; but here—'

'I shall not shrink even here, Reuben Bourne,' interrupted Malvin. 'I am a man of no weak heart; and, if I were, there is a surer support than that of earthly friends. You are young, and life is dear to you. Your last moments will need comfort far more than mine; and when you have laid me in the earth, and are alone, and night is settling on the forest, you will feel all the bitterness of the death that may now be escaped. But I will urge no selfish motive to your generous nature. Leave me for my sake, that, having said a prayer for your safety, I may have space to settle my account undisturbed by worldly sorrows.'

'And your daughter,—how shall I dare to meet her eye?' exclaimed Reuben. 'She will ask the fate of her father, whose life I vowed to defend with my own. Must I tell her that he travelled three days' march with me from the field of battle, and that then I left him to perish in the wilderness? Were it not better to lie down and die by your side than to return safe and say this to Dorcas?'

'Tell my daughter,' said Roger Malvin, 'that, though yourself sore wounded, and weak, and weary, you led my tottering footsteps many a mile, and left me only at my earnest entreaty, because I would not have your blood upon my soul. Tell her, that through pain and danger you were faithful, and that, if your life-blood could have saved me, it would have flowed to its last drop; and tell her that you will be something dearer than a father, and that my blessing is with you both, and that my dying eyes can see a long and pleasant path in which you will journey together.'

As Malvin spoke he almost raised himself from the ground, and the energy of his concluding words seemed to fill the wild and lonely forest with a vision of happiness; but, when he sank exhausted upon his bed of oak-leaves, the light which had kindled in Reuben's eye was quenched. He felt as if it were both sin and folly to think of happiness at such a moment. His companion watched his changing countenance, and sought with generous art to wile him* to his own good.

'Perhaps I deceive myself in regard to the time I have to live,' he resumed. 'It may be that, with speedy assistance, I might recover of my wound. The foremost fugitives must, ere this, have carried tidings of our fatal battle to the frontier, and parties will be out to succour those in like condition with ourselves. Should you meet one of these and guide them hither, who can tell but that I may sit by my own fireside again?'

A mournful smile strayed across the features of the dying man as he insinuated that unfounded hope; which, however, was not without its effect on Reuben. No merely selfish motive, nor even the desolate condition of Dorcas, could have induced him to desert his companion at such a moment; but his wishes seized upon the thought that Malvin's life might be preserved, and his sanguine nature heightened almost to certainty the remote possibility of procuring human aid.

'Surely there is reason, weighty reason, to hope that friends are not far distant,' he said, half aloud. 'There fled one coward,* unwounded, in the beginning of the fight, and most probably he made good speed. Every true man on the frontier would shoulder his musket at the news; and, though no party may range so far into the woods as this, I shall perhaps encounter them in one day's march. Counsel me faithfully,' he added, turning to Malvin, in distrust of his own motives. 'Were your situation mine, would you desert me while life remained?'

'It is now twenty years,' replied Roger Malvin, sighing, however, as he secretly acknowledged the wide dissimilarity between the two cases,—'it is now twenty years since I escaped with one dear friend from Indian captivity near Montreal. We journeyed many days through the woods, till at length, overcome with hunger and weariness, my friend lay down and besought me to leave him; for he knew that, if I remained, we both must perish; and, with but little hope of obtaining succour, I heaped a pillow of dry leaves beneath his head and hastened on.'

'And did you return in time to save him?' asked Reuben, hanging on Malvin's words as if they were to be prophetic of his own success.

'I did,' answered the other. 'I came upon the camp of a hunting party before sunset of the same day. I guided them to the spot where my comrade was expecting death; and he is now a hale and hearty man upon his own farm, far within the frontiers, while I lie wounded here in the depths of the wilderness.'

This example, powerful in effecting Reuben's decision, was aided, unconsciously to himself, by the hidden strength* of many another motive. Roger Malvin perceived that the victory was nearly won.

'Now, go, my son, and Heaven prosper you!' he said. 'Turn not back with your friends when you meet them, lest your wounds and weariness overcome you; but send hitherward two or three, that may be spared, to search for me; and believe me, Reuben, my heart will be lighter with every step you take towards home.' Yet there was, perhaps, a change both in his countenance and voice as he spoke thus; for, after all, it was a ghastly fate to be left expiring in the wilderness.

Reuben Bourne, but half convinced that he was acting rightly, at length raised himself from the ground and prepared himself for his departure. And first, though contrary to Malvin's wishes, he collected a stock of roots and herbs, which had been their only food during the last two days. This useless supply he placed within reach of the dying man, for whom, also, he swept together a fresh bed of dry oak-leaves. Then climbing to the summit of the rock, which on one side was rough and broken, he bent the oak sapling downward, and bound his handkerchief to the topmost branch.* This precaution was not unnecessary to direct any who might come in search of Malvin; for every part of the rock, except its broad smooth front, was concealed at a little distance by the dense undergrowth of the forest. The handkerchief had been the bandage of a wound upon Reuben's arm; and, as he bound it to the tree, he vowed by the blood that stained it that he would return, either to save his companion's life, or to lay his body in the grave. He then descended, and stood, with downcast eyes, to receive Roger Malvin's parting words.

The experience of the latter suggested much and minute advice respecting the youth's journey through the trackless forest. Upon this subject he spoke with calm earnestness, as if he were sending Reuben to the battle or the chase while he himself remained secure at home, and not as if the human countenance that was about to leave him were the last he would ever behold. But his firmness was shaken before he concluded.

'Carry my blessing to Dorcas, and say that my last prayer shall be for her and you. Bid her to have no hard thoughts because you left me here,'—Reuben's heart smote him,—'for that your life would not have weighed with you if its sacrifice could have done me good. She will marry you after she has mourned a little while for her father; and Heaven grant you long and happy days, and may your children's children stand round your death-bed! And, Reuben,' added he, as the weakness of mortality made its way at last, 'return, when your wounds are healed and your weariness refreshed,—return to this wild rock, and lay my bones in the grave, and say a prayer over them.'

An almost superstitious regard, arising perhaps from the customs of the Indians, whose war was with the dead as well as the living, was paid by the frontier inhabitants to the rites of sepulture;* and there are many instances of the sacrifice of life in the attempt to bury those who had fallen by the 'sword of the wilderness'. Reuben, therefore, felt the full importance of the promise which he most solemnly made to return and perform Roger Malvin's obsequies. It was remarkable that the latter, speaking his whole heart in his parting words, no longer endeavoured to persuade the youth that even the speediest succour might avail to the preservation of his life. Reuben was internally convinced that he should see Malvin's living face no more. His generous nature would fain have delayed him, at whatever risk, till the dying scene were past; but the desire of existence and the hope of happiness had strengthened in his heart, and he was unable to resist them.

'It is enough,' said Roger Malvin, having listened to Reuben's promise. 'Go, and God speed you!'

The youth pressed his hand in silence, turned, and was departing. His slow and faltering steps, however, had borne him but a little way before Malvin's voice recalled him.

'Reuben, Reuben,' said he, faintly; and Reuben returned and knelt down by the dying man.

'Raise me, and let me lean against the rock,' was his last request. 'My face will be turned towards home,* and I shall see you a moment longer as you pass among the trees.'

Reuben, having made the desired alteration in his companion's posture, again began his solitary pilgrimage. He walked more hastily at first than was consistent with his strength; for a sort of guilty feeling, which sometimes torments men in their most justifiable acts, caused him to seek concealment from Malvin's eyes; but after he had trodden far upon the rustling forest leaves he crept back, impelled by a wild and painful curiosity, and, sheltered by the earthy roots of an uptorn tree, gazed earnestly at the desolate man. The morning sun was unclouded, and the trees and shrubs imbibed the sweet air of the month of May; yet there seemed a gloom on Nature's face, as if she sympathized with mortal pain and sorrow. Roger Malvin's hands were uplifted in a fervent prayer, some of the words of which stole through the stillness of the woods and entered Reuben's heart, torturing it with an unutterable pang. They were the broken accents of a petition for his own happiness and that of Dorcas; and, as the youth listened, conscience, or something in its similitude, pleaded strongly with him to return and lie down again by the rock. He felt how hard was the doom of the kind and generous being whom he had deserted in his extremity. Death would come like the slow approach of a corpse, stealing gradually towards him through the forest, and showing its ghastly and motionless features from behind a nearer and yet a nearer tree. But such must have been Reuben's own fate had he tarried another sunset; and who shall impute blame to him* if he shrank from so useless a sacrifice? As he gave a parting look, a breeze waved the little banner upon the sapling oak and reminded Reuben of his vow.

*   *   *   *   *

Many circumstances contributed to retard the wounded traveller in his way to the frontiers. On the second day the clouds, gathering densely over the sky, precluded the possibility of regulating his course by the position of the sun; and he knew not but that every effort of his almost exhausted strength was removing him farther from the home he sought. His scanty sustenance was supplied by the berries and other spontaneous products of the forest. Herds of deer, it is true, sometimes bounded past him, and partridges frequently whirred up before his footsteps; but his ammunition had been expended in the fight, and he had no means of slaying them. His wounds, irritated by the constant exertion in which lay the only hope of life, wore away his strength and at intervals confused his reason. But, even in the wanderings of intellect, Reuben's young heart clung strongly to existence; and it was only through absolute incapacity of motion that he at last sank down beneath a tree, compelled there to await death.

In this situation he was discovered by a party who, upon the first intelligence of the fight, had been dispatched to the relief of the survivors. They conveyed him to the nearest settlement, which chanced to be that of his own residence.

Dorcas, in the simplicity of the olden time, watched by the bedside of her wounded lover, and administered all those comforts that are in the sole gift of woman's heart and hand. During several says Reuben's recollection strayed drowsily among the perils and hardships through which he had passed, and he was incapable of returning definite answers to the inquiries with which many were eager to harass him. No authentic particulars of the battle had yet been circulated; nor could mothers, wives, and children tell whether their loved ones were detained by captivity or by the stronger chain of death. Dorcas nourished her apprehensions in silence till one afternoon when Reuben awoke from an unquiet sleep, and seemed to recognize her more perfectly than at any previous time. She saw that his intellect had become composed, and she could no longer restrain her filial anxiety.

'My father, Reuben?' she began; but the change in her lover's countenance made her pause.

The youth shrank as if with a bitter pain, and the blood gushed vividly into his wan and hollow cheeks. His first impulse was to cover his face; but, apparently with a desperate effort, he half raised himself and spoke vehemently, defending himself against an imaginary accusation.

'Your father was sore wounded in the battle, Dorcas; and he bade me not burden myself with him, but only to lead him to the lake side, that he might quench his thirst and die. But I would not desert the old man in his extremity, and, though bleeding myself, I supported him; I gave him half my strength, and led him away with me. For three days we journeyed on together, and your father was sustained beyond my hopes; but, awaking at sunrise on the fourth day, I found him faint and exhausted; he was unable to proceed; his life had ebbed away fast; and—'

'He died!' exclaimed Dorcas, faintly.

Reuben felt it impossible to acknowledge that his selfish love of life had hurried him away before her father's fate was decided. He spoke not; he only bowed his head; and, between shame and exhaustion, sank back and hid his face in the pillow. Dorcas wept when her fears were thus confirmed; but the shock, as it had been long anticipated, was on that account the less violent.

'You dug a grave for my poor father in the wilderness, Reuben?' was the question by which her filial piety manifested itself.

'My hands were weak; but I did what I could,' replied the youth in a smothered tone. 'There stands a noble tombstone above his head; and I would to Heaven I slept as soundly as he!'

Dorcas, perceiving the wildness of his latter words, inquired no further at the time; but her heart found ease in the thought that Roger Malvin had not lacked such funeral rites as it was possible to bestow. The tale of Reuben's courage and fidelity lost nothing when she communicated it to her friends; and the poor youth, tottering from his sick chamber to breathe the sunny air, experienced from every tongue the miserable and humiliating torture of unmerited praise. All acknowledged that he might worthily demand the hand of the fair maiden to whose father he had been 'faithful unto death'; and, as my tale is not of love, it shall suffice to say that in the space of a few months Reuben became the husband of Dorcas Malvin. During the marriage ceremony the bride was covered with blushes; but the bridegroom's face was pale.

There was now in the breast of Reuben Bourne an incommunicable thought,—something which he was to conceal most heedfully from her whom he most loved and trusted. He regretted, deeply and bitterly, the moral cowardice that had restrained his words when he was about to disclose the truth to Dorcas; but pride, the fear of losing her affection, the dread of universal scorn, forbade him to rectify this falsehood. He felt that for leaving Roger Malvin he deserved no censure. His presence, the gratuitous sacrifice of his own life, would have added only another and a needless agony to the last moments of the dying man; but concealment had imparted to a justifiable act much of the secret effect of guilt; and Reuben, while reason told him that he had done right, experienced in no small degree the mental horrors which punish the perpetrator of undiscovered crime. By a certain association of ideas, he at times almost imagined himself a murderer.* For years, also, a thought would occasionally recur, which, though he perceived all its folly and extravagance, he had not power to banish from his mind. It was a haunting and torturing fancy that his father-in-law was yet sitting at the foot of the rock, on the withered forest leaves, alive and awaiting his pledged assistance. These mental deceptions, however, came and went, nor did he ever mistake them for realities; but in the calmest and clearest moods of his mind he was conscious that he had a deep vow unredeemed, and that an unburied corpse was calling to him out of the wilderness. Yet such was the consequence of his prevarication, that he could not obey the call. It was now too late to require the assistance of Roger Malvin's friends in performing his long-deferred sepulture; and superstitious fears, of which none were more susceptible than the people of the outward settlements, forbade Reuben to go alone. Neither did he know where in the pathless and illimitable forest to seek that smooth and lettered rock at the base of which the body lay; his remembrance of every portion of his travel thence was indistinct, and the latter part had left no impression upon his mind. There was, however, a continual impulse, a voice audible only to himself,* commanding him to go forth and redeem his vow; and he had a strange impression that, were he to make the trial, he would be led straight to Malvin's bones. But year after year that summons, unheard but felt, was disobeyed. His one secret thought became like a chain binding down his spirit and like a serpent gnawing into his heart; and he was transformed into a sad and downcast yet irritable man.

In the course of a few years after their marriage changes began to be visible in the external prosperity of Reuben and Dorcas. The only riches of the former had been his stout heart and strong arm; but the latter, her father's sole heiress, had made her husband master of a farm, under older cultivation, larger, and better stocked than most of the frontier establishments. Reuben Bourne, however, was a neglectful husbandman; and, while the lands of the other settlers became

annually more fruitful, his deteriorated in the same proportion. The discouragements to agriculture were greatly
lessened by the cessation of Indian war, during which men
held the plough in one hand and the musket in the other, and
were fortunate if the products of their dangerous labour were
not destroyed, either in the field or in the barn, by the savage
enemy. But Reuben did not profit by the altered condition
of the country, nor can it be denied that his intervals of
industrious attention to his affairs were but scantily rewarded
with success. The irritability by which he had recently
become distinguished was another cause of his declining
prosperity, as it occasioned frequent quarrels in his unavoidable intercourse with the neighbouring settlers. The
results of these were innumerable lawsuits; for the people of
New England, in the earliest stages and wildest circumstances
of the country, adopted, whenever attainable, the legal mode
of deciding their differences. To be brief, the world did not
go well with Reuben Bourne; and, though not till many years
after his marriage, he was finally a ruined man, with but one
remaining expedient against the evil fate that had pursued him.
He was to throw sunlight into some deep recess of the forest,
and seek subsistence from the virgin bosom of the wilderness.

The only child of Reuben and Dorcas was a son, now
arrived at the age of fifteen years, beautiful in youth, and
giving promise of a glorious manhood. He was peculiarly
qualified for, and already began to excel in, the wild
accomplishments of frontier life. His foot was fleet, his aim
true, his apprehension quick, his heart glad and high; and all
who anticipated the return of Indian war spoke of Cyrus
Bourne as a future leader in the land. The boy was loved by
his father with a deep and silent strength, as if whatever was
good and happy in his own nature had been transferred to his
child, carrying his affections with it. Even Dorcas, though
loving and beloved, was far less dear to him; for Reuben's
secret thoughts and insulated emotions had gradually made
him a selfish man, and he could no longer love deeply except
where he saw or imagined some reflection or likeness of his
own mind. In Cyrus he recognized what he had himself been
in other days; and at intervals he seemed to partake of the

boy's spirit and to be revived with a fresh and happy life. Reuben was accompanied by his son in the expedition, for the purpose of selecting a tract of land and felling and burning the timber, which necessarily preceded the removal of the household gods. Two months of autumn were thus occupied; after which Reuben Bourne and his young hunter returned to spend their last winter in the settlements.

* * * * *

It was early in the month of May that the little family snapped asunder whatever tendrils of affection had clung to inanimate objects, and bade farewell to the few who, in the blight of fortune, called themselves their friends. The sadness of the parting moment had, to each of the pilgrims, its peculiar alleviations. Reuben, a moody man, and misanthropic because unhappy, strode onward with his usual stern brow and downcast eye, feeling few regrets and disdaining to acknowledge any. Dorcas, while she wept abundantly over the broken ties by which her simple and affectionate nature had bound itself to everything, felt that the inhabitants of her inmost heart moved on with her, and that all else would be supplied wherever she might go. And the boy dashed one teardrop from his eye, and thought of the adventurous pleasures of the untrodden forest.

Oh, who, in the enthusiasm of a day-dream, has not wished that he were a wanderer in a world of summer wilderness, with one fair and gentle being hanging lightly on his arm? In youth his free and exulting step would know no barrier but the rolling ocean or the snow-topped mountains; calmer manhood would choose a home where Nature had strewn a double wealth in the vale of some transparent stream; and when hoary age, after long years of that pure life, stole on and found him there, it would find him the father of a race, the patriarch of a people, the founder of a mighty nation yet to be. When death, like the sweet sleep which we welcome after a day of happiness, came over him, his far descendants would mourn over the venerated dust. Enveloped by tradition in mysterious attributes, the men of future generations would call him godlike; and remote posterity would see him standing, dimly glorious, far up the valley of a hundred centuries.

The tangled and gloomy forest through which the personages of my tale were wandering differed widely from the dreamer's land of fantasy; yet there was something in their way of life that Nature asserted as her own, and the gnawing cares which went with them from the world were all that now obstructed their happiness. One stout and shaggy steed, the bearer of all their wealth, did not shrink from the added weight of Dorcas; although her hardy breeding sustained her, during the latter part of each day's journey, by her husband's side. Reuben and his son, their muskets on their shoulders and their axes slung behind them, kept an unwearied pace, each watching with a hunter's eye for the game that supplied their food. When hunger bade, they halted and prepared their meal on the bank of some unpolluted forest brook, which, as they knelt down with thirsty lips to drink, murmured a sweet unwillingness, like a maiden at love's first kiss. They slept beneath a hut of branches, and awoke at peep of light refreshed for the toils of another day. Dorcas and the boy went on joyously, and even Reuben's spirit shone at intervals with an outward gladness; but inwardly there was a cold, cold sorrow, which he compared to the snow-drifts lying deep in the glens and hollows of the rivulets while the leaves were brightly green above.

Cyrus Bourne was sufficiently skilled in the travel of the woods to observe that his father did not adhere to the course they had pursued in their expedition of the preceding autumn. They were now keeping farther to the north, striking out more directly from the settlements, and into a region of which savage beasts and savage men were as yet the sole possessors. The boy sometimes hinted his opinions upon the subject, and Reuben listened attentively, and once or twice altered the direction of their march in accordance with his son's counsel; but, having done so, he seemed ill at ease. His quick and wandering glances were sent forward, apparently in search of enemies lurking behind the tree-trunks; and, seeing nothing there, he would cast his eyes backwards as if in fear of some pursuer. Cyrus, perceiving that his father gradually resumed the old direction, forbore to interfere; nor, though something began to weigh upon his heart, did his adventurous nature permit him to regret the increased length and the mystery of their way.

On the afternoon of the fifth day they halted, and made their simple encampment nearly an hour before sunset. The face of the country, for the last few miles, had been diversified by swells of land resembling huge waves of a petrified sea; and in one of the corresponding hollows, a wild and romantic spot, had the family reared their hut and kindled their fire. There is something chilling, and yet heart-warming, in the thought of these three, united by strong bands of love and insulated from all that breathe beside. The dark and gloomy pines looked down upon them, and as the wind swept through their tops a pitying sound was heard in the forest; or did those old trees groan in fear that men were come to lay the axe to their roots at last? Reuben and his son, while Dorcas made ready their meal, proposed to wander out in search of game, of which that day's march had afforded no supply. The boy, promising not to quit the vicinity of the encampment, bounded off with a step as light and elastic as that of the deer he hoped to slay; while his father, feeling a transient happiness as he gazed after him, was about to pursue an opposite direction. Dorcas, in the meanwhile, had seated herself near their fire of fallen branches, upon the moss-grown and mouldering trunk of a tree uprooted years before. Her employment, diversified by an occasional glance at the pot, now beginning to simmer over the blaze, was the perusal of the current year's Massachusetts Almanac, which, with the exception of an old black-letter Bible, comprised all the literary wealth of the family. None pay a greater regard to arbitrary divisions of time than those who are excluded from society; and Dorcas mentioned, as if the information were of importance, that it was now the twelfth of May.* Her husband started.

'The twelfth of May! I should remember it well,' muttered he, while many thoughts occasioned a momentary confusion in his mind. 'Where am I? Whither am I wandering? Where did I leave him?'

Dorcas, too well accustomed to her husband's wayward moods to note any peculiarity of demeanour, now laid aside the almanac and addressed him in that mournful tone which the tender-hearted appropriate to griefs long cold and dead.

'It was near this time of the month, eighteen years ago, that my poor father left this world for a better. He had a kind arm to hold his head and a kind voice to cheer him, Reuben, in his last moments; and the thought of the faithful care you took of him has comforted me many a time since. Oh, death would have been awful to a solitary man in a wild place like this!'

'Pray Heaven, Dorcas,' said Reuben, in a broken voice,—'pray Heaven that neither of us three dies solitary and lies unburied in this howling wilderness!' And he hastened away, leaving her to watch the fire beneath the gloomy pines.

Reuben Bourne's rapid pace gradually slackened as the pang, unintentionally inflicted by the words of Dorcas, became less acute. Many strange reflections, however, thronged upon him; and, straying onward rather like a sleep-walker than a hunter, it was attributable to no care of his own that his devious course kept him in the vicinity of the encampment. His steps were imperceptibly led almost in a circle; nor did he observe that he was on the verge of a tract of land heavily timbered, but not with pine trees. The place of the latter was here supplied by oaks and other of the harder woods; and around their roots clustered a dense and bushy undergrowth, leaving, however, barren spaces between the trees, thick strewn with withered leaves. Whenever the rustling of the branches or the creaking of the trunks made a sound, as if the forest were waking from slumber, Reuben instinctively raised the musket that rested on his arm, and cast a quick, sharp glance on every side; but, convinced by a partial observation that no animal was near, he would again give himself up to his thoughts. He was musing on the strange influence that had led him away from his premeditated course and so far into the depths of the wilderness. Unable to penetrate to the secret place of his soul where his motives lay hidden, he believed that a supernatural voice had called him onward and that a supernatural power had obstructed his retreat. He trusted that it was Heaven's intent to afford him an opportunity of expiating his sin; he hoped that he might find the bones so long unburied; and that having laid the earth over them, peace would throw its sunlight into the sepulchre of his heart. From these thoughts he was aroused by a rustling in the forest at some distance from the spot to which he had wandered. Perceiving the motion of some object behind a thick veil of undergrowth, he fired, with the instinct of a hunter and the aim of a practised marksman.* A low moan, which told his success, and by which even animals can express their dying agony, was unheeded by Reuben Bourne. What were the recollections now breaking upon him?

The thicket into which Reuben had fired was near the summit of a swell of land, and was clustered around the base of a rock, which, in the shape and smoothness of one of its surfaces, was not unlike a gigantic gravestone. As if reflected in a mirror, its likeness was in Reuben's memory. He even recognized the veins which seemed to form an inscription in forgotten characters: everything remained the same, except that a thick covert of bushes shrouded the lower part of the rock, and would have hidden Roger Malvin had he still been sitting there. Yet in the next moment Reuben's eye was caught by another change that time had effected since he last stood where he was now standing again behind the earthy roots of the uptorn tree. The sapling to which he had bound the blood-stained symbol of his vow had increased and strengthened into an oak, far indeed from its maturity, but with no mean spread of shadowy branches. There was one singularity observable in this tree which made Reuben tremble. The middle and lower branches were in luxuriant life, and an excess of vegetation had fringed the trunk almost to the ground; but a blight had apparently stricken the upper part of the oak, and the very topmost bough was withered, sapless, and utterly dead. Reuben remembered how the little banner had fluttered on that topmost bough, when it was green and lovely, eighteen years before. Whose guilt had blasted it?

*   *   *   *   *

Dorcas, after the departure of the two hunters, continued her preparations for the evening repast. Her sylvan table was the moss-covered trunk of a large fallen tree, on the broadest part of which she had spread a snow-white cloth and arranged what were left of the bright pewter vessels that had been her pride in the settlements. It had a strange aspect, that one little spot of homely comfort in the desolate heart of Nature. The sunshine yet lingered upon the higher branches of the trees that grew on rising ground; but the shadows of evening had deepened into the hollow where the encampment was made, and the firelight began to redden as it gleamed up the tall trunks of the pines or hovered on the dense and obscure mass of foliage that circled round the spot. The heart of Dorcas was not sad; for she felt that it was better to journey in the wilderness with two whom she loved than to be a lonely woman in a crowd that cared not for her. As she busied herself in arranging seats of mouldering wood covered with leaves, for Reuben and her son, her voice danced through the gloomy forest in the measure of a song that she had learned in youth. The rude melody, the production of a bard who won no name, was descriptive of a winter evening in a frontier cottage, when, secured from savage inroad by the high-piled snow-drifts, the family rejoiced by their own fireside. The whole song possessed the nameless charm peculiar to unborrowed thought, but four continually recurring lines shone out from the rest like the blaze of the hearth whose joys they celebrated. Into them, working magic with a few simple words, the poet had instilled the very essence of domestic love and household happiness, and they were poetry an d picture joined in one. As Dorcas sang, the walls of her forsaken home seemed to encircle her; she no longer saw the gloomy pines, nor heard the wind, which still, as she began each verse, sent a heavy breath through the branches and died away in a hollow moan from the burden of the song. She was aroused by the report of a gun in the vicinity of the encampment; and either the sudden sound or her loneliness by the glowing fire caused her to tremble violently. The next moment she laughed in the pride of a mother's heart.

'My beautiful young hunter! My boy has slain a deer!' she exclaimed, recollecting that in the direction whence the shot proceeded Cyrus had gone to the chase.

She waited a reasonable time to hear her son's light step bounding over the rustling leaves to tell of his success. But he did not immediately appear; and she sent her cheerful voice among the trees in search of him.

'Cyrus! Cyrus!'

His coming was still delayed; and she determined, as the report had apparently been very near, to seek for him in person. Her assistance, also, might be necessary in bringing home the venison which she flattered herself he had obtained. She therefore set forward, directing her steps by the long-past sound, and singing as she went, in order that the boy might be aware of her approach and run to meet her. From behind the trunk of every tree and from every hiding-place in the thick foliage of the undergrowth she hoped to discover the countenance of her son, laughing with the sportive mischief that is born of affection. The sun was now beneath the horizon, and the light that came down among the trees was sufficiently dim to create many illusions in her expecting fancy. Several times she seemed indistinctly to see his face gazing out from among the leaves; and once she imagined that he stood beckoning to her at the base of a craggy rock. Keeping her eyes on this object, however, it proved to be no more than the trunk of an oak, fringed to the very ground with little branches, one of which, thrust out farther than the rest, was shaken by the breeze. Making her way round to the foot of the rock, she suddenly found herself close to her husband, who had approached in another direction. Leaning upon the butt of his gun, the muzzle of which rested upon the withered leaves, he was apparently absorbed in the contemplation of some object at his feet.

'How is this, Reuben? Have you slain the deer and fallen asleep over him?' exclaimed Dorcas, laughing cheerfully, on her first slight observation of his posture and appearance.

He stirred not, neither did he turn his eyes towards her; and a cold shuddering fear, indefinite in its source and object, began to creep into her blood. She now perceived that her husband's face was ghastly pale, and his features were rigid, as if incapable of assuming any other expression than the strong despair which had hardened upon them. He gave not the slightest evidence that he was aware of her approach.

'For the love of Heaven, Reuben, speak to me!' cried

Dorcas; and the strange sound of her own voice affrighted her even more than the dead silence.

Her husband started, stared into her face, drew her to the front of the rock, and pointed with his finger.

Oh, there lay the boy, asleep, but dreamless, upon the fallen forest leaves! His cheek rested upon his arm,—his curled locks were thrown back from his brow,—his limbs were slightly relaxed. Had a sudden weariness overcome the youthful hunter? Would his mother's voice arouse him? She knew that it was death.

'This broad rock is the gravestone of your near kindred, Dorcas,' said her husband. 'Your tears will fall at once over your father and your son.'

She heard him not. With one wild shriek, that seemed to force its way from the sufferer's inmost soul, she sank insensible by the side of her dead boy. At that moment the withered topmost bough of the oak loosened itself in the stilly air, and fell in soft, light fragments upon the rock, upon the leaves, upon Reuben, upon his wife and child, and upon Roger Malvin's bones. Then Reuben's heart was stricken, and the tears gushed out like water from a rock. The vow that the wounded youth had made, the blighted man had come to redeem. His sin was expiated,*—the curse was gone from him; and in the hour when he had shed blood dearer to him than his own, a prayer, the first for years, went up to Heaven from the lips of Reuben Bourne.

THE CANTERBURY PILGRIMS*

THE summer moon, which shines in so many a tale, was beaming over a broad extent of uneven country. Some of its brightest rays were flung into a spring of water, where no traveller, toiling, as the writer has,* up the hilly road beside which it gushes, ever failed to quench his thirst. The work of neat hands and considerate art was visible about this blessed fountain. An open cistern, hewn and hollowed out of solid stone, was placed above the waters, which filled it to the brim, but, by some invisible outlet, were conveyed away without dripping down its sides. Though the basin had not room for another drop, and the continual gush of water made a tremor on the surface, there was a secret charm that forbade it to overflow. I remember, that when I had slaked my summer thirst, and sat panting by the cistern, it was my fanciful theory that Nature could not afford to lavish so pure a liquid, as she does the waters of all meaner fountains.

While the moon was hanging almost perpendicularly over this spot, two figures appeared on the summit of the hill, and came with noiseless footsteps down towards the spring. They were then in the first freshness of youth; nor is there a wrinkle now on either of their brows, and yet they wore a strange, old-fashioned garb. One, a young man with ruddy cheeks, walked beneath the canopy of a broad-brimmed grey hat; he seemed to have inherited his great-grandsire's square-skirted coat, and a waistcoat that extended its immense flaps to his knees; his brown locks, also, hung down behind, in a mode unknown to our times. By his side was a sweet young damsel, her fair features sheltered by a prim little bonnet, within which appeared the vestal muslin of a cap; her close, long-waisted gown, and indeed her whole attire, might have been worn by some rustic beauty who had faded half a century before. But that there was something too warm and lifelike in them, I would here have compared this couple to the ghosts of two young lovers, who had died long since in the glow of passion, and now were straying out of their graves, to renew the old vows, and shadow forth the unforgotten kiss of their earthly lips, beside the moonlit spring.

'Thee and I* will rest here a moment, Miriam,' said the young man, as they drew near the stone cistern, 'for there is no fear that the elders know what we have done; and this may be the last time we shall ever taste this water.'

Thus speaking, with a little sadness in his face, which was also visible in that of his companion, he made her sit down on a stone, and was about to place himself very close to her side; she, however, repelled him, though not unkindly.

'Nay, Josiah,' said she, giving him a timid push with her maiden hand, 'thee must sit farther off, on that other stone, with the spring between us. What would the sisters say, if thee were to sit so close to me?'

'But we are of the world's people now, Miriam,' answered Josiah.

The girl persisted in her prudery, nor did the youth, in fact, seem altogether free from a similar sort of shyness; so they sat apart from each other, gazing up the hill, where the moonlight discovered the tops of a group of buildings. While their attention was thus occupied, a party of travellers, who had come wearily upon the long ascent, made a halt to refresh themselves at the spring. There were three men, a woman, and a little girl and boy. Their attire was mean, covered with the dust of the summer's day, and damp with the night-dew; they all looked woebegone, as if the cares and sorrows of the world had made their steps heavier as they climbed the hill; even the two little children appeared older in evil days than the young man and maiden who had first approached the spring.

'Good evening to you, young folks,' was the salutation of the travellers; and 'Good evening, friends,' replied the youth and damsel.

'Is that white building the Shaker meeting-house?' asked one of the strangers. 'And are those the red roofs of the Shaker village?'

'Friend, it is the Shaker village,' answered Josiah, after some hesitation.

The travellers, who, from the first, had looked suspiciously at the garb of these young people, now taxed them with an intention which all the circumstances, indeed, rendered too obvious to be mistaken.

'It is true, friends,' replied the young man, summoning up his courage. 'Miriam and I have a gift to love each other, and we are going among the world's people, to live after their fashion. And ye know that we do not transgress the law of the land; and neither ye, nor the elders themselves, have a right to hinder us.'

'Yet you think it expedient to depart without leave-taking,' remarked one of the travellers.

'Yea, ye-a,' said Josiah, reluctantly, 'because father Job is a very awful man to speak with; and being aged himself, he has but little charity* for what he calls the iniquities of the flesh.'

'Well,' said the stranger, 'we will neither use force to bring you back to the village, nor will we betray you to the elders. But sit you here awhile, and when you have heard what we shall tell you of the world which we have left, and into which you are going, perhaps you will turn back with us of your own accord. What say you?' added he, turning to his companions. 'We have travelled thus far without becoming known to each other. Shall we tell our stories, here by this pleasant spring, for our own pastime, and the benefit of these misguided young lovers?'

In accordance with this proposal, the whole party stationed themselves round the stone cistern; the two children, being very weary, fell asleep upon the damp earth, and the pretty Shaker girl, whose feelings were those of a nun or a Turkish lady, crept as close as possible to the female traveller, and as far as she well could from the unknown men. The same person who had hitherto been the chief spokesman now stood up, waving his hat in his hand, and suffered the moonlight to fall full upon his front.

'In me,' said he, with a certain majesty of utterance,—'in me, you behold a poet.'

Though a lithographic print of this gentleman is extant, it may be well to notice that he was now nearly forty, a thin and stooping figure, in a black coat, out at elbows; notwithstanding the ill condition of his attire, there were about him several tokens of a peculiar sort of foppery, unworthy of a mature man, particularly in the arrangement of his hair, which was so disposed as to give all possible loftiness and breadth to his forehead. However, he had an intelligent eye, and, on the whole, a marked countenance.

'A poet!' repeated the young Shaker, a little puzzled how to understand such a designation, seldom heard in the utilitarian community where he had spent his life. 'O, ay, Miriam, he means a varse-maker, thee must know.'

This remark jarred upon the susceptible nerves of the poet; nor could he help wondering what strange fatality had put into this young man's mouth an epithet which ill-natured people had affirmed to be more proper to his merit than the one assumed by himself.

'True, I am a verse-maker,' he resumed, 'but my verse is no more than the material body into which I breathe the celestial soul of thought. Alas! how many a pang has it cost me, this same insensibility to the ethereal essence of poetry, with which you have here tortured me again, at the moment when I am to relinquish my profession for ever! O Fate! why hast thou warred with Nature, turning all her higher and more perfect gifts to the ruin of me, their possessor? What is the voice of song, when the world lacks the ear of taste? How can I rejoice in my strength and delicacy of feeling, when they have but made great sorrows out of little ones? Have I dreaded scorn like death, and yearned for fame as others pant for vital air, only to find myself in a middle state between obscurity and infamy? But I have my revenge! I could have given existence to a thousand bright creations. I crush them into my heart, and there let them putrefy! I shake off the dust of my feet against my countrymen! But posterity, tracing my footsteps up this weary hill, will cry shame upon the unworthy age that drove one of the fathers of American song to end his days in a Shaker village!'

During this harangue, the speaker gesticulated with great energy; and, as poetry is the natural language of passion, there appeared reason to apprehend his final explosion into an ode extempore. The reader must understand that, for all these bitter words, he was a kind, gentle, harmless, poor fellow enough, whom Nature, tossing her ingredients together without looking at her recipe, had sent into the world with too much of one sort of brain, and hardly any of another.

'Friend,' said the young Shaker, in some perplexity, 'thee seemest to have met with great troubles; and doubtless, I should pity them, if—if I could but understand what they were.'

'Happy in your ignorance!' replied the poet, with an air of sublime superiority. 'To your coarser mind, perhaps, I may seem to speak of more important griefs, when I add, what I had wellnigh forgotten, that I am out at elbows, and almost starved to death. At any rate, you have the advice and example of one individual to warn you back; for I am come hither, a disappointed man, flinging aside the fragments of my hopes, and seeking shelter in the calm retreat which you are so anxious to leave.'

'I thank thee, friend,' rejoined the youth, 'but I do not mean to be a poet, nor, Heaven be praised! do I think Miriam ever made a varse in her life. So we need not fear thy disappointments. But, Miriam,' he added, with real concern, 'thee knowest that the elders admit nobody that has not a gift to be useful. Now, what under the sun can they do with this poor varse-maker?'

'Nay, Josiah, do not thee discourage the poor man,' said the girl, in all simplicity and kindness. 'Our hymns are very rough, and perhaps they may trust him to smooth them.'

Without noticing this hint of professional employment, the poet turned away, and gave himself up to a sort of vague revery,* which he called thought. Sometimes he watched the moon, pouring a silvery liquid on the clouds, through which it slowly melted till they became all bright; then he saw the same sweet radiance dancing on the leafy trees which rustled as if to shake it off, or sleeping on the high tops of hills, or hovering down in distant valleys, like the material of unshaped dreams; lastly, he looked into the spring, and there the light was mingling with the water. In its crystal bosom, too, beholding all heaven reflected there, he found an emblem of a pure and tranquil breast. He listened to that most ethereal of all sounds, the song of crickets, coming in full choir upon the wind, and fancied that, if moonlight could be heard, it would sound just like that. Finally, he took a draught at the Shaker spring, and as if it were true Castalia,* was forthwith moved to compose a lyric, a Farewell to his Harp, which he swore should be its closing strain, the last verse that an ungrateful world should have from him. This effusion, with two or three other little pieces, subsequently written, he took the first opportunity to send, by one of the Shaker brethren, to Concord, where they were published in the New Hampshire Patriot.

Meantime, another of the Canterbury pilgrims, one so different from the poet that the delicate fancy of the latter could hardly have conceived of him, began to relate his sad experience. He was a small man, of quick and unquiet gestures, about fifty years old, with a narrow forehead, all wrinkled and drawn together. He held in his hand a pencil, and a card of some commission-merchant in foreign parts, on the back of which, for there was light enough to read or write by, he seemed ready to figure out a calculation.

'Young man,' said he, abruptly, 'what quantity of land do the Shakers own here, in Canterbury?'

'That is more than I can tell thee, friend,' answered Josiah, 'but it is a very rich establishment,* and for a long way by the roadside thee may guess the land to be ours, by the neatness of the fences.'

'And what may be the value of the whole,' continued the stranger, 'with all the buildings and improvements, pretty nearly, in round numbers?'

'Oh, a monstrous sum,—more than I can reckon,' replied the young Shaker.

'Well, sir,' said the pilgrim, 'there was a day, and not very long ago, neither, when I stood at my counting-room window, and watched the signal flags of three of my own ships entering the harbour, from the East Indies, from Liverpool, and from up the Straits, and I would not have given the invoice of the least of them for the title-deeds of this whole Shaker settlement. You stare. Perhaps, now, you won't believe that I could have put more value on a little slip of paper, no bigger than the palm of your hand, than all these solid acres of grain, grass, and pasture-land would sell for?'

'I won't dispute it, friend,' answered Josiah, 'but I know I had rather have fifty acres of this good land than a whole sheet of thy paper.'

'You may say so now,' said the ruined merchant, bitterly, 'for my name would not be worth the paper I should write it on. Of course, you must have heard of my failure?'

And the stranger mentioned his name, which, however mighty it might have been in the commercial world, the young Shaker had never heard of among the Canterbury hills.

'Not heard of my failure!' exclaimed the merchant, considerably piqued. 'Why, it was spoken of on 'Change in London, and from Boston to New Orleans men trembled in their shoes. At all events, I did fail, and you see me here on my road to the Shaker village, where, doubtless (for the Shakers are a shrewd sect), they will have a due respect for my experience, and give me the management of the trading part of the concern, in which case I think I can pledge myself to double their capital in four or five years. Turn back with me, young man; for though you will never meet with my good luck, you can hardly escape my bad.'

'I will not turn back for this,' replied Josiah, calmly, 'any more than for the advice of the varse-maker, between whom and thee, friend, I see a sort of likeness, though I can't justly say where it lies. But Miriam and I can earn our daily bread among the world's people, as well as in the Shaker village. And do we want anything more, Miriam?'

'Nothing more, Josiah,' said the girl, quietly.

'Yea, Miriam, and daily bread for some other little mouths, if God send them,' observed the simple Shaker lad.

Miriam did not reply, but looked down into the spring, where she encountered the image of her own pretty face, blushing within the prim little bonnet. The third pilgrim now took up the conversation. He was a sunburnt countryman, of tall frame and bony strength, on whose rude and manly face there appeared a darker, more sullen and obstinate despondency, than on those of either the poet or the merchant.

'Well, now, youngster,' he began, 'these folks have had their say, so I'll take my turn. My story will cut but a poor figure by the side of theirs; for I never supposed that I could have a right to meat and drink, and great praise besides, only for tagging rhymes together, as it seems this man does; nor ever tried to get the substance of hundreds into my own hands, like the trader there. When I was about your years, I married me a wife,—just such a neat and pretty young woman as Miriam, if that's her name,—and all I asked of Providence was an ordinary blessing on the sweat of my brow, so that we might be decent and comfortable, and have daily bread for ourselves, and for some other little mouths that we soon had to feed. We had no very great prospects before us; but I never wanted to be idle; and I thought it a matter of course that the Lord would help me, because I was willing to help myself.'

'And didn't He help thee, friend?' demanded Josiah, with some eagerness.

'No,' said the yeoman, sullenly; 'for then you would not have seen me here. I have laboured hard for years; and my means have been growing narrower, and my living poorer, and my heart colder and heavier, all the time; till at last I could bear it no longer. I set myself down to calculate whether I had best go on the Oregon expedition,* or come here to the Shaker village; but I had not hope enough left in me to begin the world over again; and, to make my story short, here I am. And now, youngster, take my advice, and turn back; or else, some few years hence, you'll have to climb this hill, with as heavy a heart as mine.'

This simple story had a strong effect on the young fugitives. The misfortunes of the poet and merchant had won little sympathy for their plain good sense and unworldly feelings, qualities which made them such unprejudiced and inflexible judges, that few men would have chosen to take the opinion of this youth and maiden as to the wisdom or folly of their pursuits. But here was one whose simple wishes had resembled their own, and who, after efforts which almost gave him a right to claim success from fate, had failed in accomplishing them.

'But thy wife, friend?' exclaimed the young man. 'What became of the pretty girl, like Miriam? Oh, I am afraid she is dead!'

'Yea, poor man, she must be dead,—she and the children, too,' sobbed Miriam.

The female pilgrim had been leaning over the spring, wherein latterly a tear or two might have been seen to fall, and form its little circle on the surface of the water. She now looked up, disclosing features still comely, but which had acquired an expression of fretfulness, in the same long course of evil fortune that had thrown a sullen gloom over the temper of the unprosperous yeoman.

'I am his wife,' said she, a shade of irritability just perceptible in the sadness of her tone. 'These poor little things, asleep on the ground, are two of our children. We had two more, but God has provided better for them than we could, by taking them to Himself.'

'And what would thee advise Josiah and me to do?' asked Miriam, this being the first question which she had put to either of the strangers.

' 'Tis a thing almost against nature for a woman to try to part true lovers,' answered the yeoman's wife, after a pause; 'but I'll speak as truly to you as if these were my dying words. Though my husband told you some of our troubles, he didn't mention the greatest, and that which makes all the rest so hard to bear. If you and your sweetheart marry, you'll be kind and pleasant to each other for a year or two, and while that's the case, you never will repent; but, by and by, he'll grow gloomy, rough, and hard to please, and you'll be peevish, and full of little angry fits, and apt to be complaining by the fireside, when he comes to rest himself from his troubles out of doors; so your love will wear away by little and little, and leave you miserable at last. It has been so with us; and yet my husband and I were true lovers once, if ever two young folks were.'

As she ceased, the yeoman and his wife exchanged a glance, in which there was more and warmer affection than they had supposed to have escaped the frost of a wintry fate in either of their breasts. At that moment, when they stood on the utmost verge of married life, one word fitly spoken, or perhaps one peculiar look, had they had mutual confidence enough to reciprocate it, might have renewed all their old feelings, and sent them back, resolved to sustain each other amid the struggles of the world. But the crisis passed, and never came again. Just then, also, the children, roused by their mother's voice, looked up, and added their wailing accents to the testimony borne by all the Canterbury pilgrims against the world from which they fled.

'We are tired and hungry!' cried they. 'Is it far to the Shaker village?'

The Shaker youth and maiden looked mournfully into each other's eyes. They had but stepped across the threshold of their homes, when lo! the dark array of cares and sorrows that rose up to warn them back. The varied narratives of the strangers had arranged themselves into a parable; they seemed not merely instances of woful fate that had befallen others, but shadowy omens of disappointed hope and unavailing toil, domestic grief and estranged affection, that would cloud the onward path of these poor fugitives. But after one instant's hesitation they opened their arms, and sealed their resolve with as pure and fond an embrace as ever youthful love had hallowed.

'We will not go back,' said they. 'The world never can be dark to us, for we will always love one another.'

Then the Canterbury pilgrims went up the hill, while the poet chanted a drear and desperate stanza of the Farewell to his Harp, fitting music for that melancholy band. They sought a home where all former ties of nature or society would be sundered,* and all old distinctions levelled, and a cold and passionless security be substituted for mortal hope and fear, as in that other refuge of the world's weary outcasts, the grave. The lovers drank at the Shaker spring, and then, with chastened hopes, but more confiding affections, went on to mingle in an untried life.

THE SEVEN VAGABONDS

RAMBLING on foot in the spring of my life and the summer of the year, I came one afternoon to a point which gave me the choice of three directions. Straight before me, the main road extended its dusty length to Boston; on the left a branch went towards the sea, and would have lengthened my journey a trifle of twenty or thirty miles; while by the right-hand path, I might have gone over hills and lakes to Canada,* visiting in my way the celebrated town of Stamford.* On a level spot of grass, at the foot of the guide-post, appeared an object which, though locomotive on a different principle, reminded me of Gulliver's portable mansion among the Brobdignags. It was a huge covered wagon, or, more properly, a small house on wheels, with a door on one side and a window shaded by green blinds on the other. Two horses, munching provender out of the baskets which muzzled them, were fastened near the vehicle: a delectable sound of music proceeded from the interior; and I immediately conjectured that this was some itinerant show, halting at the confluence of the roads to intercept such idle travellers as myself. A shower had long been climbing up the western sky, and now hung so blackly over my onward path that it was a point of wisdom to seek shelter here.

'Halloo! Who stands guard here? Is the doorkeeper asleep?' cried I, approaching a ladder of two or three steps which was let down from the wagon.

The music ceased at my summons, and there appeared at the door, not the sort of figure that I had mentally assigned to the wandering showman, but a most respectable old personage, whom I was sorry to have addressed in so free a style. He wore a snuff-coloured coat and small-clothes, with white-top boots, and exhibited the mild dignity of aspect and manner which may often be noticed in aged schoolmasters, and sometimes in deacons, selectmen, or other potentates of that kind. A small piece of silver was my passport within his premises, where I found only one other person, hereafter to be described.

'This is a dull day for business,' said the old gentleman, as he ushered me in; 'but I merely tarry here to refresh the cattle, being bound for the camp-meeting at Stamford.'

Perhaps the movable scene of this narrative is still peregrinating New England, and may enable the reader to test the accuracy of my description. The spectacle—for I will not use the unworthy term of puppet-show—consisted of a multitude of little people assembled on a miniature stage. Among them were artisans of every kind, in the attitudes of their toil, and a group of fair ladies and gay gentlemen standing ready for the dance; a company of foot-soldiers formed a line across the stage, looking stern, grim, and terrible enough, to make it a pleasant consideration that they were but three inches high; and conspicuous above the whole was seen a Merry-Andrew,* in the pointed cap and motley coat of his profession. All the inhabitants of this mimic world were motionless, like the figures in a picture, or like that people who one moment were alive in the midst of their business and delights, and the next were transformed to statues, preserving an eternal semblance of labour that was ended and pleasure that could be felt no more. Anon, however, the old gentleman turned the handle of a barrel-organ, the first note of which produced a most enlivening effect upon the figures, and awoke them all to their proper occupations and amusements. By the selfsame impulse the tailor plied his needle, the blacksmith's hammer descended upon the anvil, and the dancers whirled away on feathery tiptoes; the company of soldiers broke into platoons, retreated from the stage, and were succeeded by a troop of horse, who came prancing onward with such a sound of trumpets and trampling of hoofs as might have startled Don Quixote* himself; while an old toper,* of inveterate ill habits, uplifted his black bottle and took off a hearty swig. Meantime the Merry-Andrew began to caper and turn somersaults, shaking his sides, nodding his head, and winking his eyes in as life-like a manner as if he were ridiculing the nonsense of all human affairs, and making fun of the whole multitude beneath him. At length the old magician (for I compared the showman to Prospero, entertaining his guests with a mask of shadows) paused that I might give utterance to my wonder.

'What an admirable piece of work is this!' exclaimed I, lifting up my hands in astonishment.

Indeed, I liked the spectacle, and was tickled with the old man's gravity as he presided at it, for I had none of that foolish wisdom which reproves every occupation that is not useful in this world of vanities. If there be a faculty which I possess more perfectly than most men, it is that of throwing myself mentally into situations foreign to my own, and detecting, with a cheerful eye, the desirable circumstances of each. I could have envied the life of this grey-headed showman, spent as it had been in a course of safe and pleasurable adventure, in driving his huge vehicle sometimes through the sands of Cape Cod, and sometimes over the rough forest roads of the north and east, and halting now on the green before a village meeting-house, and now in a paved square of the metropolis. How often must his heart have been gladdened by the delight of children, as they viewed these animated figures! or his pride indulged, by haranguing learnedly to grown men on the mechanical powers which produced such wonderful effects! or his gallantry brought into play (for this is an attribute which such grave men do not lack) by the visits of pretty maidens!

And then with how fresh a feeling must he return, at intervals, to his own peculiar home!

'I would I were assured of as happy a life as his,' thought I.

Though the showman's wagon might have accommodated fifteen or twenty spectators, it now contained only himself and me, and a third person at whom I threw a glance on entering. He was a neat and trim young man of two or three and twenty; his drab hat and green frock-coat with velvet collar were smart, though no longer new; while a pair of green spectacles, that seemed needless to his brisk little eyes, gave him something of a scholar-like and literary air. After allowing me a sufficient time to inspect the puppets, he advanced with a bow, and drew my attention to some books in a corner of the wagon. These he forthwith began to extol, with an amazing volubility of well-sounding words, and an ingenuity of praise that won him my heart, as being myself one of the most merciful of critics. Indeed, his stock required some considerable powers of commendation in the salesman; there were several ancient friends of mine, the novels of those happy days when my affections wavered between the Scottish Chiefs* and Thomas Thumb; besides a few of later date, whose merits had not been acknowledged by the public. I was glad to find that dear little venerable volume, the New England Primer*, looking as antique as ever, though in its thousandth new edition; a bundle of superannuated gilt picture-books made such a child of me, that, partly for the glittering covers, and partly for the fairy-tales within, I bought the whole; and an assortment of ballads and popular theatrical songs drew largely on my purse. To balance these expenditures, I meddled neither with sermons, nor science, nor morality, though volumes of each were there; nor with a Life of Franklin* in the coarsest of paper, but so showily bound that it was emblematical of the Doctor himself, in the court dress which he refused to wear at Paris; nor with Webster's Spelling-Book,* nor some of Byron's minor poems, nor half-a-dozen little Testaments at twenty-five cents each.

Thus far the collection might have been swept from some great bookstore, or picked up at an evening auction-room; but there was one small blue-covered pamphlet, which the pedlar handed me with so peculiar an air, that I purchased it immediately at his own price; and then, for the first time, the thought struck me, that I had spoken face to face with the veritable author of a printed book. The literary man now evinced a great kindness for me, and I ventured to inquire which way he was travelling.

'Oh,' said he, 'I keep company with this old gentleman here, and we are moving now towards the camp-meeting at Stamford!'

He then explained to me, that for the present season he had rented a corner of the wagon as a bookstore, which, as he wittily observed, was a true Circulating Library, since there were few parts of the country where it had not gone its rounds. I approved of the plan exceedingly, and began to sum up within my mind the many uncommon felicities in the life of a book-pedlar, especially when his character resembled that of the individual before me. At a high rate was to be reckoned the daily and hourly enjoyment of such interviews as the present, in which he seized upon the admiration of a passing stranger, and made him aware that a man of literary taste, and even of literary achievement, was travelling the country in a showman's wagon. A more valuable, yet not infrequent triumph, might be won in his conversation with some elderly clergyman, long vegetating in a rocky, woody, watery back settlement of New England, who, as he recruited his library from the pedlar's stock of sermons, would exhort him to seek a college education and become the first scholar in his class. Sweeter and prouder yet would be his sensations, when, talking poetry while he sold spelling-books, he should charm the mind, and haply touch the heart of a fair country schoolmistress, herself an unhonoured poetess, a wearer of blue stockings which none but himself took pains to look at. But the scene of his completest glory would be when the wagon had halted for the night, and his stock of books was transferred to some crowded bar-room. Then would he recommend to the multifarious company, whether traveller from the city, or teamster from the hills, or neighbouring squire, or the landlord himself, or his loutish ostler, works suited to each particular taste and capacity; proving, all the while, by acute criticism and profound remark, that the lore in his books was even exceeded by that in his brain.

Thus happily would he traverse the land; sometimes a herald before the march of Mind; sometimes walking arm in arm with awful Literature; and reaping everywhere a harvest of real and sensible popularity, which the secluded bookworms, by whose toil he lived, could never hope for.

'If ever I meddle with literature,' thought I, fixing myself in adamantine resolution, 'it shall be as a travelling bookseller.'

Though it was still mid-afternoon, the air had now grown dark about us, and a few drops of rain came down upon the roof of our vehicle, pattering like the feet of birds that had flown thither to rest. A sound of pleasant voices made us listen, and there soon appeared half-way up the ladder the pretty person of a young damsel, whose rosy face was so cheerful, that even amid the gloomy light it seemed as if the sunbeams were peeping under her bonnet. We next saw the dark and handsome features of a young man, who, with easier gallantry than might have been expected in the heart of Yankee-land, was assisting her into the wagon. It became immediately evident to us, when the two strangers stood within the door, that they were of a profession kindred to those of my companions; and I was delighted with the more than hospitable, the even paternal kindness, of the old showman's manner, as he welcomed them; while the man of literature hastened to lead the merry-eyed girl to a seat on the long bench.

'You are housed but just in time, my young friends,' said the master of the wagon. 'The sky would have been down upon you within five minutes.'

The young man's reply marked him as a foreigner, not by any variation from the idiom and accent of good English, but because he spoke with more caution and accuracy, than if perfectly familiar with the language.

'We knew that a shower was hanging over us,' said he, 'and consulted whether it were best to enter the house on the top of yonder hill, but seeing your wagon in the road—'

'We agreed to come hither,' interrupted the girl, with a

smile, 'because we should be more at home in a wandering house like this.'

I, meanwhile, with many a wild and undetermined fantasy, was narrowly inspecting these two doves that had flown into our ark. The young man, tall, agile, an athletic, wore a mass of black shining curls clustering round a dark and vivacious countenance, which, if it had not greater expression, was at least more active, and attracted readier notice, than the quiet faces of our countrymen. At his first appearance, he had been laden with a neat mahogany box, of about two feet square, but very light in proportion to its size, which he had immediately unstrapped from his shoulders and deposited on the floor of the wagon.

The girl had nearly as fair a complexion as our own beauties, and a brighter one than most of them; the lightness of her figure, which seemed calculated to traverse the whole world without weariness, suited well with the glowing cheerfulness of her face; and her gay attire, combining the rainbow hues of crimson, green, and a deep orange, was as proper to her lightsome aspect as if she had been born in it.* This gay stranger was appropriately burdened with that mirth-inspiring instrument, the fiddle, which her companion took from her hands, and shortly began the process of tuning. Neither of us—the previous company of the wagon—needed to inquire their trade; for this could be no mystery to frequenters of brigade-musters, ordinations, cattle-shows, commence-ments,* and other festal meetings in our sober land; and there is a dear friend of mine, who will smile when this page recalls to his memory a chivalrous deed performed by us, in rescuing the show-box of such a couple from a mob of great double-fisted countrymen.

'Come,' said I to the damsel of gay attire, 'shall we visit all the wonders of the world together?'

She understood the metaphor at once; though indeed it would not much have troubled me if she had assented to the literal meaning of my words. The mahogany box was placed in a proper position, and I peeped in through its small round magnifying window, while the girl sat by my side, and gave short descriptive sketches, as one after another the pictures were unfolded to my view. We visited together, at least our imaginations did, full many a famous city, in the streets of which I had long yearned to tread; once, I remember, we were in the harbour of Barcelona, gazing townwards; next, she bore me through the air to Sicily, and bade me look up at blazing Etna; then we took wing to Venice, and sat in a gondola beneath the arch of the Rialto; and anon she sat me down among the thronged spectators at the coronation of Napoleon. But there was one scene, its locality she could not tell, which charmed my attention longer than all those gorgeous palaces and churches, because the fancy haunted me, that I myself, the preceding summer, had beheld just such a humble meeting-house, in just such a pine-surrounded nook, among our own green mountains. All these pictures were tolerably executed though far inferior to the girl's touches of description; nor was it easy to comprehend, how in so few sentences, and these, as I supposed, in a language foreign to her, she contrived to present in airy copy of each varied scene. When we had travelled through the vast extent of the mahogany box, I looked into my guide's face.

'Where are you going, my pretty maid?' inquired I, in the words of an old song.*

'Ah,' said the gay damsel, 'you might as well ask where the summer wind is going. We are wanderers here, and there, and everywhere. Wherever there is mirth, our merry hearts are drawn to it. To-day, indeed, the people have told us of a great frolic and festival in these parts; so perhaps we may be needed at what you call the camp-meeting* at Stamford.'

Then in my happy youth, and while her pleasant voice yet sounded in my ears, I sighed; for none but myself, I thought, should have been her companion in a life which seemed to realize my own wild fancies, cherished all through visionary boyhood to that hour. To these two strangers the world was in its golden age, not that indeed it was less dark and sad than ever, but because its weariness and sorrow had no community with their ethereal nature. Wherever they might appear in their pilgrimage of bliss, Youth would echo back their gladness, care-stricken Maturity would rest a moment from its toil, and Age, tottering among the graves, would smile in withered joy for their sakes. The lonely cot, the narrow and gloomy street, the sombre shade, would catch a passing gleam like that now shining on ourselves, as these bright spirits wandered by. Blessed pair, whose happy home was throughout all the earth! I looked at my shoulders, and thought them broad enough to sustain those pictured towns and mountains; mine, too, was an elastic foot, as tireless as the wing of the bird of paradise; mine was then an untroubled heart, that would have gone singing on its delightful way.

'O maiden!' said I aloud, 'why did you not come hither alone?'

While the merry girl and myself were busy with the show-box, the unceasing rain had driven another wayfarer into the wagon. He seemed pretty nearly of the old showman's age, but much smaller, leaner, and more withered than he, and less respectably clad in a patched suit of grey; withal, he had a thin, shrewd countenance, and a pair of diminutive grey eyes, which peeped rather too keenly out of their puckered sockets. This old fellow had been joking with the showman, in a manner which intimated previous acquaintance; but perceiving that the damsel and I had terminated our affairs, he drew forth a folded document, and presented it to me. As I had anticipated, it proved to be a circular, written in a very fair and legible hand, and signed by several distinguished gentlemen whom I had never heard of, stating that the bearer had encountered every variety of misfortune, and recommending him to the notice of all charitable people. Previous disbursements had left me no more than a five-dollar bill, out of which, however, I offered to make the beggar a donation, provided he would give me change for it. The object of my beneficence looked keenly in my face, and discerned that I had none of that abominable spirit, characteristic though it be, of a full-blooded Yankee, which takes pleasure in detecting every little harmless piece of knavery.

'Why, perhaps,' said the ragged old mendicant, 'if the bank is in good standing, I can't say but I may have enough about me to change your bill.'

'It is a bill of the Suffolk Bank,'* said I, 'and better than the specie.'*

As the beggar had nothing to object, he now produced a small buff-leather bag, tied up carefully with a shoestring. When this was opened, there appeared a very comfortable treasure of silver coins of all sorts and sizes; and I even fancied that I saw, gleaming among them, the golden plumage of that rare bird in our currency, the American Eagle. In this precious heap was my banknote deposited, the rate of exchange being considerably against me. His wants being thus relieved, the destitute man pulled out of his pocket an old pack of greasy cards, which had probably contributed to fill the buff-leather bag in more ways than one.

'Come,' said he, 'I spy a rare fortune in your face, and for twenty-five cents more I'll tell you what it is.'

I never refuse to take a glimpse into futurity; so, after shuffling the cards, and when the fair damsel had cut them, I dealt a portion to the prophetic beggar. Like others of his profession, before predicting the shadowy events that were moving on to meet me, he gave proof of his preternatural science by describing scenes through which I had already passed. Here let me have credit for a sober fact. When the old man had read a page in his book of fate, he bent his keen grey eyes on mine, and proceeded to relate, in all its minute particulars, what was then the most singular event of my life. It was one which I had no purpose to disclose, till the general unfolding of all secrets; nor would it be a much stranger instance of inscrutable knowledge, or fortunate conjecture, if the beggar were to meet me in the street today, and repeat, word for word, the page which I have here written. The fortune-teller, after predicting a destiny which time seems loath to make good, put up his cards, secreted his treasure-bag, and began to converse with the other occupants of the wagon.

'Well, old friend,' said the showman, 'you have not yet told us which way your face is turned this afternoon.'

'I am taking a trip northward, this warm weather,' replied the conjurer, 'across the Connecticut first, and then up through Vermont, and may be into Canada before the fall. But I must stop and see the breaking up of the camp-meeting at Stamford.'

I began to think that all the vagrants in New England were converging to the camp-meeting, and had made this wagon their rendezvous by the way. The showman now proposed that, when the shower was over, they should pursue the road to Stamford together, it being sometimes the policy of these people to form a sort of league and confederacy.

'And the young lady too,' observed the gallant bibliopolist,* bowing to her profoundly, 'and this foreign gentleman, as I understand, are on a jaunt of pleasure to the same spot. It would add incalculably to my own enjoyment, and I presume to that of my colleague and his friend, if they could be prevailed upon to join our party.'

This arrangement met with approbation on all hands, nor were any of those concerned more sensible of its advantages than myself, who had no title to be included in it. Having already satisfied myself as to the several modes in which the four others attained felicity, I next set my mind at work to discover what enjoyments were peculiar to the old 'Straggler', as the people of the country would have termed the wandering mendicant and prophet. As he pretended to familiarity with the Devil, so I fancied that he was fitted to pursue and take delight in his way of life, by possessing some of the mental and moral characteristics, the lighter and more comic ones, of the Devil in popular stories. Among them might be reckoned a love of deception for its own sake, a shrewd eye and keen relish for human weakness and ridiculous infirmity, and the talent of petty fraud. Thus to this old man there would be pleasure even in the consciousness, so insupportable to some minds, that his whole life was a cheat upon the world, and that, so far as he was concerned with the public, his little cunning had the upper hand of its united wisdom. Every day would furnish him with a succession of minute and pungent triumphs: as when, for instance, his importunity wrung a pittance out of the heart of a miser, or when my silly good-nature transferred a part of my slender purse to his plump leather bag; or when some ostentatious gentleman should throw a coin to the ragged beggar who was richer than himself; or when, though he would not always be so decidedly diabolical, his pretended wants should make him a sharer in the scanty living of real indigence. And then what an inexhaustible field of enjoyment, both as enabling him to discern so much folly and achieve such quantities of minor mischief, was opened to his sneering spirit by his pretensions to prophetic knowledge.

All this was a sort of happiness which I could conceive of, though I had little sympathy with it. Perhaps, had I been then inclined to admit it, I might have found that the roving life was more proper to him than to either of his companions; for Satan, to whom I had compared the poor man, has delighted, ever since the time of Job, in 'wandering up and down* upon the earth'; and indeed a crafty disposition, which operates not in deep-laid plans, but in disconnected tricks, could not have an adequate scope, unless naturally impelled to a continual change of scene and society. My reflections were here interrupted.

'Another visitor!' exclaimed the old showman.

The door of the wagon had been closed against the tempest, which was roaring and blustering with prodigious fury and commotion, and beating violently against our shelter, as if it claimed all those homeless people for its lawful prey, while we, caring little for the displeasure of the elements, sat comfortably talking. There was now an attempt to open the door, succeeded by a voice, uttering some strange, unintelligible gibberish, which my companions mistook for Greek, and I suspected to be thieves' Latin. However, the showman stepped forward, and gave admittance to a figure which made me imagine, either that our wagon had rolled back two hundred years into past ages, or that the forest and its old inhabitants had sprung up around us by enchantment.

It was a red Indian, armed with his bow and arrow. His dress was a sort of cap, adorned with a single feather of some wild bird, and a frock of blue cotton, girded tight about him; on his breast, like orders of knighthood, hung a crescent and a circle, and other ornaments of silver; while a small crucifix betokened that our Father the Pope had interposed between the Indian and the Great Spirit, whom he had worshipped in his simplicity. This son of the wilderness, and pilgrim of the storm, took his place silently in the midst of us. When the first surprise was over, I rightly conjectured him to be one of the Penobscot tribe,* parties of which I had often seen, in their summer excursions down our Eastern rivers. There they paddle their birch canoes among the coasting schooners, and build their wigwam beside some roaring mill-dam, and drive a little trade in basket-work where their fathers hunted deer. Our new visitor was probably wandering through the country towards Boston, subsisting on the careless charity of the people, while he turned his archery to profitable account by shooting at cents, which were to be the prize of his successful aim.

The Indian had not long been seated, ere our merry damsel sought to draw him into conversation. She, indeed, seemed all made up of sunshine in the month of May; for there was nothing so dark and dismal that her pleasant mind could not cast a glow over it; and the wild man, like a fir-tree in his native forest, soon began to brighten into a sort of sombre cheerfulness. At length, she inquired whether his journey had any particular end or purpose.

'I go shoot at the camp-meeting at Stamford,' replied the Indian.

'And here are five more,' said the girl, 'all aiming at the camp-meeting too. You shall be one of us, for we travel with light hearts; and as for me, I sing merry songs, and tell merry tales, and am full of merry thoughts, and I dance merrily along the road, so that there is never any sadness among them that keep me company. But, oh, you would find it very dull indeed, to go all the way to Stamford alone!'

My ideas of the aboriginal character led me to fear that the Indian would prefer his own solitary musings to the gay society thus offered him; on the contrary, the girl's proposal met with immediate acceptance, and seemed to animate him with a misty expectation of enjoyment. I now gave myself up to a course of thought which, whether it flowed naturally from this combination of events, or was drawn forth by a wayward fancy, caused my mind to thrill as if I were listening to deep music. I saw mankind, in this weary old age of the world, either enduring a sluggish existence amid the smoke and dust of cities, or, if they breathed a purer air, still lying down at

night with no hope but to wear out to-morrow, and all the
tomorrows which make up life, among the same dull scenes
and in the same wretched toil that had darkened the sunshine
of to-day. But there were some, full of the primaeval instinct,
who preserved the freshness of youth to their latest years by
the continual excitement of new objects, new pursuits, and
new associates; and cared little, though their birthplace might
have been here in New England, if the grave should close over
them in Central Asia. Fate was summoning a parliament of
these free spirits; unconscious of the impulse which directed
them to a common centre, they had come hither from far and
near; and last of all appeared the representative of those
mighty vagrants, who had chased the deer during thousands
of years, and were chasing it now in the Spirit Land.
Wandering down through the waste of ages, the woods had
vanished around his path; his arm had lost somewhat of its
strength, his foot of its fleetness, his mien of its wild regality,
his heart and mind of their savage virtue and uncultured force;
but here, untamable to the routine of artificial life, roving now
along the dusty road, as of old over the forest leaves, here was
the Indian still.

'Well,' said the old showman, in the midst of my meditations, 'here is an honest company of us,—one, two, three,
four, five, six,—all going to the camp-meeting at Stamford.
Now, hoping no offence, I should like to know where this
young gentleman may be going?'

I started. How came I among these wanderers? The free
mind, that preferred its own folly to another's wisdom; the
open spirit, that found companions everywhere; above all, the
restless impulse, that had so often made me wretched in the
midst of enjoyments: these were my claims to be of their
society.

'My friends!' cried I, stepping into the centre of the wagon,
'I am going with you to the camp-meeting at Stamford.'

'But in what capacity?' asked the old showman, after a
moment's silence. 'All of us here can get our bread in some
creditable way. Every honest man should have his livelihood.
You, sir, as I take it, are a mere strolling gentleman.'

I proceeded to inform the company, that, when Nature gave

me a propensity to their way of life, she had not left me altogether destitute of qualifications for it; though I could not deny that my talent was less respectable, and might be less profitable, than the meanest of theirs. My design, in short, was to imitate the story-tellers of whom Oriental travellers* have told us, and become an itinerant novelist, reciting my own extemporaneous fictions to such audiences as I could collect.

'Either this,' said I, 'is my vocation, or I have been born in vain.'

The fortune-teller, with a sly wink to the company, proposed to take me as an apprentice to one or other of his professions, either of which, undoubtedly, would have given full scope to whatever inventive talent I might possess. The bibliopolist spoke a few words in opposition to my plan, influenced partly, I suspect, by the jealousy of authorship, and partly by an apprehension that the *viva voce* practice would become general among novelists, to the infinite detriment of the book-trade. Dreading a rejection, I solicited the interest of the merry damsel.

'Mirth,' cried I, most aptly appropriating the words of L'Allegro,* 'to thee I sue! Mirth, admit me of thy crew!'

'Let us indulge the poor youth,' said Mirth, with a kindness which made me love her dearly, though I was no such coxcomb as to misinterpret her motives. 'I have espied much promise in him. True, a shadow sometimes flits across his brow, but the sunshine is sure to follow in a moment. He is never guilty of a sad thought, but a merry one is twin-born with it. We will take him with us; and you shall see that he will set us all a-laughing before we reach the camp-meeting at Stamford.'

Her voice silenced the scruples of the rest, and gained me admittance into the league, according to the terms of which, without a community of goods or profits, we were to lend each other all the aid, and avert all the harm, that might be in our power. This affair settled, a marvellous jollity entered into the whole tribe of us, manifesting itself characteristically in each individual. The old showman, sitting down to his barrel-organ, stirred up the souls of the pygmy people with one of the quickest tunes in the music-book; tailors, blacksmiths, gentlemen, and ladies, all seemed to share in the spirit of the occasion; and the Merry-Andrew played his part more facetiously than ever, nodding and winking particularly at me. The young foreigner flourished his fiddle-bow with a master's hand, and gave an inspiring echo to the showman's melody. The bookish man and the merry damsel started up simultaneously to dance; the former enacting the double shuffle in a style which everybody must have witnessed, ere Election week was blotted out of time; while the girl, setting her arms akimbo with both hands at her slim waist, displayed such light rapidity of foot, and harmony of varying attitude and motion, that I could not conceive how she ever was to stop; imagining, at the moment, that Nature had made her, as the old showman had made his puppets, for no earthly purpose but to dance jigs. The Indian bellowed forth a succession of most hideous outcries, somewhat affrighting us, till we interpreted them as the war-song, with which, in imitation of his ancestors, he was prefacing the assault on Stamford. The conjurer, meanwhile, sat demurely in a corner, extracting a sly enjoyment from the whole scene, and, like the facetious Merry-Andrew, directing his queer glance particularly at me.

As for myself, with great exhilaration of fancy, I began to arrange and colour the incidents of a tale, wherewith I proposed to amuse an audience that very evening; for I saw that my associates were a little ashamed of me, and that no time was to be lost in obtaining a public acknowledgement of my abilities.

'Come, fellow-labourers,' at last said the old showman, whom we had elected President; 'the shower is over, and we must be doing our duty by these poor souls at Stamford.'

'We'll come among them in procession, with music and dancing,' cried the merry damsel.

Accordingly—for it must be understood that our pilgrimage* was to be performed on foot—we sallied joyously out of the wagon, each of us, even the old gentleman in his white-top boots, giving a great skip as we came down the ladder. Above our heads there was such a glory of sunshine and splendour of clouds, and such brightness of verdure below, that, as I modestly remarked at the time, Nature seemed to have washed her face, and put on the best of her jewellery and a fresh green gown, in honour of our confederation. Casting our eyes northward, we beheld a horseman approaching leisurely, and splashing through the little puddles on the Stamford road. Onward he came, sticking up in his saddle with rigid perpendicularity, a tall, thin figure in rusty black, whom the showman and the conjurer shortly recognized to be, what his aspect sufficiently indicated, a travelling preacher* of great fame among the Methodists. What puzzled us was the fact, that his face appeared turned from, instead of to, the camp-meeting at Stamford. However, as this new votary of the wandering life drew near the little green space, where the guidepost and our wagon were situated, my six fellow-vagabonds and myself rushed forward and surrounded him, crying out with united voices,—

'What news, what news from the camp-meeting at Stamford?'

The missionary looked down, in surprise, at as singular a knot of people as could have been selected from all his heterogeneous auditors. Indeed, considering that we might all be classified under the general head of Vagabond, there was great diversity of character among the grave old showman, the sly, prophetic beggar, the fiddling foreigner and his merry damsel, the smart bibliopolist, the sombre Indian, and myself, the itinerant novelist, a slender youth of eighteen. I even fancied that a smile was endeavouring to disturb the iron gravity of the preacher's mouth.

'Good people,' answered he, 'the camp-meeting is broke up.'

So saying, the Methodist minister switched his steed, and rode westward. Our union being thus nullified, by the removal of its object, we were sundered at once to the four winds of heaven. The fortune-teller, giving a nod to all, and a peculiar wink to me, departed on his northern tour, chuckling within himself as he took the Stamford road. The old showman and his literary co-adjutor were already tackling their horses to the wagon, with a design to peregrinate southwest along the sea-coast. The foreigner and the merry damsel took their laughing leave, and pursued the eastern road, which I had that day trodden; as they passed away, the young man played a lively strain, and the girl's happy spirit broke into a dance; and thus, dissolving, as it were into sunbeams and gay music, that pleasant pair departed from my view. Finally, with a pensive shadow thrown across my mind, yet emulous of the light philosophy of my late companions, I joined myself to the Penobscot Indian, and set forth towards the distant city.

THE GREY CHAMPION

THERE was once a time when New England groaned under the actual pressure of heavier wrongs than those threatened ones which brought on the Revolution. James II, the bigoted successor of Charles the Voluptuous, had annulled the charters* of all the colonies, and sent a harsh and unprincipled soldier to take away our liberties and endanger our religion. The administration of Sir Edmund Andros* lacked scarcely a single characteristic of tyranny: a Governor and Council, holding office from the King, and wholly independent of the country; laws made and taxes levied without concurrence of the people, immediate or by their representatives; the rights of private citizens violated, and the titles of all landed property declared void; the voice of complaint stifled by restrictions on the press; and, finally, disaffection overawed by the first band of mercenary troops that ever marched on our free soil. For two years our ancestors were kept in sullen submission by that filial love which had invariably secured their allegiance to the mother country, whether its head chanced to be a Parliament, Protector, or Popish Monarch. Till these evil times, however, such allegiance had been merely nominal, and the colonists had ruled themselves, enjoying far more freedom than is even yet the privilege of the native subjects of Great Britain.

At length a rumour reached our shores that the Prince of Orange* had ventured on an enterprise, the success of which would be the triumph of civil and religious rights and the salvation of New England. It was but a doubtful whisper; it might be false, or the attempt might fail; and, in either case, the man that stirred against King James would lose his head. Still, the intelligence produced a marked effect. The people smiled mysteriously in the streets, and threw bold glances at their oppressors; while, far and wide, there was a subdued and silent agitation, as if the slightest signal would rouse the whole land from its sluggish despondency. Aware of their danger, the rulers resolved to avert it by an imposing display of strength, and perhaps to confirm their despotism by yet harsher measures. One afternoon in April 1689, Sir Edmund Andros and his favourite councillors, being warm with wine, assembled the redcoats of the Governor's Guard, and made their appearance in the streets of Boston. The sun was near setting when the march commenced.

The roll of the drum, at that unquiet crisis, seemed to go through the streets, less as the martial music of the soldiers, than as a muster-call to the inhabitants themselves. A multitude, by various avenues, assembled in King Street,* which was destined to be the scene, nearly a century afterwards, of another encounter between the troops of Britain and a people struggling against her tyranny. Though more than sixty years* had elapsed since the Pilgrims came, this crowd of their descendants still showed the strong and sombre features of their character, perhaps more strikingly in such a stern emergency than on happier occasions. There were the sober garb, the general severity of mien, the gloomy but undismayed expression, the Scriptural forms of speech, and the confidence in Heaven's blessing on a righteous cause,* which would have marked a band of the original Puritans, when threatened by some peril of the wilderness. Indeed, it was not yet time for the old spirit to be extinct; since there were men in the street, that day, who had worshipped there beneath the trees, before a house was reared to the God for whom they had become exiles. Old soldiers of the Parliament were here, too, smiling grimly at the thought that their aged arms might strike another blow against the house of Stuart. Here, also, were the veterans of King Philip's war,* who had burned villages and slaughtered young and old, with pious fierceness, while the godly souls throughout the land were helping them with prayer. Several ministers were scattered among the crowd, which, unlike all other mobs, regarded them with such reverence, as if there were sanctity in their very garments. These holy men exerted their influence to quiet the people, but not to disperse them. Meantime, the purpose of the Governor, in disturbing the peace of the town, at a period when the slightest commotion might throw the country into a ferment, was almost the universal subject of inquiry, and variously explained.

'Satan will strike his master-stroke presently,' cried some, 'because he knoweth that his time is short. All our godly pastors are to be dragged to prison! We shall see them at a Smithfield fire* in King Street!'

Hereupon the people of each parish gathered closer round their minister, who looked calmly upwards and assumed a more apostolic dignity, as well befitted a candidate for the highest honour of his profession, the crown of martyrdom. It was actually fancied, at that period, that New England might have a John Rogers* of her own, to take the place of that worthy in the Primer.*

'The Pope of Rome has given orders for a new St. Bartholomew!'* cried others. 'We are to be massacred,* man and male child!'

Neither was this rumour wholly discredited, although the wiser class believed the Governor's object somewhat less atrocious. His predecessor under the old charter, Bradstreet,* a venerable companion of the first settlers, was known to be in town. There were grounds for conjecturing that Sir Edmund Andros intended, at once, to strike terror, by a parade of military force, and to confound the opposite faction by possessing himself of their chief.

'Stand firm for the old charter Governor!' shouted the crowd, seizing upon the idea. 'The good old Governor Bradstreet!'

While this cry was at the loudest, the people were surprised by the well-known figure of Governor Bradstreet himself, a patriarch of nearly ninety, who appeared on the elevated steps of a door, and, with characteristic mildness, besought them to submit to the constituted authorities.

'My children,' concluded this venerable person, 'do nothing rashly. Cry not aloud, but pray for the welfare of New England, and expect patiently what the Lord will do in this matter!'

The event was soon to be decided. All this time, the roll of the drum had been approaching through Cornhill, louder and deeper, till with reverberations from house to house, and the regular tramp of martial footsteps, it burst into the street. A double rank of soldiers made their appearance, occupying the whole breadth of the passage, with shouldered matchlocks, and matches burning, so as to present a row of fires in the dusk. Their steady march was like the progress of a machine, that would roll irresistibly over everything in its way. Next, moving slowly, with a confused clatter of hoofs on the pavement, rode a party of mounted gentlemen, the central figure being Sir Edmund Andros, elderly, but erect and soldier-like. Those around him were his favourite councillors, and the bitterest foes of New England. At his right hand rode Edward Randolph,* our arch-enemy, that 'blasted wretch', as Cotton Mather* calls him, who achieved the downfall of our ancient government, and was followed with a sensible curse, through life and to his grave. On the other side was Bullivant,* scattering jests and mockery as he rode along. Dudley* came behind, with a downcast look, dreading, as well he might, to meet the indignant gaze of the people, who beheld him, their only countryman by birth, among the oppressors of his native land. The captain of a frigate in the harbour, and two or three civil officers under the Crown, were also there. But the figure which most attracted the public eye, and stirred up the deepest feeling, was the Episcopal clergyman of King's Chapel,* riding haughtily among the magistrates in his priestly vestments, the fitting representative of prelacy and persecution, the union of Church and State, and all those abominations which had driven the Puritans to the wilderness. Another guard of soldiers, in double rank, brought up the rear.

The whole scene was a picture of the condition of New England, and its moral, the deformity of any government that does not grow out of the nature of things and the character of the people. On one side the religious multitude, with their sad visages and dark attire, and on the other, the group of despotic rulers, with the High Churchman in the midst, and here and there a crucifix at their bosoms, all magnificently clad, flushed with wine, proud of unjust authority, and scoffing at the universal groan. And the mercenary soldiers, waiting but the word to deluge the street with blood, showed the only means by which obedience could be secured.

'O Lord of Hosts,' cried a voice among the crowd, 'provide a Champion* for thy people!'

This ejaculation was loudly uttered, and served as a herald's cry, to introduce a remarkable personage. The crowd had rolled back, and were now huddled together nearly at the extremity of the street, while the soldiers had advanced no more than a third of its length. The intervening space was empty,—a paved solitude, between lofty edifices, which threw almost a twilight shadow over it. Suddenly, there was seen the figure of an ancient man, who seemed to have emerged from among the people, and was walking by himself along the centre of the street, to confront the armed band. He wore the old Puritan dress, a dark cloak and a steeple-crowned hat, in the fashion of at least fifty years before, with a heavy sword upon his thigh, but a staff in his hand to assist the tremulous gait of age.

When at some distance from the multitude, the old man turned slowly round, displaying a face of antique majesty, rendered doubly venerable by the hoary beard that descended on his breast. He made a gesture at once of encouragement and warning, then turned again, and resumed his way.

'Who is this grey patriarch?' asked the young men of their sires.

'Who is this venerable brother?' asked the old men among themselves.

But none could make reply. The fathers of the people, those of four score years and upwards, were disturbed, deeming it strange that they should forget one of such evident authority, whom they must have known in their early days, the associate of Winthrop,* and all the old councillors, giving laws, and making prayers, and leading them against the savage. The elderly men ought to have remembered him, too, with locks as grey in their youth as their own were now. And the young! How could he have passed so utterly from their memories,— that hoary sire, the relic of long-departed times, whose awful benediction had surely been bestowed on their uncovered heads, in childhood?

'Whence did he come? What is his purpose? Who can this old man be?' whispered the wondering crowd.

Meanwhile, the venerable stranger, staff in hand, was pursuing his solitary walk along the centre of the street. As he drew near the advancing soldiers, and as the roll of their drums came full upon his ear, the old man raised himself to a loftier mien, while the decrepitude of age seemed to fall from his shoulders, leaving him in grey but unbroken dignity. Now, he marched onward with a warrior's step, keeping time to the military music. Thus the aged form advanced on one side, and the whole parade of soldiers and magistrates on the other, till, when scarcely twenty yards remained between, the old man grasped his staff by the middle, and held it before him like a leader's truncheon.

'Stand!' cried he.

The eye, the face, and attitude of command; the solemn, yet warlike peal of that voice, fit either to rule a host in the battle-field or be raised to God in prayer, were irresistible. At the old man's word and outstretched arm, the roll of the drum was hushed at once, and the advancing line stood still. A tremulous enthusiasm seized upon the multitude. That stately form, combining the leader and the saint, so grey, so dimly seen, in such an ancient garb, could only belong to some old champion of the righteous cause, whom the oppressor's drum had summoned from his grave. They raised a shout of awe and exultation, and looked for the deliverance of New England.

The Governor, and the gentlemen of his party, perceiving themselves brought to an unexpected stand, rode hastily forward, as if they would have pressed their snorting and affrighted horses right against the hoary apparition. He, however, blenched not a step, but glancing his severe eye round the group, which half encompassed him, at last bent it sternly on Sir Edmund Andros. One would have thought that the dark old man was chief ruler there, and that the Governor and Council, with soldiers at their back, representing the whole power and authority of the Crown, had no alternative but obedience.

'What does this old fellow here?' cried Edward Randolph, fiercely. 'On, Sir Edmund! Bid the soldiers forward, and give the dotard the same choice that you give all his countrymen,—to stand aside or be trampled on!'

'Nay, nay, let us show respect to the good grandsire,' said Bullivant, laughing. 'See you not, he is some old round-headed dignitary, who hath lain asleep these thirty years, and knows nothing of the change of times? Doubtless, he thinks to put us down with a proclamation in Old Noll's name!'*

'Are you mad, old man?' demanded Sir Edmund Andros, in loud and harsh tones, 'How dare you stay the march of King James's Governor?'

'I have stayed the march of a king* himself, ere now,' replied the grey figure, with stern composure. 'I am here, Sir Governor, because the cry of an oppressed people hath disturbed me in my secret place; and beseeching this favour earnestly of the Lord, it was vouchsafed me to appear once again on earth, in the good old cause of the saints. And what speak ye of James? There is no longer a Popish tyrant on the throne of England, and by to-morrow noon his name shall be a byword in this very street, where ye would make it a word of terror. Back, thou that wast a Governor, back! With this night thy power is ended,—to-morrow, the prison!—back, lest I foretell the scaffold!'

The people had been drawing nearer and nearer, and drinking in the words of their champion, who spoke in accents long disused, like one unaccustomed to converse, except with the dead of many years ago. But his voice stirred their souls. They confronted the soldiers, not wholly without arms, and ready to convert the very stones of the street into deadly weapons. Sir Edmund Andros looked at the old man; then he cast his hard and cruel eye over the multitude, and beheld them burning with that lurid wrath, so difficult to kindle or to quench; and again he fixed his gaze on the aged form, which stood obscurely in an open space, where neither friend nor foe had thrust himself. What were his thoughts, he uttered no word which might discover. But whether the oppressor were overawed by the Grey Champion's look, or perceived his peril in the threatening attitude of the people, it is certain that he gave back, and ordered his soldiers to commence a slow and guarded retreat. Before another sunset, the Governor, and all that rode so proudly with him, were prisoners, and long ere it was known that James had abdicated, King William was proclaimed throughout New England.

But where was the Grey Champion? Some reported, that when the troops had gone from King Street, and the people were thronging tumultuously in their rear, Bradstreet, the aged Governor, was seen to embrace a form more aged than his own. Others soberly affirmed, that while they marvelled at the venerable grandeur of his aspect, the old man had faded from their eyes, melting slowly into the hues of twilight, till, where he stood, there was an empty space. But all agreed that the hoary shape was gone. The men of that generation watched for his reappearance, in sunshine and in twilight, but never saw him more, nor knew when his funeral passed, nor where his gravestone was.

And who was the Grey Champion? Perhaps his name might be found in the records of that stern Court of Justice, which passed a sentence, too mighty for the age, but glorious in all after times, for its humbling lesson to the monarch and its high example to the subject. I have heard, that whenever the descendants of the Puritans are to show the spirit of their sires, the old man appears again. When eighty years had passed,* he walked once more in King Street. Five years later, in the twilight of an April morning, he stood on the green, beside the meeting-house, at Lexington,* where now the obelisk of granite, with a slab of slate inlaid, commemorates the first fallen of the Revolution. And when our fathers were toiling at the breastwork on Bunker's Hill,* all through that night the old warrior walked his rounds. Long, long may it be, ere he comes again! His hour is one of darkness, and adversity and peril. But should domestic tyranny oppress us, or the invader's step pollute our soil, still may the Grey Champion come, for he is the type of New England's hereditary spirit, and his shadowy march, on the eve of danger, must ever be the pledge that New England's sons will vindicate their ancestry.

YOUNG GOODMAN BROWN

YOUNG Goodman* Brown came forth at sunset into the street of Salem village;* but put his head back, after crossing the threshold, to exchange a parting kiss with his young wife. And Faith, as the wife was aptly named, thrust her own pretty head into the street, letting the wind play with the pink ribbons of her cap while she called to Goodman Brown.

'Dearest heart,' whispered she, softly and rather sadly, when her lips were close to his ear, 'prithee put off your journey until sunrise and sleep in your own bed to-night. A lone woman is troubled with such dreams and such thoughts that she's afeared of herself sometimes. Pray tarry with me this night, dear husband, of all nights in the year.'*

'My love and my Faith,' replied young Goodman Brown, 'of all nights in the year, this one night must I tarry away from thee. My journey, as thou callest it, forth and back again, must needs be done 'twixt now and sunrise. What, my sweet, pretty wife, dost thou doubt me already, and we but three months married?'

'Then God bless you!' said Faith, with the pink ribbons; 'and may you find all well when you come back.'

'Amen!' cried Goodman Brown. 'Say thy prayers, dear Faith, and go to bed at dusk, and no harm will come to thee.'

So they parted; and the young man pursued his way until, being about to turn the corner by the meeting-house, he looked back and saw the head of Faith still peeping after him with a melancholy air, in spite of her pink ribbons.

'Poor little Faith!' thought he, for his heart smote him. 'What a wretch am I to leave her on such an errand! She talks of dreams, too. Methought as she spoke, there was trouble in her face, as if a dream had warned her what work is to be done to-night. But no, no; 'twould kill her to think it. Well, she's a blessed angel on earth; and after this one night I'll cling to her skirts and follow her to heaven.'

With this excellent resolve for the future, Goodman Brown felt himself justified in making more haste on his present evil purpose. He had taken a dreary road, darkened by all the gloomiest trees of the forest, which barely stood aside to let the narrow path creep through, and closed immediately behind. It was all as lonely as could be; and there is this peculiarity in such a solitude, that the traveller knows not who may be concealed by the innumerable trunks and the thick boughs overhead; so that with lonely footsteps he may yet be passing through an unseen multitude.

'There may be a devilish Indian behind every tree,' said Goodman Brown to himself; and he glanced fearfully behind him as he added, 'What if the Devil himself should be at my very elbow!'

His head being turned back, he passed a crook of the road, and, looking foward again, beheld the figure of a man, in grave and decent attire, seated at the foot of an old tree. He arose at Goodman Brown's approach and walked onward side by side with him.

'You are late, Goodman Brown,' said he. 'The clock of the Old South* was striking as I came through Boston; and that is full fifteen minutes* agone.'

'Faith kept me back awhile,' replied the young man, with a tremor in his voice, caused by the sudden appearance of his companion, though not wholly unexpected.

It was now deep dusk in the forest, and deepest in that part of it where these two were journeying. As nearly as could be discerned, the second traveller was about fifty years old, apparently in the same rank of life as Goodman Brown, and bearing a considerable resemblance to him, though perhaps more in expression than features. Still they might have been taken for father and son. And yet, though the elder person was as simply clad as the younger and as simple in manner too, he had an indescribable air of one who knew the world, and who would not have felt abashed at the governor's dinner-table or in King William's court,* were it possible that his affairs should call him thither. But the only thing about him that could be fixed upon as remarkable was his staff, which bore the likeness of a great black snake, so curiously wrought that it might almost be seen to twist and wriggle itself like a living serpent. This, of course, must have been an ocular deception, assisted by the uncertain light.

'Come, Goodman Brown,' cried his fellow-traveller, 'this is a dull pace for the beginning of a journey. Take my staff, if you are so soon weary.'

'Friend,' said the other, exchanging his slow pace for a full stop, 'having kept covenant by meeting thee here, it is my purpose now to return whence I came. I have scruples touching the matter thou wot'st of.'

'Sayest thou so?' replied he of the serpent, smiling apart. 'Let us walk on, nevertheless, reasoning as we go; and if I convince thee not, thou shalt turn back. We are but a little way in the forest yet.'

'Too far! too far!' exclaimed the goodman, unconsciously resuming his walk. 'My father never went into the woods on such an errand, nor his father before him. We have been a race of honest men and good Christians since the days of the martyrs; and shall I be the first by the name of Brown that ever took this path and kept—'

'Such company, thou wouldst say,' observed the elder person, interpreting his pause. 'Well said, Goodman Brown! I have been as well acquainted with your family as with ever a one among the Puritans; and that's no trifle to say. I helped your grandfather, the constable,* when he lashed the Quaker woman so smartly through the streets of Salem; and it was I that brought your father a pitch-pine knot, kindled at my own hearth, to set fire to an Indian village,* in King Philip's war. They were my good friends both; and many a pleasant walk have we had along this path, and returned merrily after midnight. I would fain be friends with you for their sake.'

'If it be as thou sayest,' replied Goodman Brown, 'I marvel they never spoke of these matters; or, verily, I marvel not, seeing that the least rumour of the sort would have driven them from New England. We are a people of prayer, and good works to boot, and abide no such wickedness.'

'Wickedness or not,' said the traveller with the twisted staff, 'I have a very general acquaintance here in New England. The deacons of many a church have drunk the communion wine with me; the selectmen of divers towns make me their chairman; and a majority of the Great and General Court are firm supporters of my interest. The governor and I, too— But these are state secrets.'

'Can this be so?'* cried Goodman Brown, with a stare of amazement at his undisturbed companion. 'Howbeit, I have nothing to do with the governor and council; they have their own ways, and are no rule for a simple husbandman like me. But, were I to go on with thee, how should I meet the eye of that good old man, our minister, at Salem village? Oh, his voice would make me tremble both Sabbath day and lecture day!'

Thus far the elder traveller had listened with due gravity; but now burst into a fit of irrepressible mirth, shaking himself so violently that his snake-like staff actually seemed to wriggle in sympathy.

'Ha! ha! ha!' shouted he again and again; then composing himself, 'Well, go on, Goodman Brown, go on; but, prithee, don't kill me with laughing.'

'Well, then, to end the matter at once,' said Goodman Brown, considerably nettled, 'there is my wife, Faith. It would break her dear little heart; and I'd rather break my own.'

'Nay, if that be the case,' answered the other, 'e'en go thy ways, Goodman Brown. I would not for twenty old women like the one hobbling before us that Faith should come to any harm.'

As he spoke, he pointed his staff at a female figure on the path, in whom Goodman Brown recognized a very pious and exemplary dame, who had taught him his catechism in youth, and was still his moral and spiritual adviser, jointly with the minister and Deacon Gookin.*

'A marvel, truly, that Goody Cloyse* should be so far in the wilderness at nightfall,' said he. 'But, with your leave, friend, I shall take a cut through the woods until we have left this Christian woman behind. Being a stranger to you, she might ask whom I was consorting with and whither I was going.'

'Be it so,' said his fellow-traveller. 'Betake you to the woods, and let me keep the path.'

Accordingly the young man turned aside, but took care to watch his companion, who advanced softly along the road until he had come within a staff's length of the old dame. She, meanwhile, was making the best of her way, with singular speed for so aged a woman, and mumbling some indistinct words—a prayer, doubtless—as she went. The traveller put forth his staff and touched her withered neck with what seemed the serpent's tail.

'The Devil!' screamed the pious old lady.

'Then Goody Cloyse knows her old friend?' observed the traveller, confronting her and leaning on his writhing stick.

'Ah, forsooth, and is it your worship indeed?' cried the good dame. 'Yea, truly is it, and in the very image of my old gossip,* Goodman Brown, the grandfather of the silly fellow that now is. But—would your worship believe it?—my broomstick hath strangely disappeared, stolen, as I suspect, by that unhanged witch, Goody Cory,* and that, too, when I was all anointed* with the juice of smallage, and cinquefoil, and wolf's-bane—'*

'Mingled with fine wheat and the fat of a new-born babe,' said the shape of old Goodman Brown.

'Ah, your worship knows the recipe,' cried the old lady, cackling aloud. 'So, as I was saying, being all ready for the meeting, and no horse to ride on, I made up my mind to foot it; for they tell me there is a nice young man to be taken into communion to-night. But now your good worship will lend me your arm, and we shall be there in a twinkling.'

'That can hardly be,' answered her friend. 'I may not spare you my arm, Goody Cloyse; but here is my staff, if you will.'

So saying, he threw it down at her feet, where, perhaps, it assumed life, being one of the rods which its owner had formerly lent to the Egyptian magi.* Of this fact, however, Goodman Brown could not take cognizance. He had cast up his eyes in astonishment, and, looking down again, beheld neither Goody Cloyse nor the serpentine staff, but his fellow-traveller alone, who waited for him as calmly as if nothing had happened.

'That old woman taught me my catechism,' said the young man; and there was a world of meaning in this simple comment.

They continued to walk onward, while the elder traveller exhorted his companion to make good speed and persevere in the path, discoursing so aptly that his arguments seemed rather to spring up in the bosom of his auditor than to be suggested by himself. As they went, he plucked a branch of maple to serve for a walking-stick, and began to strip it of the twigs and little boughs, which were wet with evening dew. The moment his fingers touched them they became strangely withered and dried up as with a week's sunshine. Thus the pair proceeded, at a good free pace, until suddenly, in a gloomy hollow of the road, Goodman Brown sat himself down on the stump of a tree and refused to go any farther.

'Friend,' said he, stubbornly, 'my mind is made up. Not another step will I budge on this errand. What if a wretched old woman do choose to go to the Devil when I thought she was going to heaven: is that any reason why I should quit my dear Faith and go after her?'

'You will think better of this by and by,' said his acquaintance, composedly. 'Sit here and rest yourself awhile; and when you feel like moving again, there is my staff to help you along.'

Without more words, he threw his companion the maple-stick, and was as speedily out of sight as if he had vanished into the deepening gloom. The young man sat a few moments by the roadside, applauding himself greatly, and thinking with how clear a conscience he should meet the minister in his morning walk, nor shrink from the eye of good old Deacon Gookin. And what calm sleep would be his that very night, which was to have been spent so wickedly, but so purely and sweetly now, in the arms of Faith! Amidst these pleasant and praiseworthy meditations, Goodman Brown heard the tramp of horses along the road, and deemed it advisable to conceal himself within the verge of the forest, conscious of the guilty purpose that had brought him thither, though now so happily turned from it.

On came the hoof-tramps and the voices of the riders, two grave old voices, conversing soberly as they drew near. These mingled sounds appeared to pass along the road, within a few yards of the young man's hiding-place; but, owing doubtless to the depth of the gloom at that particular spot, neither the travellers nor their steeds were visible. Though their figures brushed the small boughs by the wayside, it could not be seen that they intercepted, even for a moment, the faint gleam from the strip of bright sky athwart which they must have passed. Goodman Brown alternately crouched and stood on tiptoe, pulling aside the branches and thrusting forth his head as far as he durst, without discerning so much as a shadow. It vexed him the more, because he could have sworn, were such a thing possible, that he recognized the voices of the minister and Deacon Gookin, jogging along quietly, as they were wont to do, when bound to some ordination or ecclesiastical council. While yet within hearing, one of the riders stopped to pluck a switch.

'Of the two, reverend sir,' said the voice like the deacon's, 'I had rather miss an ordination dinner than tonight's meeting. They tell me that some of our community are to be here from Falmouth* and beyond, and others from Connecticut and Rhode Island, besides several of the Indian pow-wows,* who, after their fashion, know almost as much deviltry as the best of us. Moreover, there is a goodly young woman to be taken into communion.'

'Mighty well, Deacon Gookin!' replied the solemn old tones of the minister. 'Spur up, or we shall be late. Nothing can be done, you know, until I get on the ground.'

The hoofs clattered again; and the voices, talking so strangely in the empty air, passed on through the forest, where no church had ever been gathered or solitary Christian prayed. Whither, then, could these holy men be journeying so deep into the heathen wilderness? Young Goodman Brown caught hold of a tree for support, being ready to sink down on the ground, faint and overburdened with the heavy sickness of his heart. He looked up to the sky, doubting whether there really was a heaven above him. Yet there was the blue arch, and the stars brightening in it.

'With heaven above and Faith below, I will yet stand firm against the Devil!' cried Goodman Brown.

While he still gazed upward into the deep arch of the firmament and had lifted his hands to pray, a cloud, though no wind was stirring, hurried across the zenith and hid the brightening stars. The blue sky was still visible except directly overhead, where this black mass of cloud was sweeping swiftly northward. Aloft in the air, as if from the depths of the cloud, came a confused and doubtful sound of voices. Once the listener fancied that he could distinguish the accents of townspeople of his own, men and women, both pious and ungodly, many of whom he had met at the communion-table, and had seen others rioting at the tavern. The next morning, so indistinct were the sounds, he doubted whether he had heard aught but the murmur of the old forest, whispering without a wind. Then came a stronger swell of those familiar tones, heard daily in the sunshine at Salem village, but never until now from a cloud of night. There was one voice, of a young woman, uttering lamentations, yet with an uncertain sorrow, and entreating for some favour, which, perhaps, it would grieve her to obtain; and all the unseen multitude, both saints and sinners, seemed to encourage her onward.

'Faith!' shouted Goodman Brown, in a voice of agony and desperation; and the echoes of the forest mocked him, crying, 'Faith! Faith!' as if bewildered wretches were seeking her all through the wilderness.

The cry of grief, rage, and terror was yet piercing the night, when the unhappy husband held his breath for a response. There was a scream, drowned immediately in a louder murmur of voices, fading into far-off laughter, as the dark cloud swept away, leaving the clear and silent sky above Goodman Brown. But something fluttered lightly down through the air and caught on the branch of a tree. The young man seized it, and beheld a pink ribbon.

'My Faith is gone!' cried he, after one stupefied moment. 'There is no good on earth; and sin is but a name. Come, Devil; for to thee is this world given.'

And, maddened with despair, so that he laughed loud and long, did Goodman Brown grasp his staff and set forth again, at such a rate that he seemed to fly along the forest path rather than to walk or run. The road grew wilder and drearier and more faintly traced, and vanished at length, leaving him in the heart of the dark wilderness, still rushing onward with the instinct that guides mortal man to evil. The whole forest was peopled with frightful sounds,—the creaking of the trees, the howling of wild beasts, and the yell of Indians; while sometimes the wind tolled like a distant church-bell, and sometimes gave a broad roar around the traveller, as if all Nature were laughing him to scorn. But he was himself the chief horror of the scene, and shrank not from its other horrors.

'Ha! ha! ha!' roared Goodman Brown when the wind laughed at him. 'Let us hear which will laugh loudest. Think not to frighten me with your deviltry. Come witch, come wizard, come Indian pow-wow, come Devil himself, and here comes Goodman Brown. You may as well fear him as he fear you.'

In truth, all through the haunted forest there could be nothing more frightful than the figure of Goodman Brown. On he flew* among the black pines, brandishing his staff with frenzied gestures, now giving vent to an inspiration of horrid blasphemy, and now shouting forth such laughter as set all the echoes of the forest laughing like demons around him. The fiend in his own shape is less hideous than when he rages in the breast of man. Thus sped the demoniac on his course, until, quivering among the trees, he saw a red light before him, as when the felled trunks and branches of a clearing have been set on fire, and throw up their lurid blaze against the sky, at the hour of midnight. He paused, in a lull of the tempest that had driven him onward, and heard the swell of what seemed a hymn rolling solemnly from a distance with the weight of many voices. He knew the tune; it was a familiar one in the choir of the village meeting-house. The verse died heavily away, and was lengthened by a chorus, not of human voices, but of all the sounds of the benighted wilderness pealing in awful harmony together. Goodman Brown cried out; and his cry was lost to his own ear by its unison with the cry of the desert.

In the interval of silence he stole forward until the light glared full upon his eyes. At one extremity of an open space, hemmed in by the dark wall of the forest, arose a rock, bearing some rude, natural resemblance either to an altar or a pulpit,* and surrounded by four blazing pines, their tops aflame, their stems untouched, like candles at an evening meeting. The mass of foliage that had overgrown the summit of the rock was all on fire, blazing high into the night and fitfully illuminating the whole field. Each pendent twig and leafy festoon was in a blaze. As the red light arose and fell, a numerous congregation alternately shone forth, then disappeared in shadow, and again grew, as it were, out of the darkness, peopling the heart of the solitary woods at once.

'A grave and dark-clad company,' quoth Goodman Brown.

In truth they were such. Among them, quivering to and fro between gloom and splendour, appeared faces that would be seen next day at the council board of the province, and others which, Sabbath after Sabbath, looked devoutly heavenward, and benignantly over the crowded pews, from the holiest pulpits in the land. Some affirm that the lady of the governor* was there. At least there were high dames well known to her, and wives of honoured husbands, and widows, a great multitude, and ancient maidens, all of excellent repute, and fair young girls, who trembled lest their mothers should espy them. Either the sudden gleams of light flashing over the obscure field bedazzled Goodman Brown, or he recognized a score of the church-members of Salem village famous for their especial sanctity. Good old Deacon Gookin had arrived, and waited at the skirts of that venerable saint, his revered pastor. But, irreverently consorting with these grave, reputable, and pious people, these elders of the church, these chaste dames and dewy virgins, there were men of dissolute lives and women of spotted fame, wretches given over to all mean and filthy vice, and suspected even of horrid crimes. It was strange to see that the good shrank not from the wicked, nor were the sinners abashed by the saints. Scattered also among their pale-faced enemies were the Indian priests, or pow-wows, who had often scared their native forest with more hideous incantations than any known to English witchcraft.

'But where is Faith?' thought Goodman Brown; and, as hope came into his heart, he trembled.

Another verse of the hymn arose, a slow and mournful strain, such as the pious love, but joined to words which expressed all that our nature can conceive of sin, and darkly hinted at far more. Unfathomable to mere mortals is the lore of fiends. Verse after verse was sung; and still the chorus of the desert swelled between like the deepest tone of a mighty organ; and with the final peal of that dreadful anthem there came a sound, as if the roaring wind, the rushing streams, and howling beasts, and every other voice of the unconverted wilderness were mingling and according with the voice of guilty man in homage to the prince of all. The four blazing pines threw up a loftier flame, and obscurely discovered shapes and visages of horror on the smoke-wreaths above the impious assembly. At the same moment the fire on the rock shot redly forth and formed a glowing arch above its base, where now appeared a figure. With reverence be it spoken, the figure* bore no slight similitude, both in garb and manner, to some grave divine* of the New England churches.

'Bring forth the converts!' cried a voice that echoed through the field and rolled into the forest.

At the word, Goodman Brown stepped forth from the shadow of the trees and approached the congregation, with whom he felt a loathful brotherhood by the sympathy of all that was wicked in his heart. He could have wellnigh sworn that the shape of his own dead father beckoned him to advance, looking downward from a smoke-wreath, while a woman, with dim features of despair, threw out her hand to warn him back. Was it his mother? But he had no power to retreat one step, nor to resist, even in thought, when the minister and good old Deacon Gookin seized his arms and led him to the blazing rock. Thither came also the slender form of a veiled female, led between Goody Cloyse, that pious teacher of the catechism, and Martha Carrier, who had received the Devil's promise to be queen of hell.* A rampant hag was she. And there stood the proselytes beneath the canopy of fire.

'Welcome, my children,' said the dark figure, 'to the communion of your race. Ye have found thus young your nature and your destiny. My children, look behind you!'

They turned; and flashing forth, as it were, in a sheet of flame, the fiend worshippers were seen; the smile of welcome gleamed darkly on every visage.

'There,' resumed the sable form, 'are all whom ye have

reverenced from youth. Ye deemed them holier than yourselves, and shrank from your own sin, contrasting it with their lives of righteousness and prayerful aspirations heavenward. Yet here are they all in my worshipping assembly. This night it shall be granted you to know their secret deeds; how hoary-bearded elders of the church have whispered wanton words to the young maids of their households; how many a woman, eager for widow's weeds, has given her husband a drink at bedtime and let him sleep his last sleep in her bosom; how beardless youths have made haste to inherit their father's wealth; and how fair damsels—blush not, sweet ones—have dug little graves in the garden, and bidden me, the sole guest, to an infant's funeral. By the sympathy of your human hearts for sin ye shall scent out all the places— whether in church, bedchamber, street, field, or forest—where crime has been committed, and shall exult to behold the whole earth one stain of guilt, one mighty blood-spot. Far more than this. It shall be yours to penetrate, in every bosom, the deep mystery of sin, the fountain of all wicked arts, and which inexhaustibly supplies more evil impulses than human power—than my power at its utmost—can make manifest in deeds. And now, my children, look upon each other.'

They did so; and, by the blaze of the hell-kindled torches, the wretched man beheld his Faith, and the wife her husband, trembling before that unhallowed altar.

'Lo, there ye stand, my children,' said the figure, in a deep and solemn tone, almost sad with its despairing awfulness, as if his once angelic nature could yet mourn for our miserable race. 'Depending upon one another's hearts, ye had still hoped that virtue were not all a dream. Now are ye undeceived. Evil is the nature of mankind. Evil must be your only happiness. Welcome again, my children, to the communion of your race.'

'Welcome,' repeated the fiend worshippers, in one cry of despair and triumph.

And there they stood, the only pair, as it seemed, who were yet hesitating on the verge of wickedness in this dark world. A basin was hollowed, naturally, in the rock. Did it contain water, reddened by the lurid light? or was it blood? or, perchance, a liquid flame? Herein did the shape of evil dip his hand and prepare to lay the mark of baptism upon their foreheads, that they might be partakers of the mystery of sin, more conscious of the secret guilt of others, both in deed and thought, than they could now be of their own. The husband cast one look at his pale wife, and Faith at him. What polluted wretches would the next glance show them to each other, shuddering alike at what they disclosed and what they saw!

'Faith! Faith!' cried the husband, 'look up to Heaven, and resist the wicked one.'

Whether Faith obeyed, he knew not. Hardly had he spoken, when he found himself amid calm night and solitude, listening to a roar of the wind which died heavily away through the forest. He staggered against the rock, and felt it chill and damp; while a hanging twig, that had been all on fire, besprinkled his cheek with the coldest dew.

The next morning young Goodman Brown came slowly into the street of Salem village, staring around him like a bewildered man. The good old minister was taking a walk along the graveyard to get an appetite for breakfast and meditate his sermon, and bestowed a blessing, as he passed, on Goodman Brown. He shrank from the venerable saint as if to avoid an anathema. Old Deacon Gookin was at domestic worship, and the holy words of his prayer were heard through the open window. 'What God doth the wizard pray to?' quoth Goodman Brown. Goody Cloyse, that excellent old Christian, stood in the early sunshine at her own lattice, catechizing a little girl who had brought her a pint of morning's milk. Goodman Brown snatched away the child as from the grasp of the fiend himself. Turning the corner by the meeting-house, he spied the head of Faith, with the pink ribbons, gazing anxiously forth, and bursting into such joy at sight of him that she skipped along the street and almost kissed her husband before the whole village. But Goodman Brown looked sternly and sadly into her face, and passed on without a greeting.

Had Goodman Brown fallen asleep in the forest, and only dreamed a wild dream of a witch-meeting?

Be it so, if you will; but, alas! it was a dream of evil omen for young Goodman Brown. A stern, a sad, a darkly meditative, a distrustful, if not a desperate, man did he become from the night of that fearful dream. On the Sabbath day, when the congregation were singing a holy psalm, he could not listen, because an anthem of sin rushed loudly upon his ear and drowned all the blessed strain. When the minister spoke from the pulpit, with power and fervid eloquence, and with his hand on the open Bible, of the sacred truths of our religion, and of saint-like lives and triumphant deaths, and of future bliss or misery unutterable, then did Goodman Brown turn pale, dreading lest the roof should thunder down upon the grey blasphemer and his hearers. Often, awaking suddenly at midnight, he shrank from the bosom of Faith; and at morning or eventide, when the family knelt down to prayer, he scowled, and muttered to himself, and gazed sternly at his wife, and turned away. And when he had lived long, and was borne to his grave, a hoary corpse, followed by Faith, an aged woman, and children and grandchildren, a goodly procession, besides neighbours not a few, they carved no hopeful verse upon his tombstone; for his dying hour was gloom.

WAKEFIELD

IN some old magazine or newspaper,* I recollect a story, told as truth, of a man—let us call him Wakefield—who absented himself for a long time from his wife. The fact thus abstractedly stated is not very uncommon, nor—without a proper distinction of circumstances—to be condemned either as naughty or nonsensical. Howbeit, this, though far from the most aggravated, is perhaps the strangest instance on record of marital delinquency; and, moreover, as remarkable a freak as may be found in the whole list of human oddities. The wedded couple lived in London. The man, under pretence of going a journey, took lodgings in the next street to his own house, and there, unheard of by his wife or friends, and without the shadow of a reason for such self-banishment, dwelt upwards of twenty years. During that period, he beheld his home every day, and frequently the forlorn Mrs. Wakefield. And after so great a gap in his matrimonial felicity—when his death was reckoned certain, his estate settled, his name dismissed from memory, and his wife, long, long ago, resigned to her autumnal widowhood—he entered the door one evening, quietly, as from a day's absence, and became a loving spouse till death.*

This outline is all that I remember. But the incident, though of the purest originality, unexampled, and probably never to be repeated, is one, I think, which appeals to the generous sympathies of mankind. We know, each for himself, that none of us would perpetrate such a folly, yet feel as if some other might. To my own contemplations, at least, it has often recurred, always exciting wonder, but with a sense that the story must be true, and a conception of its hero's character. Whenever any subject so forcibly affects the mind, time is well spent in thinking of it. If the reader choose, let him do his own meditation; or if he prefer to ramble with me through the twenty years of Wakefield's vagary, I bid him welcome; trusting that there will be a pervading spirit and a moral, even should we fail to find them, done up neatly, and condensed into the final sentence. Thought has always its efficacy, and every striking incident its moral.

What sort of a man was Wakefield? We are free to shape out our own idea, and call it by his name. He was now in the meridian of life; his matrimonial affections, never violent, were sobered into a calm, habitual sentiment; of all husbands, he was likely to be the most constant, because a certain sluggishness would keep his heart at rest, wherever it might be placed. He was intellectual, but not actively so; his mind occupied itself in long and lazy musings, that tended to no purpose, or had not vigour to attain it; his thoughts were seldom so energetic as to seize hold of words. Imagination, in the proper meaning of the term, made no part of Wakefield's gifts. With a cold but not depraved* nor wandering heart, and a mind never feverish with riotous thoughts, nor perplexed with originality, who could have anticipated that our friend would entitle himself to a foremost place among the doers of eccentric deeds? Had his acquaintances been asked, who was the man in London, the surest to perform nothing to-day which should be remembered on the morrow, they would have thought of Wakefield. Only the wife of his bosom might have hesitated. She, without having analysed his character, was partly aware of a quiet selfishness, that had rusted into his inactive mind,—of a peculiar sort of vanity, the most uneasy attribute about him,—of a disposition to craft, which had seldom produced more positive effects than the keeping of petty secrets, hardly worth revealing,—and, lastly, of what she called a little strangeness, sometimes, in the good man. This latter quality is indefinable, and perhaps non-existent.

Let us now imagine Wakefield bidding adieu to his wife. It is the dusk of an October evening. His equipment is a drab great-coat, a hat covered with an oil-cloth, top-boots, an umbrella in one hand and a small portmanteau in the other. He has informed Mrs. Wakefield that he is to take the night coach into the country. She would fain inquire the length of his journey, its object, and the probable time of his return; but, indulgent to his harmless love of mystery, interrogates him only by a look. He tells her not to expect him positively by the return coach, not to be alarmed should he tarry three or four days; but, at all events, to look for him at supper on Friday evening. Wakefield himself, be it considered, has no suspicion of what is before him. He holds out his hand; she gives her own, and meets his parting kiss, in the matter-of-course way of a ten years' matrimony; and forth goes the middle-aged Mr. Wakefield, almost resolved to perplex his good lady by a whole week's absence. After the door has closed behind him, she perceives it thrust partly open, and a vision of her husband's face, through the aperture, smiling on her, and gone in a moment. For the time, this little incident is dismissed without a thought. But, long afterwards, when she has been more years a widow than a wife, that smile recurs, and flickers across all her reminiscences of Wakefield's visage. In her many musings, she surrounds the original smile with a multitude of fantasies, which make it strange and awful; as, for instance, if she imagines him in a coffin, that parting look is frozen on his pale features; or, if she dreams of him in heaven, still his blessed spirit wears a quiet and crafty smile. Yet, for its sake, when all others have given him up for dead, she sometimes doubts whether she is a widow.

But our business is with the husband. We must hurry after him, along the street, ere he lose his individuality, and melt into the great mass of London life. It would be vain searching for him there. Let us follow close at his heels, therefore, until, after several superflous turns and doublings, we find him comfortably established by the fireside of a small apartment, previously bespoken. He is in the next street to his own, and at his journey's end. He can scarcely trust his good fortune in having got thither unperceived,—recollecting that, at one time, he was delayed by the throng, in the very focus of a lighted lantern; and, again, there were footsteps, that seemed to tread behind his own, distinct from the multitudinous tramp around him; and, anon, he heard a voice shouting afar, and fancied that it called his name. Doubtless, a dozen busybodies had been watching him, and told his wife the whole affair. Poor Wakefield! Little knowest thou thine own insignificance in this great world! No mortal eye but mine has traced thee. Go quietly to thy bed, foolish man; and, on the morrow, if thou wilt be wise, get thee home to good Mrs. Wakefield, and tell her the truth. Remove not thyself, even for a little week, from thy place in her chaste bosom. Were she, for a single moment, to deem thee dead, or lost, or lastingly divided from her, thou wouldst be woefully conscious of a change in thy true wife, forever after. It is perilous to make a chasm in human affections; not that they gape so long and wide, but so quickly close again!

Almost repenting of his frolic, or whatever it may be termed, Wakefield lies down betimes, and starting from his first nap, spreads forth his arms into the wide and solitary waste of the unaccustomed bed. 'No,'—thinks he, gathering the bedclothes about him—'I will not sleep alone another night.'

In the morning, he rises earlier than usual, and sets himself to consider what he really means to do. Such are his loose and rambling modes of thought, that he has taken this very singular step, with the consciousness of a purpose, indeed, but without being able to define it sufficiently for his own contemplation. The vagueness of the project, and the convulsive effort with which he plunges into the execution of it, are equally characteristic of a feeble-minded man. Wake-field sifts his ideas, however, as minutely as he may, and finds himself curious to know the progress of matters at home,— how his exemplary wife will endure her widowhood of a week; and, briefly, how the little sphere of creatures and circumstances, in which he was a central object, will be affected by his removal. A morbid vanity,* therefore, lies nearest the bottom of the affair. But, how is he to attain his ends? Not, certainly, by keeping close in this comfortable lodging, where, though he slept and awoke in the next street to his home, he is as effectually abroad, as if the stage-coach had been whirling him away all night. Yet, should he reappear, the whole project is knocked on the head. His poor brains being hopelessly puzzled with this dilemma, he at length ventures out, partly resolving to cross the head of the street, and send one hasty glance towards his forsaken domicile. Habit—for he is a man of habits—takes him by the hand, and guides him, wholly unaware, to his own door, where, just at the critical moment, he is aroused by the scraping of his foot upon the step. Wakefield! whither are you going?

At that instant, his fate was turning on the pivot. Little dreaming of the doom to which his first backward step devotes him, he hurries away, breathless with agitation hitherto unfelt, and hardly dares turn his head, at the distant corner. Can it be that nobody caught sight of him? Will not the whole household—the decent Mrs. Wakefield, the smart maid-servant, and the dirty little footboy—raise a hue and cry, through London streets, in pursuit of their fugitive lord and master? Wonderful escape! He gathers courage to pause and look homeward, but is perplexed with a sense of change about the familiar edifice, such as affects us all, when, after a separation of months or years, we again see some hill or lake, or work of art, with which we were friends of old. In ordinary cases, this indescribable impression is caused by the comparison and contrast between our imperfect reminiscences and the reality. In Wakefield, the magic of a single night has wrought a similar transformation, because, in that brief period, a great moral change has been effected. But this is a secret from himself. Before leaving the spot, he catches a far and momentary glimpse of his wife, passing athwart the front window, with her face turned towards the head of the street. The crafty nincompoop takes to his heels, scared with the idea, that, among a thousand such atoms of mortality, her eye must have detected him. Right glad is his heart, though his brain be somewhat dizzy, when he finds himself by the coalfire of his lodgings.

So much for the commencement of this long whim-wham. After the initial conception, and the stirring up of the man's sluggish temperament to put it in practice, the whole matter evolves itself in a natural train. We may suppose him, as the result of deep deliberation, buying a new wig,* of reddish hair, and selecting sundry garments, in a fashion unlike his customary suit of brown, from a Jew's old-clothes bag. It is accomplished. Wakefield is another man. The new system being now established, a retrograde movement to the old would be almost as difficult as the step that placed him in his unparalleled position. Furthermore, he is rendered obstinate by a sulkiness, occasionally incident to his temper, and brought on, at present, by the inadequate sensation which he conceives to have been produced in the bosom of Mrs. Wakefield. He will not go back until she be frightened half to death. Well; twice or thrice has she passed before his sight, each time with a heavier step, a paler cheek, and more anxious brow; and in the third week of his non-appearance, he detects a portent of evil entering the house, in the guise of an apothecary. Next day, the knocker is muffled. Towards nightfall comes the chariot of a physician, and deposits its big-wigged and solemn burden at Wakefield's door, whence, after a quarter of an hour's visit, he emerges, perchance the herald of a funeral. Dear woman! Will she die? By this time, Wakefield is excited to something like energy of feeling, but still lingers away from his wife's bedside, pleading with his conscience, that she must not be disturbed at such a juncture. If aught else restrains him, he does not know it. In the course of a few weeks, she gradually recovers; the crisis is over; her heart is sad, perhaps, but quiet; and, let him return soon or late, it will never be feverish for him again. Such ideas glimmer through the mist of Wakefield's mind, and render him indistinctly conscious that an almost impassable gulf divides his hired apartment from his former home. 'It is but in the next street!' he sometimes says. Fool! it is in another world. Hitherto, he has put off his return from one particular day to another; henceforward, he leaves the precise time undetermined. Not to-morrow,—probably next week,—pretty soon. Poor man! The dead have nearly as much chance of revisiting their earthly homes, as the self-banished Wakefield.

Would that I had a folio to write, instead of an article of a dozen pages! Then might I exemplify how an influence, beyond our control, lays its strong hand on every deed which we do, and weaves its consequences into an iron tissue of necessity. Wakefield is spellbound. We must leave him, for ten years or so, to haunt around his house, without once crossing the threshold, and to be faithful to his wife, with all the affection of which his heart is capable, while he is slowly fading out of hers. Long since, it must be remarked, he has lost the perception of singularity in his conduct.

Now for a scene! Amid the throng of a London street, we distinguish a man, now waxing elderly, with few characteristics to attract careless observers, yet bearing, in his whole aspect, the handwriting of no common fate, for such as have the skill to read it. He is meagre; his low and narrow forehead is deeply wrinkled; his eyes, small and lustreless, sometimes wander apprehensively about him, but oftener seem to look inward. He bends his head, and moves with an indescribable obliquity of gait, as if unwilling to display his full front to the world. Watch him, long enough to see what we have described, and you will allow, that circumstances—which often produce remarkable men from nature's ordinary handiwork—have produced one such here. Next, leaving him to sidle along the footwalk, cast your eyes in the opposite direction, where a portly female, considerably in the wane of life, with a prayer-book in her hand, is proceeding to yonder church.* She has the placid mien of settled widowhood. Her regrets have either died away, or have become so essential to her heart, that they would be poorly exchanged for joy. Just as the lean man and well-conditioned woman are passing, a slight obstruction occurs, and brings these two figures directly in contact. Their hands touch; the pressure of the crowd forces her bosom against his shoulder; they stand, face to face, staring into each other's eyes. After a ten years' separation, thus Wakefield meets his wife!

The throng eddies away, and carries them asunder. The sober widow, resuming her former pace, proceeds to church, but pauses in the portal, and throws a perplexed glance along the street. She passes in, however, opening her prayer-book as she goes. And the man! with so wild a face, that busy and selfish London* stands to gaze after him, he hurries to his lodgings, bolts the door, and throws himself upon the bed. The latent feelings of years break out; his feeble mind acquires a brief energy from their strength; all the miserable strangeness of his life is revealed to him at a glance: and he cries out, passionately, 'Wakefield! Wakefield! You are mad!'

Perhaps he was so. The singularity of his situation must have so moulded him to himself, that, considered in regard to his fellow-creatures and the business of life, he could not be said to possess his right mind. He had contrived, or rather he had happened, to dissever himself from the world,—to vanish,—to give up his place and privileges with living men, without being admitted among the dead. The life of a hermit is nowise parallel to his. He was in the bustle of the city, as of old; but the crowd swept by, and saw him not; he was, we may figuratively say, always beside his wife, and at his hearth, yet must never feel the warmth of the one, nor the affection of the other. It was Wakefield's unprecedented fate, to retain his original share of human sympathies, and to be still involved in human interests, while he had lost his reciprocal influence on them. It would be a most curious speculation, to trace out the effect of such circumstances on his heart and intellect, separately, and in unison. Yet, changed as he was, he would seldom be conscious of it, but deem himself the same man as ever; glimpses of the truth, indeed, would come, but only for the moment; and still he would keep saying, 'I shall soon go back!' nor reflect that he had been saying so for twenty years.

I conceive, also, that these twenty years would appear, in the retrospect, scarcely longer than the week to which

Wakefield had at first limited his absence. He would look on the affair as no more than an interlude in the main business of his life. When, after a little while more, he should deem it time to re-enter his parlour, his wife would clap her hands for joy, on beholding the middle-aged Mr. Wakefield. Alas, what a mistake! Would Time but await the close of our favourite follies, we should be young men, all of us, and till Doomsday.

One evening, in the twentieth year since he vanished, Wakefield is taking his customary walk towards the dwelling which he still calls his own. It is a gusty night of autumn, with frequent showers, that patter down upon the pavement, and are gone, before a man can put up his umbrella. Pausing near the house, Wakefield discerns, through the parlour windows of the second floor, the red glow, and the glimmer and fitful flash of a comfortable fire. On the ceiling appears a grotesque shadow of good Mrs. Wakefield. The cap, the nose and chin, and the broad waist form an admirable caricature, which dances, moreover, with the up-flickering and down-sinking blaze, almost too merrily for the shade of an elderly widow. At this instant, a shower chances to fall, and is driven, by the unmannerly gust, full into Wakefield's face and bosom. He is quite penetrated with its autumnal chill. Shall he stand, wet and shivering* here, when his own hearth has a good fire to warm him, and his own wife will run to fetch the grey coat and small clothes, which doubtless she has kept carefully in the closet of their bedchamber? No! Wakefield is no such fool. He ascends the steps,—heavily!—for twenty years have stiffened his legs, since he came down,—but he knows it not. Stay, Wakefield! Would you go to the sole home that is left you? Then step into your grave! The door opens. As he passes in, we have a parting glimpse of his visage, and recognize the crafty smile, which was the precursor of the little joke that he has ever since been playing off at his wife's expense. How unmercifully has he quizzed the poor woman! Well, a good night's rest to Wakefield!

This happy event—supposing it to be such—could only have occurred at an unpremeditated moment. We will not follow our friend across the threshold. He has left us much food for thought, a portion of which shall lend its wisdom to a moral, and be shaped into a figure. Amid the seeming confusion of our mysterious world, individuals are so nicely adjusted to a system, and systems to one another, and to a whole, that, by stepping aside for a moment, a man exposes himself to a fearful risk of losing his place for ever. Like Wakefield, he may become, as it were, the Outcast of the Universe.*

THE MAYPOLE OF MERRY MOUNT

There is an admirable foundation for a philosophic romance, in the curious history of the early settlement of Mount Wollaston,* or Merry Mount. In the slight sketch here attempted, the facts recorded on the grave pages of our New England annalists* have wrought themselves, almost spontaneously, into a sort of allegory. The masques, mummeries, and festive customs, described in the text, are in accordance with the manners of the age. Authority on these points may be found in Strutt's *Book of English Sports and Pastimes*.*

BRIGHT were the days at Merry Mount, when the Maypole was the banner staff of that gay colony! They who reared it, should their banner be triumphant, were to pour sunshine over New England's rugged hills, and scatter flower-seeds throughout the soil. Jollity and gloom were contending for an empire. Midsummer eve had come, bringing deep verdure to the forest, and roses in her lap, of a more vivid hue than the tender buds of Spring. But May, or her mirthful spirit, dwelt all the year round at Merry Mount, sporting with the Summer months, and revelling with Autumn, and basking in the glow of Winter's fireside. Through a world of toil and care she flitted with dreamlike smile, and came hither to find a home among the lightsome hearts of Merry Mount.

Never had the Maypole been so gaily decked as at sunset on midsummer eve. This venerated emblem was a pine-tree, which had preserved the slender grace of youth, while it equalled the loftiest height of the old wood monarchs. From its top streamed a silken banner, coloured like a rainbow. Down nearly to the ground, the pole was dressed with birchen boughs, and others of the liveliest green, and some silvery leaves, fastened by ribbons* that fluttered in fantastic knots of

twenty different colours, but no sad ones. Garden flowers and
blossoms of the wilderness laughed gladly forth amid the
verdure, so fresh and dewy, that they must have grown by
magic on that happy pine-tree. Where this green and flowery
splendour terminated, the shaft of the Maypole was stained
with the seven brilliant hues of the banner at its top. On the
lowest green bough hung an abundant wreath of roses, some
that had been gathered in the sunniest spots of the forest, and
others, of still richer blush, which the colonists had reared
from English seed. Oh people of the Golden Age,* the chief
of your husbandry was to raise flowers!

But what was the wild throng that stood hand in hand about
the Maypole? It could not be, that the fauns and nymphs,
when driven from their classic groves and homes of ancient
fable, had sought refuge, as all the persecuted did, in the fresh
woods of the West. These were Gothic monsters, though
perhaps of Grecian ancestry. On the shoulders of a comely
youth uprose the head and branching antlers of a stag; a
second, human in all other points, had the grim visage of a
wolf; a third, still with the trunk and limbs of a mortal man,
showed the beard and horns of a venerable he-goat. There was
the likeness of a bear* erect, brute in all but his hind legs,
which were adorned with pink silk stockings. And here again,
almost as wondrous, stood a real bear of the dark forest,
lending each of his fore-paws to the grasp of a human hand
and as ready for the dance as any in that circle. His inferior
nature rose half-way, to meet his companions as they stooped.
Other faces wore the similitude of man or woman, but distorted
or extravagant, with red noses pendulous before their mouths,
which seemed of awful depth, and stretched from ear to ear
in an eternal fit of laughter. Here might be seen the Salvage
Man,* well known in heraldry, hairy as a baboon, and girdled
with green leaves. By his side, a nobler figure, but still a
counterfeit, appeared an Indian hunter, with feathery crest
and wampum* belt. Many of this strange company wore
foolscaps, and had little bells appended to their garments,
tinkling with a silvery sound, responsive to the inaudible
music of their gleesome spirits. Some youths and maidens
were of soberer garb, yet well maintained their places in the

irregular throng, by the expression of wild revelry upon their features. Such were the colonists of Merry Mount, as they stood in the broad smile of sunset, round their venerated Maypole.

Had a wanderer, bewildered in the melancholy forest, heard their mirth, and stolen a half-affrighted glance, he might have fancied them the crew of Comus, some already transformed to brutes, some midway between man and beast, and the others rioting in the flow of tipsy jollity that foreran the change. But a band of Puritans, who watched the scene, invisible themselves, compared the masques to those devils and ruined souls with whom their superstition peopled the black wilderness.

Within the ring of monsters appeared the two airiest forms* that had ever trodden on any more solid footing than a purple and golden cloud. One was a youth in glistening apparel, with a scarf of the rainbow pattern crosswise on his breast. His right hand held a gilded staff, the ensign of high dignity among the revellers, and his left grasped the slender fingers of a fair maiden, not less gaily decorated than himself. Bright roses glowed in contrast with the dark and glossy curls of each, and were scattered round their feet, or had sprung up spontaneously there. Behind this lightsome couple, so close to the Maypole that its boughs shaded his jovial face, stood the figure of an English priest, canonically dressed, yet decked with flowers, in heathen fashion, and wearing a chaplet of the native vine-leaves. By the riot of his rolling eye, and the pagan decorations of his holy garb, he seemed the wildest monster there, and the very Comus of the crew.

'Votaries of the Maypole,' cried the flower-decked priest, 'merrily, all day long, have the woods echoed to your mirth. But be this your merriest hour, my hearts! Lo, here stand the Lord and Lady of the May, whom I, a clerk* of Oxford, and high-priest of Merry Mount, am presently to join in holy matrimony. Up with your nimble spirits, ye morris dancers, green men, and glee maidens, bears and wolves, and horned gentlemen! Come; a chorus now, rich with the old mirth of Merry England, and the wilder glee of this fresh forest; and then a dance, to show the youthful pair what life is made of, and how airily they should go through it! All ye that love the Maypole, lend your voices to the nuptial song of the Lord and Lady of the May!'

This wedlock was more serious than most affairs of Merry Mount, where jest and delusion, trick and fantasy, kept up a continual carnival. The Lord and Lady of the May, though their titles must be laid down at sunset, were really and truly to be partners for the dance of life, beginning the measure that same bright eve. The wreath of roses, that hung from the lowest green bough of the Maypole, had been twined for them, and would be thrown over both their heads, in symbol of their flowery union. When the priest had spoken, therefore, a riotous uproar burst from the rout of monstrous figures.

'Begin you the stave, reverend Sir,' cried they all; 'and never did the woods ring to such a merry peal, as we of the Maypole shall send up!'

Immediately a prelude of pipe, cithern,* and viol, touched with practised minstrelsy, began to play from a neighbouring thicket, in such a mirthful cadence that the boughs of the Maypole quivered to the sound. But the May Lord, he of the gilded staff, chancing to look into his Lady's eyes, was wonder-struck at the almost pensive glance* that met his own.

'Edith, sweet Lady of the May,' whispered he, reproach-fully, 'is yon wreath of roses a garland to hang above our graves, that you look so sad? O Edith, this is our golden time! Tarnish it not by any pensive shadow of the mind; for it may be that nothing of futurity will be brighter than the mere remembrance of what is now passing.'

'That was the very thought that saddened me! How came it in your mind too?' said Edith, in a still lower tone than he; for it was high treason to be sad at Merry Mount. 'Therefore do I sigh amid this festive music. And besides, dear Edgar, I struggle as with a dream, and fancy that these shapes of our jovial friends are visionary, and their mirth unreal, and that we are no true Lord and Lady of the May. What is the mystery in my heart?'

Just then, as if a spell had loosened them, down came a little shower of withering rose-leaves from the Maypole. Alas, for the young lovers! No sooner had their hearts glowed with real passion, than they were sensible of something vague and unsubstantial in their former pleasures, and felt a dreary presentiment of inevitable change. From the moment that they truly loved, they had subjected themselves to earth's doom of care and sorrow, and troubled joy, and had no more a home at Merry Mount. That was Edith's mystery. Now leave we the priest to marry them, and the masquers to sport round the Maypole, till the last sunbeam be withdrawn from its summit, and the shadows of the forest mingle gloomily in the dance. Meanwhile, we may discover who these gay people were.

Two hundred years ago, and more,* the Old World and its inhabitants became mutually weary of each other. Men voyaged by thousands to the West; some to barter glass beads, and such-like jewels, for the furs of the Indian hunter, some to conquer virgin empires; and one stern band to pray. But none of these motives had much weight with the colonists of Merry Mount. Their leaders were men who had sported so long with life, that when Thought and Wisdom came, even these unwelcome guests were led astray by the crowd of vanities which they should have put to flight. Erring Thought and perverted Wisdom were made to put on masques, and play the fool. The men of whom we speak, after losing the heart's fresh gaiety, imagined a wild philosophy of pleasure, and came hither to act out their latest day-dream. They gathered followers from all that giddy tribe, whose whole life is like the festal days of soberer men. In their train were minstrels,* not unknown in London streets; wandering players, whose theatres had been the halls of noblemen; mummers, rope-dancers, and mountebanks, who would long be missed at wakes, church ales, and fairs; in a word, mirth-makers of every sort,* such as abounded in that age, but now began to be discountenanced by the rapid growth of Puritanism. Light had their footsteps been on land, and as lightly they came across the sea. Many had been maddened by their previous troubles into a gay despair; others were as madly gay in the flush of youth, like the May Lord and his Lady; but whatever might be the quality of their mirth, old and young were gay at Merry Mount. The young deemed themselves happy. The elder spirits, if they knew that mirth was but the counterfeit of happiness, yet followed the false shadow wilfully, because at least her garments glittered brightest. Sworn triflers of a lifetime, they would not venture among the sober truths of life, not even to be truly blest.

All the hereditary pastimes of Old England were transplanted hither. The King of Christmas was duly crowned, and the Lord of Misrule* bore potent sway. On the eve of Saint John,* they felled whole acres of the forest to make bonfires, and danced by the blaze all night, crowned with garlands, and throwing flowers into the flame. At harvest-time, though their crop was of the smallest, they made an image with the sheaves of Indian corn, and wreathed it with autumnal garlands, and bore it home triumphantly. But what chiefly characterized the colonists of Merry Mount was their veneration for the Maypole. It has made their true history a poet's tale. Spring decked the hallowed emblem with young blossoms and fresh green boughs; Summer brought roses of the deepest blush, and the perfected foliage of the forest; Autumn enriched it with that red and yellow gorgeousness, which converts each wildwood leaf into a painted flower; and Winter silvered it with sleet, and hung it round with icicles, till it flashed in the cold sunshine, itself a frozen sunbeam. Thus each alternate season did homage to the Maypole, and paid it a tribute of its own richest splendour. Its votaries danced round it, once, at least, in every month; sometimes they called it their religion, or their altar; but always, it was the banner staff of Merry Mount.

Unfortunately, there were men in the New World of a sterner faith than these Maypole worshippers. Not far from Merry Mount was a settlement of Puritans, most dismal wretches, who said their prayers before daylight, and then wrought in the forest or the cornfield till evening made it prayer-time again. Their weapons were always at hand, to shoot down the straggling savage. When they met in conclave, it was never to keep up the old English mirth, but to hear sermons three hours long, or to proclaim bounties on the heads of wolves and the scalps of Indians. Their festivals were fast-days, and their chief pastime the singing of psalms. Woe to the youth or maiden who did but dream of a dance! The selectman nodded to the constable; and there sat the light-heeled reprobate in the stocks; or if he danced, it was round the whipping-post, which might be termed the Puritan Maypole.

A party of these grim Puritans, toiling through the difficult woods, each with a horse-load of iron armour to burden his footsteps, would sometimes draw near the sunny precincts of Merry Mount. There were the silken colonists, sporting round their Maypole; perhaps teaching a bear to dance, or striving to communicate their mirth to the grave Indian; or masquerading in the skins of deer and wolves, which they had hunted for that especial purpose. Often, the whole colony were playing at blind-man's-buff, magistrates and all with their eyes bandaged, except a single scape-goat, whom the blinded sinners pursued by the tinkling of the bells at his garments. Once, it is said, they were seen following a flower-decked corpse, with merriment and festive music, to his grave. But did the dead man laugh? In their quietest times, they sang ballads and told tales, for the edification of their pious visitors; or perplexed them with juggling tricks; or grinned at them through horse-collars; and when sport itself grew wearisome, they made game of their own stupidity, and began a yawning match. At the very least of these enormities, the men of iron shook their heads and frowned so darkly, that the revellers looked up, imagining that a momentary cloud had overcast the sunshine, which was to be perpetual there. On the other hand, the Puritans affirmed that, when a psalm was pealing from their place of worship, the echo which the forest sent them back seemed often like the chorus of a jolly catch, closing with a roar of laughter. Who but the fiend, and his bond slaves, the crew of Merry Mount, had thus disturbed them? In due time, a feud arose, stern and bitter on one side, and as serious on the other as anything could be among such light spirits as had sworn allegiance to the Maypole. The future complexion of New England was involved in this important quarrel. Should the grizzly saints establish their jurisdiction over the gay sinners, then would their spirits darken all the clime, and make it a land of clouded visages, of hard toil, of sermon and psalm for ever. But should the banner staff of Merry Mount be fortunate, sunshine would break upon the hills, and flowers would beautify the forest, and late posterity do homage to the Maypole.

After these authentic passages from history, we return to the nuptials of the Lord and Lady of the May. Alas! we have delayed too long, and must darken our tale too suddenly. As we glance again at the Maypole, a solitary sunbeam is fading from the summit, and leaves only a faint, golden tinge, blended with the hues of the rainbow banner. Even that dim light is now withdrawn, relinquishing the whole domain of Merry Mount to the evening gloom, which has rushed so instantaneously from the black surrounding woods. But some of these black shadows have rushed forth in human shape.

Yes, with the setting sun, the last day of mirth had passed from Merry Mount. The ring of gay masquers was disordered and broken; the stag lowered his antlers in dismay; the wolf grew weaker than a lamb; the bells of the morris dancers tinkled with tremulous affright. The Puritans had played a characteristic part in the Maypole mummeries. Their darksome figures were intermixed with the wild shapes of their foes, and made the scene a picture of the moment, when waking thoughts start up amid the scattered fantasies of a dream. The leader of the hostile party stood in the centre of the circle, while the rout of monsters cowered around him, like evil spirits in the presence of a dread magician. No fantastic foolery could look him in the face. So stern was the energy of his aspect, that the whole man, visage, frame, and soul, seemed wrought of iron, gifted with life and thought, yet all of one substance with his headpiece and breastplate. It was the Puritan of Puritans; it was Endicott himself!

'Stand off, priest of Baal!'* said he, with a grim frown, and laying no reverent hand upon the surplice. 'I know thee, Blackstone!¹* Thou art the man, who couldst not abide the rule even of thine own corrupted church, and hast come hither to preach iniquity, and to give example of it in thy life.

---

¹ Did Governor Endicott speak less positively, we should suspect a mistake here. The Rev. Mr. Blackstone, though an eccentric, is not known to have been an immoral man. We rather doubt his identity with the priest of Merry Mount.

But now shall it be seen that the Lord hath sanctified this wilderness for his peculiar people. Woe unto them that would defile it! And first, for this flower-decked abomination, the altar of thy worship!'

And with his keen sword Endicott assaulted the hallowed Maypole.* Nor long did it resist his arm. It groaned with a dismal sound; it showered leaves and rosebuds upon the remorseless enthusiast; and finally, with all its green boughs, and ribbons, and flowers, symbolic of departed pleasures, down fell the banner staff of Merry Mount. As it sank, tradition says, the evening sky drew darker, and the woods threw forth a more sombre shadow.

'There,' cried Endicott, looking triumphantly on his work,—'there lies the only Maypole* in New England! The thought is strong within me, that, by its fall, is shadowed forth the fate of light and idle mirth-makers, amongst us and our posterity. Amen, saith John Endicott.'

'Amen!' echoed his followers.

But the votaries of the Maypole gave one groan for their idol. At the sound, the Puritan leader glanced at the crew of Comus, each a figure of broad mirth, yet, at this moment, strangely expressive of sorrow and dismay.

'Valiant captain,' quoth Peter Palfrey, the Ancient* of the band, 'what order shall be taken with the prisoners?'

'I thought not to repent me of cutting down a Maypole,' replied Endicott, 'yet now I could find in my heart to plant it again, and give each of these bestial pagans one other dance round their idol. It would have served rarely for a whipping-post!'

'But there are pine-trees enow,' suggested the lieutenant.

'True, good Ancient,' said the leader. 'Wherefore, bind the heathen crew, and bestow on them a small matter of stripes apiece, as earnest of our future justice. Set some of the rogues in the stocks to rest themselves, so soon as Providence shall bring us to one of our own well-ordered settlements, where such accommodations may be found. Further penalties, such as branding and cropping of ears, shall be thought of hereafter.'

'How many stripes for the priest?' inquired Ancient Palfrey.

'None as yet,' answered Endicott, bending his iron frown upon the culprit. 'It must be for the Great and General Court* to determine whether stripes and long imprisonment, and other grievous penalty, may atone for his transgressions. Let him look to himself! For such as violate our civil order, it may be permitted us to show mercy. But woe to the wretch that troubleth our religion!'

'And this dancing bear,' resumed the officer. 'Must he share the stripes of his fellows?'

'Shoot him through the head!' said the energetic Puritan. 'I suspect witchcraft in the beast.'

'Here be a couple of shining ones,' continued Peter Palfrey, pointing his weapon at the Lord and Lady of the May. 'They seem to be of high station among these misdoers. Methinks their dignity will not be fitted with less than a double share of stripes.'

Endicott rested on his sword, and closely surveyed the dress and aspect of the hapless pair. There they stood, pale, downcast and apprehensive. Yet there was an air of mutual support, and of pure affection, seeking aid and giving it, that showed them to be man and wife, with the sanction of a priest upon their love. The youth, in the peril of the moment, had dropped his gilded staff, and thrown his arm about the Lady of the May, who leaned against his breast, too lightly to burden him, but with weight enough to express that their destinies were linked together, for good or evil. They looked first at each other, and then into the grim captain's face. There they stood, in the first hour of wedlock, while the idle pleasures, of which their companions were the emblems, had given place to the sternest cares of life, personified by the dark Puritans. But never had their youthful beauty seemed so pure and high, as when its glow was chastened by adversity.

'Youth,' said Endicott, 'ye stand in an evil case, thou and thy maiden wife. Make ready presently; for I am minded that ye shall both have a token to remember your wedding-day!'

'Stern man,' cried the May Lord, 'how can I move thee? Were the means at hand, I would resist to the death. Being powerless, I entreat! Do with me as thou wilt, but let Edith go untouched!'

'Not so,' replied the immitigable zealot. 'We are not wont to show an idle courtesy to that sex, which requireth the stricter discipline. What sayest thou, maid? Shall thy silken bridegroom suffer thy share of the penalty, besides his own?'

'Be it death,' said Edith, 'and lay it all on me!'

Truly, as Endicott had said, the poor lovers stood in a woful case. Their foes were triumphant, their friends captive and abased, their home desolate, the benighted wilderness around them, and rigorous destiny, in the shape of the Puritan leader, their only guide. Yet the deepening twilight could not altogether conceal that the iron man was softened; he smiled at the fair spectacle of early love; he almost sighed for the inevitable blight of early hopes.

'The troubles of life have come hastily on this young couple,' observed Endicott. 'We will see how they comport themselves under their present trials, ere we burden them with greater. If, among the spoil, there be any garments of a more decent fashion, let them be put upon this May Lord and his Lady, instead of their glistening vanities. Look to it, some of you.'

'And shall not the youth's hair be cut?' asked Peter Palfrey, looking with abhorrence at the lovelock and long glossy curls of the young man.

'Crop it forthwith, and that in the true pumpkin-shell fashion,' answered the captain. 'Then bring them along with us, but more gently than their fellows. There be qualities in the youth, which may make him valiant to fight, and sober to toil, and pious to pray; and in the maiden, that may fit her to become a mother in our Israel,* bringing up babes in better nurture than her own hath been. Nor think ye, young ones, that they are the happiest, even in our lifetime of a moment, who mis-spend it in dancing round a Maypole!'

And Endicott, the severest Puritan of all who laid the rock foundation of New England, lifted the wreath of roses from the ruin of the Maypole, and threw it, with his own gauntleted hand, over the heads of the Lord and Lady of the May. It was a deed of prophecy. As the moral gloom of the world overpowers all systematic gaiety, even so was their home of wild mirth made desolate amid the sad forest. They returned to it no more. But, as their flowery garland was wreathed of the brightest roses that had grown there, so, in the tie that united them, were intertwined all the purest and best of their early joys. They went heavenward,* supporting each other along the difficult path which it was their lot to tread, and never wasted one regretful thought on the vanities of Merry Mount.

THE MINISTER'S BLACK VEIL

A PARABLE[1]*

THE sexton stood in the porch of Milford* meeting-house, pulling busily at the bell-rope. The old people of the village came stooping along the street. Children with bright faces tripped merrily beside their parents, or mimicked a graver gait, in the conscious dignity of their Sunday clothes. Spruce bachelors* looked sidelong at the pretty maidens, and fancied that the Sabbath sunshine made them prettier than on week-days. When the throng had mostly streamed into the porch, the sexton began to toll the bell, keeping his eye on the Reverend Mr. Hooper's door. The first glimpse of the clergyman's figure was the signal for the bell to cease its summons.

'But what has good Parson Hooper got upon his face?' cried the sexton, in astonishment.

All within hearing immediately turned about, and beheld the semblance of Mr. Hooper, pacing slowly his meditative way towards the meeting-house. With one accord they started, expressing more wonder than if some stranger minister were coming to dust the cushions of Mr. Hooper's pulpit.

'Are you sure it is our parson?' inquired Goodman Gray of the sexton.

---

[1] Another clergyman in New England, Mr. Joseph Moody,* of York, Maine, who died about eighty years since, made himself remarkable by the same eccentricity that is here related of the Reverend Mr. Hooper. In his case, however, the symbol had a different import. In early life he had accidentally killed a beloved friend; and from that day till the hour of his own death, he hid his face from men.

'Of a certainty it is good Mr. Hooper,' replied the sexton. 'He was to have exchanged pulpits with Parson Shute, of Westbury;* but Parson Shute sent to excuse himself yesterday, being to preach a funeral sermon.'

The cause of so much amazement may appear sufficiently slight. Mr. Hooper, a gentlemanly person, of about thirty, though still a bachelor, was dressed with due clerical neatness, as if a careful wife had starched his band and brushed the weekly dust from his Sunday's garb. There was but one thing remarkable in his appearance. Swathed about his forehead, and hanging down over his face, so low as to be shaken by his breath, Mr. Hooper had on a black veil. On a nearer view, it seemed to consist of two folds of crape, which entirely concealed his features, except the mouth and chin, but probably did not intercept his sight, further than to give a darkened aspect to all living and inanimate things. With this gloomy shade before him, good Mr. Hooper walked onward, at a slow and quiet pace, stooping somewhat, and looking on the ground, as is customary with abstracted men, yet nodding kindly to those of his parishioners who still waited on the meeting-house steps. But so wonder-struck were they, that his greeting hardly met with a return.

'I can't really feel as if good Mr. Hooper's face was behind that piece of crape,' said the sexton.

'I don't like it,' muttered an old woman, as she hobbled into the meeting-house. 'He has changed himself into something awful,* only by hiding his face.'

'Our parson has gone mad!' cried Goodman Gray, following him across the threshold.

A rumour of some unaccountable phenomenon had preceded Mr. Hooper into the meeting-house, and set all the congregation astir. Few could refrain from twisting their heads towards the door; many stood upright, and turned directly about; while several little boys clambered upon the seats, and came down again with a terrible racket. There was a general bustle, a rustling of the women's gowns and shuffling of the men's feet, greatly at variance with that hushed repose which should attend the entrance of the minister. But Mr. Hooper appeared not to notice the perturbation of his people. He entered with an almost noiseless step, bent his head mildly to the pews on each side, and bowed as he passed his oldest parishioner, a white-haired great-grandsire, who occupied an armchair in the centre of the aisle. It was strange to observe how slowly this venerable man became conscious of something singular in the appearance of his pastor. He seemed not fully to partake of the prevailing wonder, till Mr. Hooper had ascended the stairs, and showed himself in the pulpit, face to face with his congregation, except for the black veil. The mysterious emblem was never once withdrawn. It shook with his measured breath as he gave out the psalm; it threw its obscurity between him and the holy page, as he read the Scriptures; and while he prayed, the veil lay heavily on his uplifted countenance. Did he seek to hide it from the dread Being whom he was addressing?

Such was the effect of this simple piece of crape, that more than one woman of delicate nerves was forced to leave the meeting-house. Yet perhaps the pale-faced congregation was almost as fearful a sight to the minister, as his black veil to them.

Mr. Hooper had the reputation of a good preacher, but not an energetic one: he strove to win his people heavenward by mild, persuasive influences, rather than to drive them thither by the thunders of the Word. The sermon which he now delivered was marked by the same characteristics of style and manner as the general series of his pulpit oratory. But there was something, either in the sentiment of the discourse itself, or in the imagination of the auditors, which made it greatly the most powerful effort that they had ever heard from their pastor's lips. It was tinged, rather more darkly than usual, with the gentle gloom of Mr. Hooper's temperament. The subject had reference to secret sin, and those sad mysteries which we hide from our nearest and dearest, and would fain conceal from our own consciousness, even forgetting that the Omniscient can detect them. A subtile power was breathed into his words. Each member of the congregation, the most innocent girl and the man of hardened breast, felt as if the preacher had crept upon them, behind his awful veil, and discovered their hoarded iniquity of deed or thought.

Many spread their clasped hands on their bosoms. There was nothing terrible in what Mr. Hooper said; at least, no violence; and yet, with every tremor of his melancholy voice, the hearers quaked. An unsought pathos came hand in hand with awe. So sensible were the audience of some unwonted attribute in their minister, that they longed for a breath of wind to blow aside the veil, almost believing that a stranger's visage would be discovered, though the form, gesture, and voice were those of Mr. Hooper.

At the close of the service, the people hurried out with indecorous confusion, eager to communicate their pent-up amazement, and conscious of lighter spirits,* the moment they lost sight of the black veil. Some gathered in little circles, huddled closely together, with their mouths all whispering in the centre; some went homeward alone, wrapt in silent meditation; some talked loudly, and profaned the Sabbath day with ostentatious laughter. A few shook their sagacious heads, intimating that they could penetrate the mystery; while one or two affirmed that there was no mystery at all, but only that Mr. Hooper's eyes were so weakened by the midnight lamp, as to require a shade. After a brief interval, forth came good Mr. Hooper also, in the rear of his flock. Turning his veiled face from one group to another, he paid due reverence to the hoary heads, saluted the middle-aged with kind dignity, as their friend and spiritual guide, greeted the young with mingled authority and love, and laid his hands on the little children's heads to bless them. Such was always his custom on the Sabbath day. Strange and bewildered looks repaid him for his courtesy. None, as on former occasions, aspired to the honour of walking by their pastor's side. Old Squire Saunders, doubtless by an accidental lapse of memory, neglected to invite Mr. Hooper to his table, where the good clergyman had been wont to bless the food, almost every Sunday since his settlement. He returned, therefore, to the parsonage, and, at the moment of closing the door, was observed to look back upon the people, all of whom had their eyes fixed upon the minister. A sad smile gleamed faintly from beneath the black veil, and flickered about his mouth, glimmering as he disappeared.

'How strange,' said a lady, 'that a simple black veil, such as

any woman might wear on her bonnet, should become such
a terrible thing on Mr. Hooper's face!'

'Something must surely be amiss with Mr. Hooper's
intellects,' observed her husband, the physician of the village.
'But the strangest part of the affair is the effect of this vagary,
even on a sober-minded man like myself. The black veil,
though it covers only our pastor's face, throws its influence
over his whole person, and makes him ghost-like from head to
foot. Do you not feel it so?'

'Truly do I,' replied the lady; 'and I would not be alone with
him for the world. I wonder he is not afraid to be alone with
himself!'

'Men sometimes are so,' said her husband.

The afternoon service was attended with similar circumstances. At its conclusion, the bell tolled for the funeral of a
young lady. The relatives and friends were assembled in the
house, and the more distant acquaintances stood about the
door, speaking of the good qualities of the deceased, when
their talk was interrupted by the appearance of Mr. Hooper,
still covered with his black veil. It was now an appropriate
emblem. The clergyman stepped into the room where the
corpse was laid, and bent over the coffin, to take a last farewell
of his deceased parishioner. As he stooped, the veil hung
straight down from his forehead, so that, if her eyelids had not
been closed for ever, the dead maiden might have seen his
face. Could Mr. Hooper be fearful of her glance,* that he so
hastily caught back the black veil? A person who watched the
interview between the dead and living scrupled not to affirm
that, at the instant when the clergyman's features were
disclosed, the corpse had slightly shuddered, rustling the
shroud and muslin cap, though the countenance retained the
composure of death. A superstitious old woman was the only
witness of this prodigy. From the coffin Mr. Hooper passed
into the chamber of the mourners, and thence to the head of
the staircase, to make the funeral prayer. It was a tender and
heart-dissolving prayer, full of sorrow, yet so imbued with
celestial hopes, that the music of a heavenly harp, swept by
the fingers of the dead, seemed faintly to be heard among the
saddest accents of the minister. The people trembled, though

they but darkly understood him when he prayed that they, and himself, and all of mortal race, might be ready, as he trusted this young maiden had been, for the dreadful hour that should snatch the veil from their faces. The bearers went heavily forth, and the mourners followed, saddening all the street, with the dead before them, and Mr. Hooper in his black veil behind.

'Why do you look back?' said one in the procession to his partner.

'I had a fancy,' replied she, 'that the minister and the maiden's spirit were walking hand in hand.'

'And so had I, at the same moment,' said the other.

That night, the handsomest couple in Milford village were to be joined in wedlock. Though reckoned a melancholy man, Mr. Hooper had a placid cheerfulness for such occasions, which often excited a sympathetic smile, where livelier merriment would have been thrown away. There was no quality of his disposition which made him more beloved than this. The company at the wedding awaited his arrival with impatience, trusting that the strange awe, which had gathered over him throughout the day, would now be dispelled. But such was not the result. When Mr. Hooper came, the first thing that their eyes rested on was the same horrible black veil, which had added deeper gloom to the funeral, and could portend nothing but evil to the wedding. Such was its immediate effect on the guests, that a cloud seemed to have rolled duskily from beneath the black crape, and dimmed the light of the candles. The bridal pair stood up before the minister. But the bride's cold fingers quivered in the tremulous hand of the bridegroom, and her death-like paleness caused a whisper that the maiden who had been buried a few hours before was come from her grave to be married. If ever another wedding were so dismal, it was that famous one where they tolled the wedding knell.* After performing the ceremony, Mr. Hooper raised a glass of wine to his lips, wishing happiness to the new-married couple, in a strain of mild pleasantry that ought to have brightened the features of the guests, like a cheerful gleam from the hearth. At that instant, catching a glimpse of his figure in the looking-glass, the black veil involved his own spirit in the horror with which it overwhelmed all others. His frame shuddered,—his lips grew white,—he spilt the untasted wine upon the carpet,—and rushed forth into the darkness. For the Earth, too, had on her Black Veil.

The next day, the whole village of Milford talked of little else than Parson Hooper's black veil. That, and the mystery concealed behind it, supplied a topic for discussion between acquaintances meeting in the street and good women gossiping at their open windows. It was the first item of news that the tavern-keeper told to his guests. The children babbled of it on their way to school. One imitative little imp covered his face with an old black handkerchief, thereby so affrighting his playmates that the panic seized himself, and he wellnigh lost his wits by his own waggery.

It was remarkable that, of all the busybodies and impertinent people in the parish, not one ventured to put the plain question to Mr. Hooper, wherefore he did this thing. Hitherto, whenever there appeared the slightest call for such interference, he had never lacked advisers, nor shown himself averse to be guided by their judgement. If he erred at all, it was by so painful a degree of self-distrust, that even the mildest censure would lead him to consider an indifferent action as a crime. Yet, though so well acquainted with this amiable weakness, no individual among his parishioners chose to make the black veil a subject of friendly remonstrance. There was a feeling of dread, neither plainly confessed nor carefully concealed, which caused each to shift the responsibility upon another, till at length it was found expedient to send a deputation of the church, in order to deal with Mr. Hooper about the mystery, before it should grow into a scandal. Never did an embassy so ill discharge its duties. The minister received them with friendly courtesy, but became silent, after they were seated, leaving to his visitors the whole burden of introducing their important business. The topic, it might be supposed, was obvious enough. There was the black veil, swathed round Mr. Hooper's forehead, and concealing every feature above his placid mouth, on which, at times, they could perceive the glimmering of a melancholy smile.* But that piece of crape, to their imagination, seemed to hang down before his heart, the symbol of a fearful secret between him and them. Were the veil but cast aside, they might speak freely of it, but not till then. Thus they sat a considerable time, speechless, confused, and shrinking uneasily from Mr. Hooper's eye, which they felt to be fixed upon them with an invisible glance. Finally, the deputies returned abashed to their constituents, pronouncing the matter too weighty to be handled, except by a council of the churches, if, indeed, it might not require a general synod.*

But there was one person in the village, unappalled by the awe with which the black veil had impressed all beside herself. When the deputies returned without an explanation, or even venturing to demand one, she, with the calm energy of her character, determined to chase away the strange cloud that appeared to be settling round Mr. Hooper, every moment more darkly than before. As his plighted wife, it should be her privilege to know what the black veil concealed. At the minister's first visit, therefore, she entered upon the subject, with a direct simplicity which made the task easier both for him and her. After he had seated himself, she fixed her eyes steadfastly upon the veil, but could discern nothing of the dreadful gloom that had so overawed the multitude; it was but a double fold of crape, hanging down from his forehead to his mouth, and slightly stirring with his breath.

'No,' said she aloud, and smiling, 'there is nothing terrible in this piece of crape, except that it hides a face which I am always glad to look upon. Come, good sir, let the sun shine from behind the cloud. First lay aside your black veil: then tell my why you put it on.'

Mr. Hooper's smile glimmered faintly.

'There is an hour to come,' said he, 'when all of us shall cast aside our veils. Take it not amiss, beloved friend, if I wear this piece of crape till then.'

'Your words are a mystery too,' returned the young lady. 'Take away the veil from them, at least.'

'Elizabeth, I will,' said he, 'so far as my vow may suffer me. Know, then, this veil is a type and a symbol, and I am bound to wear it ever, both in light and darkness, in solitude and before the gaze of multitudes, and as with strangers, so with my familiar friends. No mortal eye will see it withdrawn. This dismal shade must separate me from the world: even you, Elizabeth, can never come behind it!'

'What grievous affliction hath befallen you,' she earnestly inquired, 'that you should thus darken your eyes for ever?'

'If it be a sign of mourning,' replied Mr. Hooper, 'I, perhaps, like most other mortals, have sorrows dark enough to be typified by a black veil.'

'But what if the world will not believe that it is the type of an innocent sorrow?' urged Elizabeth. 'Beloved and respected as you are, there may be whispers, that you hide your face under the consciousness of secret sin. For the sake of your holy office, do away this scandal!'

The colour rose into her cheeks as she intimated the nature of the rumours that were already abroad in the village. But Mr. Hooper's mildness did not forsake him. He even smiled again,—that same sad smile, which always appeared like a faint glimmering of light, proceeding from the obscurity beneath the veil.

'If I hide my face for sorrow, there is cause enough,' he merely replied; 'and if I cover it for secret sin, what mortal might not do the same?'*

And with this gentle, but unconquerable obstinacy did he resist all her entreaties. At length Elizabeth sat silent. For a few moments she appeared lost in thought, considering, probably, what new methods might be tried to withdraw her lover from so dark a fantasy, which, if it had no other meaning, was perhaps a symptom of mental disease. Though of a firmer character than his own the tears rolled down her cheeks. But, in an instant, as it were, a new feeling took the place of sorrow; her eyes were fixed insensibly on the black veil, when, like a sudden twilight in the air, its terrors fell around her. She arose, and stood trembling before him.

'And do you feel it then at last?' said he, mournfully.

She made no reply, but covered her eyes with her hand, and turned to leave the room. He rushed forward and caught her arm.

'Have patience with me, Elizabeth!' cried he, passionately.

'Do not desert me, though this veil must be between us here on earth. Be mine, and hereafter there shall be no veil over my face, no darkness between our souls! It is but a mortal veil,—it is not for eternity! Oh, you know not how lonely I am, and how frightened, to be alone behind my black veil! Do not leave me in this miserable obscurity for ever!'

'Lift the veil but once, and look me in the face,' said she.

'Never! It cannot be!' replied Mr. Hooper.

'Then, farewell!' said Elizabeth.

She withdrew her arm from his grasp, and slowly departed, pausing at the door, to give one long, shuddering gaze, that seemed almost to penetrate the mystery of the black veil. But, even amid his grief, Mr. Hooper smiled to think that only a material emblem had separated him from happiness, though the horrors which it shadowed forth must be drawn darkly between the fondest of lovers.

From that time no attempts were made to remove Mr. Hooper's black veil, or, by a direct appeal, to discover the secret which it was supposed to hide. By persons who claimed a superiority to popular prejudice, it was reckoned merely an eccentric whim, such as often mingles with the sober actions of men otherwise rational, and tinges them all with its own semblance of insanity. But with the multitude, good Mr. Hooper was irreparably a bugbear. He could not walk the street with any peace of mind, so conscious was he that the gentle and timid would turn aside to avoid him, and that others would make it a point of hardihood to throw themselves in his way. The impertinence of the latter class compelled him to give up his customary walk, at sunset, to the burial-ground; for when he leaned pensively over the gate, there would always be faces behind the gravestones, peeping at his black veil. A fable went the rounds, that the stare of the dead people drove him thence. It grieved him, to the very depth of his kind heart, to observe how the children fled from his approach, breaking up their merriest sports, while his melancholy figure was yet afar off. Their instinctive dread caused him to feel, more strongly than aught else, that a preternatural horror was interwoven with the threads of the black crape. In truth, his own antipathy to the veil was known to be so great, that he never willingly passed before a mirror, nor stooped to drink at a still fountain, lest, in its peaceful bosom, he should be affrighted by himself. This was what gave plausibility to the whispers, that Mr. Hooper's conscience tortured him for some great crime too horrible to be entirely concealed, or otherwise than so obscurely intimated. Thus, from beneath the black veil, there rolled a cloud into the sunshine, an ambiguity of sin or sorrow, which enveloped the poor minister, so that love or sympathy could never reach him. It was said, that ghost and fiend consorted with him there. With self-shudderings and outward terrors, he walked continually in its shadow, groping darkly within his own soul, or gazing through a medium that saddened the whole world. Even the lawless wind, it was believed, respected his dreadful secret, and never blew aside the veil. But still good Mr. Hooper sadly smiled at the pale visages of the worldly throng as he passed by.

Among all its bad influences, the black veil had the one desirable effect of making its wearer a very efficient clergyman. By the aid of his mysterious emblem—for there was no other apparent cause—he became a man of awful power, over souls that were in agony for sin. His converts always regarded him with a dread peculiar to themselves, affirming, though but figuratively, that, before he brought them to celestial light, they had been with him behind the black veil. Its gloom, indeed, enabled him to sympathize with all dark affections. Dying sinners cried aloud for Mr. Hooper, and would not yield their breath till he appeared; though ever, as he stooped to whisper consolation, they shuddered at the veiled face so near their own. Such were the terrors of the black veil, even when Death had bared his visage! Strangers came long distances to attend service at his church, with the mere idle purpose of gazing at his figure, because it was forbidden them to behold his face. But many were made to quake ere they departed! Once, during Governor Belcher's* administration, Mr. Hooper was appointed to preach the election sermon. Covered with his black veil, he stood before the chief magistrate, the council, and the representatives, and wrought so deep an impression, that the legislative measures of that year were characterized by all the gloom and piety of our earliest ancestral sway.

In this manner Mr. Hooper spent a long life, irreproachable in outward act, yet shrouded in dismal suspicions; kind and loving, though unloved, and dimly feared; a man apart from men, shunned in their health and joy, but ever summoned to their aid in mortal anguish. As years wore on, shedding their snows above his sable veil, he acquired a name throughout the New England churches, and they called him Father Hooper. Nearly all his parishioners, who were of mature age when he was settled, had been borne away by many a funeral: he had one congregation in the church, and a more crowded one in the churchyard; and having wrought so late into the evening, and done his work so well, it was now good Father Hooper's turn to rest.

Several persons were visible by the shaded candlelight, in the death-chamber of the old clergyman. Natural connexions he had none. But there was the decorously grave, though unmoved physician, seeking only to mitigate the last pangs of the patient whom he could not save. There were the deacons, and other eminently pious members of his church. There, also, was the Reverend Mr. Clark, of Westbury, a young and zealous divine, who had ridden in haste to pray by the bedside of the expiring minister. There was the nurse, no hired handmaiden of death, but one whose calm affection had endured thus long in secrecy, in solitude, amid the chill of age, and would not perish, even at the dying hour. Who, but Elizabeth! And there lay the hoary head of good Father Hooper upon the death-pillow, with the black veil still swathed about his brow, and reaching down over his face, so that each more difficult gasp of his faint breath caused it to stir. All through life that piece of crape had hung between him and the world; it had separated him from cheerful brotherhood and woman's love, and kept him in that saddest of all prisons, his own heart; and still it lay upon his face, as if to deepen the gloom of his darksome chamber, and shade him from the sunshine of eternity.

For some time previous, his mind had been confused,

wavering doubtfully between the past and the present, and hovering forward, as it were, at intervals, into the indistinctness of the world to come. There had been feverish turns, which tossed him from side to side, and wore away what little strength he had. But in his most convulsive struggles, and in the wildest vagaries of his intellect, when no other thought retained its sober influence, he still showed an awful solicitude lest the black veil should slip aside. Even if his bewildered soul could have forgotten, there was a faithful woman at his pillow, who, with averted eyes, would have covered that aged face, which she had last beheld in the comeliness of manhood. At length the death-stricken old man lay quietly in the torpor of mental and bodily exhaustion, with an imperceptible pulse, and breath that grew fainter and fainter, except when a long, deep, and irregular inspiration seemed to prelude the flight of his spirit.

The minister of Westbury approached the bedside.

'Venerable Father Hooper,' said he, 'the moment of your release is at hand. Are you ready for the lifting of the veil, that shuts in time from eternity?'

Father Hooper at first replied merely by a feeble motion of his head; then, apprehensive, perhaps, that his meaning might be doubtful, he exerted himself to speak.

'Yea,' said he, in faint accents, 'my soul hath a patient weariness until that veil be lifted.'

'And is it fitting,' resumed the Reverend Mr. Clark, 'that a man so given to prayer, of such a blameless example, holy in deed and thought, so far as mortal judgement may pronounce, —is it fitting that a father in the church should leave a shadow on his memory, that may seem to blacken a life so pure? I pray you, my venerable brother, let not this thing be! Suffer us to be gladdened by your triumphant aspect, as you go to your reward. Before the veil of eternity be lifted, let me cast aside this black veil from your face!'

And thus speaking, the Reverend Mr. Clark bent forward to reveal the mystery of so many years. But, exerting a sudden energy, that made all the beholders stand aghast, Father Hooper snatched both his hands from beneath the bedclothes, and pressed them strongly on the black veil, resolute to struggle, if the minister of Westbury would contend with a dying man.

'Never!' cried the veiled clergyman. 'On earth, never!'

'Dark old man!' exclaimed the affrighted minister, 'with what horrible crime upon your soul are you now passing to the judgement?'

Father Hooper's breath heaved; it rattled in his throat; but, with a mighty effort, grasping forward with his hands, he caught hold of life, and held it back till he should speak. He even raised himself in bed; and there he sat, shivering with the arms of death around him, while the black veil hung down, awful, at that last moment, in the gathered terrors of a lifetime. And yet the faint, sad smile, so often there, now seemed to glimmer from its obscurity, and linger on Father Hooper's lips.

'Why do you tremble at me alone?' cried he, turning his veiled face round the circle of pale spectators. 'Tremble also at each other! Have men avoided me, and women shown no pity, and children screamed and fled, only for my black veil? What, but the mystery which it obscurely typifies, has made this piece of crape so awful? When the friend shows his inmost heart to his friend; the lover to his best beloved; when man does not vainly shrink from the eye of his Creator, loathsomely treasuring up the secret of his sin; then deem me a monster, for the symbol beneath which I have lived, and die! I look around me, and, lo! on every visage a Black Veil!'

While his auditors shrank from one another, in mutual affright, Father Hooper fell back upon his pillow, a veiled corpse, with a faint smile lingering on the lips. Still veiled, they laid him in his coffin and a veiled corpse they bore him to the grave. The grass of many years has sprung up and withered on that grave, the burial stone is moss-grown, and good Mr. Hooper's face is dust; but awful is still the thought, that it mouldered beneath the Black Veil!

DR. HEIDEGGER'S EXPERIMENT

THAT very singular man, old Dr. Heidegger, once invited four venerable friends to meet him in his study. There were three white-bearded gentlemen, Mr. Medbourne, Colonel Killigrew, and Mr. Gascoigne, and a withered gentlewoman, whose name was the Widow Wycherly. They were all melancholy old creatures, who had been unfortunate in life, and whose greatest misfortune it was that they were not long ago in their graves. Mr. Medbourne, in the vigour of his age, had been a prosperous merchant, but had lost his all by a frantic speculation, and was now little better than a mendicant. Colonel Killigrew had wasted his best years, and his health and substance, in the pursuit of sinful pleasures, which had given birth to a brood of pains, such as the gout, and divers other torments of soul and body. Mr. Gascoigne was a ruined politician, a man of evil fame, or at least had been so, till time had buried him from the knowledge of the present generation, and made him obscure instead of infamous. As for the Widow Wycherly, tradition tells us that she was a great beauty in her day; but, for a long while past, she had lived in deep seclusion, on account of certain scandalous stories, which had prejudiced the gentry of the town against her. It is a circumstance worth mentioning, that each of these three old gentlemen, Mr. Medbourne, Colonel Killigrew, and Mr. Gascoigne, were early lovers of the Widow Wycherly, and had once been on the point of cutting each other's throats for her sake. And, before proceeding farther, I will merely hint, that Dr. Heidegger and all his four guests were sometimes thought to be a little beside themselves; as is not unfrequently the case with old people, when worried either by present troubles or woful recollections.

'My dear old friends,' said Dr. Heidegger, motioning them to be seated, 'I am desirous of your assistance in one of those little experiments* with which I amuse myself here in my study.'

If all stories were true, Dr. Heidegger's study must have

been a very curious place. It was a dim, old-fashioned chamber, festooned with cobwebs and besprinkled with antique dust. Around the walls stood several oaken bookcases, the lower shelves of which were filled with rows of gigantic folios and black-letter quartos, and the upper with little parchment-covered duodecimos. Over the central bookcase was a bronze bust of Hippocrates,* with which, according to some authorities, Dr. Heidegger was accustomed to hold consultations, in all difficult cases of his practice. In the obscurest corner of the room stood a tall and narrow oaken closet, with its door ajar, within which doubtfully appeared a skeleton. Between two of the bookcases hung a looking-glass, presenting its high and dusty plate within a tarnished gilt frame. Among many wonderful stories related of this mirror, it was fabled that the spirits of all the doctor's deceased patients dwelt within its verge, and would stare him in the face whenever he looked thitherward. The opposite side of the chamber was ornamented with the full-length portrait of a young lady, arrayed in the faded magnificence of silk, satin, and brocade, and with a visage as faded as her dress. Above half a century ago, Dr. Heidegger had been on the point of marriage with his young lady; but, being affected with some slight disorder, she had swallowed one of her lover's prescriptions, and died on the bridal evening. The greatest curiosity of the study remains to be mentioned; it was a ponderous folio volume, bound in black leather, with massive silver clasps. There were no letters on the back, and nobody could tell the title of the book. But it was well known to be a book of magic;* and once, when a chambermaid had lifted it, merely to brush away the dust, the skeleton had rattled in its closet, the picture of the young lady had stepped one foot upon the floor, and several ghastly faces had peeped forth from the mirror; while the brazen head of Hippocrates frowned, and said, 'Forbear!'

Such was Dr. Heidegger's study. On the summer afternoon of our tale, a small round table, as black as ebony, stood in the centre of the room, sustaining a cut-glass vase, of beautiful form and elaborate workmanship. The sunshine came through the window, between the heavy festoons of two faded damask curtains, and fell directly across this vase; so that a mild splendour was reflected from it on the ashen visages of the five old people who sat around. Four champagne-glasses were also on the table.

'My dear old friends,' repeated Dr. Heidegger, 'may I reckon on your aid in performing an exceedingly curious experiment?'

Now Dr. Heidegger was a very strange old gentleman, whose eccentricity had become the nucleus for a thousand fantastic stories. Some of these fables, to my shame be it spoken, might possibly be traced back to mine own veracious self; and if any passages of the present tale should startle the reader's faith, I must be content to bear the stigma of a fiction-monger.

When the doctor's four guests heard him talk of his proposed experiment, they anticipated nothing more wonderful than the murder of a mouse in an airpump, or the examination of a cobweb by the microscope, or some similar nonsense, with which he was constantly in the habit of pestering his intimates. But without waiting for a reply, Dr. Heidegger hobbled across the chamber, and returned with the same ponderous folio, bound in black leather, which common report affirmed to be a book of magic. Undoing the silver clasps, he opened the volume, and took from among its black-letter pages a rose, or what was once a rose, though now the green leaves and crimson petals had assumed one brownish hue, and the ancient flower seemed ready to crumble to dust in the doctor's hands.

'This rose,' said Dr. Heidegger, with a sigh, 'this same withered and crumbling flower, blossomed five-and-fifty years ago. It was given me by Sylvia Ward, whose portrait hangs yonder; and I meant to wear it in my bosom at our wedding. Five-and-fifty years it has been treasured between the leaves of this old volume. Now, would you deem it possible that this rose of half a century could ever bloom again?'

'Nonsense!' said the Widow Wycherly, with a peevish toss of her head. 'You might as well ask whether an old woman's wrinkled face could ever bloom again.'

'See!' answered Dr. Heidegger.

He uncovered the vase, and threw the faded rose into the water which it contained. At first, it lay lightly on the surface of the fluid, appearing to imbibe none of its moisture. Soon, however, a singular change began to be visible. The crushed and dried petals stirred, and assumed a deepening tinge of crimson, as if the flower were reviving from a deathlike slumber; the slender stalk and twigs of foliage became green; and there was the rose of half a century, looking as fresh as when Sylvia Ward had first given it to her lover. It was scarcely full-blown; for some of its delicate red leaves curled modestly around its moist bosom, within which two or three dewdrops were sparkling.

'That is certainly a very pretty deception,' said the doctor's friends; carelessly, however, for they had witnessed greater miracles at a conjurer's show; 'pray how was it effected?'

'Did you never hear of the "Fountain of Youth",' asked Dr. Heidegger, 'which Ponce de Leon,* the Spanish adventurer, went in search of, two or three centuries ago?'

'But did Ponce de Leon ever find it?' said the Widow Wycherly.

'No,' answered Dr. Heidegger, 'for he never sought it in the right place. The famous Fountain of Youth, if I am rightly informed, is situated in the southern part of the Floridan peninsula, not far from Lake Macaco. Its source is over-shadowed by several gigantic magnolias, which, though numberless centuries old, have been kept as fresh as violets, by the virtues of this wonderful water. An acquaintance of mine, knowing my curiosity in such matters, has sent me what you see in the vase.'

'Ahem!' said Colonel Killigrew, who believed not a word of the doctor's story; 'and what may be the effect of this fluid on the human frame?'

'You shall judge for yourself, my dear Colonel,' replied Dr. Heidegger; 'and all of you, my respected friends, are welcome to so much of this admirable fluid as may restore to you the bloom of youth.* For my own part, having had much trouble in growing old, I am in no hurry to grow young again. With your permission, therefore, I will merely watch the progress of the experiment.'

While he spoke, Dr. Heidegger had been filling the four champagne-glasses with the water of the Fountain of Youth. It was apparently impregnated with an effervescent gas, for little bubbles were continually ascending from the depths of the glasses, and bursting in silvery spray at the surface. As the liquor diffused a pleasant perfume, the old people doubted not that it possessed cordial and comfortable properties; and, though utter sceptics as to its rejuvenescent power, they were inclined to swallow it at once. But Dr. Heidegger besought them to stay a moment.

'Before you drink, my respectable old friends,' said he, 'it would be well that, with the experience of a lifetime to direct you, you should draw up a few general rules for your guidance, in passing a second time through the perils of youth. Think what a sin and shame it would be, if, with your peculiar advantages, you should not become patterns of virtue and wisdom to all the young people of the age.'

The doctor's four venerable friends made him no answer, except by a feeble and tremulous laugh; so very ridiculous was the idea, that, knowing how closely repentance treads behind the steps of error, they should ever go astray again.

'Drink, then,' said the doctor, bowing. 'I rejoice that I have so well selected the subjects of my experiment.'

With palsied hands, they raised the glasses to their lips. The liquor, if it really possessed such virtues as Dr. Heidegger imputed to it, could not have been bestowed on four human beings who needed it more wofully. They looked as if they had never known what youth or pleasure was, but had been the offspring of Nature's dotage, and always the grey, decrepit, sapless, miserable creatures who now sat stooping round the doctor's table, without life enough in their souls or bodies to be animated even by the prospect of growing young again. They drank off the water, and replaced their glasses on the table.

Assuredly there was an almost immediate improvement in the aspect of the party, now unlike what might have been produced by a glass of generous wine, together with a sudden glow of cheerful sunshine, brightening over all their visages at once. There was a healthful suffusion on their cheeks, instead of the ashen hue that had made them look so corpse-like. They gazed at one another, and fancied that some magic power had really begun to smooth away the deep and sad inscription which Father Time had been so long engraving on their brows. The Widow Wycherly adjusted her cap, for she felt almost like a woman again.

'Give us more of this wondrous water!' cried they, eagerly. 'We are younger,—but we are still too old! Quick,—give us more!'

'Patience, patience!' quoth Dr. Heidegger, who sat watching the experiment, with philosophic coolness. 'You have been a long time growing old. Surely, you might be content to grow young in half-an-hour! But the water is at your service.'

Again he filled their glasses with the liquor of youth, enough of which still remained in the vase to turn half the old people in the city to the age of their own grandchildren. While the bubbles were yet sparkling on the brim, the doctor's four guests snatched their glasses from the table, and swallowed the contents at a single gulp. Was it delusion? even while the draught was passing down their throats, it seemed to have wrought a change on their whole systems. Their eyes grew clear and bright; a dark shade deepened among their silvery locks; they sat around the table, three gentlemen of middle age, and a woman, hardly beyond her buxom prime.

'My dear widow, you are charming!' cried Colonel Killigrew, whose eyes had been fixed upon her face, while the shadows of age were flitting from it like darkness from the crimson daybreak.

The fair widow knew, of old, that Colonel Killigrew's compliments were not always measured by sober truth; so she started up and ran to the mirror, still dreading that the ugly visage of an old woman would meet her gaze. Meanwhile, the three gentlemen behaved in such a manner, as proved that the water of the Fountain of Youth possessed some intoxicating qualities; unless, indeed, their exhilaration of spirits were merely a lightsome dizziness, caused by the sudden removal of the weight of years. Mr. Gascoigne's mind seemed to run on political topics, but whether relating to the past, present, or future, could not easily be determined, since the same ideas and phrases have been in vogue these fifty years. Now he rattled forth full-throated sentences about patriotism, national glory, and the people's right; now he muttered some perilous stuff or other, in a sly and doubtful whisper, so cautiously that even his own conscience could scarely catch the secret; and now, again, he spoke in measured accents, and a deeply deferential tone, as if a royal ear were listening to his well-turned periods. Colonel Killigrew all this time had been trolling forth a jolly bottle-song, and ringing his glass in symphony with the chorus, while his eyes wandered toward the buxom figure of the Widow Wycherly. On the other side of the table, Mr. Medbourne was involved in a calculation of dollars and cents, with which was strangely intermingled a project for supplying the East Indies with ice, by harnessing a team of whales to the polar icebergs.

As for the Widow Wycherly, she stood before the mirror curtsying and simpering to her own image, and greeting it as the friend whom she loved better than all the world beside. She thrust her face close to the glass, to see whether some long-remembered wrinkle or crow's-foot had indeed vanished. She examined whether the snow had so entirely melted from her hair, that the venerable cap could be safely thrown aside. At last, turning briskly away, she came with a sort of dancing step to the table.

'My dear old doctor,' cried she, 'pray favour me with another glass!'

'Certainly, my dear madam, certainly!' replied the complaisant doctor; 'see! I have already filled the glasses.'

There, in fact, stood the four glasses, brimful of this wonderful water, the delicate spray of which, as it effervesced from the surface, resembled the tremulous glitter of diamonds. It was now so nearly sunset, that the chamber had grown duskier than ever; but a mild and moonlike splendour gleamed from within the vase, and rested alike on the four guests, and on the doctor's venerable figure. He sat in a high-backed, elaborately carved oaken armchair, with a grey dignity of aspect that might have well befitted that very Father Time, whose power had never been disputed, save by this fortunate company. Even while quaffing the third draught of the

Fountain of Youth, they were almost awed by the expression of his mysterious visage.

But, the next moment, the exhilarating gush of young life shot through their veins. They were now in the happy prime of youth. Age, with its miserable train of cares, and sorrows, and diseases, was remembered only as the trouble of a dream, from which they had joyously awoke. The fresh gloss of the soul, so early lost, and without which the world's successive scenes had been but a gallery of faded pictures, again threw its enchantment over all their prospects. They felt like new-created beings, in a new-created universe.

'We are young! We are young!' they cried exultingly.

Youth, like the extremity of age, had effaced the strongly marked characteristics of middle life, and mutually assimilated them all. They were a group of merry youngsters,* almost maddened with the exuberant frolicsomeness of their years. The most singular effect of their gaiety was an impulse to mock the infirmity and decrepitude of which they had so lately been the victims. They laughed loudly at their old-fashioned attire, the wide-skirted coats and flapped waistcoats of the young men, and the ancient cap and gown of the blooming girl. One limped across the floor, like a gouty grandfather; one set a pair of spectacles astride of his nose, and pretended to pore over the black-letter pages of the book of magic; a third seated himself in an armchair, and strove to imitate the venerable dignity of Dr. Heidegger. Then all shouted mirthfully, and leaped about the room. The Widow Wycherly—if so fresh a damsel could be called a widow—tripped up to the doctor's chair, with a mischievous merriment in her rosy face.

'Doctor, you dear old soul,' cried she, 'get up and dance with me!' And then the four young people laughed louder than ever, to think what a queer figure the poor old doctor would cut.

'Pray excuse me,' answered the doctor, quietly. 'I am old and rheumatic, and my dancing days were over long ago. But either of these gay young gentlemen will be glad of so pretty a partner.'

'Dance with me, Clara!' cried Colonel Killigrew.

'No, no, I will be her partner!' shouted Mr. Gascoigne.

'She promised me her hand, fifty years ago!' exclaimed Mr. Medbourne.

They all gathered round her. One caught both her hands in his passionate grasp,—another threw his arm about her waist,—the third buried his hand among the glossy curls that clustered beneath the widow's cap. Blushing, panting, struggling, chiding, laughing, her warm breath fanning each of their faces by turns, she strove to disengage herself, yet still remained in their triple embrace. Never was there a livelier picture of youthful rivalship, with bewitching beauty for the prize. Yet, by a strange deception, owing to the duskiness of the chamber, and the antique dresses which they still wore, the tall mirror is said to have reflected the figures of three old, grey, withered grandsires, ridiculously contending for the skinny ugliness of a shrivelled grandam.

But they were young: their burning passions proved them so. Inflamed to madness by the coquetry of the girl-widow, who neither granted nor quite withheld her favours, the three rivals began to interchange threatening glances. Still keeping hold of the fair prize, they grappled fiercely at one another's throats. As they struggled to and fro, the table was overturned, and the vase dashed into a thousand fragments. The precious Water of Youth flowed in a bright stream across the floor, moistening the wings of a butterfly, which, grown old in the decline of summer, had alighted there to die. The insect fluttered lightly through the chamber, and settled on the snowy head of Dr. Heidegger.

'Come, come, gentlemen!—come, Madam Wycherly,' exclaimed the doctor, 'I really must protest against this riot.'

They stood still and shivered; for it seemed as if grey Time were calling them back from their sunny youth, far down into the chill and darksome vale of years. They looked at old Dr. Heidegger, who sat in his carved armchair, holding the rose of half a century, which he had rescued from among the fragments of the shattered vase. At the motion of his hand, the four rioters resumed their seats; the more readily, because their violent exertions had wearied them, youthful though they were.

'My poor Sylvia's rose!' ejaculated Dr. Heidegger, holding it in the light of the sunset clouds; 'it appears to be fading again.'

And so it was. Even while the party were looking at it, the flower continued to shrivel up, till it became as dry and fragile as when the doctor had first thrown it into the vase. He shook off the few drops of moisture which clung to its petals.

'I love it as well thus, as in its dewy freshness,' observed he, pressing the withered rose to his withered lips. While he spoke, the butterfly fluttered down from the doctor's snowy head, and fell upon the floor.

His guests shivered again. A strange chilliness, whether of the body or spirit they could not tell, was creeping gradually over them all. They gazed at one another, and fancied that each fleeting moment snatched away a charm, and left a deepening furrow where none had been before. Was it an illusion? Had the changes of a lifetime been crowded into so brief a space, and were they now four aged people, sitting with their old friend, Dr. Heidegger?

'Are we grown old again, so soon?' cried they, dolefully.

In truth, they had. The Water of Youth possessed merely a virtue more transient than that of wine. The delirium which it created had effervesced away. Yes! they were old again. With a shuddering impulse, that showed her a woman still, the widow clasped her skinny hands before her face, and wished that the coffin-lid were over it, since it could be no longer beautiful.

'Yes, friends, ye are old again,' said Dr. Heidegger; 'and lo! the Water of Youth is all lavished on the ground. Well, I bemoan it not; for if the fountain gushed at my very doorstep, I would not stoop to bathe my lips in it; no, though its delirium were for years instead of moments. Such is the lesson ye have taught me!'

But the doctor's four friends had taught no such lesson to themselves. They resolved forthwith to make a pilgrimage to Florida, and quaff at morning, noon, and night from the Fountain of Youth.

Note. In an English Review,* not long since, I have been accused of plagiarizing the idea of this story from a chapter in one of the novels of Alexandre Dumas. There has undoubtedly been a plagiarism on one side or the other; but as my story was written a good deal more than twenty years ago, and as the novel is of considerably more recent date, I take pleasure in thinking that M. Dumas has done me the honour to appropriate one of the fanciful conceptions of my earlier days. He is heartily welcome to it; nor is it the only instance, by many, in which the great French romancer has exercised the privilege of commanding genius by confiscating the intellectual property of less famous people to his own use and behoof.

September, 1860.

ENDICOTT AND THE RED CROSS

AT noon of an autumnal day, more than two centuries ago,* the English colours were displayed by the standard-bearer of the Salem trainband, which had mustered for martial exercise under the orders of John Endicott. It was a period when the religious exiles were accustomed often to buckle on their armour, and practise the handling of their weapons of war. Since the first settlement of New England, its prospects had never been so dismal. The dissensions between Charles the First and his subjects were then, and for several years afterwards, confined to the floor of Parliament. The measures of the King and ministry were rendered more tyranically violent by an opposition, which had not yet acquired sufficient confidence in its own strength to resist royal injustice with the sword. The bigoted and haughty primate, Laud,* Archbishop of Canterbury, controlled the religious affairs of the realm, and was consequently invested with powers which might have wrought the utter ruin of the two Puritan colonies, Plymouth and Massachusetts. There is evidence on record, that our forefathers perceived their danger, but were resolved that their infant country should not fall without a struggle, even beneath the giant strength of the King's right arm.*

Such was the aspect of the times, when the folds of the English banner, with the Red Cross in its field, were flung out over a company of Puritans. Their leader, the famous

Endicott, was a man of stern and resolute countenance, the effect of which was heightened by a grizzled beard that swept the upper portion of his breastplate.* This piece of armour was so highly polished, that the whole surrounding scene had its image in the glittering steel. The central object in the mirrored picture was an edifice of humble architecture, with neither steeple nor bell to proclaim it—what nevertheless it was—the house of prayer. A token of the perils of the wilderness was seen in the grim head of a wolf, which had just been slain within the precincts of the town, and according to the regular mode of claiming the bounty, was nailed on the porch of the meeting-house. The blood was still plashing on the doorstep. There happened to be visible, at the same noontide hour, so many other characteristics of the times and manners of the Puritans, that we must endeavour to represent them in a sketch, though far less vividly than they were reflected in the polished breastplate of John Endicott.

In close vicinity to the sacred edifice appeared that important engine of Puritanic authority, the whipping-post, with the soil around it well trodden by the feet of evil-doers, who had there been disciplined. At one corner of the meeting-house was the pillory, and at the other the stocks; and, by a singular good fortune for our sketch, the head of an Episcopalian and suspected Catholic was grotesquely incased in the former machine; while a fellow-criminal, who had boisterously quaffed a health to the King,* was confined by the legs in the latter. Side by side, on the meeting-house steps, stood a male and a female figure. The man was a tall, lean, haggard personification of fanaticism, bearing on his breast this label,—A WANTON GOSPELLER,*—which betokened that he had dared to give interpretations of Holy Writ unsanctioned by the infallible judgement of the civil and religious rulers. His aspect showed no lack of zeal to maintain his heterodoxies, even at the stake. The woman wore a cleft stick on her tongue, in appropriate retribution for having wagged that unruly member against the elders of the church; and her countenance and gestures gave much cause to apprehend, that, the moment the stick should be removed, a repetition of the offence would demand new ingenuity in chastising it.

The above-mentioned individuals had been sentenced to undergo their various modes of ignominy, for the space of one hour at noonday. But among the crowd were several whose punishment* would be lifelong; some, whose ears had been cropped, like those of puppy-dogs; others, whose cheeks had been branded with the initials of their misdemeanours; one, with his nostrils slit and seared; and another, with a halter about his neck, which he was forbidden ever to take off, or to conceal beneath his garments. Methinks he must have been grievously tempted to affix the other end of the rope to some convenient beam or bough. There was likewise a young woman, with no mean share of beauty, whose doom it was to wear the letter A on the breast of her gown,* in the eyes of all the world and her own children. And even her own children knew what that initial signified. Sporting with her infamy, the lost and desperate creature had emboidered the fatal token in scarlet cloth, with golden thread and the nicest art of needlework; so that the capital A might have been thought to mean Admirable, or anything rather than Adulteress.

Let not the reader argue, from any of these evidences of iniquity, that the times of the Puritans were more vicious than our own, when, as we pass along the very street of this sketch, we discern no badge of infamy on man or woman. It was the policy of our ancestors to search out even the most secret sins and expose them to shame, without fear or favour, in the broadest light of the noonday sun. Were such the custom now, perchance we might find materials for a no less piquant sketch than the above.

Except the malefactors whom we have described, and the diseased or infirm persons, the whole male population of the town, between sixteen years and sixty, were seen in the ranks of the trainband. A few stately savages, in all the pomp and dignity of the primaeval Indian, stood gazing at the spectacle. Their flint-headed arrows were but childish weapons, compared with the matchlocks of the Puritans, and would have rattled harmlessly against the steel caps and hammered iron breastplates, which enclosed each soldier in an individual fortress. The valiant John Endicott glanced with an eye of pride at his sturdy followers, and prepared to renew the martial toils of the day.

'Come, my stout hearts!' quoth he, drawing his sword. 'Let us show these poor heathen that we can handle our weapons like men of might. Well for them, if they put us not to prove it in earnest!'

The iron-breasted company straightened their line, and each man drew the heavy butt of his matchlock close to his left foot, thus awaiting the orders of the captain. But, as Endicott glanced right and left along the front, he discovered a personage at some little distance, with whom it behoved him to hold a parley. It was an elderly gentleman, wearing a black cloak and band, and a high-crowned hat, beneath which was a velvet skullcap, the whole being the garb of a Puritan minister. This reverend person bore a staff, which seemed to have been recently cut in the forest, and his shoes were bemired, as if he had been travelling on foot through the swamps of the wilderness. He aspect was perfectly that of a pilgrim, heightened also by an apostolic dignity. Just as Endicott perceived him, he laid aside his staff, and stooped to drink at a bubbling fountain, which gushed into the sunshine about a score of yards from the corner of the meeting-house. But, ere the good man drank, he turned his face heavenward in thankfulness, and then, holding back his grey beard with one hand, he scooped up his simple draught in the hollow of the other.

'What, ho! good Mr. Williams,' shouted Endicott. 'You are welcome back again to our town of peace. How does our worthy Governor Winthrop? And what news from Boston?'

'The Governor hath his health, worshipful Sir,' answered Roger Williams,* now resuming his staff, and drawing near. 'And, for the news, here is a letter, which, knowing I was to travel hitherward today, his Excellency committed to my charge. Belike it contains tidings of much import; for a ship arrived yesterday from England.'

Mr. Williams, the minister of Salem, and of course known to all the spectators, and now reached the spot where Endicott was standing under the banner of his company, and put the Governor's epistle into his hand. The broad seal was impressed with Winthrop's coat of arms. Endicott hastily unclosed the letter, and began to read; while, as his eye passed down the page, a wrathful change came over his manly countenance. The blood glowed through it, till it seemed to be kindling with an internal heat; nor was it unnatural to suppose that his breastplate would likewise become red-hot, with the angry fire of the bosom which it covered. Arriving at the conclusion, he shook the letter fiercely in his hand, so that it rustled as loud as the flag above his head.

'Black tidings* these, Mr. Williams,' said he; 'blacker never came to New England. Doubtless you know their purport?'

'Yea, truly,' replied Roger Williams; 'for the Governor consulted, respecting this matter, with my brethren in the ministry at Boston; and my opinion was likewise asked. And his Excellency entreats you by me, that the news be not suddenly noised abroad, lest the people be stirred up unto some outbreak, and thereby give the King and the Archbishop a handle against us.'

'The Governor is a wise man,—a wise man, and a meek and moderate,' said Endicott, setting his teeth grimly. 'Nevertheless, I must do according to my own best judgement.* There is neither man, woman, nor child in New England but has a concern as dear as life in these tidings; and if John Endicott's voice be loud enough, man, woman, and child shall hear them. Soldiers, wheel into a hollow square!* Ho, good people! Here are news for one and all of you.'

The soldiers closed in around their captain; and he and Roger Williams stood together under the banner of the Red Cross; while the women and the aged men pressed forward, and the mothers held up their children to look Endicott in the face. A few taps of the drum gave signal for silence and attention.

'Fellow-soldiers,—fellow-exiles,' began Endicott, speaking under strong excitement, yet powerfully restraining it, 'wherefore did ye leave your native country? Wherefore, I say, have we left the green and fertile fields, the cottages, or, perchance, the old grey halls, where we were born and bred, the churchyards where our forefathers lie buried? Wherefore have we come hither to set up our own tombstones in a wilderness? A howling wilderness it is! The wolf and the bear meet us within halloo of our dwellings. The savage lieth in wait for us in the dismal shadow of the woods. The stubborn roots of the trees break our ploughshares, when we would till the earth. Our children cry for bread, and we must dig in the sands of the sea-shore to satisfy them. Wherefore, I say again, have we sought this country of a rugged soil and wintry sky? Was it not for the enjoyment of our civil rights? Was it not for liberty to worship God according to our conscience?'

'Call you this liberty of conscience?'* interrupted a voice on the steps of the meeting-house.

It was the Wanton Gospeller. A sad and quiet smile flitted across the mild visage of Roger Williams. But Endicott, in the excitement of the moment, shook his sword wrathfully at the culprit,—an ominous gesture from a man like him.

'What hast thou to do with conscience, thou knave?' cried he. 'I said liberty to worship God, not licence to profane and ridicule him. Break not in upon my speech; or I will lay thee neck and heels till this time to-morrow! Hearken to me, friends, nor heed that accursed rhapsodist. As I was saying, we have sacrificed all things, and have come to a land whereof the old world hath scarcely heard, that we might make a new world unto ourselves, and painfully seek a path from hence to heaven. But what think ye now? This son of a Scotch tyrant,*—this grandson of a Papistical and adulterous Scotchwoman, whose death proved that a golden crown doth not always save an anointed head from the block—'

'Nay, brother, nay,' interposed Mr. Williams; 'thy words are not meet for a secret chamber, far less for a public street.'

'Hold thy peace, Roger Williams!' answered Endicott, imperiously. 'My spirit is wiser than thine, for the business now in hand. I tell ye, fellow-exiles, that Charles of England, and Laud, our bitterest persecutor, arch-priest of Canterbury, are resolute to pursue us even hither. They are taking counsel, saith this letter, to send over a governor-general, in whose breast shall be deposited all the law and equity of the land. They are minded, also, to establish the idolatrous forms of English Episcopacy; so that, when Laud shall kiss the Pope's toe, as cardinal of Rome, he may deliver New England, bound hand and foot, into the power of his master!'

A deep groan from the auditors—a sound of wrath, as well as fear and sorrow—responded to this intelligence.

'Look ye to it, brethren,' resumed Endicott, with increasing energy. 'If this King and this arch-prelate have their will, we shall briefly behold a cross on the spire of this tabernacle which we have builded, and a high altar within its walls, with wax tapers burning round it at noonday. We shall hear the sacring bell, and the voices of the Romish priests saying the mass. But think ye, Christian men, that these abominations may be suffered without a sword drawn? without a shot fired? without blood spilt, yea, on the very stairs of the pulpit? No,—be ye strong of hand, and stout of heart! Here we stand on our own soil, which we have bought with our goods, which we have won with our swords, which we have cleared with our axes, which we have tilled with the sweat of our brows, which we have sanctified with our prayers to the God that brought us hither! Who shall enslave us here? What have we to do with this mitred prelate,—with this crowned King? What have we to do with England?'

Endicott gazed round at the excited countenances of the people, now full of his own spirit, and then turned suddenly to the standard-bearer, who stood close behind him.

'Officer, lower your banner!' said he.

The officer obeyed; and, brandishing his sword, Endicott thrust it through the cloth, and, with his left hand, rent the Red Cross completely out of the banner. He then waved the tattered ensign above his head.

'Sacrilegious wretch!' cried the High-Churchman in the pillory, unable longer to restrain himself; 'thou hast rejected the symbol of our holy religion!'

'Treason, treason!' roared the royalist in the stocks. 'He hath defaced the King's banner!'

'Before God and man, I will avouch the deed,' answered Endicott. 'Beat a flourish, drummer! shout, soldiers and people! in honour of the Ensign of New England. Neither Pope nor Tyrant hath part in it now!'

With a cry of triumph, the people gave their sanction to one of the boldest exploits which our history records. And, for ever honoured* be the name of Endicott! We look back through the mist of ages, and recognize, in the rending of the Red Cross from New England's banner, the first omen of that deliverance which our fathers consummated, after the bones of the stern Puritan had lain more than a century in the dust.

THE BIRTHMARK

IN the latter part of the last century* there lived a man of science, an eminent proficient in every branch of natural philosophy, who not long before our story opens had made experience of a spiritual affinity more attractive than any chemical one. He had left his laboratory to the care of an assistant, cleared his fine countenance from the furnace-smoke, washed the stain of acids from his fingers, and persuaded a beautiful woman to become his wife. In those days, when the comparatively recent discovery of electricity and other kindred mysteries of Nature seemed to open paths into the region of miracle, it was not unusual for the love of science to rival the love of woman in its depths and absorbing energy. The higher intellect,* the imagination, the spirit, and even the heart might all find their congenial aliment in pursuits which, as some of their ardent votaries believed, would ascend from one step of powerful intelligence to another, until the philosopher should lay his hand on the secret of creative force* and perhaps make new worlds for himself. We know not whether Aylmer possessed this degree of faith in man's ultimate control over nature. He had devoted himself, however, too unreservedly to scientific studies ever to be weaned from them by any second passion. His love for his young wife might prove the stronger of the two; but it could only be by intertwining itself with his love of science* and uniting the strength of the latter to his own.

Such a union accordingly took place, and was attended with truly remarkable consequences and a deeply impressive moral. One day, very soon after their marriage Aylmer sat gazing at his wife with a trouble in his countenance that grew stronger until he spoke.

'Georgiana,' said he, 'has it never occurred to you that the mark upon your cheek might be removed?'

'No, indeed,' said she, smiling; but, perceiving the seriousness of his manner, she blushed deeply. 'To tell you the truth, it has been so often called a charm, that I was simple enough to imagine it might be so.'

'Ah, upon another face perhaps it might,' replied her husband; 'but never on yours. No, dearest Georgiana, you came so nearly perfect from the hand of Nature, that this slightest possible defect, which we hesitate whether to term a defect or a beauty, shocks me, as being the visible mark of earthly imperfection.'

'Shocks you, my husband!' cried Georgiana, deeply hurt; at first reddening with momentary anger, but then bursting into tears. 'Then why did you take me from my mother's side? You cannot love what shocks you!'

To explain this conversation, it must be mentioned that in the centre of Georgiana's left cheek there was a singular mark, deeply interwoven, as it were, with the texture and substance of her face. In the usual state of her complexion—a healthy though delicate bloom—the mark wore a tint of deeper crimson, which imperfectly defined its shape amid the surrounding rosiness. When she blushed it gradually became more indistinct, and finally vanished amid the triumphant rush of blood that bathed the whole cheek with its brilliant glow. But if any shifting motion caused her to turn pale there was the mark again, a crimson stain upon the snow,* in what Aylmer sometimes deemed an almost fearful distinctness. Its shape bore not a little similarity to the human hand, though of the smallest pygmy size. Georgiana's lovers were wont to say that some fairy at her birth-hour had laid her tiny hand upon the infant's cheek, and left this impress there in token of the magic endowments that were to give her such sway over all hearts. Many a desperate swain would have risked life for the privilege of pressing his lips to the mysterious hand. It must not be concealed, however, that the impression wrought by this fairy sign-manual varied exceedingly according to the difference of temperament in the beholders. Some fastidious persons—but they were exclusively of her own sex—affirmed that the bloody hand, as they chose to call it, quite destroyed the effect of Georgiana's beauty and rendered her countenance even hideous. But it would be as reasonable to say that one of those small blue stains which sometimes occur in the purest statuary marble would convert the Eve of Powers* to a monster. Masculine observers, if the birthmark did not heighten their admiration, contented themselves with wishing it away, that the world might possess one living specimen of ideal loveliness without the semblance of a flaw. After his marriage,—for he thought little or nothing of the matter before,—Aylmer discovered that this was the case with himself.

Had she been less beautiful,—if Envy's self could have found aught else to sneer at,—he might have felt his affection heightened by the prettiness of this mimic hand, now vaguely portrayed, now lost, now stealing forth again and glimmering to and fro with every pulse of emotion that throbbed within her heart; but, seeing her otherwise so perfect, he found this one defect grow more and more intolerable with every moment of their united lives. It was the fatal flaw of humanity* which Nature, in one shape or another, stamps ineffaceably on all her productions, either to imply that they are temporary and finite, or that their perfection must be wrought by toil and pain. The crimson hand expressed the ineludible grip in which mortality clutches the highest and purest of earthly mould, degrading them into kindred with the lowest, and even with the very brutes, like whom their visible frames return to dust. In this manner, selecting it as the symbol of his wife's liability to sin, sorrow, decay, and death, Aylmer's sombre imagination was not long in rendering the birthmark a frightful object, causing him more trouble and horror than ever Georgiana's beauty, whether of soul or sense, had given him delight.

At all the seasons which should have been their happiest he invariably, and without intending it, nay, in spite of a purpose to the contrary, reverted to this one disastrous topic. Trifling as it at first appeared, it so connected itself with innumerable trains of thought and modes of feeling that it became the central point of all. With the morning twilight Aylmer opened his eyes upon his wife's face and recognized the symbol of imperfection; and when they sat together at the evening hearth his eyes wandered stealthily to her cheek, and beheld, flickering with the blaze of the wood-fire, the spectral hand that wrote mortality where he would fain have worshipped. Georgiana soon learned to shudder at his gaze. It needed but a glance with the peculiar expression that his face often wore to change the roses of her cheek into a death-like paleness, amid which the crimson hand was brought strongly out, like a bas-relief of ruby on the whitest marble.

Late one night, when the lights were growing dim so as hardly to betray the stain on the poor wife's cheek, she herself, for the first time, voluntarily took up the subject.

'Do you remember, my dear Aylmer,' said she, with a feeble attempt at a smile, 'have you any recollection of a dream last night about this odious hand?'

'None! none whatever!' replied Aylmer, starting; but then he added, in a dry, cold tone, affected for the sake of concealing the real depth of his emotion, 'I might well dream of it; for, before I fell asleep, it had taken a pretty firm hold of my fancy.'

'And you did dream of it?' continued Georgiana, hastily; for she dreaded lest a gush of tears should interrupt what she had to say. 'A terrible dream! I wonder that you can forget it. Is it possible to forget this one expression?—"It is in her heart now; we must have it out!" Reflect, my husband; for by all means I would have you recall that dream.'

The mind is in a sad state when Sleep, the all-involving, cannot confine her spectres within the dim region of her sway, but suffers them to break forth, affrighting this actual life with secrets that perchance belong to a deeper one.* Aylmer now remembered his dream. He had fancied himself with his servant Aminadab attempting an operation for the removal of the birthmark; but the deeper went the knife, the deeper sank the hand, until at length its tiny grasp appeared to have caught hold of Georgiana's heart; whence, however, her husband was inexorably resolved to cut or wrench it away.

When the dream had shaped itself perfectly in his memory, Aylmer sat in his wife's presence with a guilty feeling. Truth often finds its way to the mind close muffled in robes of sleep, and then speaks with uncompromising directness of matters in regard to which we practise an unconscious self-deception during our waking moments. Until now he had not been aware of the tyrannizing influence acquired by one idea over his mind, and of the lengths which he might find in his heart to go for the sake of giving himself peace.

'Aylmer,' resumed Georgiana, solemnly, 'I know not what may be the cost to both of us to rid me of this fatal birthmark. Perhaps its removal may cause cureless deformity; or it may be the stain goes as deep as life itself. Again: do we know that there is a possibility, on any terms, of unclasping the firm grip of this little hand which was laid upon me before I came into the world?'

'Dearest Georgiana, I have spent much thought upon the subject,' hastily interrupted Aylmer. 'I am convinced of the perfect practicability of its removal.'

'If there be the remotest possibility of it,' continued Georgiana, 'let the attempt be made, at whatever risk. Danger is nothing to me; for life, while this hateful mark makes me the object of your horror and disgust,—life is a burden which I would fling down with joy. Either remove this dreadful hand, or take my wretched life! You have deep science. All the world bears witness of it. You have achieved great wonders. Cannot you remove this little, little mark, which I cover with the tips of two small fingers? Is this beyond your power, for the sake of your own peace, and to save your poor wife from madness?'

'Noblest, dearest, tenderest wife,' cried Aylmer, rapturously, 'doubt not my power. I have already given this matter the deepest thought,—thought which might almost have enlightened me to create a being less perfect than yourself. Georgiana, you have led me deeper than ever into the heart of science. I feel myself fully competent to render this dear cheek as faultless as its fellow; and then, most beloved, what will be my triumph when I shall have corrected what Nature left imperfect in her fairest work! Even Pygmalion,* when his sculptured woman assumed life, felt not greater ecstasy than mine will be.'

'It is resolved, then,' said Georgiana, faintly smiling. 'And, Aylmer, spare me not, though you should find the birthmark take refuge in my heart at last.'

Her husband tenderly kissed her cheek,—her right cheek,—not that which bore the impress of the crimson hand.

The next day Aylmer apprised his wife of a plan that he had formed whereby he might have opportunity for the intense thought and constant watchfulness which the proposed operation would require; while Georgiana, likewise, would enjoy the perfect repose essential to its success. They were to seclude themselves in the extensive apartments occupied by Aylmer as a laboratory, and where, during his toilsome youth, he had made discoveries in the elemental powers of nature that had roused the admiration of all the learned societies in Europe. Seated calmly in this laboratory, the pale philosopher had investigated the secrets of the highest cloud-region and of the profoundest mines; he had satisfied himself of the causes that kindled and kept alive the fires of the volcano; and had explained the mystery of fountains, and how it is that they gush forth, some so bright and pure, and others with such rich medicinal virtues, from the dark bosom of the earth. Here, too, at an earlier period, he had studied the wonders of the human frame, and attempted to fathom the very process by which Nature assimilates all her precious influences from earth and air, and from the spiritual world, to create and foster man, her masterpiece. The latter pursuit, however, Aylmer had long laid aside in unwilling recognition of the truth—against which all seekers sooner or later stumble—that our great creative Mother, while she amuses us with apparently working in the broadest sunshine, is yet severely careful to keep her own secrets, and, in spite of her pretended openness, shows us nothing but results. She permits us, indeed, to mar, but seldom to mend, and, like a jealous patentee, on no account to make. Now, however, Aylmer resumed these half-forgotten investigations; not, of course, with such hopes or wishes as first suggested them; but because they involved much physiological truth and lay in the path of his proposed scheme for the treatment of Georgiana.

As he led her over the threshold of the laboratory Georgiana was cold and tremulous. Aylmer looked cheerfully into her face, with intent to reassure her, but was so startled with the intense glow of the birthmark upon the whiteness of her cheek that he could not restrain a strong convulsive shudder. His wife fainted.

'Aminadab!* Aminadab!' shouted Aylmer, stamping violently on the floor.

Forthwith there issued from an inner apartment a man of low stature, but bulky frame, with shaggy hair hanging about his visage, which was grimed with the vapours of the furnace. This personage had been Aylmer's underworker during his whole scientific career, and was admirably fitted for that office by his great mechanical readiness, and the skill with which, while incapable of comprehending a single principle, he executed all the details of his master's experiments. With his vast strength, his shaggy hair, his smoky aspect, and the indescribable earthiness that encrusted him, he seemed to represent man's physical nature; while Aylmer's slender figure, and pale, intellectual face, were no less apt a type of the spiritual element.

'Throw open the door of the boudoir, Aminadab,' said Aylmer, 'and burn a pastille.'

'Yes, master,' answered Aminadab, looking intently at the lifeless form of Georgiana; and then he muttered to himself, 'If she were my wife, I'd never part with that birthmark.'

When Georgiana recovered consciousness she found herself breathing an atmosphere of penetrating fragrance, the gentle potency of which had recalled her from her death-like faintness. The scene around her looked like enchantment. Aylmer had converted those smoky, dingy, sombre rooms, where he had spent his brightest years in recondite pursuits, into a series of beautiful apartments not unfit to be the secluded abode of a lovely woman. The walls were hung with gorgeous curtains, which imparted the combination of grandeur and grace that no other species of adornment can achieve; and, as they fell from the ceiling to the floor, their rich and ponderous folds concealing all angles and straight lines, appeared to shut in the scene from infinite space. For aught Georgiana knew, it might be a pavilion among the clouds. And Aylmer, excluding the sunshine, which would have interfered with his chemical processes, had supplied its place with perfumed lamps, emitting flames of various hue, but all uniting in a soft, empurpled radiance. He now knelt by his wife's side, watching her earnestly, but without alarm; for he was confident in his science, and felt that he could draw a magic circle round her within which no evil might intrude.

'Where am I? Ah, I remember,' said Georgiana, faintly; and she placed her hand over her cheek to hide the terrible mark from her husband's eyes.

'Fear not, dearest!' exclaimed he. 'Do not shrink from me! Believe me, Georgiana, I even rejoice in this single imperfection, since it will be such a rapture to remove it.'

'Oh, spare me!' sadly replied his wife. 'Pray do not look at it again. I never can forget that convulsive shudder.'

In order to soothe Georgiana, and, as it were, to release her mind from the burden of actual things, Aylmer now put in practice some of the light and playful secrets which science had taught him among its profounder lore. Airy figures, absolutely bodiless ideas, and forms of unsubstantial beauty came and danced before her, imprinting their momentary footsteps on beams of light. Though she had some indistinct idea of the method of these optical phenomena, still the illusion was almost perfect enough to warrant the belief that her husband possessed sway over the spiritual world. Then again, when she felt a wish to look forth from her seclusion, immediately, as if her thoughts were answered, the procession of external existence flitted across a screen. The scenery and the figures of actual life were perfectly represented, but with that bewitching yet indescribable difference which always makes a picture, an image, or a shadow so much more attractive than the original. When wearied of this, Aylmer bade her cast her eyes upon a vessel containing a quantity of earth. She did so, with little interest at first; but was soon startled to perceive the germ of a plant shooting upward from the soil. Then came the slender stalk; the leaves gradually unfolded themselves; and amid them was a perfect and lovely flower.

'It is magical!' cried Georgiana. 'I dare not touch it.'

'Nay, pluck it,' answered Aylmer,—'pluck it, and inhale its brief perfume while you may. The flower will wither in a few moments and leave nothing save its brown seed-vessels; but thence may be perpetuated a race as ephemeral as itself.'

But Georgiana had no sooner touched the flower than the whole plant suffered a blight, its leaves turning coal-black as if by the agency of fire.

'There was too powerful a stimulus,' said Aylmer, thoughtfully.

To make up for this abortive experiment, he proposed to take her portrait by a scientific process of his own invention. It was to be effected by rays of light striking upon a polished plate of metal.* Georgiana assented; but, on looking at the result, was affrighted to find the features of the portrait blurred and indefinable; while the minute figure of a hand appeared where the cheek should have been. Aylmer snatched the metallic plate and threw it into a jar of corrosive acid.

Soon, however, he forgot these mortifying failures. In the intervals of study and chemical experiment he came to her flushed and exhausted, but seemed invigorated by her presence, and spoke in glowing language of the resources of his art. He gave a history of the long dynasty of the alchemists,* who spent so many ages in quest of the universal solvent by which the golden principle might be elicited from all things vile and base. Aylmer appeared to believe that, by the plainest scientific logic, it was altogether within the limits of possibility to discover this long-sought medium. 'But,' he added, 'a philosopher who should go deep enough to acquire the power would attain too lofty a wisdom to stoop to the exercise of it.' Not less singular were his opinions in regard to the elixir vitae.* He more than intimated that it was at his option to concoct a liquid that should prolong life for years, perhaps interminably; but that it would produce a discord in nature which all the world, and chiefly the quaffer of the immortal nostrum, would find cause to curse.

'Aylmer, are you in earnest?' asked Georgiana, looking at him with amazement and fear. 'It is terrible to possess such power, or even to dream of possessing it.'

'Oh, do not tremble, my love,' said her husband. 'I would

not wrong either you or myself by working such inharmonious effects upon our lives; but I would have you consider how trifling, in comparison, is the skill requisite to remove this little hand.'

At the mention of the birthmark, Georgiana, as usual, shrank as if a red-hot iron had touched her cheek.

Again Aylmer applied himself to his labours. She could hear his voice in the distant furnace-room giving directions to Aminadab, whose harsh, uncouth, misshapen tones were audible in response, more like the grunt or growl of a brute than human speech. After hours of absence, Aylmer re-appeared and proposed that she should now examine his cabinet of chemical products and natural treasures of the earth. Among the former he showed her a small vial, in which, he remarked, was contained a gentle yet most powerful fragrance, capable of impregnating all the breezes that blow across the kingdom. They were of inestimable value, the contents of that little vial; and, as he said so, he threw some of the perfume into the air and filled the room with piercing and invigorating delight.

'And what is this?' asked Georgiana, pointing to a small crystal globe containing a gold-coloured liquid. 'It is so beautiful to the eye that I could imagine it the elixir of life.'

'In one sense it is,' replied Aylmer; 'or rather, the elixir of immortality. It is the most precious poison that ever was concocted in this world. By its aid I could apportion the lifetime of any mortal at whom you might point your finger. The strength of the dose would determine whether he were to linger out years, or drop dead in the midst of a breath. No king on his guarded throne could keep his life if I, in my private station, should deem that the welfare of millions justified me in depriving him of it.'

'Why do you keep such a terrific drug?' inquired Georgiana, in horror.

'Do not mistrust me, dearest,' said her husband, smiling; 'its virtuous potency is yet greater than its harmful one. But see! here is a powerful cosmetic. With a few drops of this in a vase of water, freckles may be washed away as easily as the hands are cleansed. A stronger infusion would take the blood out of the cheek, and leave the rosiest beauty a pale ghost.'

'It is with this lotion that you intend to bathe my cheek?' asked Georgiana, anxiously.

'Oh no,' hastily replied her husband; 'this is merely superficial. Your case demands a remedy that shall go deeper.'

In his interviews with Georgiana, Aylmer generally made minute inquiries as to her sensations, and whether the confinement of the rooms and the temperature of the atmosphere agreed with her. These questions had such a particular drift that Georgiana began to conjecture that she was already subjected to certain physical influences, either breathed in with the fragrant air or taken with her food. She fancied likewise, but it might be altogether fancy, that there was a stirring up of her system,—a strange, indefinite, sensation creeping through her veins, and tingling, half painfully, half pleasurably, at her heart. Still, whenever she dared to look into the mirror, there she beheld herself pale as a white rose and with the crimson birthmark stamped upon her cheek. Not even Aylmer now hated it so much as she.

To dispel the tedium of the hours which her husband found it necessary to devote to the processes of combination and analysis, Georgiana turned over the volumes of his scientific library. In many dark old tomes she met with chapters full of romance and poetry. They were the works of the philosophers of the Middle Ages,* such as Albertus Magnus, Cornelius Agrippa, Paracelsus, and the famous friar who created the prophetic Brazen Head. All these antique naturalists stood in advance of their centuries, yet were imbued with some of their credulity, and therefore were believed, and perhaps imagined themselves, to have acquired from the investigation of nature a power above nature, and from physics a sway over the spiritual world. Hardly less curious and imaginative were the early volumes of the *Transactions of the Royal Society*,* in which the members, knowing little of the limits of natural possibility, were continually recording wonders or proposing methods whereby wonders might be wrought.

But, to Georgiana, the most engrossing volume was a large folio from her husband's own hand, in which he had recorded every experiment of his scientific career, its original aim, the methods adopted for its development, and its final success or failure, with the circumstances to which either event was attributable. The book, in truth, was both the history and emblem of his ardent, ambitious, imaginative, yet practical and laborious life. He handled physical details as if there were nothing beyond them; yet spiritualized them all, and redeemed himself from materialism by his strong and eager aspiration towards the infinite. In his grasp the veriest clod of earth assumed a soul. Georgiana, as she read, reverenced Aylmer and loved him more profoundly than ever, but with a less entire dependence on his judgement than heretofore. Much as he had accomplished, she could not but observe that his most splendid successes were almost invariably failures, if compared with the ideal at which he aimed. His brightest diamonds were the merest pebbles, and felt to be so by himself, in comparison with the inestimable gems which lay hidden beyond his reach. The volume, rich with achievements that had won renown for its author, was yet as melancholy a record as ever mortal hand had penned. It was the sad confession and continual exemplification of the shortcomings of the composite man, the spirit burdened with clay and working in matter, and of the despair that assails the higher nature at finding itself so miserably thwarted by the earthly part. Perhaps every man of genius, in whatever sphere, might recognize the image of his own experience in Aylmer's journal.

So deeply did these reflections affect Georgiana that she laid her face upon the open volume and burst into tears. In this situation she was found by her husband.

'It is dangerous to read in a sorcerer's books,' said he with a smile, though his countenance was uneasy and displeased. 'Georgiana, there are pages in that volume which I can scarcely glance over and keep my senses. Take heed lest it prove as detrimental to you.'

'It has made me worship you more than ever,' said she.

'Ah, wait for this one success,' rejoined he, 'then worship me if you will. I shall deem myself hardly unworthy of it. But come, I have sought you for the luxury of your voice. Sing to me, dearest.'

So she poured out the liquid music* of her voice to quench the thirst of his spirit. He then took his leave with a boyish exuberance of gaiety, assuring her that her seclusion would endure but a little longer, and that the result was already certain. Scarcely had he departed when Georgiana felt irresistibly impelled to follow him. She had forgotten to inform Aylmer of a symptom which for two or three hours past had begun to excite her attention. It was a sensation in the fatal birthmark, not painful, but which induced a restlessness throughout her system. Hastening after her husband, she intruded for the first time into the laboratory.

The first thing that struck her eye was the furnace, that hot and feverish worker, with the intense glow of its fire, which by the quantities of soot clustered above it seemed to have been burning for ages. There was a distilling apparatus in full operation. Around the room were retorts, tubes, cylinders, crucibles, and other apparatus of chemical research. An electrical machine stood ready for immediate use. The atmosphere felt oppressively close, and was tainted with gaseous odours which had been tormented forth by the processes of science. The severe and homely simplicity of the apartment, with its naked walls and brick pavement, looked strange, accustomed as Georgiana had become to the fantastic elegance of her boudoir. But what chiefly, indeed almost solely, drew her attention, was the aspect of Aylmer himself.

He was pale as death, anxious and absorbed, and hung over the furnace as if it depended upon his utmost watchfulness whether the liquid which it was distilling should be the draught of immortal happiness or misery. How different from the sanguine and joyous mien that he had assumed for Georgiana's encouragement!

'Carefully now, Aminadab; carefully, thou human machine; carefully, thou man of clay,' muttered Aylmer, more to himself than his assistant. 'Now, if there be a thought too much or too little, it is all over.'

'Ho! ho!' mumbled Aminadab. 'Look, master! look!'

Aylmer raised his eyes hastily, and at first reddened, then grew paler than ever, on beholding Georgiana. He rushed towards her and seized her arm with a grip that left the print of his fingers upon it.

'Why do you come hither? Have you no trust in your husband?' cried he, impetuously. 'Would you throw the blight of that fatal birthmark over my labours? It is not well done. Go, prying woman! go!'

'Nay, Aylmer,' said Georgiana with the firmness of which she possessed no stinted endowment, 'it is not you that have a right to complain. You mistrust your wife; you concealed the anxiety with which you watch the development of this experiment. Think not so unworthily of me, my husband. Tell me all the risk we run, and fear not that I shall shrink; for my share in it is far less than your own.'

'No, no, Georgiana!' said Aylmer, impatiently; 'it must not be.'

'I submit,' replied she, calmly. 'And, Aylmer, I shall quaff whatever draught you bring me; but it will be on the same principle that would induce me to take a dose of poison if offered by your hand.'

'My noble wife,' said Aylmer, deeply moved, 'I knew not the height and depth of your nature until now. Nothing shall be concealed. Know, then, that this crimson hand, superficial as it seems, has clutched its grasp into your being with a strength of which I had no previous conception. I have already administered agents powerful enough to do aught except to change your entire physical system. Only one thing remains to be tried. If that fail us we are ruined.'

'Why did you hesitate to tell me this?' asked she.

'Because, Georgiana,' said Aylmer, in a low voice, 'there is danger.'

'Danger? There is but one danger,—that this horrible stigma shall be left upon my cheek!' cried Georgiana. 'Remove it, remove it, whatever be the cost, or we shall both go mad!'

'Heaven knows your words are too true,' said Aylmer, sadly. 'And now, dearest, return to your boudoir. In a little while all will be tested.'

He conducted her back and took leave of her with a solemn tenderness which spoke far more than his words how much was now at stake. After his departure Georgiana became rapt in musings. She considered the character of Aylmer, and did it completer justice than at any previous moment. Her heart exulted, while it trembled, at his honourable love,—so pure and lofty* that it would accept nothing less than perfection, nor miserably make itself contented with an earthlier nature than he had dreamed of. She felt how much more precious was such a sentiment than that meaner kind which would have borne with the imperfection for her sake, and have been guilty of treason to holy love by degrading its perfect idea to the level of the actual; and with her whole spirit she prayed that, for a single moment, she might satisfy his highest and deepest conception. Longer than one moment she well knew it could not be; for his spirit was ever on the march, ever ascending, and each instant required something that was beyond the scope of the instant before.

The sound of her husband's footsteps aroused her. He bore a crystal goblet containing a liquor colourless as water, but bright enough to be the draught of immortality. Aylmer was pale; but it seemed rather the consequence of a highly wrought state of mind and tension of spirit than of fear or doubt.

'The concoction of the draught has been perfect,' said he, in answer to Georgiana's look. 'Unless all my science have deceived me, it cannot fail.'

'Save on your account, my dearest Aylmer,' observed his wife, 'I might wish to put off this birthmark of mortality by relinquishing mortality itself in preference to any other mode. Life is but a sad possession to those who have attained precisely the degree of moral advancement at which I stand. Were I weaker and blinder, it might be happiness. Were I stronger, it might be endured hopefully. But, being what I find myself, methinks I am of all mortals the most fit to die.'

'You are fit for heaven without tasting death!' replied her husband. 'But why do we speak of dying? The draught cannot fail. Behold its effect upon this plant.'

On the window-seat there stood a geranium* diseased with yellow blotches, which had overspread all its leaves. Aylmer poured a small quantity of the liquid upon the soil in which it grew. In a little time, when the roots of the plant had taken up the moisture, the unsightly blotches began to be extinguished in a living verdure.

'There needed no proof,' said Georgiana, quietly. 'Give me the goblet. I joyfully stake all upon your word.'

'Drink, then, thou lofty creature!' exclaimed Aylmer, with fervid admiration. 'There is no taint of imperfection on thy spirit. Thy sensible frame, too, shall soon be all perfect.'

She quaffed the liquid and returned the goblet to his hand.

'It is grateful,' said she, with a placid smile. 'Methinks it is like water from a heavenly fountain; for it contains I know not what of unobtrusive fragrance and deliciousness. It allays a feverish thirst that had parched me for many days. Now, dearest, let me sleep. My earthly senses are closing over my spirit like the leaves around the heart of a rose at sunset.'

She spoke the last words with a gentle reluctance, as if it required almost more energy than she could command to pronounce the faint and lingering syllables. Scarcely had they loitered through her lips ere she was lost in slumber. Aylmer sat by her side, watching her aspect with the emotions proper to a man the whole value of whose existence was involved in the process now to be tested. Mingled with this mood, however, was the philosophic investigation characteristic of the man of science. Not the minutest symptom escaped him. A heightened flush of the cheek, a slight irregularity of breath, a quiver of the eyelid, a hardly perceptible tremor through the frame,—such were the details which, as the moments passed, he wrote down in his folio volume. Intense thought had set its stamp upon every previous page of that volume; but the thoughts of years were all concentrated upon the last.

While thus employed, he failed not to gaze often at the fatal hand, and not without a shudder. Yet once, by a strange and unaccountable impulse, he pressed it with his lips. His spirit recoiled, however, in the very act; and Georgiana, out of the midst of her deep sleep, moved uneasily and murmured, as if in remonstrance. Again Aylmer resumed his watch. Nor was it without avail. The crimson hand, which at first had been strongly visible upon the marble paleness of Georgiana's cheek, now grew more faintly outlined. She remained not less pale than ever; but the birthmark, with every breath that came and went, lost somewhat of its former distinctness. Its presence had been awful; its departure was more awful still. Watch the stain of the rainbow fading out of the sky, and you will know how that mysterious symbol passed away.

'By Heaven! it is wellnigh gone!' said Aylmer to himself, in almost irrepressible ecstasy. 'I can scarcely trace it now. Success! success! And now it is like the faintest rose colour. The lightest flush of blood across her cheek would overcome it. But she is so pale!'

He drew aside the window-curtain and suffered the light of natural day to fall into the room and rest upon her cheek. At the same time he heard a gross, hoarse chuckle, which he had long known as his servant Aminadab's expression of delight.

'Ah, clod! ah, earthly mass!' cried Aylmer, laughing in a sort of frenzy, 'you have served me well! Matter and spirit—earth and heaven—have both done their part in this! Laugh, thing of the senses! You have earned the right to laugh.'

These exclamations broke Georgiana's sleep. She slowly unclosed her eyes and gazed into the mirror which her husband had arranged for that purpose. A faint smile flitted over her lips when she recognized how barely perceptible was now that crimson hand which had once blazed forth with such disastrous brilliancy as to scare away all their happiness. But then her eyes sought Aylmer's face with a trouble and anxiety that he could by no means account for.

'My poor Aylmer!' murmured she.

'Poor? Nay, richest, happiest, most favoured!' exclaimed he. 'My peerless bride, it is successful! You are perfect!'

'My poor Aylmer,' she repeated, with a more than human tenderness, 'you have aimed loftily; you have done nobly. Do not repent that, with so high and pure a feeling, you have rejected the best the earth could offer. Aylmer, dearest Aylmer, I am dying!'

Alas! it was too true! The fatal hand had grappled with the mystery of life, and was the bond by which an angelic spirit kept itself in union with a mortal frame. As the last crimson tint of the birthmark—that sole token of human imperfection—faded from her cheek, the parting breath of the now perfect woman passed into the atmosphere, and her soul, lingering a moment near her husband, took its heavenward flight. Then a hoarse, chuckling laugh was heard again! Thus ever does the gross fatality of earth exult in its invariable triumph over the immortal essence which, in this dim sphere of half-development, demands the completeness of a higher state. Yet, had Aylmer reached a profounder wisdom, he need not thus have flung away the happiness which would have woven his mortal life of the self-same texture with the celestial. The momentary circumstance was too strong for him; he failed to look beyond the shadowy scope of time, and, living once for all in eternity, to find the perfect future in the present.

THE CELESTIAL RAILROAD

NOT a great while ago, passing through the gate of dreams,* I visited that region of the earth in which lies the famous City of Destruction.* It interested me much to learn that by the public spirit of some of the inhabitants a railroad has recently been established between this populous and flourishing town and the Celestial City. Having a little time upon my hands, I resolved to gratify a liberal curiosity* by making a trip thither. Accordingly, one fine morning after paying my bill at the hotel and directing the porter to stow my luggage behind a coach, I took my seat in the vehicle and set out for the station-house. It was my good fortune to enjoy the company of a gentleman—one Mr. Smooth-it-away*—who, though he had never actually visited the Celestial City, yet seemed as well acquainted with its laws, customs, policy, and statistics as with those of the City of Destruction, of which he was a native townsman. Being, moreover, a director of the railroad corporation and one of its largest stockholders, he had it in his power to give me all desirable information respecting that praiseworthy enterprise.*

Our coach rattled out of the city, and at a short distance from its outskirts passed over a bridge of elegant construction, but somewhat too slight, as I imagined, to sustain any considerable weight. On both sides lay an extensive quagmire, which could not have been more disagreeable, either to sight or smell, had all the kennels of the earth emptied their pollution there.

'This,' remarked Mr. Smooth-it-away, 'is the famous Slough of Despond,*—a disgrace to all the neighbourhood; and the greater, that it might so easily be converted into firm ground.'

'I have understood,' said I, 'that efforts have been made for that purpose from time immemorial. Bunyan mentions that above twenty thousand cartloads of wholesome instructions had been thrown in here without effect.'

'Very probably! And what effect could be anticipated from such unsubstantial stuff?' cried Mr. Smooth-it-away. 'You observe this convenient bridge. We obtained a sufficient foundation for it by throwing into the slough some editions of books of morality; volumes of French philosophy and German rationalism; tracks, sermons, and essays of modern clergymen; extracts from Plato, Confucius, and various Hindu sages, together with a few ingenious commentaries upon texts of Scripture,—all of which, by some scientific process, have been converted into a mass like granite. The whole bog might be filled up with similar matter.'

It really seemed to me, however, that the bridge vibrated and heaved up and down in a very formidable manner; and, spite of Mr. Smooth-it-away's testimony to the solidity of its foundation, I should be loath to cross it in a crowded omnibus, especially if each passenger were encumbered with as heavy luggage as that gentlemen and myself. Nevertheless, we got over without accident, and soon found ourselves at the station-house. This very neat and spacious edifice is erected on the site of the little wicket-gate,* which, formerly, as all old pilgrims will recollect, stood directly across the highway, and, by its inconvenient narrowness, was a great obstruction to the traveller of liberal mind and expansive stomach. The reader of John Bunyan will be glad to know that Christian's old friend Evangelist, who was accustomed to supply each pilgrim with a mystic roll, now presides at the ticket-office. Some malicious persons, it is true, deny the identity of this reputable character with the Evangelist of old times, and even

pretend to bring competent evidence of an imposture.*
Without involving myself in a dispute, I shall merely observe
that, so far as my experience goes, the square pieces of
pasteboard now delivered to passengers are much more
convenient and useful along the road than the antique roll of
parchment. Whether they will be as readily received at the
gate of the Celestial City I decline giving an opinion.

A large number of passengers were already at the station-
house awaiting the departure of the cars. By the aspect and
demeanour of these persons, it was easy to judge that the
feelings of the community had undergone a very favourable
change in reference to the celestial pilgrimage. It would have
done Bunyan's heart good to see it. Instead of a lonely and
ragged man, with a huge burden on his back, plodding along
sorrowfully on foot while the whole city hooted after him,
here were parties of the first gentry and most respectable
people in the neighbourhood setting forth towards the
Celestial City as cheerfully as if the pilgrimage were merely
a summer tour. Among the gentlemen were characters of
deserved eminence,—magistrates, politicans, and men of
wealth, by whose example religion could not but be greatly
recommended to their meaner brethren. In the ladies'
apartment, too, I rejoiced to distinguish some of those flowers
of fashionable society who are so well fitted to adorn the most
elevated circles of the Celestial City. There was much pleasant
conversation about the news of the day, topics of business, and
politics, or the lighter matters of amusement; while religion,
though indubitably the main thing at heart, was thrown
tastefully into the background.* Even an infidel would have
heard little or nothing to shock his sensibility.

One great convenience of the new method of going on
pilgrimage I must not forget to mention. Our enormous
burdens, instead of being carried on our shoulders as had been
the custom of old, were all snugly deposited in the baggage-
car, and, as I was assured, would be delivered to their
respective owners at the journey's end. Another thing, likewise, the benevolent reader will be delighted to understand.
It may be remembered that there was an ancient feud between
Prince Beelzebub* and the keeper of the wicket-gate, and that

the adherents of the former distinguished personage were accustomed to shoot deadly arrows at honest pilgrims while knocking at the door. This dispute, much to the credit as well of the illustrious potentate above mentioned as of the worthy and enlightened directors of the railroad, has been pacifically arranged on the principle of mutual compromise. The prince's subjects are now pretty numerously employed about the station-house, some in taking care of the baggage, others in collecting fuel, feeding the engines, and such congenial occupations; and I can conscientiously affirm that persons more attentive to their business, more willing to accommodate, or more generally agreeable to the passengers, are not to be found on any railroad. Every good heart must surely exult at so satisfactory an arrangement of an immemorial difficulty.

'Where is Mr. Greatheart?'* inquired I. 'Beyond a doubt the directors have engaged that famous old champion to be chief conductor on the railroad?'

'Why, no,' said Mr. Smooth-it-away, with a dry cough. 'He was offered the situation of brakeman; but, to tell you the truth, our friend Greatheart has grown preposterously stiff and narrow in his old age. He has so often guided pilgrims over the road on foot, that he considers it a sin to travel in any other fashion. Besides, the old fellow had entered so heartily into the ancient feud with Prince Beelzebub, that he would have been perpetually at blows or ill language with some of the prince's subjects, and thus have embroiled us anew. So, on the whole, we were not sorry when honest Greatheart went off to the Celestial City in a huff and left us at liberty to choose a more suitable and accommodating man. Yonder comes the engineer of the train. You will probably recognize him at once.'

The engine at this moment took its station in advance of the cars, looking, I must confess, much more like a sort of mechanical demon that would hurry us to the infernal regions than a laudable contrivance for smoothing our way to the Celestial City. On its top sat a personage almost enveloped in smoke and flame, which, not to startle the reader, appeared to gush from his own mouth and stomach as well as from the engine's brazen abdomen.

'Do my eyes deceive me?' cried I. 'What on earth is this! A living creature? If so, he is own brother to the engine he rides upon!'

'Poh, poh, you are obtuse!' said Mr. Smooth-it-away, with a hearty laugh. 'Don't you know Apollyon,* Christian's old enemy, with whom he fought so fierce a battle in the Valley of Humiliation? He was the very fellow to manage the engine; and so we have reconciled him to the custom of going on pilgrimage, and engaged him as chief engineer.'

'Bravo, bravo!' exclaimed I, with irrepressible enthusiasm; 'this shows the liberality of the age; this proves, if anything can, that all musty prejudices are in a fair way to be obliterated. And how will Christian rejoice to hear of this happy transformation of his old antagonist! I promise myself great pleasure in informing him of it when we reach the Celestial City.'

The passengers being all comfortably seated, we now rattled away merrily, accomplishing a greater distance in ten minutes than Christian probably trudged over in a day. It was laughable, while we glanced along, as it were, at the tail of a thunderbolt, to observe two dusty foot-travellers in the old pilgrim guise, with cockle-shell and staff, their mystic rolls of parchment in their hands, and their intolerable burdens on their backs. The preposterous obstinacy of these honest people in persisting to groan and stumble along the difficult pathway, rather than take advantage of modern improvements,* excited great mirth among our wiser brotherhood. We greeted the two pilgrims with many pleasant gibes and a roar of laughter; whereupon they gazed at us with such woful and absurdly compassionate visages, that our merriment grew tenfold more obstreperous. Apollyon also entered heartily into the fun, and contrived to flirt the smoke and flame of the engine, or of his own breath, into their faces, and envelop them in an atmosphere of scalding steam. These little practical jokes amused us mightily, and doubtless afforded the pilgrims the gratification of considering themselves martyrs.

At some distance from the railroad Mr. Smooth-it-away pointed to a large, antique edifice, which, he observed, was a tavern of long standing, and had formerly been a noted stopping-place for pilgrims. In Bunyan's road-book it is mentioned as the Interpreter's House.*

'I have long had a curiosity to visit that old mansion,' remarked I.

'It is not one of our stations, as you perceive,' said my companion. 'The keeper was violently opposed to the railroad; and well he might be, as the track left his house of entertainment on one side, and thus was pretty certain to deprive him of all his reputable customers. But the footpath still passes his door; and the old gentleman now and then receives a call from some simple traveller, and entertains him with fare as old-fashioned as himself.'

Before our talk on this subject came to a conclusion, we were rushing by the place where Christian's burden fell from his shoulders at the sight of the Cross. This served as a theme for Mr. Smooth-it-away, Mr. Live-for-the-world, Mr. Hide-sin-in-the-heart, Mr. Scaly-conscience, and a knot of gentlemen from the town of Shun-repentance, to descant upon the inestimable advantages resulting from the safety of our baggage. Myself, and all the passengers indeed, joined with great unanimity in this view of the matter; for our burdens were rich in many things esteemed precious throughout the world; and, especially, we each of us possessed a great variety of favourite Habits, which we trusted would not be out of fashion even in the polite circles of the Celestial City. It would have been a sad spectacle to see such an assortment of valuable articles tumbling into the sepulchre. Thus pleasantly conversing on the favourable circumstances of our position as compared with those of past pilgrims and of narrow-minded ones at the present day, we soon found ourselves at the foot of the Hill Difficulty.* Through the very heart of this rocky mountain a tunnel has been constructed of most admirable architecture, with a lofty arch and a spacious double track; so that, unless the earth and rocks should chance to crumble down, it will remain an eternal monument of the builder's skill and enterprise. It is a great though incidental advantage that the materials from the heart of the Hill Difficulty have been employed in filling up the Valley of Humiliation, thus obviating the necessity of descending into that disagreeable and unwholesome hollow.

'This is a wonderful improvement, indeed,' said I. 'Yet I should have been glad of an opportunity to visit the Palace Beautiful and be introduced to the charming young ladies—Miss Prudence, Miss Piety, Miss Charity, and the rest—who have the kindness to entertain pilgrims there.'

'Young ladies!' cried Mr. Smooth-it-away, as soon as he could speak for laughing. 'And charming young ladies! Why, my dear fellow, they are old maids, every soul of them,—prim, starched, dry, and angular; and not one of them, I will venture to say, has altered so much as the fashion of her gown since the days of Christian's pilgrimage.'

'Ah, well,' said I, much comforted, 'then I can very readily dispense with their acquaintance.'

The respectable Apollyon was now putting on the steam at a prodigious rate, anxious, perhaps, to get rid of the unpleasant reminiscences connected with the spot where he had so disastrously encountered Christian. Consulting Mr. Bunyan's road-book, I perceived that we must now be within a few miles of the Valley of the Shadow of Death,* into which doleful region, at our present speed, we should plunge much sooner than seemed at all desirable. In truth, I expected nothing better than to find myself in the ditch on one side or the quag on the other; but on communicating my apprehensions to Mr. Smooth-it-away, he assured me that the difficulties of this passage, even in its worst condition, had been vastly exaggerated, in that, in its present state of improvement, I might consider myself as safe as on any railroad in Christendom.

Even while we were speaking, the train shot into the entrance of this dreaded Valley. Though I plead guilty to some foolish palpitations of the heart during our headlong rush over the causeway here constructed, yet it were unjust to withhold the highest encomiums on the boldness of its original conception and the ingenuity of those who executed it. It was gratifying, likewise, to observe how much care had been taken to dispel the everlasting gloom and supply the defect of cheerful sunshine, not a ray of which has ever penetrated among these awful shadows. For this purpose, the inflammable gas which exudes plentifully from the soil is collected by means of pipes, and thence communicated to a quadruple row of lamps along the whole extent of the passage. Thus a radiance has been created even out of the fiery and sulphurous curse that rests forever upon the Valley,— a radiance hurtful, however, to the eyes, and somewhat bewildering, as I discovered by the changes which it wrought in the visages of my companions. In this respect, as compared with natural daylight, there is the same difference as between truth and falsehood; but if the reader have ever travelled through the dark Valley, he will have learned to be thankful for any light that he could get,—if not from the sky above, then from the blasted soil beneath. Such was the red brilliancy of these lamps that they appeared to build walls of fire on both sides of the track, between which we held our course at lightning speed, while a reverberating thunder filled the Valley with its echoes. Had the engine run off the track,—a catastrophe, it is whispered, by no means unprecedented,—the bottomless pit, if there be any such place, would undoubtedly have received us. Just as some dismal fooleries of this nature had made my heart quake there came a tremendous shriek, careering along the Valley as if a thousand devils had burst their lungs to utter it, but which proved to be merely the whistle of the engine on arriving at a stopping-place.

The spot where we had now paused is the same that our friend Bunyan—a truthful man, but infected with many fantastic notions—has designated, in terms plainer than I like to repeat, as the mouth of the infernal region. This, however, must be a mistake, inasmuch as Mr. Smooth-it-away, while we remained in the smoky and lurid cavern, took occasion to prove that Tophet* has not even a metaphorical existence. The place, he assured us, is no other than the crater of a half-extinct volcano, in which the directors had caused forges to be set up for the manufacture of railroad-iron. Hence, also, is obtained a plentiful supply of fuel for the use of the engines. Whoever had gazed into the dismal obscurity of the broad cavern-mouth, whence ever and anon darted huge tongues of dusky flame, and had seen the strange, half-shaped monsters, and visions of faces horribly grotesque, into which the smoke seemed to wreathe itself, and had heard the awful murmurs, and shrieks, and deep, shuddering whispers of the blast sometimes forming themselves into words almost articulate, would have seized upon Mr. Smooth-it-away's comfortable explanation as greedily as we did. The inhabitants of the cavern, moreover, were unlovely personages, dark, smoke-begrimed, generally deformed, with misshapen feet, and a glow of dusky redness in their eyes as if their hearts had caught fire and were blazing out of the upper windows. It struck me as a peculiarity that the labourers at the forge and those who brought fuel to the engine, when they began to draw short breath, positively emitted smoke from their mouth and nostrils.

Among the idlers about the train, most of whom were puffing cigars which they had lighted at the flame of the crater, I was perplexed to notice several who, to my certain knowledge, had heretofore set forth by railroad for the Celestial City. They looked dark, wild, and smoky, with a singular resemblance, indeed, to the native inhabitants, like whom, also, they had a disagreeable propensity to ill-natured gibes and sneers, the habit of which had wrought a settled contortion of their visages. Having been on speaking terms with one of these persons,—an indolent, good-for-nothing fellow, who went by the name of Take-it-easy,—I called him, and inquired what was his business there.

'Did you not start,' said I, 'for the Celestial City?'

'That 's a fact,' said Mr. Take-it-easy, carelessly puffing some smoke into my eyes. 'But I heard such bad accounts that I never took pains to climb the hill on which the city stands. No business doing, no fun going on, nothing to drink, and no smoking allowed, and a thrumming of church-music from morning till night. I would not stay in such a place if they offered me house-room and living free.'

'But, my good Mr. Take-it-easy,' cried I, 'why take up your residence here, of all places in the world?'

'Oh,' said the loafer, with a grin, 'it is very warm hereabouts, and I meet with plenty of old acquaintances, and altogether the place suits me. I hope to see you back again some day soon. A pleasant journey to you.'

While he was speaking, the bell of the engine rang, and we

dashed away, after dropping a few passengers, but receiving no new ones. Rattling onward through the Valley, we were dazzled with the fiercely gleaming gas-lamps, as before. But sometimes, in the dark of intense brightness, grim faces, that bore the aspect and expression of individual sins, or evil passions, seemed to thrust themselves through the veil of light, glaring upon us, and stretching forth a great, dusky hand, as if to impede our progress. I almost thought that they were my own sins that appalled me there. These were freaks of imagination,—nothing more, certainly,—mere delusions, which I ought to be heartily ashamed of; but all through the Dark Valley I was tormented and pestered and dolefully bewildered with the same kind of waking dreams. The mephitic gases of that region intoxicate the brain. As the light of natural day, however, began to struggle with the glow of the lanterns, these vain imaginations lost their vividness, and finally vanished with the first ray of sunshine that greeted our escape from the Valley of the Shadow of Death. Ere we had gone a mile beyond it, I could wellnigh have taken my oath that this whole gloomy passage was a dream.

At the end of the Valley, as John Bunyan mentions, is a cavern, where, in his days, dwelt two cruel giants, Pope and Pagan,* who had strewn the ground about their residence with the bones of slaughtered pilgrims. These vile old troglodytes are no longer there; but into their deserted cave another terrible giant has thrust himself, and makes it his business to seize upon honest travellers and fatten them for his table with plentiful meals of smoke, mist, moonshine, raw potatoes, and sawdust. He is a German by birth, and is called Giant Transcendentalist;* but as to his form, his features, his substance, and his nature generally, it is the chief peculiarity of this huge miscreant, that neither he for himself, nor anybody for him, has ever been able to describe them. As we rushed by the cavern's mouth we caught a hasty glimpse of him, looking somewhat like an ill-proportioned figure, but considerably more like a heap of fog and duskiness. He shouted after us, but in so strange a phraseology that we knew not what he meant, nor whether to be encouraged or affrighted.

It was late in the day when the train thundered into the ancient city of Vanity, where Vanity Fair* is still at the height of prosperity, and exhibits an epitome of whatever is brilliant, gay, and fascinating beneath the sun. As I purposed to make a considerable stay here, it gratified me to learn that there is no longer the want of harmony between the townspeople and pilgrims, which impelled the former to such lamentably mistaken measures as the persecution of Christian and the fiery martyrdom of Faithful. On the contrary, as the new railroad brings with it great trade and a constant influx of strangers, the lord of Vanity Fair is its chief patron, and the capitalists of the city are among the largest stockholders. Many passengers stop to take their pleasure or make their profit in the Fair, instead of going onward to the Celestial City. Indeed, such are the charms of the place that people often affirm it to be the true and only heaven; stoutly contending that there is no other, that those who seek farther are mere dreamers, and that, if the fabled brightness of the Celestial City lay but a bare mile beyond the gates of Vanity, they would not be fools enough to go thither. Without subscribing to these perhaps exaggerated encomiums, I can truly say that my abode in the city was mainly agreeable, and my intercourse with the inhabitants productive of much amusement and instruction.

Being naturally of a serious turn, my attention was directed to the solid advantages derivable from a residence here, rather than to the effervescent pleasures which are the grand object with too many visitants. The Christian reader, if he have had no accounts of the city later than Bunyan's time, will be surprised to hear that almost every street has its church, and that the reverend clergy are nowhere held in higher respect than at Vanity Fair. And well do they deserve such honourable estimation; for the maxims of wisdom and virtue which fall from their lips come from as deep a spiritual source, and tend to as lofty a religious aim, as those of the sagest philosophers of old. In justification of this high praise I need only mention the names of the Rev. Mr. Shallow-deep, the Rev. Mr. Stumble-at-truth, that fine old clerical character the Rev. Mr. This-to-day, who expects shortly to resign his pulpit to the Rev. Mr. That-to-morrow; together with the Rev. Mr.

Bewilderment, the Rev. Mr. Clog-the-spirit, and, last and greatest, the Rev. Dr. Wind-of-doctrine. The labours of these eminent divines are aided by those of innumerable lecturers, who diffuse such a various profundity, in all subjects of human or celestial science, that any man may acquire an omnigenous erudition without the trouble of even learning to read. Thus literature is etherealized by assuming for its medium the human voice; and knowledge, depositing all its heavier particles, except, doubtless, its gold, becomes exhaled into a sound, which forthwith steals into the ever-open ear of the community. These ingenious methods constitute a sort of machinery, by which thought and study are done to every person's hand without his putting himself to the slightest inconvenience in the matter. There is another species of machine for the wholesale manufacture of individual morality. This excellent result is effected by societies for all manner of virtuous purposes, with which a man has merely to connect himself, throwing, as it were, his quota of virtue into the common stock, and the president and directors will take care that the aggregate amount be well applied. All these, and other wonderful improvements in ethics, religion, and literature, being made plain to my comprehension by the ingenious Mr. Smooth-it-away, inspired me with a vast admiration of Vanity Fair.

It would fill a volume, in an age of pamphlets, were I to record all my observations in this great capital of human business and pleasure. There was an unlimited range of society,—the powerful, the wise, the witty, and the famous in every walk of life; princes, presidents, poets, generals, artists, actors, and philanthropists,—all making his own market at the fair, and deeming no price too exorbitant for such commodities as hit their fancy. It was well worth one's while, even if he had no idea of buying or selling, to loiter through the bazaars and observe the various sorts of traffic that were going forward.

Some of the purchasers, I thought, made very foolish bargains. For instance, a young man having inherited a splendid fortune, laid out a considerable portion of it in the purchase of diseases, and finally spent all the rest for a heavy lot of repentance and a suit of rags. A very pretty girl bartered a heart as clear as crystal, and which seemed her most valuable possession, for another jewel of the same kind, but so worn and defaced as to be utterly worthless. In one shop there were a great many crowns of laurel and myrtle, which soldiers, authors, statesmen, and various other people pressed eagerly to buy; some purchased these paltry wreaths with their lives, others by a toilsome servitude of years, and many sacrificed whatever was most valuable, yet finally slunk away without the crown. There was a sort of stock or scrip, called Conscience, which seemed to be in great demand, and would purchase almost anything. Indeed, few rich commodities were to be obtained without paying a heavy sum in this particular stock, and a man's business was seldom very lucrative unless he knew precisely when and how to throw his hoard of conscience into the market. Yet, as this stock was the only thing of permanent value, whoever parted with it was sure to find himself a loser in the long run. Several of the speculations were of a questionable character. Occasionally a member of Congress recruited his pocket by the sale of his constituents; and I was assured that public officers have often sold their country at very moderate prices. Thousands sold their happiness for a whim. Gilded chains were in great demand, and purchased with almost any sacrifice. In truth, those who desired, according to the old adage, to sell anything valuable for a song, might find customers all over the Fair; and there were innumerable messes of pottage, piping hot, for such as chose to buy them with their birthrights. A few articles, however, could not be found genuine at Vanity Fair. If a customer wished to renew his stock of youth, the dealers offered him a set of false teeth and an auburn wig; if he demanded peace of mind, they recommended opium or a brandy-bottle.

Tracts of land and golden mansions, situate in the Celestial City, were often exchanged, at very disadvantageous rates, for a few years' lease of small, dismal, inconvenient tenements in Vanity Fair. Prince Beelzebub himself took great interest in this sort of traffic, and sometimes condescended to meddle with smaller matters. I once had the pleasure to see him bargaining with a miser for his soul, which, after much ingenious skirmishing on both sides, his highness succeeded in obtaining at about the value of sixpence. The prince remarked, with a smile, that he was a loser by the transaction.

Day after day, as I walked the streets of Vanity, my manners and deportment became more and more like those of the inhabitants. The place began to seem like home; the idea of pursuing my travels to the Celestial City was almost obliterated from my mind. I was reminded of it, however, by the sight of the same pair of simple pilgrims at whom we had laughed so heartily when Apollyon puffed smoke and steam into their faces at the commencement of our journey. There they stood, amid the densest bustle of Vanity; the dealers offering them their purple and fine linen and jewels, the men of wit and humour gibing at them, a pair of buxom ladies ogling them askance, while the benevolent Mr. Smooth-it-away whispered some of his wisdom at their elbows, and pointed to a newly erected temple; but there were these worthy simpletons, making the scene look wild and monstrous, merely by their sturdy repudiation of all part in its business or pleasures.

One of them—his name was Stick-to-the-right—perceived in my face, I suppose, a species of sympathy and almost admiration, which, to my own great surprise, I could not help feeling for this pragmatic couple. It prompted him to address me.

'Sir,' inquired he, with a sad, yet mild and kindly voice, 'do you call yourself a pilgrim?'

'Yes,' I replied, 'my right to that appellation is indubitable. I am merely a sojourner here in Vanity Fair, being bound to the Celestial City by the new railroad.'

'Alas, friend,' rejoined Mr. Stick-to-the-right, 'I do assure you, and beseech you to receive the truth of my words, that that whole concern is a bubble. You may travel on it all your lifetime, were you to live thousands of years, and yet never get beyond the limits of Vanity Fair. Yea, though you should deem yourself entering the gates of the blessed city, it will be nothing but a miserable delusion.'

'The Lord of the Celestial City,' began the other pilgrim,

whose name was Mr. Foot-it-to-heaven, 'has refused, and will ever refuse, to grant an act of incorporation for this railroad; and, unless that be obtained, no passenger can ever hope to enter his dominions. Wherefore every man who buys a ticket must lay his account with losing the purchase-money, which is the value of his own soul.'

'Poh, nonsense!' said Mr. Smooth-it-away, taking my arm and leading me off, 'these fellows ought to be indicted for a libel. If the law stood as it once did in Vanity Fair, we should see them grinning through the iron bars of the prison-window.'

This incident made a considerable impression on my mind, and contributed with other circumstances to indispose me to a permanent residence in the city of Vanity; although, of course, I was not simple enough to give up my original plan of gliding along easily and commodiously by railroad. Still, I grew anxious to be gone. There was one strange thing that troubled me. Amid the occupations or amusements of the Fair, nothing was more common than for a person—whether at feast, theatre, or church, or trafficking for wealth and honours, or whatever he might be doing, and however unseasonable the interruption—suddenly to vanish like a soap-bubble, and be never more seen of his fellows; and so accustomed were the latter to such little accidents, that they went on with their business as quietly as if nothing had happened. But it was otherwise with me.

Finally, after a pretty long residence at the Fair, I resumed my journey towards the Celestial City, still with Mr. Smooth-it-away at my side. At a short distance beyond the suburbs of Vanity we passed the ancient silver-mine, of which Demas* was the first discoverer, and which is now wrought to great advantage, supplying nearly all the coined currency of the world. A little farther onward is the spot where Lot's wife had stood forever under the semblance of a pillar of salt. Curious travellers have long since carried it away piecemeal. Had all regrets been punished as rigorously as this poor dame's were, my yearning for the relinquished delights of Vanity Fair might have produced a similar change in my own corporeal substance, and left me a warning to future pilgrims.

The next remarkable object was a large edifice, constructed of moss-grown stone, but in a modern and airy style of architecture. The engine came to a pause in its vicinity, with the usual tremendous shriek.

'This was formerly the castle of the redoubted Giant Despair,' observed Mr. Smooth-it-away; 'but since his death Mr. Flimsy-faith has repaired it, and keeps an excellent house of entertainment here. It is one of our stopping-places.'

'It seems but slightly put together,' remarked I, looking at the frail yet ponderous walls. 'I do not envy Mr. Flimsy-faith his habitation. Some day it will thunder down upon the heads of the occupants.'

'We shall escape, at all events,' said Mr. Smooth-it-away, 'for Apollyon is putting on the steam again.'

The road now plunged into a gorge of the Delectable Mountains,* and traversed the field where in former ages the blind men wandered and stumbled among the tombs. One of these ancient tombstones had been thrust across the track by some malicious person, and gave the train of cars a terrible jolt. Far up the rugged side of a mountain I perceived a rusty iron door, half overgrown with bushes and creeping plants, but with smoke issuing from its crevices.

'It that,' inquired I, 'the very door in the hillside which the shepherds assured Christian was a byway to hell?'*

'That was a joke on the part of the shepherds,' said Mr. Smooth-it-away, with a smile. 'It is neither more nor less than the door of a cavern which they use as a smoke-house for the preparation of mutton hams.'

My recollections of the journey are now, for a little space, dim and confused, inasmuch as a singular drowsiness here overcame me, owing to the fact that we were passing over the enchanted ground, the air of which encourages a disposition to sleep. I awoke, however, as soon as we crossed the borders of the pleasant land of Beulah.* All the passengers were rubbing their eyes, comparing watches, and congratulating one another on the prospect of arriving so seasonably at the journey's end. The sweet breezes of this happy clime came refreshingly to our nostrils; we beheld the glimmering gush of silver fountains, overhung by trees of beautiful foliage and delicious fruit, which were propagated by grafts from the celestial gardens. Once, as we dashed onward like a hurricane, there was a flutter of wings and the bright appearance of an angel in the air, speeding forth on some heavenly mission. The engine now announced the close vicinity of the final station-house, by one last and horrible scream, in which there seemed to be distinguishable every kind of wailing and woe, and bitter fierceness of wrath, all mixed up with the wild laughter of a devil or a madman. Throughout our journey, at every stopping-place, Apollyon had exercised his ingenuity in screwing the most abominable sounds out of the whistle of the steam-engine; but in this closing effort he outdid himself and created an infernal uproar, which, besides disturbing the peaceful inhabitants of Beulah, must have sent its discord even through the celestial gates.

While the horrid clamour was still ringing in our ears, we heard an exulting strain, as if a thousand instruments of music, with height and depth and sweetness in their tones, at once tender and triumphant, were struck in unison, to greet the approach of some illustrious hero, who had fought the good fight and won a glorious victory, and was come to lay aside his battered arms forever. Looking to ascertain what might be the occasion of this glad harmony, I perceived, on alighting from the cars, that a multitude of shining ones had assembled on the other side of the river, to welcome two poor pilgrims, who were just emerging from its depths. They were the same whom Apollyon and ourselves had persecuted with taunts and gibes and scalding steam, at the commencement of our journey,—the same whose unworldly aspect and impressive words had stirred my conscience amid the wild revellers of Vanity Fair.

'How amazingly well those men have got on!' cried I to Mr. Smooth-it-away. 'I wish we were secure of as good a reception.'

'Never fear, never fear!' answered my friend. 'Come, make haste; the ferry-boat* will be off directly, and in three minutes you will be on the other side of the river. No doubt you will find coaches to carry you up to the city gates.'

A steam ferry-boat, the last improvement on this important

route, lay at the river-side, puffing, snorting, and emitting all those other disagreeable utterances which betoken the departure to be immediate. I hurried on board with the rest of the passengers, most of whom were in great perturbation; some bawling out for their baggage; some tearing their hair and exclaiming that the boat would explode or sink; some already pale with the heaving of the stream; some gazing affrighted at the ugly aspect of the steersman; and some still dizzy with the slumberous influences of the Enchanted Ground. Looking back to the shore, I was amazed to discern Mr. Smooth-it-away waving his hand in token of farewell.

'Don't you go over to the Celestial City?' exclaimed I.

'Oh no!' answered he with a queer smile, and that same disagreeable contortion of visage which I had remarked in the inhabitants of the Dark Valley. 'Oh no! I have come thus far only for the sake of your pleasant company. Good-bye! We shall meet again.'

And then did my excellent friend Mr. Smooth-it-away laugh outright, in the midst of which cachinnation a smoke-wreath issued from his mouth and nostrils, while a twinkle of lurid flame darted out of either eye, proving indubitably that his heart was all of a red blaze. The impudent fiend! To deny the existence of Tophet, when he felt its fiery tortures raging within his breast. I rushed to the side of the boat, intending to fling myself on shore; but the wheels, as they began their revolutions, threw a dash of spray over me so cold—so deadly cold, with the chill that will never leave those waters until Death be drowned in his own river—that, with a shiver and a heartquake, I awoke. Thank Heaven it was a Dream!

THE CHRISTMAS BANQUET

[From the unpublished 'Allegories of the Heart'.] *

'I HAVE here attempted,' said Roderick,* unfolding a few sheets of manuscript, as he sat with Rosina and the sculptor in the summer-house,—'I have attempted to seize hold of a personage who glides past me, occasionally, in my walk through life. My former sad experience, as you know, has gifted me with some degree of insight into the gloomy mysteries of the human heart, through which I have wandered like one astray in a dark cavern,* with his torch fast flickering to extinction. But this man, this class of men, is a hopeless puzzle.'

'Well, but propound him,' said the sculptor. 'Let us have an idea of him, to begin with.'

'Why, indeed,' replied Roderick, 'he is such a being as I could conceive you to carve out of marble, and some yet unrealized perfection of human science to endow with an exquisite mockery of intellect; but still there lacks the last inestimable touch of a divine Creator. He looks like man; and, perchance, like a better specimen of man than you ordinarily meet. You might esteem him wise; he is capable of cultivation and refinement, and has at least an external conscience; but the demands that spirit makes upon spirit are precisely those to which he cannot respond. When at last you come close to him you find him chill and unsubstantial,—a mere vapour.'

'I believe,' said Rosina, 'I have a glimmering idea of what you mean.'

'Then be thankful,' answered her husband, smiling; 'but do not anticipate any further illumination from what I am about to read. I have here imagined such a man to be—what, probably, he never is—conscious of the deficiency in his spiritual organization. Methinks the result would be a sense of cold unreality wherewith he would go shivering through the world, longing to exchange his load of ice for any burden of real grief that fate could fling upon a human being.'

Contenting himself with this preface, Roderick began to read.

In a certain old gentleman's last will and testament there appeared a bequest, which, as his final thought and deed, was singularly in keeping with a long life of melancholy eccentricity. He devised a considerable sum for establishing a fund, the interest of which was to be expended annually for ever, in preparing a Christmas Banquet for ten of the most miserable persons that could be found. It seemed not to be the testator's purpose to make these half a score of sad hearts merry, but to provide that the stern or fierce expression of human discontent should not be drowned, even for that one holy and joyful day, amid the acclamations of festal gratitude which all Christendom sends up. And he desired, likewise, to perpetuate his own remonstrance against the earthly course of Providence, and his sad and sour dissent from those systems of religion or philosophy which either find sunshine in the world or draw it down from heaven.

The task of inviting the guests, or of selecting among such as might advance their claims to partake of this dismal hospitality, was confided to the two trustees or stewards of the fund. These gentlemen, like their deceased friend, were sombre humorists, who made it their principal occupation to number the sable threads in the web of human life, and drop all the golden ones out of the reckoning. They performed their present office with integrity and judgement. The aspect of the assembled company, on the day of the first festival, might not, it is true, have satisfied every beholder that these were especially the individuals, chosen forth from all the world, whose griefs were worthy to stand as indicators of the mass of human suffering. Yet after due consideration, it could not be disputed that here was a variety of hopeless discomfort, which, if it sometimes arose from causes apparently inadequate, was thereby only the shrewder imputation against the nature and mechanism of life.

The arrangements and decorations of the banquet were probably intended to signify that death in life which had been the testator's definition of existence. The hall, illuminated by torches, was hung round with curtains of deep and dusky purple, and adorned with branches of cypress and wreaths of artificial flowers, imitative of such as used to be strewn over the dead. A sprig of parsley was laid by every plate. The main reservoir of wine was a sepulchral urn of silver, whence the liquor was distributed around the table in small vases, accurately copied from those that held tears of ancient mourners. Neither had the stewards—if it were their taste that arranged these details—forgotten the fantasy of the old Egyptians, who seated a skeleton at every festive board, and mocked their own merriment with the imperturbable grin of a death's-head. Such a fearful guest, shrouded in a black mantle, sat now at the head of the table. It was whispered, I know not with what truth, that the testator himself had once walked the visible world with the machinery of that same skeleton, and that it was one of the stipulations of his will, that he should thus be permitted to sit, from year to year, at the banquet which he had instituted. If so, it was perhaps covertly implied that he had cherished no hopes of bliss beyond the grave to compensate for the evils which he felt or imagined here. And if, in their bewildered conjectures as to the purpose of earthly existence, the banqueters should throw aside the veil, and cast an inquiring glance at this figure of death, as seeking thence the solution otherwise unattainable, the only reply would be a stare of the vacant eye caverns and a grin of the skeleton jaws. Such was the response that the dead man had fancied himself to receive when he asked of Death to solve the riddle of his life; and it was his desire to repeat it when the guests of his dismal hospitality should find themselves perplexed with the same question.

'What means that wreath?' asked several of the company, while viewing the decorations of the table.

They alluded to a wreath of cypress, which was held on high by a skeleton arm, protruding from within the black mantle.

'It is a crown,' said one of the stewards, 'not for the worthiest, but for the wofulest, when he shall prove his claim to it.'

The guest earliest bidden to the festival was a man of soft and gentle character, who had not energy to struggle against the heavy despondency to which his temperament rendered him liable; and therefore with nothing outwardly to excuse him from happiness, he had spent a life of quiet misery that made his blood torpid, and weighed upon his breath, and sat like a ponderous night-fiend upon every throb of his unresisting heart. His wretchedness seemed as deep as his original nature, if not identical with it. It was the misfortune of a second guest to cherish within his bosom a diseased heart, which had become so wretchedly sore that the continual and unavoidable rubs of the world, the blow of an enemy, the careless jostle of a stranger, and even the faithful and loving touch of a friend, alike made ulcers in it. As is the habit of people thus afflicted, he found his chief employment in exhibiting these miserable sores to any who would give themselves the pain of viewing them. A third guest was a hypochondriac, whose imagination wrought necromancy in his outward and inward world, and caused him to see monstrous faces in the household fire, and dragons in the clouds of sunset, and fiends in the guise of beautiful women, and something ugly or wicked beneath all the pleasant surfaces of nature. His neighbour at table was one who, in his early youth, had trusted mankind too much, and hoped too highly in their behalf, and, in meeting with many disappointments, had become desperately soured. For several years back this misanthrope had employed himself in accumulating motives for hating and despising his race,—such as murder, lust, treachery, ingratitude, faithlessness of trusted friends, instinctive vices of children, impurity of women, hidden guilt in men of saint-like aspect,—and, in short, all manner of black realities that sought to decorate themselves with outward grace or glory. But at every atrocious fact that was added to his catalogue, at every increase of the sad knowledge which he spent his life to collect, the native impulses of the poor man's loving and confiding heart made him groan with anguish. Next, with his heavy brow bent downward, there stole into the hall a man naturally earnest and impassioned, who, from his immemorial infancy, had felt the consciousness of a high message to the world; but, essaying to deliver it, had found either no voice or form of speech, or else no ears to listen. Therefore his whole life was a bitter questioning of himself: 'Why have not men acknowledged my mission? Am I not a self-deluding fool? What business have I on earth? Where is my grave?' Throughout the festival, he quaffed frequent draughts from the sepulchral urn of wine, hoping thus to quench the celestial fire that tortured his own breast and could not benefit his race.

Then there entered, having flung away a ticket for a ball, a gay gallant of yesterday, who had found four or five wrinkles in his brow, and more grey hairs than he could well number

on his head. Endowed with sense and feeling, he had
nevertheless spent his youth in folly, but had reached at last
that dreary point in life where Folly quits us of her own
accord, leaving us to make friends with Wisdom if we can.
Thus, cold and desolate, he had come to seek Wisdom at the
banquet, and wondered if the skeleton were she. To eke out
the company, the stewards had invited a distressed poet from
his home in the almshouse, and a melancholy idiot from the
street-corner. The latter had just the glimmering of sense that
was sufficient to make him conscious of a vacancy, which
the poor fellow, all his life long, had mistily sought to fill up
with intelligence, wandering up and down* the streets, and
groaning miserably because his attempts were ineffectual. The
only lady in the hall was one who had fallen short of absolute
and perfect beauty, merely by the trifling defect of a slight cast
in her left eye. But this blemish, minute as it was, so shocked
the pure ideal of her soul, rather than her vanity, that she
passed her life in solitude, and veiled her countenance even
from her own gaze. So the skeleton sat shrouded at one end
of the table, and this poor lady at the other.

One other guest remains to be described. He was a young
man of smooth brow, fair cheeks, and fashionable mien. So far
as his exterior developed him, he might much more suitably
have found a place at some merry Christmas table, than have
been numbered among the blighted, fate-stricken, fancy-
tortured set of ill-starred banqueters. Murmurs arose among
the guests as they noted the glance of general scrutiny which
the intruder threw over his companions. What had he to do
among them? Why did not the skeleton of the dead founder
of the feast unbend its rattling joints, arise, and motion the
unwelcome stranger from the board?

'Shameful!' said the morbid man, while a new ulcer broke
out in his heart. 'He comes to mock us!—we shall be the jest
of his tavern friends!—he will make a farce of our miseries,
and bring it out upon the stage!'

'Oh, never mind him!' said the hypochondriac, smiling
sourly. 'He shall feast from yonder tureen of viper-soup; and
if there is a fricassee of scorpions on the table, pray let him
have his share of it. For the dessert, he shall taste the apples

of Sodom.* Then, if he like our Christmas fare, let him return again next year!'

'Trouble him not,' murmured the melancholy man, with gentleness. 'What matters it whether the consciousness of misery come a few years sooner or later? If this youth deem himself happy now, yet let him sit with us for the sake of the wretchedness to come.'

The poor idiot approached the young man with that mournful aspect of vacant inquiry which his face continually wore, and which caused people to say that he was always in search of his missing wits. After no little examination he touched the stranger's hand, but immediately drew back his own, shaking his head and shivering.

'Cold, cold, cold!' muttered the idiot.

The young man shivered too, and smiled.

'Gentlemen, and you, madam,' said one of the stewards of the festival, 'do not conceive so ill either of our caution or judgement, as to imagine that we have admitted this young stranger—Gervayse Hastings by name—without a full investigation and thoughtful balance of his claims. Trust me, not a guest at the table is better entitled to his seat.'

The steward's guaranty was perforce satisfactory. The company, therefore, took their places, and addressed themselves to the serious business of the feast, but were soon disturbed by the hypochondriac, who thrust back his chair, complaining that a dish of stewed toads and vipers was set before him, and that there was green ditchwater in his cup of wine. This mistake being amended, he quietly resumed his seat. The wine, as it flowed freely from the sepulchral urn, seemed to come imbued with all gloomy inspirations; so that its influence was not to cheer, but either to sink the revellers into a deeper melancholy, or elevate their spirits to an enthusiasm of wretchedness. The conversation was various. They told sad stories about people who might have been worthy guests at such a festival as the present. They talked of grisly incidents in human history; of strange crimes, which, if truly considered were but convulsions of agony; of some lives that had been altogether wretched, and of others which, wearing a general semblance of happiness, had yet

been deformed, sooner or later, by misfortune, as by the
intrusion of a grim face at a banquet; of deathbed scenes, and
what dark intimations might be gathered from the words of
dying men; of suicide, and whether the more eligible mode
were by halter, knife, poison, drowning, gradual starvation, or
the fumes of charcoal. The majority of the guests, as is the
custom with people thoroughly and profoundly sick at heart,
were anxious to make their own woes the theme of discussion, and prove themselves most excellent in anguish. The
misanthropist went deep into the philosophy of evil, and
wandered about in the darkness, with now and then a gleam
of discoloured light hovering on ghastly shapes and horrid
scenery. Many a miserable thought, such as men have
stumbled upon from age to age, did he now rake up again, and
gloat over it as an inestimable gem, a diamond, a treasure far
preferable to those bright, spiritual revelations of a better
world, which are like precious stones from heaven's pavement. And then, amid his lore of wretchedness he hid his face
and wept.

It was a festival at which the woful man of Uz* might
suitably have been a guest, together with all, in each
succeeding age, who have tasted deepest of the bitterness of
life. And be it said, too, that every son or daughter of woman,
however favoured with happy fortune, might, at one sad
moment or another, have claimed the privilege of a stricken
heart, to sit down at this table. But throughout the feast it was
remarked that the young stranger, Gervayse Hastings, was
unsuccessful in his attempts to catch its pervading spirit. At
any deep, strong thought that found utterance, and which was
torn out, as it were, from the saddest recesses of human
consciousness, he looked mystified and bewildered; even more
than the poor idiot, who seemed to grasp at such things with
his earnest heart, and thus occasionally to comprehend them.
The young man's conversation was of a colder and lighter
kind, often brilliant, but lacking the powerful characteristics
of a nature that had been developed by suffering.

'Sir,' said the misanthropist, bluntly, in reply to some
observation by Gervayse Hastings, 'pray do not address me
again. We have no right to talk together. Our minds have

nothing in common. By what claim you appear at this banquet I cannot guess; but methinks, to a man who could say what you have just now said, my companions and myself must seem no more than shadows flickering on the wall. And precisely such a shadow are you to us.'

The young man smiled and bowed, but, drawing himself back in his chair, he buttoned his coat over his breast, as if the banqueting-hall were growing chill. Again the idiot fixed his melancholy stare upon the youth, and murmured, 'Cold! cold! cold!'

The banquet drew to its conclusion, and the guests departed. Scarcely had they stepped across the threshold of the hall, when the scene that had there passed seemed like the vision of a sick fancy, or an exhalation from a stagnant heart. Now and then, however, during the year that ensued, these melancholy people caught glimpses of one another, transient, indeed, but enough to prove that they walked the earth with the ordinary allotment of reality. Sometimes a pair of them came face to face, while stealing through the evening twilight, enveloped in their sable cloaks. Sometimes they casually met in churchyards. Once, also, it happened that two of the dismal banqueters mutually started at recognizing each other in the noonday sunshine of a crowded street, stalking there like ghosts astray. Doubtless they wondered why the skeleton did not come abroad at noonday too.

But whenever the necessity of their affairs compelled these Christmas guests into the bustling world, they were sure to encounter the young man who had so unaccountably been admitted to the festival. They saw him among the gay and fortunate; they caught the sunny sparkle of his eye; they heard the light and careless tones of his voice, and muttered to themselves with such indignation as only the aristocracy of wretchedness could kindle, 'The traitor! The vile impostor! Providence, in its own good time, may give him a right to feast among us!' But the young man's unabashed eye dwelt upon their gloomy figures as they passed him, seeming to say, perchance with somewhat of a sneer, 'First, know my secret!—then, measure your claims with mine!'

The steps of Time stole onward, and soon brought merry

Christmas round again, with glad and solemn worship in the churches, and sports, games, festivals, and everywhere the bright face of Joy beside the household fire. Again likewise the hall, with its curtains of dusky purple, was illuminated by the death-torches gleaming on the sepulchral decorations of the banquet. The veiled skeleton sat in state, lifting the cypress-wreath above its head, as the guerdon of some guest illustrious in the qualifications which there claimed precedence. As the stewards deemed the world inexhaustible in misery, and were desirous of recognizing it in all its forms, they had not seen fit to reassemble the company of the former year. New faces now threw their gloom across the table.

There was a man of nice conscience, who bore a bloodstain in his heart—the death of a fellow-creature—which, for his more exquisite torture, had chanced with such a peculiarity of circumstances, that he could not absolutely determine whether his will had entered into the deed or not. Therefore his whole life was spent in the agony of an inward trial for murder, with a continual sifting of the details of his terrible calamity, until his mind had no longer any thought, nor his soul any emotion, disconnected with it. There was a mother, too—a mother once, but a desolation now,—who, many years before, had gone out on a pleasure-party, and, returning, found her infant smothered in its little bed. And ever since she has been tortured with the fantasy that her buried baby lay smothering in its coffin. Then there was an aged lady, who had lived from time immemorial with a constant tremor quivering through her frame. It was terrible to discern her dark shadow tremulous upon the wall; her lips, likewise, were tremulous; and the expression of her eye seemed to indicate that her soul was trembling too. Owing to the bewilderment and confusion which made almost a chaos of her intellect, it was impossible to discover what dire misfortune had thus shaken her nature to its depths; so that the stewards had admitted her to the table, not from any acquaintance with her history, but on the safe testimony of her miserable aspect. Some surprise was expressed at the presence of a bluff, red-faced gentleman, a certain Mr. Smith, who had evidently the fat of many a rich feast within him, and the habitual twinkle of whose eye betrayed a disposition to break forth into uproarious laughter for little cause or none. It turned out, however, that, with the best possible flow of spirits, our poor friend was afflicted with a physical disease of the heart, which threatened instant death on the slightest cachinnatory indulgence, or even that titillation of the bodily frame produced by merry thoughts. In this dilemma he had sought admittance to the banquet, on the ostensible plea of his irksome and miserable state, but, in reality, with the hope of imbibing a life-preserving melancholy.

A married couple had been invited from a motive of bitter humour, it being well understood that they rendered each other unutterably miserable whenever they chanced to meet, and therefore must necessarily be fit associates at the festival. In contrast with these was another couple still unmarried, who had interchanged their hearts in early life, but had been divided by circumstances as impalpable as morning mist, and kept apart so long that their spirits now found it impossible to meet. Therefore, yearning for communion, yet shrinking from one another and choosing none beside, they felt themselves companionless in life, and looked upon eternity as a boundless desert. Next to the skeleton sat a mere son of earth,—a hunter of the Exchange,—a gatherer of shining dust,—a man whose life's record was in his ledger, and whose soul's prison-house the vaults of the bank where he kept his deposits. This person had been greatly perplexed at his invitation, deeming himself one of the most fortunate men in the city; but the stewards persisted in demanding his presence, assuring him that he had no conception how miserable he was.

And now appeared a figure which we must acknowledge as our acquaintance of the former festival. It was Gervayse Hastings, whose presence had then caused so much question and criticism, and who now took his place with the composure of one whose claims were satisfactory to himself and must needs be allowed by others. Yet his easy and unruffled face betrayed no sorrow. The well-skilled beholders gazed a moment into his eyes and shook their heads, to miss the unuttered sympathy—the countersign never to be falsified—of those whose hearts are cavern-mouths through which they descend into a region of illimitable woe and recognize other wanderers there.

'Who is this youth?' asked the man with a bloodstain on his conscience. 'Surely he has never gone down into the depths! I know all the aspects of those who have passed through the dark valley. By what right is he among us?'

'Ah, it is a sinful thing to come hither without a sorrow,' murmured the aged lady, in accents that partook of the eternal tremor which pervaded her whole being. 'Depart, young man! Your soul has never been shaken, and, therefore, I tremble so much the more to look at you.'

'His soul shaken! No; I'll answer for it,' said bluff Mr. Smith, pressing his hand upon his heart and making himself as melancholy as he could, for fear of a fatal explosion of laughter. 'I know the lad well; he has as fair prospects as any young man about town, and has no more right among us miserable creatures than the child unborn. He never was miserable, and probably never will be!'

'Our honoured guests,' interposed the stewards, 'pray have patience with us, and believe, at least, that our deep veneration for the sacredness of this solemnity would preclude any wilful violation of it. Receive this young man to your table. It may not be too much to say, that no guest here would exchange his own heart for the one that beats within that youthful bosom!'

'I'd call it a bargain, and gladly, too,' muttered Mr. Smith, with a perplexing mixture of sadness and mirthful conceit. 'A plague upon their nonsense! My own heart is the only really miserable one in the company; it will certainly be the death of me at last!'

Nevertheless, as on the former occasion, the judgement of the stewards being without appeal, the company sat down. The obnoxious guest made no more attempt to obtrude his conversation on those about him, but appeared to listen to the table-talk with peculiar assiduity, as if some inestimable secret, otherwise beyond his reach, might be conveyed in a casual word. And in truth, to those who could understand and value it, there was rich matter in the upgushings and outpourings of these initiated souls to whom sorrow had been a talisman, admitting them into spiritual depths which no other spell can open. Sometimes out of the midst of densest gloom there flashed a momentary radiance, pure as crystal, bright as the flame of stars, and shedding such a glow upon the mysteries of life, that the guests were ready to exclaim, 'Surely the riddle is on the point of being solved!' At such illuminated intervals the saddest mourners felt it to be revealed that mortal griefs are but shadowy and external; no more than the sable robes voluminously shrouding a certain divine reality, and thus indicating what might otherwise be altogether invisible to mortal eye.

'Just now,' remarked the trembling old woman, 'I seemed to see beyond the outside. And then my everlasting tremor passed away!'

'Would that I could dwell always in these momentary gleams of light!' said the man of stricken conscience. 'Then the bloodstain in my heart would be washed clean away.'

This strain of conversation appeared so unintelligibly absurd to good Mr. Smith, that he burst into precisely the fit of laughter which his physicians had warned him against, as likely to prove instantaneously fatal. In effect, he fell back in his chair a corpse, with a broad grin upon his face, while his ghost, perchance, remained beside it bewildered at its unpremeditated exit. This catastrophe of course broke up the festival.

'How is this? You do not tremble!' observed the tremulous old woman to Gervayse Hastings, who was gazing at the dead man with singular intentness. 'Is it not awful to see him so suddenly vanish out of the midst of life,—this man of flesh and blood, whose earthly nature was so warm and strong? There is a never-ending tremor in my soul, but it trembles afresh at this! And you are calm!'

'Would that he could teach me somewhat!' said Gervayse Hastings, drawing a long breath. 'Men pass before me like shadows on the wall; their actions, passions, feelings, are flickerings of the light, and then they vanish! Neither the corpse, nor yonder skeleton, nor this old woman's everlasting tremor, can give me what I seek.'

And then the company departed.

We cannot linger to narrate, in such detail, more circumstances of these singular festivals, which, in accordance with the founder's will, continued to be kept with the regularity of an established institution. In process of time the stewards adopted the custom of inviting, from far and near, those individuals whose misfortunes were prominent above other men's, and whose mental and moral development might, therefore, be supposed to possess a corresponding interest. The exiled noble of the French Revolution and the broken soldier of the Empire were alike represented at the table. Fallen monarchs, wandering about the earth, have found places at that forlorn and miserable feast. The statesman, when his party flung him off, might, if he chose it, be once more a great man for the space of a single banquet. Aaron Burr's* name appears on the record at a period when his ruin—the profoundest and most striking, with more of moral circumstance in it than that of almost any other man—was complete in his lonely age. Stephen Girard,* when his wealth weighed upon him like a mountain, once sought admittance of his own accord. It is not probable, however, that these men had any lesson to teach in the lore of discontent and misery which might not equally well have been studied in the common walks of life. Illustrious unfortunates attract a wider sympathy, not because their griefs are more intense, but because, being set on lofty pedestals, they the better serve mankind as instances and bywords of calamity.

It concerns our present purpose to say that, at each successive festival, Gervayse Hastings showed his face, gradually changing from the smooth beauty of his youth to the thoughtful comeliness of manhood, and thence to the bald, impressive dignity of age. He was the only individual invariably present. Yet on every occasion there were murmurs, both from those who knew his character and position, and from them whose hearts shrank back as denying his companionship in their mystic fraternity.

'Who is this impassive man?' had been asked a hundred times. 'Has he suffered? Has he sinned? There are no traces of either. Then wherefore is he here?'

'You must inquire of the stewards or of himself,' was the

constant reply. 'We seem to know him well here in our city, and know nothing of him but what is creditable and fortunate. Yet hither he comes, year after year, to this gloomy banquet, and sits among the guests like a marble statue. Ask yonder skeleton, perhaps that may solve the riddle!'

It was in truth a wonder. The life of Gervayse Hastings was not merely a prosperous, but a brilliant one. Everything had gone well with him. He was wealthy, far beyond the expenditure that was required by habits of magnificence, a taste of rare purity and cultivation, a love of travel, a scholar's instinct to collect a splendid library, and, moreover, what seemed a magnificent liberality to the distressed. He had sought happiness, and not vainly, if a lovely and tender wife, and children of fair promise, could ensure it. He had, besides, ascended above the limit which separates the obscure from the distinguished, and had won a stainless reputation in affairs of the widest public importance. Not that he was a popular character, or had within him the mysterious attributes which are essential to that species of success. To the public he was a cold abstraction, wholly destitute of those rich hues of personality, that living warmth, and the peculiar faculty of stamping his own heart's impression on a multitude of hearts, by which the people recognize their favourites. And it must be owned that, after his most intimate associates had done their best to know him thoroughly, and love him warmly, they were startled to find how little hold he had upon their affections. They approved, they admired, but still in those moments when the human spirit most craves reality, they shrank back from Gervayse Hastings, as powerless to give them what they sought. It was the feeling of distrustful regret with which we should draw back the hand after extending it, in an illusive twilight, to grasp the hand of a shadow upon the wall.

As the superficial fervency of youth decayed, this peculiar effect of Gervayse Hastings's character grew more perceptible. His children, when he extended his arms, came coldly to his knees, but never climbed them of their own accord. His wife wept secretly, and almost adjudged herself a criminal because she shivered in the chill of his bosom. He, too, occasionally appeared not unconscious of the chillness of his moral atmosphere, and willing, if it might be so, to warm himself at a kindly fire. But age stole onward and benumbed him more and more. As the hoarfrost began to gather on him his wife went to her grave, and was doubtless warmer there; his children either died or were scattered to different homes of their own; and old Gervayse Hastings, unscathed by grief,—alone, but needing no companionship,—continued his steady walk through life, and still on every Christmas day attended at the dismal banquet. His privilege as a guest had become prescriptive now. Had he claimed the head of the table, even the skeleton would have been ejected from its seat.

Finally, at the merry Christmas-tide, when he had numbered fourscore years complete, this pale, high-browed, marble-featured old man once more entered the long-frequented hall, with the same impassive aspect that had called forth so much dissatisfied remark at his first attendance. Time, except in matters merely external, had done nothing for him, either of good or evil. As he took his place he threw a calm, inquiring glance around the table, as if to ascertain whether any guest had yet appeared, after so many unsuccessful banquets, who might impart to him the mystery—the deep, warm secret—the life within the life—which, whether manifested in joy or sorrow, is what gives substance to a world of shadows.

'My friends,' said Gervayse Hastings, assuming a position which his long conversance with the festival caused to appear natural, 'you are welcome! I drink to you all in this cup of sepulchral wine.'

The guests replied courteously, but still in a manner that proved them unable to receive the old man as a member of their sad fraternity. It may be well to give the reader an idea of the present company at the banquet.

One was formerly a clergyman, enthusiastic in his profession, and apparently of the genuine dynasty of those old Puritan divines whose faith in their calling, and stern exercise of it, had placed them among the mighty of the earth. But yielding to the speculative tendency of the age, he had gone astray from the firm foundation of an ancient faith, and wandered into a cloud-region, where everything was misty and deceptive, ever mocking him with a semblance of reality, but still dissolving when he flung himself upon it for support and rest. His instinct and early training demanded something steadfast; but, looking forward, he beheld vapours piled on vapours, and behind him an impassable gulf between the man of yesterday and to-day, on the borders of which he paced to and fro, sometimes wringing his hands in agony, and often making his own woe a theme of scornful merriment. This surely was a miserable man. Next, there was a theorist,—one of a numerous tribe, although he deemed himself unique since the creation,—a theorist, who had conceived a plan by which all the wretchedness of earth, moral and physical, might be done away, and the bliss of the millennium at once accomplished. But, the incredulity of mankind debarring him from action, he was smitten with as much grief as if the whole mass of woe which he was denied the opportunity to remedy were crowded into his own bosom. A plain old man in black attracted much of the company's notice, on the supposition that he was no other than Father Miller,* who, it seemed, had given himself up to despair at the tedious delay of the final conflagration. Then there was a man distinguished for native pride and obstinacy, who, a little while before, had possessed immense wealth, and held the control of a vast moneyed interest which he had wielded in the same spirit as a despotic monarch would wield the power of his empire, carrying on a tremendous moral warfare, the roar and tremor of which was felt at every fireside in the land. At length came a crushing ruin,—a total overthrow of fortune, power, and character,—the effect of which on his imperious and, in many respects, noble and lofty nature might have entitled him to a place, not merely at our festival, but among the peers of Pandemonium.*

There was a modern philanthropist, who had become so deeply sensible of the calamities of thousands and millions of his fellow-creatures, and of the impracticableness of any general measures for their relief, that he had no heart to do what little good lay immediately within his power, but contented himself with being miserable for sympathy. Near him sat a gentleman in a predicament hitherto unprecedented, but of which the present epoch probably affords numerous examples. Ever since he was of capacity to read a newspaper, this person had prided himself on his consistent adherence to one political party, but, in the confusion of these latter days, had got bewildered and knew not whereabouts his party was. This wretched condition, so morally desolate and disheartening to a man who has long accustomed himself to merge his individuality in the mass of a great body, can only be conceived by such as have experienced it. His next companion was a popular orator who had lost his voice, and— as it was pretty much all that he had to lose—had fallen into a state of hopeless melancholy. The table was likewise graced by two of the gentler sex,—one, a half-starved, consumptive seamstress, the representative of thousands just as wretched; the other, a woman of unemployed energy, who found herself in the world with nothing to achieve, nothing to enjoy, and nothing even to suffer. She had, therefore, driven herself to the verge of madness by dark broodings over the wrongs of her sex, and its exclusion from a proper field of action. The roll of guests being thus complete, a side-table had been set for three or four disappointed office-seekers, with hearts as sick as death, whom the stewards had admitted partly because their calamities really entitled them to entrance here, and partly that they were in especial need of a good dinner. There was likewise a homeless dog, with his tail between his legs, licking up the crumbs and gnawing the fragments of the feast,—such a melancholy cur as one sometimes sees about the streets without a master, and willing to follow the first that will accept his service.

In their own way, there were as wretched a set of people as ever had assembled at the festival. There they sat, with the veiled skeleton of the founder holding aloft the cypress-wreath, at one end of the table, and at the other, wrapped in furs, the withered figure of Gervayse Hastings, stately, calm, and cold, impressing the company with awe, yet so little interesting their sympathy that he might have vanished into thin air without their once exclaiming, 'Whither is he gone?'

'Sir,' said the philanthropist, addressing the old man, 'you have been so long a guest at this annual festival, and have thus been conversant with so many varieties of human affliction, that, not improbably, you have thence derived some great and important lessons. How blessed were your lot could you reveal a secret by which all this mass of woe might be removed!'

'I know of but one misfortune,' answered Gervayse Hastings, quietly, 'and that is my own.'

'Your own!' rejoined the philanthropist. 'And looking back on your serene and prosperous life, how can you claim to be the sole unfortunate of the human race?'

'You will not understand it,' replied Gervayse Hastings, feebly, and with a singular inefficiency of pronunciation, and sometimes putting one word for another. 'None have understood it, not even those who experience the like. It is a chillness, a want of earnestness, a feeling as if what should be my heart were a thing of vapour, a haunting perception of unreality! Thus seeming to possess all that other men have, all that men aim at, I have really possessed nothing, neither joy nor griefs. All things, all persons,—as was truly said to me at this table long and long ago,—have been like shadows flickering on the wall. It was so with my wife and children, with those who seemed my friends: it is so with yourselves, whom I see now before me. Neither have I myself any real existence, but am a shadow like the rest.'

'And how is it with your views of a future life?' inquired the speculative clergyman.

'Worse than with you,' said the old man, in a hollow and feeble tone; 'for I cannot conceive it earnestly enough to feel either hope or fear. Mine,—mine is the wretchedness! This cold heart,—this unreal life! Ah! it grows colder still.'

It so chanced that at this juncture the decayed ligaments of the skeleton gave way, and the dry bones fell together in a heap, thus causing the dusty wreath of cypress to drop upon the table. The attention of the company being thus diverted for a single instant from Gervayse Hastings, they perceived, on turning again towards him, that the old man had undergone a change. His shadow had ceased to flicker on the wall.

'Well Rosina, what is your criticism?' asked Roderick, as he rolled up the manuscript.

'Frankly, your success is by no means complete,' replied she. 'It is true, I have an idea of the character you endeavour to describe; but it is rather by dint of my own thought than your expression.'

'That is unavoidable,' observed the sculptor, 'because the characteristics are all negative. If Gervayse Hastings could have imbibed one human grief at the gloomy banquet, the task of describing him would have been infinitely easier. Of such persons—and we do meet with these moral monsters now and then—it is difficult to conceive how they came to exist here, or what there is in them capable of existence hereafter. They seem to be on the outside of everything; and nothing wearies the soul more than an attempt to comprehend them within its grasp.'

EARTH'S HOLOCAUST

ONCE upon a time—but whether in the time past or time to come is a matter of little or no moment—this wide world had become so overburdened with an accumulation of worn-out trumpery, that the inhabitants determined to rid themselves of it by a general bonfire. The site fixed upon, at the representation of the insurance companies, and as being as central a spot as any other on the globe, was one of the broadest prairies of the West,* where no human habitation would be endangered by the flames, and where a vast assemblage of spectators might commodiously admire the show. Having a taste for sights of this kind, and imagining, likewise, that the illumination of the bonfire might reveal some profundity of moral truth heretofore hidden in mist or darkness, I made it convenient to journey thither and be present. At my arrival, although the heap of condemned rubbish was as yet comparatively small, the torch had already been applied. Amid that boundless plain, in the dusk of the evening, like a far-off star alone in the firmament, there was merely visible one tremulous gleam, whence none could have anticipated so fierce a blaze as was destined to ensue. With every moment, however, there came foot-travellers, women holding up their aprons, men on horseback, wheelbarrows, lumbering baggage-wagons, and other vehicles, great and small, and from far and near, laden with articles that were judged fit for nothing but to be burned.

'What materials have been used to kindle the flame?' inquired I of a bystander; for I was desirous of knowing the whole process of the affair from beginning to end.

The person whom I addressed was a grave man, fifty years old or thereabout, who had evidently come thither as a looker-on. He struck me immediately as having weighed for himself the true value of life and its circumstances, and therefore as feeling little personal interest in whatever judgement the world might form of them. Before answering my question, he looked me in the face by the kindling light of the fire.

'Oh, some very dry combustibles,' replied he, 'and extremely suitable to the purpose,—no other, in fact, than yesterday's newspapers, last month's magazines, and last year's withered leaves. Here now comes some antiquated trash that will take fire like a handful of shavings.'

As he spoke, some rough-looking men advanced to the verge of the bonfire, and threw in, as it appeared, all the rubbish of the herald's office,—the blazonry of coat armour, the crests and devices of illustrious families, pedigrees that extended back, like lines of light, into the mist of the dark ages, together with stars, garters, and embroidered collars, each of which, as paltry a bauble as it might appear to the uninstructed eye, had once possessed vast significance, and was still, in truth, reckoned among the most precious of moral or material facts by the worshippers of the gorgeous past. Mingled with this confused heap, which was tossed into the flames by armfuls at once, were innumerable badges of knighthood, comprising those of all the European sovereignties, and Napoleon's decoration of the Legion of Honour, the ribbons of which were entangled with those of the ancient order of St. Louis. There, too, were the medals of our own Society of Cincinnati,* by means of which, as history tells us, an order of hereditary knights came near being constituted out of the king-quellers of the Revolution. And besides, there were the patents of nobility of German counts and barons, Spanish grandees, and English peers, from the worm-eaten instruments signed by William the Conqueror down to the brand-new parchment of the latest lord who has received his honours from the fair hand of Victoria.

At sight of the dense volumes of smoke, mingled with vivid jets of flame, that gushed and eddied forth from this immense pile of earthly distinctions, the multitude of plebeian spectators set up a joyous shout, and clapped their hands with an emphasis that made the welkin echo. That was their moment of triumph, achieved, after long ages, over creatures of the same clay and the same spiritual infirmities, who had dared to assume the privileges due only to Heaven's better workmanship. But now there rushed towards the blazing heap a grey-haired man, of stately presence, wearing a coat from the breast of which a star, or other badge of rank, seemed to have been forcibly wrenched away. He had not the tokens of intellectual power in his face; but still there was the demeanour, the habitual and almost native dignity, of one who had been born to the idea of his own social superiority, and had never felt it questioned till that moment.

'People,' cried he, gazing at the ruin of what was dearest to his eyes with grief and wonder, but nevertheless with a degree of stateliness,—'people, what have you done? This fire is consuming all that marked your advance from barbarism, or that could have prevented your relapse thither. We, the men of the privileged orders,* were those who kept alive from age to age the old chivalrous spirit; the gentle and generous thought; the higher, the purer, the more refined and delicate life. With the nobles, too, you cast off the poet, the painter, the sculptor,—all the beautiful arts; for we were their patrons, and created the atmosphere in which they flourish. In abolishing the majestic distinctions of rank, society loses not only its grace, but its steadfastness——'

More he would doubtless have spoken; but here there arose an outcry, sportive, contemptuous, and indignant, that altogether drowned the appeal of the fallen nobleman, insomuch that, casting one look of despair at his own half-burned pedigree, he shrunk back into the crowd, glad to shelter himself under his new-found insignifance.

'Let him thank his stars that we have not flung him into the same fire!' shouted a rude figure, spurning the embers with his foot. 'And henceforth let no man dare to show a piece of musty parchment as his warrant for lording it over his fellows. If he have strength of arm, well and good; it is one species of superiority. If he have wit, wisdom, courage, force of character, let these attributes do for him what they may; but from this day forward no mortal must hope for place and consideration by reckoning up the mouldy bones of his ancestors.* That nonsense is done away.'

'And in good time,' remarked the grave observer by my side, in a low voice, however, 'if no worse nonsense comes in its place; but, at all events, this species of nonsense has fairly lived out its life.'

There was little space to muse or moralize over the embers of this time-honoured rubbish; for, before it was half burned out, there came another multitude from beyond the sea, bearing the purple robes of royalty, and the crowns, globes, and sceptres of emperors and kings.* All these had been condemned as useless baubles, playthings at best, fit only for the infancy of the world, or rods to govern and chastise it in its nonage, but with which universal manhood at its full-grown stature could no longer brook to be insulted. Into such contempt had these regal insignia now fallen that the gilded crown and tinselled robes of the player king from Drury Lane Theatre* had been thrown in among the rest, doubtless as a mockery of his brother monarchs on the great stage of the world. It was a strange sight to discern the crown-jewels of England glowing and flashing in the midst of the fire. Some of them had been delivered down from the time of the Saxon princes; others were purchased with vast revenues, or perchance ravished from the dead brows of the native potentates of Hindustan; and the whole now blazed with a dazzling lustre, as if a star had fallen in that spot and been shattered into fragments. The splendour of the ruined monarchy had no reflection save in those inestimable precious stones. But enough on this subject. It were but tedious to describe how the Emperor of Austria's mantle was converted to tinder, and how the posts and pillars of the French throne became a heap of coals, which it was impossible to distinguish from those of any other wood. Let me add, however, that I noticed one of the exiled Poles stirring up the bonfire with the Czar of Russia's sceptre, which he afterwards flung into the flames.

'The smell of singed garments is quite intolerable here,' observed my new acquaintance, as the breeze enveloped us in the smoke of a royal wardrobe. 'Let us get to windward and see what they are doing on the other side of the bonfire.'

We accordingly passed around, and were just in time to witness the arrival of a vast procession of Washingtonians,*— as the votaries of temperance call themselves nowadays,— accompanied by thousands of the Irish disciples of Father Mathew,* with that great apostle at their head. They brought a rich contribution to the bonfire, being nothing less than all the hogsheads and barrels of liquor in the world, which they rolled before them across the prairie.

'Now, my children,' cried Father Mathew, when they reached the verge of the fire, 'one shove more, and the work is done. And now let us stand off and see Satan deal with his own liquor.'

Accordingly, having placed their wooden vessels within reach of the flames, the procession stood off at a safe distance, and soon beheld them burst into a blaze that reached the clouds and threatened to set the sky itself on fire. And well it might; for here was the whole world's stock of spirituous liquors, which, instead of kindling a frenzied light in the eyes of individual topers as of yore, soared upwards with a bewildering gleam that startled all mankind. It was the aggregate of that fierce fire which would otherwise have scorched the hearts of millions. Meantime numberless bottles of precious wine were flung into the blaze, which lapped up the contents as if it loved them, and grew, like other drunkards, the merrier and fiercer for what it quaffed. Never again will the insatiable thirst of the fire-fiend be so pampered. Here were the treasures of famous bonvivants,—liquors that had been tossed on ocean, and mellowed in the sun, and hoarded long in the recesses of the earth,—the pale, the gold, the ruddy juice of whatever vineyards were most delicate,—

the entire vintage of Tokay,*—all mingling in one stream with the vile fluids of the common pot-house, and contributing to heighten the self-same blaze. And while it rose in a gigantic spire that seemed to wave against the arch of the firmament and combine itself with the lights of stars, the multitude gave a shout as if the broad earth were exulting in its deliverance from the curse of ages.

But the joy was not universal. Many deemed that human life would be gloomier than ever when that brief illumination should sink down. While the reformers were at work I overheard muttered expostulations from several respectable gentlemen with red noses and wearing gouty shoes, and a ragged worthy, whose face looked like a hearth where the fire is burned out, now expressed his discontent more openly and boldly.

'What is this world good for,' said the last toper, 'now that we can never be jolly any more? What is to comfort the poor man in sorrow and perplexity? How is he to keep his heart warm against the cold winds of this cheerless earth? And what do you propose to give him in exchange for the solace that you take away? How are old friends to sit together by the fireside without a cheerful glass between them? A plague upon your reformation! It is a sad world, a cold world, a selfish world, a low world, not worth an honest fellow's living in, now that good fellowship is gone for ever!'

This harangue excited great mirth among the bystanders; but, preposterous as was the sentiment, I could not help commiserating the forlorn condition of the last toper, whose boon companions had dwindled away from his side, leaving the poor fellow without a soul to countenance him in sipping his liquor, nor indeed any liquor to sip. Not that this was quite the true state of the case; for I had observed him at a critical moment filch a bottle of fourth-proof brandy that fell beside the bonfire and hide it in his pocket.

The spirituous and fermented liquors being thus disposed of, the zeal of the reformers next induced them to replenish the fire with all the boxes of tea and bags of coffee in the world. And now came the planters of Virginia, bringing their crops of tobacco. These, being cast upon the heap of inutility, aggregated it to the size of a mountain, and incensed the atmosphere with such potent fragrance that methought we should never draw pure breath again. The present sacrifice seemed to startle the lovers of the weed more than any that they had hitherto witnessed.

'Well, they've put my pipe out,' said an old gentleman, flinging it into the flames in a pet. 'What is this world coming to? Everything rich and racy—all the spice of life—is to be condemned as useless. Now that they have kindled the bonfire, if these nonsensical reformers would fling themselves into it, all would be well enough!'

'Be patient,' responded a staunch conservative; 'it will come to that in the end. They will first fling us in, and finally themselves.'

From the general and systematic measures of reform I now turn to consider the individual contributions to this memorable bonfire. In many instances these were of a very amusing character. One poor fellow threw in his empty purse, and another a bundle of counterfeit or insolvable bank-notes. Fashionable ladies threw in their last season's bonnets, together with heaps of ribbons, yellow lace, and much other half-worn milliner's ware, all of which proved even more evanescent in the fire than it had been in the fashion. A multitude of lovers of both sexes—discarded maids or bachelors and couples mutually weary of one another—tossed in bundles of perfumed letters and enamoured sonnets. A hack politician, being deprived of bread by the loss of office, threw in his teeth, which happened to be false ones. The Rev. Sydney Smith*—having voyaged across the Atlantic for that sole purpose—came up to the bonfire with a bitter grin and threw in certain repudiated bonds, fortified though they were with the broad seal of a sovereign state. A little boy of five years old, in the premature manliness of the present epoch, threw in his playthings; a college graduate, his diploma; an apothecary, ruined by the spread of homoeopathy, his whole stock of drugs and medicines; a physician, his library; a parson, his old sermons; and a fine gentleman of the old school, his code of manners, which he had formerly written down for the benefit of the next generation. A widow, resolving on a second marriage, slyly threw in her dead husband's miniature. A young man, jilted by his mistress, would willingly have flung his own desperate heart into the flames, but could find no means to wrench it out of his bosom. An American author, whose works were neglected by the public, threw his pen and paper into the bonfire and betook himself to some less discouraging occupation. It somewhat startled me to overhear a number of ladies, highly respectable in appearance, proposing to fling their gowns and petticoats into the flames, and assume the garb,* together with the manners, duties, offices, and responsibilities, of the opposite sex.

What favour was accorded to this scheme I am unable to say, my attention being suddenly drawn to a poor, deceived, and half-delirious girl, who, exclaiming that she was the most worthless thing alive or dead, attempted to cast herself into the fire amid all that wrecked and broken trumpery of the world. A good man, however, ran to her rescue.

'Patience, my poor girl!' said he, as he drew her back from the fierce embrace of the destroying angel. 'Be patient, and abide Heaven's will. So long as you possess a living soul, all may be restored to its first freshness. These things of matter and creations of human fantasy are fit for nothing but to be burned when once they have had their day; but your day is eternity!'

'Yes,' said the wretched girl, whose frenzy seemed now to have sunk down into deep despondency,—'yes, and the sunshine is blotted out of it!'

It was now rumoured among the spectators that all the weapons and munitions of war* were to be thrown into the bonfire with the exception of the world's stock of gunpowder, which, as the safest mode of disposing of it, had already been drowned in the sea. This intelligence seemed to awaken great diversity of opinion. The hopeful philanthropist esteemed it a token that the millennium was already come; while persons of another stamp, in whose view mankind was a breed of bulldogs, prophesied that all the old stoutness, fervour, nobleness, generosity, and magnanimity of the race would disappear,—these qualities, as they affirmed, requiring blood for their nourishment. They comforted themselves, however, in the belief that the proposed abolition of war was impracticable for any length of time together.

Be that as it might, numberless great guns, whose thunder had long been the voice of battle,—the artillery of the Armada, the battering trains of Marlborough, and the adverse cannon of Napoleon and Wellington,—were trundled into the midst of the fire. By the continual addition of dry combustibles, it had now waxed so intense that neither brass nor iron could withstand it. It was wonderful to behold how these terrible instruments of slaughter melted away like playthings of wax. Then the armies of the earth wheeled around the mighty furnace, with their military music playing triumphant marches, and flung in their muskets and swords. The standard-bearers, likewise, cast one look upward at their banners, all tattered with shot-holes and inscribed with the names of victorious fields; and, giving them a last flourish on the breeze, they lowered them into the flame, which snatched them upward in its rush towards the clouds. This ceremony being over, the world was left without a single weapon in its hands, except possibly a few old king's arms and rusty swords and other trophies of the Revolution in some of our State armouries. And now the drums were beaten and the trumpets brayed all together, as a prelude to the proclamation of universal and eternal peace and the announcement that glory was no longer to be won by blood, but that it would henceforth be the contention of the human race to work out the greatest mutual good, and that beneficence, in the future annals of the earth, would claim the praise of valour. The blessed tidings were accordingly promulgated, and caused infinite rejoicings among those who had stood aghast at the horror and absurdity of war.

But I saw a grim smile pass over the seared visage of a stately old commander,—by his war-worn figure and rich military dress, he might have been one of Napoleon's famous marshals,—who, with the rest of the world's soldiery, had just flung away the sword that had been familiar to his right hand for half a century.

'Ay! ay!' grumbled he. 'Let them proclaim what they please;

but, in the end, we shall find that all this foolery has only made more work for the armourers and cannon-founders.'

'Why, sir,' exclaimed I, in astonishment, 'do you imagine that the human race will ever so far return on the steps of its past madness as to weld another sword or cast another cannon?'

'There will be no need,' observed, with a sneer, one who neither felt benevolence nor had faith in it. 'When Cain wished to slay his brother, he was at no loss for a weapon.'

'We shall see,' replied the veteran commander. 'If I am mistaken, so much the better; but in my opinion, without pretending to philosophize about the matter, the necessity of war lies far deeper than these honest gentlemen suppose. What! is there a field for all the petty disputes of individuals? and shall there be no great law court for the settlement of national difficulties? The battlefield is the only court where such suits can be tried.'

'You forget, general,' rejoined I, 'that, in this advanced stage of civilization, Reason and Philanthropy combined will constitute just such a tribunal as is requisite.'

'Ah, I had forgotten that, indeed!' said the old warrior, as he limped away.

The fire was now to be replenished with materials that had hitherto been considered of even greater importance to the well-being of society than the warlike munitions which we had already seen consumed. A body of reformers had travelled all over the earth in quest of the machinery by which the different nations were accustomed to inflict the punishment of death. A shudder passed through the multitude as these ghastly emblems were dragged forward. Even the flames seemed at first to shrink away, displaying the shape and murderous contrivance to each in a full blaze of light, which of itself was sufficient to convince mankind of the long and deadly error of human law. Those old implements of cruelty; those horrible monsters of mechanism; those inventions which it seemed to demand something worse than man's natural heart to contrive, and which had lurked in the dusky nooks of ancient prisons, the subject of terror-stricken legend,—were now brought forth to view. Headsmen's axes, with the rust of noble and royal blood upon them, and a vast collection of halters that had choked the breath of plebeian victims, were thrown in together. A shout greeted the arrival of the guillotine, which was thrust forward on the same wheels that had borne it from one to another of the bloodstained streets of Paris. But the loudest roar of applause went up, telling the distant sky of the triumph of the earth's redemption, when the gallows made its appearance. An ill-looking fellow, however, rushed forward, and, putting himself in the path of the reformers, bellowed hoarsely, and fought with brute fury to stay their progress.

It was little matter of surprise, perhaps, that the executioner should thus do his best to vindicate and uphold the machinery by which he himself had his livelihood and worthier individuals their death; but it deserved special note that men of a far different sphere—even of that consecrated class in whose guardianship the world is apt to trust its benevolence—were found to take the hangman's view of the question.

'Stay, my breathren!' cried one of them. 'You are misled by a false philanthropy; you know not what you do. The gallows is a Heaven-ordained instrument. Bear it back, then, reverently, and set it up in its old place, else the world will fall to speedy ruin and desolation!'

'Onward! onward!' shouted a leader in the reform. 'Into the flames with the accursed instrument of man's bloody policy! How can human law inculcate benevolence and love while it persists in setting up the gallows as its chief symbol? One heave more, good friends, and the world will be redeemed from its greatest error.'

A thousand hands, that nevertheless loathed the touch, now lent their assistance, and thrust the ominous burden far, far into the centre of the raging furnace. There its fatal and abhorred image was beheld, first black, then a red coal, then ashes.

'That was well done!' exclaimed I.

'Yes, it was well done,' replied, but with less enthusiasm than I expected, the thoughtful observer, who was still at my side,—'well done, if the world be good enough for the measure. Death, however, is an idea that cannot easily be dispensed with in any condition between the primal innocence and that other purity and perfection which perchance we are destined to attain after travelling round the full circle; but, at all events, it is well that the experiment should now be tried.'

'Too cold! too cold!' impatiently exclaimed the young and ardent leader in this triumph. 'Let the heart have its voice here as well as the intellect. And as for ripeness, and as for progress, let mankind always do the highest, kindest, noblest thing that, at any given period, it has attained the perception of; and surely that thing cannot be wrong nor wrongly timed.'

I know not whether it were the excitement of the scene, or whether the good people around the bonfire were really growing more enlightened every instant; but they now proceeded to measures in the full length of which I was hardly prepared to keep them company. For instance, some threw their marriage certificates into the flames, and declared themselves candidates for a higher, holier, and more comprehensive union than that which had subsisted from the birth of time under the form of the connubial tie. Others hastened to the vaults of banks and to the coffers of the rich— all of which were opened to the first comer on this fated occasion—and brought entire bales of paper-money to enliven the blaze, and tons of coin to be melted down by its intensity. Henceforth, they said, universal benevolence, uncoined and exhaustless, was to be the golden currency of the world. At this intelligence the bankers and speculators in the stocks grew pale, and a pickpocket, who had reaped a rich harvest among the crowd, fell down in a deadly fainting fit. A few men of business burned their day-books and ledgers, the notes and obligations of their creditors, and all other evidences of debts · due to themselves; while perhaps a somewhat larger number satisfied their zeal for reform with the sacrifice of any uncomfortable recollection of their own indebtment. There was then a cry that the period was arrived when the title-deeds of landed property* should be given to the flames, and the whole soil of the earth revert to the public, from whom it had been wrongfully abstracted and most unequally distributed among individuals. Another party demanded that all written constitutions, set forms of government, legislative acts, statute-books, and everything else on which human invention had endeavoured to stamp its arbitrary laws, should at once be destroyed, leaving the consummated world as free as the man first created.

Whether any ultimate action was taken with regard to these propositions is beyond my knowledge; for, just then, some matters were in progress that concerned my sympathies more nearly.

'See! see! What heaps of books and pamphlets!' cried a fellow, who did not seem to be a lover of literature. 'Now we shall have a glorious blaze!'

'That's just the thing!' said a modern philospher. 'Now we shall get rid of the weight of dead men's thought, which has hitherto pressed so heavily on the living intellect that it has been incompetent to any effectual self-exertion. Well done, my lads! Into the fire with them! Now you are enlightening the world indeed!'

'But what is to become of the trade?' cried a frantic bookseller.

'Oh, by all means, let them accompany their merchandise,' coolly observed an author. 'It will be a noble funeral-pile!'

The truth was, that the human race had now reached a stage of progress* so far beyond what the wisest and wittiest men of former ages had ever dreamed of, that it would have been a manifest absurdity to allow the earth to be any longer encumbered with their poor achievements in the literary line. Accordingly, a thorough and searching investigation had swept the booksellers' shops, hawkers' stands, public and private libraries, and even the little bookshelf by the country fireside, and had brought the world's entire mass of printed paper, bound or in sheets, to swell the already mountain bulk of our illustrious bonfire. Thick, heavy folios, containing the labours of lexicographers, commentators, and encyclopedists, were flung in, and, falling among the embers with a leaden thump, smouldered away to ashes like rotten wood. The small, richly gilt French tomes* of the last age, with the hundred volumes of Voltaire among them, went off in a brilliant shower of sparkles and little jets of flame; while the current literature of the same nation burned red and blue, and threw an infernal light over the visages of the spectators, converting them all to the aspect of parti-coloured fiends. A collection of German stories* emitted a scent of brimstone. The English standard authors made excellent fuel, generally exhibiting the properties of sound oak logs. Milton's works, in particular, sent up a powerful blaze, gradually reddening into a coal, which promised to endure longer than almost any other material of the pile. From Shakespeare there gushed a flame of such marvellous splendour that men shaded their eyes as against the sun's meridian glory; nor even when the works of his own elucidators were flung upon him did he cease to flash forth a dazzling radiance from beneath the ponderous heap. It is my belief that he is still blazing as fervidly as ever.

'Could a poet but light a lamp at that glorious flame,' remarked I, 'he might then consume the midnight oil to some good purpose.'

'That is the very thing which modern poets have been too apt to do, or at least to attempt,' answered a critic. 'The chief benefit to be expected from this conflagration of past literature undoubtedly is, that writers will henceforth be compelled to light their lamps at the sun or stars.'

'If they can reach so high,' said I; 'but that task requires a giant, who may afterwards distribute the light among inferior men. It is not every one that can steal the fire from heaven like Prometheus; but, when once he had done the deed, a thousand hearths were kindled by it.'

It amazed me much to observe how indefinite was the proportion between the physical mass of any given author and the property of brilliant and long-continued combustion. For instance, there was not a quarto volume of the last century—nor, indeed, of the present—that could compete in that particular with a child's little gilt-covered book, containing Mother Goose's Melodies.* The Life and Death of Tom Thumb outlasted the biography of Marlborough. An epic, indeed a dozen of them, was converted to white ashes before the single sheet of an old ballad was half consumed. In more than one case, too, when volumes of applauded verse proved incapable of anything better than a stifling smoke, an unregarded ditty of some nameless bard—perchance in the corner of a newspaper—soared up among the stars with a flame as brilliant as their own. Speaking of the properties of flame, methought Shelley's poetry emitted a purer light than almost any other productions of his day, contrasting beautifully with the fitful and lurid gleams and gushes of black vapour that flashed and eddied from the volumes of Lord Byron.* As for Tom Moore,* some of his songs diffused an odour like a burning pastille.

I felt particular interest in watching the combustion of American authors, and scrupulously noted by my watch the precise number of moments that changed most of them from shabbily printed books to indistinguishable ashes. It would be invidious, however, if not perilous, to betray these awful secrets; so that I shall content myself with observing that it was not invariably the writer most frequent in the public mouth that made the most splendid appearance in the bonfire. I especially remember that a great deal of excellent inflammability was exhibited in a thin volume of poems by Ellery Channing;* although, to speak the truth, there were certain portions that hissed and spluttered in a very disagreeable fashion. A curious phenomenon occurred in reference to several writers, native as well as foreign. Their books, though of highly respectable figure, instead of bursting into a blaze or even smouldering out their substance in smoke, suddenly melted away in a manner that proved them to be ice.

If it be no lack of modesty to mention my own works, it must here be confessed that I looked for them with a fatherly interest, but in vain. Too probably they were changed to vapour by the first action of the heat; at best, I can only hope that, in their quiet way, they contributed a glimmering spark or two to the splendour of the evening.

'Alas! and woe is me!' thus bemoaned himself a heavy-looking gentleman in green spectacles. 'The world is utterly ruined, and there is nothing to live for any longer. The business of my life is snatched from me. Not a volume to be had for love or money!'

'This,' remarked the sedate observer beside me, 'is a bookworm,—one of those men who are born to gnaw dead thoughts. His clothes, you see, are covered with the dust of libraries. He has no inward fountain of ideas; and, in good earnest, now that the old stock is abolished, I do not see what is to become of the poor fellow. Have you no word of comfort for him?'

'My dear sir,' said I to the desperate bookworm, 'is not nature better than a book? Is not the human heart deeper than any system of philosophy? Is not life replete with more instruction than past observers have found it possible to write down in maxims? Be of good cheer. The great book of Time is still spread wide open before us; and, if we read it aright, it will be to us a volume of eternal truth.'

'Oh, my books, my books, my precious printed books!' reiterated the forlorn bookworm. 'My only reality was a bound volume; and now they will not leave me even a shadowy pamphlet!'

In fact, the last remnant of the literature of all the ages was now descending upon the blazing heap in the shape of a cloud of pamphlets from the press of the New World. These likewise were consumed in the twinkling of an eye, leaving the earth, for the first time since the days of Cadmus,* free from the plague of letters,—an enviable field for the authors of the next generation.

'Well, and does anything remain to be done?' inquired I, somewhat anxiously. 'Unless we set fire to the earth itself, and then leap boldly off into infinite space, I know not that we can carry reform to any farther point.'*

'You are vastly mistaken, my good friend,' said the observer. 'Believe me, the fire will not be allowed to settle down without the addition of fuel that will startle many persons who have lent a willing hand thus far.'

Nevertheless there appeared to be a relaxation of effort for a little time, during which, probably, the leaders of the movement were considering what should be done next. In the interval, a philosopher threw his theory into the flames,—a sacrifice which, by those who knew how to estimate it, was pronounced the most remarkable that had yet been made. The combustion, however, was by no means brilliant. Some indefatigable people, scorning to take a moment's ease, now employed themselves in collecting all the withered leaves and fallen boughs of the forest, and thereby recruited the bonfire to a greater height than ever. But this was mere by-play.

'Here comes the fresh fuel that I spoke of,' said my companion.

To my astonishment the persons who now advanced into the vacant space around the mountain fire bore surplices and other priestly garments, mitres, crosiers, and a confusion of Popish and Protestant emblems with which it seemed their purpose to consummate the great act of faith. Crosses from the spires of old cathedrals were cast upon the heap with as little remorse as if the reverence of centuries passing in long array beneath the lofty towers had not looked up to them as the holiest of symbols. The font in which infants were consecrated to God, the sacramental vessels whence piety received the hallowed draught, were given to the same destruction. Perhaps it most nearly touched my heart to see among these devoted relics fragments of the humble communion-tables and undecorated pulpits which I recognized as having been torn from the meeting-houses of New England. Those simple edifices might have been permitted to retain all of sacred embellishment that their Puritan founders had bestowed, even though the mighty structure of St. Peter's had sent its spoils to the fire of this terrible sacrifice. Yet I felt that these were but the externals of religion, and might most safely be relinquished by spirits that best knew their deep significance.

'All is well,' said I, cheerfully. 'The wood-paths shall be the aisles of our cathedral, the firmament itself shall be its ceiling. What needs an earthly roof between the Deity and his worshippers? Our faith can well afford to lose all the drapery that even the holiest men have thrown around it, and be only the more sublime in its simplicity.'

'True,' said my companion; 'but will they pause here?'

The doubt implied in his question was well founded. In the general destruction of books already described, a holy volume, that stood apart from the catalogue of human literature, and yet, in one sense, was at its head, had been spared. But the Titan of innovation,—angel or fiend, double in his nature, and capable of deeds befitting both characters,—at first shaking down only the old and rotten shapes of things, had now, as it appeared, laid his terrible hand upon the main pillars which supported the whole edifice of our moral and spiritual state. The inhabitants of the earth had grown too enlightened to define their faith within a form of words, or to limit the spiritual by any analogy to our material existence. Truths which the heavens trembled at were now but a fable of the world's infancy. Therefore, as the final sacrifice of human error, what else remained to be thrown upon the embers of that awful pile, except the book which, though a celestial revelation to past ages, was but a voice from a lower sphere as regarded the present race of man? It was done! Upon the blazing heap of falsehood and worn-out truth—things that the earth had never needed, or had ceased to need, or had grown childishly weary of—fell the ponderous church Bible, the great old volume that had lain so long on the cushion of the pulpit, and whence the pastor's solemn voice had given holy utterance on so many a Sabbath day. There, likewise, fell the family Bible, which the long-buried patriarch had read to his children,—in prosperity or sorrow, by the fireside and in the summer shade of trees,—and had bequeathed downward as the heirloom of generations. There fell the bosom Bible, the little volume that had been the soul's friend of some sorely tried child of dust, who thence took courage, whether his trial were for life or death, steadfastly confronting both in the strong assurances of immortality.

All these were flung into the fierce and riotous blaze; and then a mighty wind came roaring across the plain with a desolate howl, as if it were the angry lamentation of the earth for the loss of heaven's sunshine; and it shook the gigantic pyramid of flame and scattered the cinders of half-consumed abominations around upon the spectators.

'This is terrible!' said I, feeling that my cheek grew pale, and seeing a like change in the visages about me.

'Be of good courage yet,' answered the man with whom I had so often spoken. He continued to gaze steadily at the spectacle with singular calmness, as if it concerned him merely as an observer. 'Be of good courage, nor yet exult too much; for there is far less both of good and evil in the effect of this bonfire than the world might be willing to believe.'

'How can that be?' exclaimed, I, impatiently. 'Has it not consumed everything? Has it not swallowed up or melted down every human or divine appendage of our mortal state that had substance enough to be acted on by fire? Will there be anything left us to-morrow morning better or worse than a heap of embers and ashes?'

'Assuredly there will,' said my grave friend. 'Come hither to-morrow morning, or whenever the combustible portion of the pile shall be quite burned out, and you will find among the ashes everything really valuable that you have seen cast into the flames. Trust me, the world of to-morrow will again enrich itself with the gold and diamonds which have been cast off by the world of to-day. Not a truth is destroyed nor buried so deep among the ashes but it will be raked up at last.'

This was a strange assurance. Yet I felt inclined to credit it, the more especially as I beheld among the wallowing flames a copy of the Holy Scriptures, the pages of which, instead of being blackened into tinder, only assumed a more dazzling whiteness as the fingermarks of human imperfection were purified away. Certain marginal notes and commentaries, it is true, yielded to the intensity of the fiery test, but without detriment to the smallest syllable that had flamed from the pen of inspiration.

'Yes; there is the proof of what you say,' answered I, turning to the observer; 'but if only what is evil can feel the action of the fire, then, surely, the conflagration has been of inestimable utility. Yet, if I understand aright, you intimate a doubt whether the world's expectation of benefit would be realized by it.'

'Listen to the talk of these worthies,' said he, pointing to a group in front of the blazing pile; 'possibly they may teach you something useful, without intending it.'

The persons whom he indicated consisted of that brutal and most earthly figure who had stood forth so furiously in defence of the gallows,—the hangman, in short,—together with the last thief and the last murderer, all three of whom were clustered about the last toper. The latter was liberally passing the brandy-bottle, which he had rescued from the general destruction of wines and spirits. This little convivial party seemed at the lowest pitch of despondency, as considering that the purified world must needs be utterly unlike the sphere that they had hitherto known, and therefore but a strange and desolate abode for gentlemen of their kidney.

'The best counsel for all of us is,' remarked the hangman, 'that, as soon as we have finished the last drop of liquor, I help you, my three friends, to a comfortable end upon the nearest tree, and then hang myself on the same bough. This is no world for us any longer.'

'Poh, poh, my good fellows!' said a dark-complexioned personage, who now joined the group,—his complexion was indeed fearfully dark, and his eyes glowed with a redder light than that of the bonfire; 'be not so cast down, my dear friends; you shall see good days yet. There is one thing that these wiseacres have forgotten to throw into the fire, and without which all the rest of the conflagration is just nothing at all; yes, though they had burned the earth itself to a cinder.'

'And what may that be?' eagerly demanded the last murderer.

'What but the human heart itself?' said the dark-visaged stranger, with a portentous grin. 'And, unless they hit upon some method of purifying that foul cavern,* forth from it will reissue all the shapes of wrong and misery—the same old shapes or worse ones—which they have taken such a vast deal of trouble to consume to ashes. I have stood by this live-long night and laughed in my sleeve at the whole business. Oh, take my word for it, it will be the old world yet!'

This brief conversation supplied me with a theme for lengthened thought. How sad a truth, if true it were, that man's age-long endeavour for perfection had served only to render him the mockery of the evil principle, from the fatal circumstance of an error at the very root of the matter! The heart, the heart,—there was the little yet boundless sphere wherein existed the original wrong of which the crime and misery of this outward world were merely types. Purify that inward sphere, and the many shapes of evil that haunt the outward, and which now seem almost our only realities, will turn to shadowy phantoms and vanish of their own accord; but if we go no deeper than the intellect, and strive, with merely that feeble instrument, to discern and rectify what is wrong, our whole accomplishment will be a dream, so unsubstantial that it matters little whether the bonfire, which I have so faithfully described, were what we choose to call a real event and a flame that would scorch the finger, or only a phosphoric radiance and a parable of my own brain.

THE ARTIST OF THE BEAUTIFUL

AN elderly man, with his pretty daughter on his arm, was passing along the street, and emerged from the gloom of the cloudy evening into the light that fell across the pavement from the window of a small shop. It was a projecting window; and on the inside were suspended a variety of watches, pinchbeck, silver, and one or two of gold, all with their faces turned from the street, as if churlishly disinclined to inform the wayfarers what o'clock it was. Seated within the shop, sidelong to the window, with his pale face bent earnestly over some delicate piece of mechanism on which was thrown the concentrated lustre of a shade-lamp, appeared a young man.

'What can Owen Warland be about?' muttered old Peter Hovenden, himself a retired watchmaker and the former master of this same young man whose occupation he was now wondering at. 'What can the fellow be about? These six months past I have never come by his shop without seeing him just as steadily at work as now. It would be a flight beyond his usual foolery to seek for the perpetual motion; and yet I know enough of my old business to be certain that what he is now so busy with is no part of the machinery of a watch.'

'Perhaps, father,' said Annie, without showing much interest in the question, 'Owen is inventing a new kind of timekeeper. I am sure he has ingenuity enough.'

'Poh, child! He has not the sort of ingenuity to invent anything better than a Dutch toy,' answered her father, who had formerly been put to much vexation by Owen Warland's irregular genius. 'A plague on such ingenuity! All the effect that ever I knew of it was to spoil the accuracy of some of the best watches* in my shop. He would turn the sun out of its orbit and derange the whole course of time, if, as I said before, his ingenuity could grasp anything bigger than a child's toy!'

'Hush, father! He hears you!' whispered Annie, pressing the old man's arm. 'His ears are as delicate as his feelings; and you know how easily disturbed they are. Do let us move on.'

So Peter Hovenden and his daughter Annie plodded on without further conversation, until in a by-street of the town they found themselves passing the open door of a blacksmith's shop. Within was seen the forge, now blazing up and illuminating the high and dusky roof, and now confining its lustre to a narrow precinct of the coal-strewn floor, according as the breath of the bellows was puffed forth or again inhaled into its vast leather lungs. In the intervals of brightness it was easy to distinguish objects in remote corners of the shop and the horseshoes that hung upon the wall; in the momentary gloom the fire seemed to be glimmering amidst the vagueness of unenclosed space. Moving about in this red glare and alternate dusk was the figure of the blacksmith, well worthy to be viewed in so picturesque an aspect of light and shade, where the bright blaze struggled with the black night, as if each would have snatched his comely strength from the other. Anon he drew a white-hot bar of iron from the coals, laid it on the anvil, uplifted his arm of might, and was soon enveloped in the myriads of sparks which the strokes of his hammer scattered into the surrounding gloom.

'Now that is a pleasant sight,' said the old watchmaker. 'I know what it is to work in gold; but give me the worker in iron after all is said and done. He spends his labour upon a reality.* What say you, daughter Annie?'

'Pray don't speak so loud, father,' whispered Annie. 'Robert Danforth will hear you.'

'And what if he should hear me?' said Peter Hovenden. 'I say again, it is a good and a wholesome thing to depend upon main strength and reality, and to earn one's bread with the bare and brawny arm of a blacksmith. A watchmaker gets his brain puzzled by his wheels within a wheel, or loses his health or the nicety of his eyesight, as was my case, and finds himself at middle age, or a little after, past labour at his own trade, and fit for nothing else, yet too poor to live at his ease. So I say once again, give me main strength for my money. And then, how it takes the nonsense out of a man! Did you ever hear of a blacksmith being such a fool as Owen Warland yonder?'

'Well said, Uncle Hovenden!' shouted Robert Danforth from the forge, in a full, deep, merry voice, that made the roof re-echo. 'And what says Miss Annie to that doctrine? She, I suppose, will think it a genteeler business to tinker up a lady's watch than to forge a horseshoe or make a gridiron.'

Annie drew her father onward without giving him time for reply.

But we must return to Owen Warland's shop, and spend more meditation upon his history and character than either Peter Hovenden, or probably his daughter Annie, or Owen's old schoolfellow, Robert Danforth, would have thought due to so slight a subject. From the time that his little fingers could grasp a penknife, Owen had been remarkable for a delicate ingenuity, which sometimes produced pretty shapes in wood, principally figures of flowers and birds, and sometimes seemed to aim at the hidden mysteries of mechanism. But it was always for purposes of grace, and never with any mockery of the useful. He did not, like the crowd of schoolboy artisans, construct little windmills on the angle of a barn or watermills across the neighbouring brook. Those who discovered such peculiarity in the boy as to think it worth their while to observe him closely, sometimes saw reason to suppose that he was attempting to imitate the beautiful movements of nature* as exemplified in the flight of birds or the activity of little animals. It seemed, in fact, a new development of the love of the beautiful, such as might have made him a poet, a painter, or a sculptor, and which was as completely refined from all utilitarian coarseness as it could have been in either of the fine arts. He looked with singular distaste at the stiff and regular processes of ordinary machinery. Being once carried to see a steam-engine,* in the expectation that his intuitive comprehension of mechanical principles would be gratified, he turned pale and grew sick, as if something monstrous and unnatural had been presented to him. This horror was partly owing to the size and terrible energy of the iron labourer; for the character of Owen's mind was microscopic, and tended naturally to the minute, in accordance with his diminutive frame and the marvellous smallness and delicate power of his fingers. Not that his sense of beauty was thereby diminished into a sense of prettiness. The beautiful idea has no relation to size, and may be as perfectly developed in a space too minute for any but microscopic investigation as within the ample verge that is measured by the arc of the rainbow. But, at all events, this characteristic minuteness in his objects and accomplishments made the world even more incapable than it might otherwise have been of appreciating Owen Warland's genius. The boy's relatives saw nothing better to be done,—as perhaps there was not,—than to bind him apprentice to a watchmaker, hoping that his strange ingenuity might thus be regulated and put to utilitarian purposes.

Peter Hovenden's opinion of his apprentice has already been expressed. He could make nothing of the lad. Owen's apprehension of the professional mysteries, it is true, was inconceivably quick; but he altogether forgot or despised the grand object of a watchmaker's business, and cared no more for the measurement of time than if it had been merged into eternity. So long, however, as he remained under his old master's care, Owen's lack of sturdiness made it possible, by strict injunctions and sharp oversight, to restrain his creative eccentricity within bounds; but when his apprenticeship was served out, and he had taken the little shop which Peter Hovenden's failing eyesight compelled him to relinquish, then did people recognize how unfit a person was Owen Warland to lead old blind Father Time along his daily course. One of his most rational projects was to connect a musical operation with the machinery of his watches, so that all the harsh dissonances of life might be rendered tuneful, and each flitting moment fall into the abyss of the past in golden drops of harmony. If a family clock was entrusted to him for repair,— one of those tall, ancient clocks that have grown nearly allied to human nature by measuring out the lifetime of many generations,—he would take upon himself to arrange a dance or funeral procession of figures across its venerable face, representing twelve mirthful or melancholy hours. Several freaks of this kind quite destroyed the young watchmaker's credit with that steady and matter-of-fact class of people who hold the opinion that time is not to be trifled with,* whether considered as the medium of advancement and prosperity in this world or preparation for the next. His custom rapidly diminished,—a misfortune, however, that was probably reckoned among his better accidents by Owen Warland, who was becoming more and more absorbed in a secret occupation which drew all his science and manual dexterity into itself, and likewise gave full employment to the characteristic tendencies of his genius. This pursuit had already consumed many months.

After the old watchmaker and his pretty daughter had gazed at him out of the obscurity of the street, Owen Warland was seized with a fluttering of the nerves, which made his hand tremble too violently to proceed with such delicate labour as he was now engaged upon.

'It was Annie herself!' murmured he. 'I should have known it, by this throbbing of my heart, before I heard her father's voice. Ah, how it throbs! I shall scarcely be able to work again on this exquisite mechanism to-night. Annie! dearest Annie! thou shouldst give firmness to my heart and hand, and not shake them thus; for, if I strive to put the very spirit of beauty into form and give it motion, it is for thy sake alone. O throbbing heart, be quiet! If my labour be thus thwarted, there will come vague and unsatisfied dreams, which will leave me spiritless to-morrow.'

As he was endeavouring to settle himself again to his task, the shop-door opened the gave admittance to no other than the stalwart figure which Peter Hovenden had paused to admire, as seen amid the light and shadow of the blacksmith's shop. Robert Danforth had brought a little anvil of his own manufacture, and peculiarly constructed, which the young artist had recently bespoken. Owen examined the article, and pronounced it fashioned according to his wish.

'Why, yes,' said Robert Danforth, his strong voice filling the shop as with the sound of a bass-viol, 'I consider myself equal to anything in the way of my own trade; though I should

have made but a poor figure at yours with such a fist as this,'
added he, laughing, as he laid his vast hand beside the delicate
one of Owen. 'But what then? I put more main strength into
one blow of my sledge-hammer than all you have expended
since you were a 'prentice. Is not that the truth?'

'Very probably,' answered the low and slender voice of
Owen. 'Strength is an earthly monster. I make no pretensions
to it. My force, whatever there may be of it, is altogether
spiritual.'

'Well, but, Owen, what are you about?' asked his old
schoolfellow, still in such a hearty volume of tone that it made
the artist shrink, especially as the question related to a subject
so sacred as the absorbing dream of his imagination. 'Folks do
say that you are trying to discover the perpetual motion.'

'The perpetual motion? Nonsense!' replied Owen Warland,
with a movement of disgust; for he was full of little
petulances. 'It can never be discovered. It is a dream that may
delude men whose brains are mystified with matter, but not
me. Besides, if such a discovery were possible, it would not
be worth my while to make it only to have the secret turned
to such purposes as are now effected by steam and water
power. I am not ambitious to be honoured with the paternity
of a new kind of cotton-machine.'*

'That would be droll enough!' cried the blacksmith,
breaking out into such an uproar of laughter that Owen
himself and the bell-glasses on his workboard quivered in
unison. 'No, no, Owen! No child of yours will have iron joints
and sinews. Well, I won't hinder you any more. Good-night,
Owen, and success; and if you need any assistance, so far as
a downright blow of hammer upon anvil will answer the
purpose, I'm your man.'

And with another laugh the man of main strength left the
shop.

'How strange it is,' whispered Owen Warland to himself,
leaning his head upon his hand, 'that all my musings, my
purposes, my passion for the beautiful, my consciousness of
power to create it,—a finer, more ethereal power, of which this
earthly giant can have no conception,—all, all, look so vain
and idle whenever my path is crossed by Robert Danforth! He

would drive me mad were I to meet him often. His hard brute force darkens and confuses the spiritual element within me; but I, too, will be strong in my own way. I will not yield to him.'

He took from beneath a glass a piece of minute machinery, which he set in the condensed light of his lamp, and, looking intently at it through a magnifying-glass, proceeded to operate with a delicate instrument of steel. In an instant, however, he fell back in his chair and clasped his hands, with a look of horror on his face that made its small features as impressive as those of a giant would have been.

'Heaven! What have I done?' exclaimed he. 'The vapour, the influence of that brute force,—it has bewildered me and obscured my perception. I have made the very stroke,—the fatal stroke,—that I have dreaded from the first. It is all over,—the toil of months, the object of my life. I am ruined!'

And there he sat, in strange despair, until his lamp flickered in the socket and left the Artist of the Beautiful in darkness.

Thus it is that ideas, which grow up within the imagination and appear so lovely to it and of a value beyond whatever men call valuable, are exposed to be shattered and annihilated by contact with the practical. It is requisite for the ideal artist to possess a force of character that seems hardly compatible with its delicacy; he must keep his faith in himself while the incredulous world assails him with its utter disbelief; he must stand up against mankind and be his own sole disciple, both as respects his genius and the objects to which it is directed.

For a time Owen Warland succumbed to this severe but inevitable test. He spent a few sluggish weeks with his head so continually resting in his hands that the townspeople had scarcely an opportunity to see his countenance. When at last it was again uplifted to the light of day, a cold, dull, nameless change was perceptible upon it. In the opinion of Peter Hovenden, however, and that order of sagacious understandings, who think that life should be regulated, like clockwork, with leaden weights,* the alteration was entirely for the better. Owen now, indeed, applied himself to business with dogged industry. It was marvellous to witness the obtuse gravity with which he would inspect the wheels of a great old silver watch; thereby delighting the owner, in whose fob it had been worn till he deemed it a portion of his own life, and was accordingly jealous of its treatment. In consequence of the good report thus acquired, Owen Warland was invited by the proper authorities to regulate the clock in the church-steeple. He succeeded so admirably in this matter of public interest, that the merchants gruffly acknowledged his merits on 'Change; the nurse whispered his praises as she gave the potion in the sick-chamber; the lover blessed him at the hour of appointed interview; and the town in general thanked Owen for the punctuality of dinner-time. In a word, the heavy weight upon his spirits kept everything in order, not merely within his own system, but wheresoever the iron accents of the church-clock were audible. It was a circumstance, though minute yet characteristic of his present state, that, when employed to engrave names or initials on silver spoons, he now wrote the requisite letters in the plainest possible style, omitting a variety of fanciful flourishes that had heretofore distinguished his work in this kind.

One day, during the era of this happy transformation, old Peter Hovenden came to visit his former apprentice.

'Well, Owen,' said he, 'I am glad to hear such good accounts of you from all quarters, and especially from the town clock yonder, which speaks in your commendation every hour of the twenty-four. Only get rid altogether of your nonsensical trash about the beautiful, which I nor nobody else, nor yourself to boot, could ever understand,—only free yourself of that, and your success in life is as sure as daylight. Why, if you go on in this way, I should even venture to let you doctor this precious old watch of mine; though, except my daughter Annie, I have nothing else so valuable in the world.'

'I should hardy dare touch it, sir,' replied Owen, in a depressed tone; for he was weighed down by his old master's presence.

'In time,' said the latter,—'in time you will be capable of it.'

The old watch-maker, with the freedom naturally consequent on his former authority, went on inspecting the work which Owen had in hand at the moment, together with other matters that were in progress. The artist, meanwhile, could scarcely lift his head. There was nothing so antipodal to his nature as this man's cold, unimaginative sagacity, by contact with which everything was converted into a dream except the densest matter of the physical world. Owen groaned in spirit and prayed fervently to be delivered from him.

'But what is this?' cried Peter Hovenden abruptly, taking up a dusty bell-glass, beneath which appeared a mechanical something, as delicate and minute as the system of a butterfly's anatomy. 'What have we here? Owen! Owen! there is witchcraft in these little chains,* and wheels, and paddles. See! with one pinch of my finger and thumb I am going to deliver you from all future peril.'

'For Heaven's sake,' screamed Owen Warland, springing up with wonderful energy, 'as you would not drive me mad, do not touch it! The slightest pressure of your finger would ruin me for ever.'

'Aha, young man! And is it so?' said the old watch-maker, looking at him with just enough of penetration to torture Owen's soul with the bitterness of worldly criticism. 'Well, take your own course; but I warn you again that in this small piece of mechanism lives your evil spirit. Shall I exorcise him?'

'You are my evil spirit,' answered Owen, much excited,— 'you, and the hard, coarse world! The leaden thoughts and the despondency that you fling upon me are my clogs, else I should long ago have achieved the task that I was created for.'

Peter Hovenden shook his head, with the mixture of contempt and indignation which mankind, of whom he was partly a representative, deem themselves entitled to feel towards all simpletons who seek other prizes than the dusty one along the highway. He then took his leave, with an uplifted finger and a sneer upon his face that haunted the artist's dreams for many a night afterwards. At the time of his old master's visit, Owen was probably on the point of taking up the relinquished task; but, by this sinister event, he was thrown back into the state whence he had been slowly emerging.

But the innate tendency of his soul had only been

accumulating fresh vigour during its apparent sluggishness. As the summer advanced he almost totally relinquished his business, and permitted Father Time, so far as the old gentleman was represented by the clocks and watches under his control, to stray at random through human life, making infinite confusion among the train of bewildered hours. He wasted the sunshine, as people said, in wandering through the woods and fields and along the banks of streams. There, like a child, he found amusement in chasing butterflies or watching the motions of water-insects. There was something truly mysterious in the intentness with which he contemplated these living playthings as they sported on the breeze or examined the structure of an imperial insect whom he had imprisoned. The chase of butterflies was an apt emblem of the ideal pursuit in which he had spent so many golden hours; but would the beautiful idea ever be yielded to his hand like the butterfly that symbolized it? Sweet, doubtless, were these days, and congenial to the artist's soul. They were full of bright conceptions, which gleamed through his intellectual world as the butterflies gleamed through the outward atmosphere, and were real to him, for the instant, without the toil, and perplexity, and many disappointments of attempting to make them visible to the sensual eye. Alas that the arist, whether in poetry or whatever other material, may not content himself with the inward enjoyment of the beautiful, but must chase the flitting mystery beyond the verge of his ethereal domain, and crush its frail being in seizing it with a material grasp. Owen Warland felt the impulse to give external reality to his ideas as irresistibly as any of the poets or painters who have arrayed the world in a dimmer and fainter beauty, imperfectly copied from the richness of their visions.

The night was now his time for the slow progress of re-creating the one idea to which all his intellectual activity referred itself. Always at the approach of dusk he stole into the town, locked himself within his shop, and wrought with patient delicacy of touch for many hours. Sometimes he was startled by the rap of the watchman, who, when all the world should be asleep, had caught the gleam of lamplight through the crevices of Owen Warland's shutters. Daylight, to the morbid sensibility of his mind, seemed to have an intrusiveness that interfered with his pursuits. On cloudy and inclement days, therefore, he sat with his head upon his hands, muffling, as it were, his sensitive brain in a mist of indefinite musings; for it was a relief to escape from the sharp distinctness with which he was compelled to shape out his thoughts during his nightly toil.

From one of these fits of torpor he was aroused by the entrance of Annie Hovenden, who came into the shop with the freedom of a customer and also with something of the familiarity of a childish friend. She had worn a hole through her silver thimble, and wanted Owen to repair it.

'But I don't know whether you will condescend to such a task,' said she, laughing, 'now that you are so taken up with the notion of putting spirit into machinery.'

'Where did you get that idea, Annie?' said Owen, starting in surprise.

'Oh, out of my own head,' answered she; 'and from something that I heard you say, long ago, when you were but a boy and I a little child. But come; will you mend this poor thimble of mine?'

'Anything for your sake, Annie,' said Owen Warland,— 'anything, even were it to work at Robert Danforth's forge.'

'And that would be a pretty sight!' retorted Annie, glancing with imperceptible slightness at the artist's small and slender frame. 'Well, here is the thimble.'

'But that is a strange idea of yours,' said Owen, 'about the spiritualization of matter.'

And then the thought stole into his mind that this young girl possessed the gift to comprehend him better than all the world besides. And what a help and strength would it be to him in his lonely toil if he could gain the sympathy of the only being whom he loved! To persons whose pursuits are insulated from the common business of life,—who are either in advance of mankind or apart from it,—there often comes a sensation of moral cold that makes the spirit shiver as if it had reached the frozen solitudes around the pole. What the prophet, the poet, the reformer, the criminal, or any other man with human yearnings, but separated from the multitude by a peculiar lot, might feel, poor Owen Warland felt.

'Annie,' cried he, growing pale as death at the thought, 'how gladly would I tell you the secret of my pursuit! You, methinks, would estimate it rightly. You, I know, would hear it with a reverence that I must not expect from the harsh, material world.'

'Would I not? to be sure I would!' replied Annie Hovenden, lightly laughing. 'Come; explain to me quickly what is the meaning of this little whirligig, so delicately wrought that it might be a plaything for Queen Mab. See! I will put it in motion.'

'Hold!' exlaimed Owen,—'hold!'

Annie had but given the slightest possible touch, with the point of a needle, to the same minute portion of complicated machinery which has been more than once mentioned, when the artist seized her by the wrist with a force that made her scream aloud. She was affrighted at the convulsion of intense rage and anguish that writhed across his features. The next instant he let his head sink upon his hands.

'Go, Annie,' murmured he; 'I have deceived myself, and must suffer for it. I yearned for sympathy, and thought, and fancied, and dreamed that you might give it me; but you lack the talisman, Annie, that should admit you into my secrets. That touch has undone the toil of months and the thought of a lifetime! It was not your fault, Annie; but you have ruined me!'

Poor Owen Warland! He had indeed erred, yet pardonably; for if any human spirit could have sufficiently reverenced the processes so sacred in his eyes, it must have been a woman's. Even Annie Hovenden, possibly, might not have disappointed him had she been enlightened by the deep intelligence of love.

The artist spent the ensuing winter in a way that satisfied any persons who had hitherto retained a hopeful opinion of him that he was, in truth, irrevocably doomed to inutility as regarded the world, and to an evil destiny on his own part. The decease of a relative had put him in possession of a small inheritance. Thus freed from the necessity of toil, and having lost the steadfast influence of a great purpose,—great, at least, to him,—he abandoned himself to habits from which it might have been supposed the mere delicacy of his organization would have availed to secure him. But when the ethereal portion of a man of genius is obscured, the earthly part assumes an influence the more uncontrollable, because the character is now thrown off the balance to which Providence had so nicely adjusted it, and which, in coarser natures, is adjusted by some other method. Owen Warland made proof of whatever show of bliss may be found in riot. He looked at the world through the golden medium of wine, and contemplated the visions that bubble up so gaily around the brim of the glass, and that people the air with shapes of pleasant madness, which so soon grow ghostly and forlorn. Even when this dismal and inevitable change had taken place, the young man might still have continued to quaff the cup of enchantments, though its vapour did but shroud life in gloom and fill the gloom with spectres that mocked at him. There was a certain irksomeness of spirit, which, being real, and the deepest sensation of which the artist was now conscious, was more intolerable than any fantastic miseries and horrors that the abuse of wine could summon up. In the latter case he could remember, even out of the midst of his trouble, that all was but a delusion; in the former, the heavy anguish was his actual life.

From this perilous state he was redeemed by an incident which more than one person witnessed, but of which the shrewdest could not explain or conjecture the operation on Owen Warland's mind. It was very simple. On a warm afternoon of spring, as the artist sat among his riotous companions with a glass of wine before him, a splendid butterfly flew in at the open window and fluttered about his head.

'Ah,' exclaimed Owen, who had drunk freely, 'are you alive again, child of the sun and playmate of the summer breeze, after your dismal winter's nap? Then it is time for me to be at work!'

And, leaving his unemptied glass upon the table, he departed, and was never known to sip another drop of wine.

And now, again, he resumed his wanderings in the woods and fields. It might be fancied that the bright butterfly, which had come so spirit-like into the window as Owen sat with the rude revellers, was indeed a spirit commissioned to recall him to the pure, ideal life that had so etherealized him among men. It might be fancied that he went forth to seek this spirit in its sunny haunts; for still, as in the summer-time gone by, he was seen to steal gently up wherever a butterfly had alighted, and lose himself in contemplation of it. When it took flight his eyes followed the winged vision, as if its airy track would show the path to heaven. But what could be the purpose of the unseasonable toil, which was again resumed, as the watchman knew by the lines of lamplight through the crevices of Owen Warland's shutters? The townspeople had one comprehensive explanation of all these singularities. Owen Warland had gone mad! How universally efficacious— how satisfactory, too, and soothing to the injured sensibility of narrowness and dullness*—is this easy method of accounting for whatever lies beyond the world's most ordinary scope! From St. Paul's days down to our poor little Artist of the Beautiful, the same talisman had been applied to the elucidation of all mysteries in the words or deeds of men who spoke or acted too wisely or too well. In Owen Warland's case the judgement of his townspeople may have been correct. Perhaps he was mad. The lack of sympathy—that contrast between himself and his neighbours which took away the restraint of example—was enough to make him so. Or possibly he had caught just so much of ethereal radiance as served to bewilder him, in an earthly sense, by its intermixture with the common daylight.

One evening, when the artist had returned from a customary ramble and had just thrown the lustre of his lamp on the delicate piece of work so often interrupted, but still taken up again, as if his fate were embodied in its mechanism, he was surprised by the entrance of old Peter Hovenden. Owen never met this man without a shrinking of the heart. Of all the world he was most terrible, by reason of a keen understanding which saw so distinctly what it did see, and disbelieved so uncompromisingly in what it could not see. On this occasion the old watchmaker had merely a gracious word or two to say.

'Owen, my lad,' said he, 'we must see you at my house to-morrow night.'

The artist began to mutter some excuse.

'Oh, but it must be so,' quoth Peter Hovenden, 'for the sake of the days when you were one of the household. What, my boy! don't you know that my daughter Annie is engaged to Robert Danforth? We are making an entertainment, in our humble way, to celebrate the event.'

'Ah!' said Owen.

That little monosyllable was all he uttered; its tone seemed cold and unconcerned to an ear like Peter Hovenden's; and yet there was in it the stifled outcry of the poor artist's heart, which he compressed within him like a man holding down an evil spirit. One slight outbreak, however, imperceptible to the old watch-maker, he allowed himself. Raising the instrument with which he was about to begin his work, he let it fall upon the little system of machinery that had, anew, cost him months of thought and toil. It was shattered by the stroke!

Owen Warland's story would have been no tolerable representation of the troubled life of those who strive to create the beautiful, if, amid all other thwarting influences, love had not interposed to steal the cunning from his hand. Outwardly he had been no ardent or enterprising lover; the career of his passion had confined its tumults and vicissitudes so entirely within the artist's imagination, that Annie herself had scarcely more than a woman's intuitive perception of it; but, in Owen's view, it covered the whole field of his life. Forgetful of the time when she had shown herself incapable of any deep response, he had persisted in connecting all his dreams of artistical success with Annie's image; she was the visible shape in which the spiritual power that he worshipped, and on whose altar he hoped to lay a not unworthy offering, was made manifest to him. Of course he had deceived himself; there were no such attributes in Annie Hovenden as his imagination had endowed her with. She, in the aspect which she wore to his inward vision, was as much a creature of his own as the mysterious piece of mechanism would be were it ever realized. Had he become convinced of his mistake through the medium of successful love,—had he won Annie to his bosom, and there beheld her fade from angel into ordinary woman,—the disappointment might have driven him back, with concentrated energy, upon his sole remaining object. On the other hand, had he found Annie what he fancied, his lot would have been so rich in beauty that out of its mere redundancy he might have wrought the beautiful into many a worthier type than he had toiled for; but the guise in which his sorrow came to him, the sense that the angel of his life had been snatched away and given to a rude man of earth and iron, who could neither need nor appreciate her ministrations,—this was the very perversity of fate that makes human existence appear too absurd and contradictory to be the scene of one other hope or one other fear. There was nothing left for Owen Warland but to sit down like a man that had been stunned.

He went through a fit of illness. After his recovery his small and slender frame assumed an obtuser garniture of flesh than it had ever before worn. His thin cheeks became round; his delicate little hand, so spiritually fashioned to achieve fairy task-work, grew plumper than the hand of a thriving infant. His aspect had a childishness such as might have induced a stranger to pat him on the head,—pausing, however, in the act, to wonder what manner of child was here. It was as if the spirit had gone out of him, leaving the body to flourish in a sort of vegetable existence. Not that Owen Warland was idiotic. He could talk, and not irrationally. Somewhat of a babbler, indeed, did people begin to think him; for he was apt to discourse at wearisome length of marvels of mechanism that he had read about in books, but which he had learned to consider as absolutely fabulous. Among them he enumerated the Man of Brass, constructed by Albertus Magnus, and the Brazen Head of Friar Bacon;* and, coming down to later times, the automata of a little coach and horses,* which it was pretended had been manufactured for the Dauphin of France; together with an insect that buzzed about the ear like a living fly,* and yet was but a contrivance of minute steel springs. There was a story, too, of a duck that waddled, and quacked, and ate; though, had any honest citizen purchased it for dinner, he would have found himself cheated with the mere mechanical apparition of a duck.*

'But all these accounts,' said Owen Warland, 'I am now satisfied are mere impositions.'

Then, in a mysterious way, he would confess that he once thought differently. In his idle and dreamy days he had considered it possible, in a certain sense, to spiritualize machinery, and to combine with the new species of life and motion thus produced a beauty that should attain to the ideal which Nature has proposed to herself in all her creatures, but has never taken pains to realize. He seemed, however, to retain no very distinct perception either of the process of achieving this object or of the design itself.

'I have thrown it all aside now,' he would say. 'It was a dream such as young men are always mystifying themselves with. Now that I have acquired a little common sense, it makes me laugh to think of it.'

Poor, poor and fallen Owen Warland! These were the symptoms that he had ceased to be an inhabitant of the better sphere that lies unseen around us. He had lost his faith in the invisible, and now prided himself, as such unfortunates invariably do, in the wisdom which rejected much that even his eye could see, and trusted confidently in nothing but what his hand could touch. This is the calamity of men whose spiritual part dies out of them and leaves the grosser understanding to assimilate them more and more to the things of which alone it can take cognizance; but in Owen Warland the spirit was not dead nor passed away; it only slept.

How it awoke again is not recorded. Perhaps the torpid slumber was broken by a convulsive pain. Perhaps, as in a former instance, the butterfly came and hovered about his head and reinspired him,—as indeed this creature of the sunshine had always a mysterious mission for the artist,— reinspired him with the former purpose of his life. Whether it were pain or happiness that thrilled through his veins, his first impulse was to thank Heaven for rendering him again the being of thought, imagination, and keenest sensibility that he had long ceased to be.

'Now for my task,' said he. 'Never did I feel such strength for it as now.'

Yet, strong as he felt himself, he was incited to toil the more diligently by an anxiety lest death should surprise him in the midst of his labours. This anxiety, perhaps, is common to all men who set their hearts upon anything so high, in their own view of it, that life becomes of importance only as conditional to its accomplishment. So long as we love life for itself, we seldom dread the losing it. When we desire life for the attainment of an object, we recognize the frailty of its texture. But, side by side with this sense of insecurity, there is a vital faith in our invulnerability to the shaft of death while engaged in any task that seems assigned by Providence as our proper thing to do, and which the world would have cause to mourn for should we leave it unaccomplished. Can the philosopher, big with the inspiration of an idea that is to reform mankind, believe that he is to be beckoned from this sensible existence at the very instant when he is mustering his breath to speak the word of light? Should he perish so, the weary ages may pass away—the world's whole life-sand may fall drop by drop—before another intellect is prepared to develop the truth that might have been uttered then. But history affords many an example where the most precious spirit, at any particular epoch manifested in human shape, has gone hence untimely, without space allowed him, so far as mortal judgement could discern, to perform his mission on earth. The prophet dies, and the man of torpid heart and sluggish brain lives on. The poet leaves his song half sung, or finishes it beyond the scope of mortal ears, in a celestial choir. The painter—as Allston* did—leaves half his conception on the canvas to sadden us with its imperfect beauty, and goes to picture forth the whole, if it be no irreverence to say so, in the hues of heaven. But rather such incomplete designs of this life will be perfected nowhere. This so frequent abortion of man's dearest projects must be taken as a proof that the deeds of earth, however etherealized by piety or genius, are without value, except as exercises and manifestations of the spirit. In heaven, all ordinary thought is higher and more melodious than Milton's song. Then, would he add another verse to any strain that he had left unfinished here?

But to return to Owen Warland. It was his fortune, good or ill, to achieve the purpose of his life. Pass we over a long space of intense thought, yearning effort, minute toil, and wasting anxiety, succeeded by an instant of solitary triumph: let all this be imagined; and then behold the artist, on a winter evening, seeking admittance to Robert Danforth's fireside circle. There he found the man of iron, with his massive substance, thoroughly warmed and attempered by domestic influences. And there was Annie, too, now transformed into a matron, with much of her husband's plain and sturdy nature, but imbued, as Owen Warland still believed, with a finer grace, that might enable her to be the interpreter between strength and beauty. It happened, likewise, that old Peter Hovenden was a guest this evening at his daughter's fireside; and it was his well-remembered expression of keen, cold criticism that first encountered the artist's glance.

'My old friend Owen!' cried Robert Danforth, starting up, and compressing the artist's delicate fingers within a hand that was accustomed to grip bars of iron. 'This is kind and neighbourly to come to us at last. I was afraid your perpetual motion had bewitched you out of the remembrance of old times.'

'We are glad to see you,' said Annie, while a blush reddened her matronly cheek. 'It was not like a friend to stay from us so long.'

'Well, Owen,' inquired the old watchmaker, as his first greeting, 'how comes on the beautiful? Have you created it at last?'

The artist did not immediately reply, being startled by the apparition of a young child of strength that was tumbling about on the carpet,—a little personage who had come mysteriously out of the infinite, but with something so sturdy and real in his composition that he seemed moulded out of the densest substance which earth could supply. This hopeful infant crawled towards the new-comer, and setting himself on end, as Robert Danforth expressed the posture, stared at Owen with a look of such sagacious observation that the mother could not help exchanging a proud glance with her husband. But the artist was disturbed by the child's look, as imagining a resemblance between it and Peter Hovenden's habitual expression. He could have fancied that the old watch-maker was compressed into this baby shape, and looking out of those baby eyes, and repeating, as he now did, the malicious question:

'The beautiful, Owen! How comes on the beautiful? Have you succeeded in creating the beautiful?'

'I have succeeded,' replied the artist, with a momentary light of triumph in his eyes and a smile of sunshine, yet steeped in such depth of thought that it was almost sadness. 'Yes, my friends, it is the truth. I have succeeded.'

'Indeed!' cried Annie, a look of maiden mirthfulness peeping out of her face again. 'And is it lawful, now, to inquire what the secret is?'

'Surely; it is to disclose it that I have come,' answered Owen Warland. 'You shall know, and see, and touch, and possess the secret! For, Annie,—if by that name I may still address the friend of my boyish years,—Annie, it is for your bridal gift that I have wrought this spiritualized mechanism, this harmony of motion, this mystery of beauty. It comes late indeed; but it is as we go onward in life, when objects begin to lose their freshness of hue and our souls their delicacy of perception, that the spirit of beauty is most needed. If,—forgive me, Annie,—if you know how to value this gift, it can never come too late.'

He produced, as he spoke, what seemed a jewel-box. It was carved richly out of ebony by his own hand, and inlaid with a fanciful tracery of pearl, representing a boy in pursuit of a butterfly, which, elsewhere, had become a winged spirit, and was flying heavenward; while the boy, or youth, had found such efficacy in his strong desire that he ascended from earth to cloud, and from cloud to celestial atmosphere, to win the beautiful. This case of ebony the artist opened, and bade Annie place her finger on its edge. She did so, but almost screamed as a butterfly fluttered forth, and, alighting on her finger's tip, sat waving the ample magnificence of its purple and gold-speckled wings, as if in prelude to a flight. It is impossible to express by words the glory, the splendour, the delicate gorgeousness which were softened into the beauty of this object. Nature's ideal butterfly was here realized in all its perfection; not in the pattern of such faded insects as flit among earthly flowers, but of those which hover across the meads of paradise for child-angels and the spirits of departed infants to disport themselves with. The rich down was visible upon its wings; the lustre of its eyes seemed instinct with spirit. The firelight glimmered around this wonder,—the candles gleamed upon it; but it glistened apparently by its own radiance, and illuminated the finger and outstretched hand on which it rested with a white gleam like that of precious stones. In its perfect beauty, the consideration of size was entirely lost. Had its wings overreached the firmament, the mind could not have been more filled or satisfied.

'Beautiful! beautiful!' exclaimed Annie. 'Is it alive? Is it alive?'

'Alive? To be sure it is,' answered her husband. 'Do you suppose any mortal has skill enough to make a butterfly, or would put himself to the trouble of making one, when any child may catch a score of them in a summer's afternoon? Alive? Certainly! But this pretty box is undoubtedly of our friend Owen's manufacture; and really it does him credit.'

At this moment the butterfly waved its wings anew, with a motion so absolutely life-like that Annie was startled, and even awe-stricken; for, in spite of her husband's opinion, she could not satisfy herself whether it was indeed a living creature or a piece of wondrous mechanism.

'Is it alive?' she repeated, more earnestly than before.

'Judge for yourself,' said Owen Warland, who stood gazing in her face with fixed attention.

The butterfly now flung itself upon the air, fluttered round Annie's head, and soared into a distant region of the parlour, still making itself perceptible to sight by the starry gleam in which the motion of its wings enveloped it. The infant on the floor followed its course with his sagacious little eyes. After flying about the room, it returned in a spiral curve and settled again on Annie's finger.

'But is it alive?' exclaimed she again; and the finger on which the gorgeous mystery had alighted was so tremulous that the butterfly was forced to balance himself with his wings. 'Tell me if it be alive, or whether you created it.'

'Wherefore ask who created it, so it be beautiful?' replied Owen Warland. 'Alive? Yes, Annie; it may well be said to possess life, for it has absorbed my own being into itself; and in the secret of that butterfly, and in its beauty,—which is not merely outward, but deep as its whole system,—is represented the intellect, the imagination, the sensibility, the soul of an Artist of the Beautiful! Yes; I created it. But'—and here his countenance somewhat changed—'this butterfly is not now to me what it was when I beheld it afar off in the day-dreams of my youth.'

'Be it what it may, it is a pretty plaything,' said the blacksmith, grinning with childlike delight. 'I wonder whether it would condescend to alight on such a great clumsy finger as mine? Hold it hither, Annie.'

By the artist's direction, Annie touched her finger's tip to that of her husband; and, after a momentary delay, the butterfly fluttered from one to the other. It preluded a second flight by a similar, yet not precisely the same, waving of wings as in the first experiment; then, ascending from the blacksmith's stalwart finger, it rose in a gradually enlarging curve to the ceiling, made one wide sweep around the room, and returned with an undulating movement to the point whence it had started.

'Well, that does beat all nature!' cried Robert Danforth, bestowing the heartiest praise that he could find expression for; and, indeed, had he paused there, a man of finer words and nicer perception could not easily have said more. 'That goes beyond me, I confess. But what then? There is more real use in one downright blow of my sledge-hammer than in the whole five years' labour that our friend Owen has wasted on this butterfly.'

Here the child clapped his hands and made a great babble of indistinct utterance, apparently demanding that the butterfly should be given him for a plaything.

Owen Warland, meanwhile, glanced sidelong at Annie, to discover whether she sympathized in her husband's estimate of the comparative value of the beautiful and the practical. There was, amid all her kindness towards himself, amid all the wonder and admiration with which she contemplated the marvellous work of his hands and incarnation of his idea, a secret scorn,—too secret, perhaps, for her own consciousness, and perceptible only to such intuitive discernment as that of the artist. But Owen, in the latter stages of his pursuit, had risen out of the region in which such a discovery might have been torture. He knew that the world, and Annie as the representative of the world, whatever praise might be bestowed, could never say the fitting word nor feel the fitting sentiment which should be the perfect recompense of an artist who, symbolizing a lofty moral by a material trifle,— converting what was earthly to spiritual gold,—had won the beautiful into his handiwork. Not at this latest moment was he to learn that the reward of all high performance must be sought within itself, or sought in vain. There was, however, a view of the matter which Annie and her husband, and even Peter Hovenden, might fully have understood, and which would have satisfied them that the toil of years had here been worthily bestowed. Owen Warland might have told them that this butterfly, this plaything, this bridal gift of a poor watchmaker to a blacksmith's wife, was, in truth, a gem of art that a monarch would have purchased with honours and abundant wealth, and have treasured it among the jewels of his kingdom as the most unique and wondrous of them all. But the artist smiled and kept the secret to himself.

'Father,' and Annie, thinking that a word of praise from the old watch-maker might gratify his former apprentice, 'do come and admire this pretty butterfly.'

'Let us see,' said Peter Hovenden, rising from his chair, with a sneer upon his face that always made people doubt, as he himself did, in everything but a material existence. 'Here is my finger for it to alight upon. I shall understand it better when once I have touched it.'

But, to the increased astonishment of Annie, when the tip of her father's finger was pressed against that of her husband, on which the butterfly still rested, the insect drooped its wings and seemed on the point of falling to the floor. Even the bright spots of gold upon its wings and body, unless her eyes deceived her, grew dim, and the glowing purple took a dusky hue, and the starry lustre that gleamed around the blacksmith's hand became faint and vanished.

'It is dying! it is dying!' cried Annie, in alarm.

'It has been delicately wrought,' and the artist, calmly. 'As I told you, it has imbibed a spiritual essence,—call it magnetism, or what you will. In an atmosphere of doubt and mockery its exquisite susceptibility suffers torture, as does the soul of him who instilled his own life into it. It has already lost its beauty; in a few moments more its mechanism would be irreparably injured.'

'Take away your hand, father!' entreated Annie, turning pale. 'Here is my child; let it rest on his innocent hand. There, perhaps, its life will revive and its colours glow brighter than ever.'

Her father, with an acrid smile, withdrew his finger. The butterfly then appeared to recover the power of voluntary motion, while its hues assumed much of their original lustre, and the gleam of starlight, which was its most ethereal attribute, again formed a halo round about it. At first, when transferred from Robert Danforth's hand to the small finger of the child, this radiance grew so powerful that it positively threw the little fellow's shadow back against the wall. He, meanwhile, extended his plump hand as he had seen his father and mother do, and watched the waving of the insect's wings with infantine delight. Nevertheless, there was a certain odd expression of sagacity that made Owen Warland feel as if here were old Peter Hovenden, partially, and but partially, redeemed from his hard scepticism into childish faith.

'How wise the little monkey looks!' whispered Robert Danforth to his wife.

'I never saw such a look on a child's face,' answered Annie, admiring her own infant, and with good reason, far more than the artistic butterfly. 'The darling knows more of the mystery than we do.'

As if the butterfly, like the artist, were conscious of something not entirely congenial in the child's nature, it alternately sparkled and grew dim. At length it arose from the small hand of the infant with an airy motion that seemed to bear it upward without an effort, as if the ethereal instincts with which its master's spirit had endowed it impelled this fair vision involuntarily to a higher sphere. Had there been no obstruction, it might have soared into the sky and grown immortal. But its lustre gleamed upon the ceiling; the exquisite texture of its wings brushed against that earthly medium; and a sparkle or two, as of star-dust, floated downward and lay glimmering on the carpet. Then the butterfly came fluttering down, and, instead of returning to the infant, was apparently attracted towards the artist's hand.

'Not so! not so!' murmured Owen Warland, as if his handiwork could have understood him. 'Thou hast gone forth out of thy master's heart. There is no return for thee.'

With a wavering movement, and emitting a tremulous radiance, the butterfly struggled, as it were, towards the infant, and was about to alight upon his finger; but, while it still hovered in the air, the little child of strength, with his grandsire's sharp and shrewd expression in his face, made a snatch at the marvellous insect and compressed it in his hand. Annie screamed. Old Peter Hovenden burst into a cold and scornful laugh. The blacksmith, by main force, unclosed the infant's hand, and found within the palm a small heap of glittering fragments, whence the mystery of beauty had fled for ever. And as for Owen Warland, he looked placidly at what seemed the ruin of his life's labour, and which was yet no ruin. He had caught a far other butterfly than this. When the artist rose high enough to achieve the beautiful, the symbol by which he made it perceptible to mortal senses became of little value in his eyes while his spirit possessed itself in the enjoyment of the reality.

DROWNE'S WOODEN IMAGE

ONE sunshiny morning, in the good old times of the town of Boston, a young carver in wood, well known by the name of Drowne,* stood contemplating a large oaken log, which it was his purpose to convert into the figure-head of a vessel. And while he discussed within his own mind what sort of shape or similitude it were well to bestow upon this excellent piece of timber, there came into Drowne's workshop a certain Captain Hunnewell, owner and commander of the good brig called the Cynosure, which had just returned from her first voyage to Fayal.*

'Ah! that will do, Drowne, that will do!' cried the jolly captain, tapping the log with his rattan. 'I bespeak this very piece of oak for the figure-head of the Cynosure. She has shown herself the sweetest craft that ever floated, and I mean to decorate her prow with the handsomest image that the skill of man can cut out of timber. And, Drowne, you are the fellow to execute it.'

'You give me more credit than I deserve, Captain Hunnewell,' said the carver, modestly, yet as one conscious of eminence in his art. 'But, for the sake of the good brig, I stand ready to do my best. And which of these designs do you prefer? Here,'—pointing to a staring, half-length figure, in a white wig and scarlet coat,—'here is an excellent model, the likeness of our gracious king. Here is the valiant Admiral Vernon.* Or, if you prefer a female figure, what say you to Britannia with the trident?'

'All very fine, Drowne; all very fine,' answered the mariner. 'But as nothing like the brig ever swam the ocean, so I am determined she shall have such a figure-head as old Neptune never saw in his life. And what is more, as there is a secret in the matter, you must pledge your credit not to betray it.'

'Certainly,' said Drowne, marvelling, however, what possible mystery there could be in reference to an affair so open, of necessity, to the inspection of all the world as the figure-head of a vessel. 'You may depend, Captain, on my being as secret as the nature of the case will permit.'

Captain Hunnewell then took Drowne by the button, and communicated his wishes in so low a tone that it would be unmannerly to repeat what was evidently intended for the carver's private ear. We shall, therefore, take the opportunity to give the reader a few desirable particulars about Drowne himself.

He was the first American who is known to have attempted—in a very humble line, it is true—that art in which we can now reckon so many names already distinguished, or rising to distinction. From his earliest boyhood he had exhibited a knack,—for it would be too proud a word to call it genius,—a knack, therefore, for the imitation of the human figure in whatever material came most readily to hand. The snows of a New England winter had often supplied him with a species of marble as dazzlingly white, at least, as the Parian or the

Carrara,* and if less durable, yet sufficiently so to correspond with any claims to permanent existence possessed by the boy's frozen statues. Yet they won admiration from maturer judges than his schoolfellows, and were, indeed, remarkably clever, though destitute of the native warmth that might have made the snow melt beneath his hand. As he advanced in life, the young man adopted pine and oak as eligible materials for the display of his skill, which now began to bring him a return of solid silver as well as the empty praise that had been an apt reward enough for his productions of evanescent snow. He became noted for carving ornamental pump-heads, and wooden urns for gateposts, and decorations, more grotesque than fanciful, for mantel-pieces. No apothecary would have deemed himself in the way of obtaining custom, without setting up a gilded mortar, if not a head of Galen or Hippocrates,* from the skilful hand of Drowne.

But the great scope of his business lay in the manufacture of figure-heads for vessels. Whether it were the monarch himself, or some famous British admiral or general, or the governor of the province, or perchance the favourite daughter of the ship-owner, there the image stood above the prow, decked out in gorgeous colours, magnificently gilded, and staring the whole world out of countenance, as if from an innate consciousness of its own superiority. These specimens of native sculpture had crossed the sea in all directions, and been not ignobly noticed among the crowded shipping of the Thames, and wherever else the hardy mariners of New England had pushed their adventures. It must be confessed that a family likeness pervaded these respectable progeny of Drowne's skill; that the benign countenance of the king resembled those of his subjects, and that Miss Peggy Hobart, the merchant's daughter, bore a remarkable similitude to Britannia, Victory, and other ladies of the allegoric sisterhood; and, finally, that they all had a kind of wooden aspect, which proved an intimate relationship with the unshaped blocks of timber in the carver's workshop. But at least there was no inconsiderable skill of hand, nor a deficiency of any attribute to render them really works of art, except that deep quality, be it of soul or intellect, which bestows life upon the lifeless and warmth upon the cold, and which, had it been present, would have made Drowne's wooden image instinct with spirit.

The captain of the Cynosure had now finished his instructions.

'And, Drowne,' said he, impressively, 'you must lay aside all other business and set about this forthwith. And as to the price, only do the job in first-rate style, and you shall settle that point yourself.'

'Very well, Captain,' answered the carver, who looked grave and somewhat perplexed, yet had a sort of smile upon his visage; 'depend upon it, I'll do my utmost to satisfy you.'

From that moment the men of taste about Long Wharf and the Town Dock who were wont to show their love for the arts by frequent visits to Drowne's workshop, and admiration of his wooden images, began to be sensible of a mystery in the carver's conduct. Often he was absent in the daytime. Sometimes, as might be judged by gleams of light from the shop-windows, he was at work until a late hour of the evening; although neither knock nor voice, on such occasions, could gain admittance for a visitor, or elicit any word of response. Nothing remarkable, however, was observed in the shop at those hours when it was thrown open. A fine piece of timber, indeed, which Drowne was known to have reserved for some work of especial dignity, was seen to be gradually assuming shape. What shape it was destined ultimately to take was a problem to his friends and a point on which the carver himself preserved a rigid silence. But day after day, though Drowne was seldom noticed in the act of working upon it, this rude · form began to be developed until it became evident to all observers that a female figure was growing into mimic life. At each new visit they beheld a larger pile of wooden chips and a nearer approximation to something beautiful. It seemed as if the hamadryad of the oak had sheltered herself from the unimaginative world within the heart of her native tree, and that it was only necessary to remove the strange shapelessness that had incrusted her, and reveal the grace and loveliness of a divinity. Imperfect as the design, the attitude, the costume, and especially the face of the image still remained, there was already an effect that drew the eye from the wooden cleverness of Drowne's earlier productions and fixed it upon the tantalizing mystery of this new project.

Copley,* the celebrated painter, then a young man and a resident of Boston, came one day to visit Drowne; for he had recognized so much of moderate ability in the carver as to induce him, in the dearth of professional sympathy, to cultivate his acquaintance. On entering the shop the artist glanced at the inflexible image of king, commander, dame, and allegory that stood around, on the best of which might have been bestowed the questionable praise that it looked as if a living man had here been changed to wood, and that not only the physical, but the intellectual and spiritual part, partook of the stolid transformation. But in not a single instance did it seem as if the wood were imbibing the ethereal essence of humanity. What a wide distinction is here! and how far would the slightest portion of the latter merit have outvalued the utmost degree of the former!

'My friend Drowne,' said Copley, smiling to himself, but alluding to the mechanical and wooden cleverness that so invariably distinguished the images, 'you are really a remarkable person! I have seldom met with a man in your line of business that could do so much; for one other touch might make this figure of General Wolfe,* for instance, a breathing and intelligent human creature.'

'You would have me think that you are praising me highly, Mr. Copley,' answered Drowne, turning his back upon Wolfe's image in apparent disgust. 'But there has come a light into my mind. I know, what you know as well, that the one touch which you speak of as deficient is the only one that would be truly valuable, and that without it these works of mine are no better than worthless abortions. There is the same difference between them and the works of an inspired artist as between a sign-post daub and one of your best pictures.'

'This is strange,' cried Copley, looking him in the face, which now, as the painter fancied, had a singular depth of intelligence, though hitherto it had not given him greatly the advantage over his own family of wooden images. 'What has come over you? How is it that, possessing the idea which you have now uttered, you should produce only such works as these?'

The carver smiled, but made no reply. Copley turned again to the images, conceiving that the sense of deficiency which Drowne had just expressed, and which is so rare in a merely mechanical character, must surely imply a genius, the tokens of which had heretofore been overlooked. But no; there was not a trace of it. He was about to withdraw when his eyes chanced to fall upon a half-developed figure which lay in a corner of the workshop, surrounded by scattered chips of oak. It arrested him at once.

'What is here? Who has done this?' he broke out, after contemplating it in speechless astonishment for an instant. 'Here is the divine, the life-giving touch. What inspired hand is beckoning this wood to arise and live? Whose work is this?'

'No man's work,' replied Drowne. 'The figure lies within that block of oak, and it is my business to find it.'

'Drowne,' said the true artist, grasping the carver fervently by the hand, 'you are a man of genius!'

As Copley departed, happening to glance backward from the threshold, he beheld Drowne bending over the half-created shape, and stretching forth his arms as if he would have embraced and drawn it to his heart; while, had such a miracle been possible, his countenance expressed passion enough to communicate warmth and sensibility to the lifeless oak.

'Strange enough!' said the artist to himself. 'Who would have looked for a modern Pygmalion* in the person of a Yankee mechanic!'

As yet, the image was but vague in its outward presentment; so that, as in the cloud-shapes around the western sun, the observer rather felt, or was led to imagine, than really saw what was intended by it. Day by day, however, the work assumed greater precision, and settled its irregular and misty outline into distincter grace and beauty. The general design was now obvious to the common eye. It was a female figure, in what appeared to be a foreign dress; the gown being laced over the bosom, and opening in front so as to disclose a skirt or petticoat, the folds and inequalities of which were admirably represented in the oaken substance. She wore a hat of singular gracefulness, and abundantly laden with flowers, such as never grew in the rude soil of New England, but which, with all their fanciful luxuriance, had a natural truth that it seemed impossible for the most fertile imagination to have attained without copying from real prototypes. There were several little appendages to this dress, such as a fan, a pair of earrings, a chain about the neck, a watch in the bosom, and a ring upon the finger, all of which would have been deemed beneath the dignity of sculpture. They were put on, however, with as much taste as a lovely woman might have shown in her attire, and could therefore have shocked none but a judgement spoiled by artistic rules.*

The face was still imperfect; but gradually, by a magic touch, intelligence and sensibility brightened through the features, with all the effect of light gleaming forth from within the solid oak. The face became alive. It was a beautiful, though not precisely regular, and somewhat haughty aspect, but with a certain piquancy about the eyes and mouth, which, of all expressions, would have seemed the most impossible to throw over a wooden countenance. And now, so far as carving went, this wonderful production was complete.

'Drowne,' said Copley, who had hardly missed a single day in his visits to the carver's workshop, 'if this work were in marble it would make you famous at once; nay, I would almost affirm that it would make an era in the art. It is as ideal as an antique statue,* and yet as real as any lovely woman whom one meets at a fireside or in the street. But I trust you do not mean to desecrate this exquisite creature with paint, like those staring kings and admirals yonder?'

'Not paint her!' exclaimed Captain Hunnewell, who stood by; 'not paint the figure-head of the *Cynosure*! And what sort of a figure should I cut in a foreign port with such an unpainted oaken stick as this over my prow! She must, and she shall, be painted to the life, from the topmost flower in her hat down to the silver spangles on her slippers.'

'Mr. Copley,' said Drowne, quietly, 'I know nothing of marble statuary, and nothing of the sculptor's rules of art; but of this wooden image, this work of my hands, this creature of my heart,'—and here his voice faltered and choked in a very singular manner,—'of this—of her—I may say that I know something. A wellspring of inward wisdom gushed within me as I wrought upon the oak with my whole strength, and soul, and faith. Let others do what they may with marble, and adopt what rules they choose. If I can produce my desired effect by painted wood, those rules are not for me, and I have a right to disregard them.'

'The very spirit of genius,' muttered Copley to himself. 'How otherwise should this carver feel himself entitled to transcend all rules, and make me ashamed of quoting them?'

He looked earnestly at Drowne, and again saw that expression of human love which, in a spiritual sense, as the artist could not help imagining, was the secret of the life that had been breathed into this block of wood.

The carver, still in the same secrecy that marked all his operations upon this mysterious image, proceeded to paint the habiliments in their proper colours, and the countenance with nature's red and white. When all was finished he threw open his workshop, and admitted the townspeople to behold what he had done. Most persons, at their first entrance, felt impelled to remove their hats, and pay such reverence as was due to the richly dressed and beautiful young lady who seemed to stand in a corner of the room, with oaken chips and shavings scattered at her feet. Then came a sensation of fear; as if, not being actually human, yet so like humanity, she must therefore be something preternatural. There was, in truth, an indefinable air and expression that might reasonably induce the query, Who and from what sphere this daughter of the oak should be? The strange, rich flowers of Eden on her head; the complexion, so much deeper and more brilliant than those of our native beauties; the foreign, as it seemed, and fantastic garb, yet not too fantastic to be worn decorously in the street; the delicately wrought embroidery of the skirt; the broad gold chain about her neck; the curious ring upon her finger; the fan, so exquisitely sculptured in open-work, and painted to resemble pearl and ebony;—where could Drowne, in his sober walk of life, have beheld the vision here so matchlessly embodied! And then her face! In the dark eyes and around the voluptuous mouth there played a look made up of pride, coquetry, and a gleam of mirthfulness, which impressed Copley with the idea that the image was secretly enjoying the perplexing admiration of himself and other beholders.

'And will you,' said he to the carver, 'permit this masterpiece to become the figure-head of a vessel? Give the honest captain yonder figure of Britannia,—it will answer his purpose far better,—and send this fairy queen to England, where, for aught I know, it may bring you a thousand pounds.'

'I have not wrought it for money,' said Drowne.

'What sort of a fellow is this?' thought Copley. 'A Yankee,* and throw away the chance of making his fortune! He has gone mad; and thence has come this gleam of genius.'

There was still further proof of Drowne's lunacy, if credit were due to the rumour that he had been seen kneeling at the feet of the oaken lady, and gazing with a lover's passionate ardour into the face that his own hands had created. The bigots of the day* hinted that it would be no matter of surprise if an evil spirit were allowed to enter this beautiful form and seduce the carver to destruction.

The fame of the image spread far and wide. The inhabitants visited it so universally that after a few days of exhibition there was hardly an old man or a child who had not become minutely familiar with its aspect. Even had the story of Drowne's wooden image ended here, its celebrity might have been prolonged for many years by the reminiscences of those who looked upon it in their childhood, and saw nothing else so beautiful in after life. But the town was now astounded by an event the narrative of which has formed itself into one of the most singular legends that are yet to be met with in the traditionary chimney-corners of the New England metropolis, where old men and women sit dreaming of the past, and wag their heads at the dreamers of the present and the future.

One fine morning, just before the departure of the *Cynosure* on her second voyage to Fayal, the commander of that gallant vessel was seen to issue from his residence in Hanover Street. He was stylishly dressed in a blue broadcloth coat, with gold-lace at the seams and buttonholes, an embroidered scarlet waistcoat, a triangular hat, with a loop and broad binding of gold, and wore a silver-hilted hanger at his side. But the good captain might have been arrayed in the robes of a prince or the rags of a beggar, without in either case attracting notice, while obscured by such a companion as now leaned on his arm. The people in the street started, rubbed their eyes, and either leaped aside from the path, or stood as if transfixed to wood or marble in astonishment.

'Do you see it?—do you see it?' cried one, with tremulous eagerness. 'It is the very same!'

'The same?' answered another, who had arrived in town only the night before. 'Who do you mean? I see only a sea-captain in his shore-going clothes, and a young lady in a foreign habit, with a bunch of beautiful flowers in her hat. On my word, she is as fair and bright a damsel as my eyes have looked on this many a day!'

'Yes; the same!—the very same!' repeated the other. 'Drowne's wooden image has come to life!'

Here was a miracle indeed! Yet, illuminated by the sunshine, or darkened by the alternate shade of the houses, and with its garments fluttering lightly in the morning breeze, there passed the image along the street. It was exactly and minutely the shape, the garb, and the face which the townspeople had so recently thronged to see and admire. Not a rich flower upon her head, not a single leaf, but had had its prototype in Drowne's wooden workmanship, although now their fragile grace had become flexible, and was shaken by every footstep that the wearer made. The broad gold chain upon the neck was identical with the one represented on the image, and glistened with the motion imparted by the rise and fall of the bosom which it decorated. A real diamond sparkled on her finger. In her right hand she bore a pearl and ebony fan, which she flourished with a fantastic and bewitching coquetry, that was likewise expressed in all her movements as well as in the style of her beauty and the attire that so well harmonized with it. The face, with its brilliant depth of complexion, had the same piquancy of mirthful mischief that was fixed upon the countenance of the image, but which was here varied and continually shifting, yet always essentially the same, like the sunny gleam upon a bubbling fountain. On the whole, there was something so airy and yet so real in the figure, and withal so perfectly did it represent Drowne's image, that people knew not whether to suppose the magic wood etherealized into a spirit or warmed and softened into an actual woman.

'One thing is certain,' muttered a Puritan of the old stamp, 'Drowne has sold himself to the Devil;* and doubtless this gay Captain Hunnewell is a party to the bargain.'

'And I,' said a young man who overheard him, 'would almost consent to be the third victim, for the liberty of saluting those lovely lips.'

'And so would I,' replied Copley, the painter, 'for the privilege of taking her picture.'

The image, or the apparition,* whichever it might be, still escorted by the bold captain, proceeded from Hanover Street through some of the cross lanes that make this portion of the town so intricate, to Ann Street, thence into Dock Square, and so downward to Drowne's shop, which stood just on the water's edge. The crowd still followed, gathering volume as it rolled along. Never had a modern miracle occurred in such broad daylight, nor in the presence of such a multitude of witnesses. The airy image, as if conscious that she was the object of the murmurs and disturbance that swelled behind her, appeared slightly vexed and flustered, yet still in a manner consistent with the light vivacity and sportive mischief that were written in her countenance. She was observed to flutter her fan with such vehement rapidity that the elaborate delicacy of its workmanship gave way, and it remained broken in her hand.

Arriving at Drowne's door, while the captain threw it open, the marvellous apparition paused an instant on the threshold, assuming the very attitude of the image, and casting over the crowd that glance of sunny coquetry which all remembered on the face of the oaken lady. She and her cavalier then disappeared.

'Ah!' murmured the crowd, drawing a deep breath, as with one vast pair of lungs.

'The world looks darker now that she has vanished,' said some of the young men.

But the aged, whose recollections dated as far back as witch times, shook their heads, and hinted that our forefathers would have thought it a pious deed to burn the daughter of the oak with fire.

'If she be other than a bubble of the elements,' exclaimed Copley, 'I must look upon her face again.'

He accordingly entered the shop; and there, in her usual corner, stood the image, gazing at him, as it might seem, with the very same expression of mirthful mischief that had been the farewell look of the apparition when, but a moment before, she turned her face towards the crowd. The carver stood beside his creation, mending the beautiful fan, which by some accident was broken in her hand. But there was no longer any motion in the life-like image, nor any real woman in the workshop, nor even the witchcraft of a sunny shadow, that might have deluded people's eyes as it flitted along the street. Captain Hunnewell, too, had vanished. His hoarse, sea-breezy tones, however, were audible on the other side of a door that opened upon the water.

'Sit down in the stern sheets, my lady,' said the gallant captain. 'Come, bear a hand, you lubbers, and set us on board in the turning of a minute-glass.'

And then was heard the stroke of oars.

'Drowne,' said Copley, with a smile of intelligence, 'you have been a truly fortunate man. What painter or statuary ever had such a subject! No wonder that she inspired a genius into you, and first created the artist who afterwards created her image.'

Drowne looked at him with a visage that bore the traces of tears, but from which the light of imagination and sensibility, so recently illuminating it, had departed. He was again the mechanical carver that he had been known to be all his lifetime.

'I hardly understand what you mean, Mr. Copley,' said he, putting his hand to his brow. 'This image! Can it have been my work? Well, I have wrought it in a kind of dream; and now that I am broad awake I must set about finishing yonder figure of Admiral Vernon.'

And forthwith he employed himself on the stolid countenance of one of his wooden progeny, and completed it in his own mechanical style, from which he was never known afterwards to deviate. He followed his business industriously for many years, acquired a competence, and in the latter part of his life attained to a dignified station in the church, being remembered in records and traditions as Deacon Drowne, the carver. One of his productions, an Indian chief, gilded all over, stood during the better part of a century on the cupola of the Province House, bedazzling the eyes of those who looked upward, like an angel of the sun. Another work of the good deacon's hand—a reduced likeness of his friend Captain Hunnewell, holding a telescope and quadrant—may be seen to this day, at the corner of Broad and State Streets, serving in the useful capacity of sign to the shop of a nautical-instrument maker. We know not how to account for the inferiority of this quaint old figure as compared with the recorded excellence of the Oaken Lady, unless on the supposition that in every human spirit there is imagination, sensibility, creative power, genius, which, according to circumstances, may either be developed in this world, or shrouded in a mask of dullness until another state of being. To our friend Drowne there came a brief season of excitement, kindled by love. It rendered him a genius of that one occasion, but, quenched in disappointment, left him again the mechanical carver in wood, without the power even of appreciating the work that his own hands had wrought. Yet who can doubt that the very highest state to which a human spirit can attain, in its loftiest aspirations, is its truest and most natural state, and that Drowne was more consistent with himself when he wrought the admirable figure of the mysterious lady, than when he perpetrated a whole progeny of blockheads?

There was a rumour in Boston, about this period, that a young Portuguese lady of rank, on some occasion of political or domestic disquietude, had fled from her home in Fayal and put herself under the protection of Captain Hunnewell, on board of whose vessel, and at whose residence, she was sheltered until a change of affairs. This fair stranger must have been the original of Drowne's Wooden Image.

RAPPACCINI'S DAUGHTER

[From the Writings of Aubépine]*

WE do not remember to have seen any translated specimens of the productions of M. de l'Aubépine,—a fact the less to be wondered at, as his very name is unknown to many of his own countrymen as well as to the student of foreign literature. As a writer, he seems to occupy an unfortunate position between Transcendentalists* (who, under one name or another, have their share in all the current literature of the world) and the great body of pen-and-ink men who address the intellect and sympathies of the multitude. If not too refined, at all events too remote, too shadowy and unsubstantial in his modes of development, to suit the taste of the latter class, and yet too popular to satisfy the spiritual or metaphysical requisitions of the former, he must necessarily find himself without an audience, except here and there an individual or possibly an isolated clique. His writings, to do them justice, are not altogether destitute of fancy and originality; they might have won him greater reputation but for an inveterate love of allegory,* which is apt to invest his plots and characters with the aspect of scenery and people in the clouds and to steal away the human warmth out of his conceptions. His fictions are sometimes historical, sometimes of the present day, and sometimes, so far as can be discovered, have little or no reference either to time or space. In any case, he generally contents himself with a very slight embroidery of outward manners,—the faintest possible counterfeit of real life,—and endeavours to create an interest by some less obvious peculiarity of the subject. Occasionally a breath of Nature, a raindrop of pathos and tenderness, or a gleam of humour, will find its way into the midst of his fantastic imagery, and make us feel as if, after all, we were yet within the limits of our native earth. We will only add to this very cursory notice that M. de l'Aubépine's productions, if the reader chance to take them in precisely the proper point of view, may amuse a leisure hour as well as those of a brighter man; if otherwise, they can hardly fail to look excessively like nonsense.

Our author is voluminous; he continues to write and publish with as much praiseworthy and indefatigable prolixity as if his efforts were crowned with the brilliant success that so justly attends those of Eugene Sue.* His first appearance was by a collection of stories in a long series* of volumes entitled *Contes deux fois racontées.* The titles of some of his more recent works (we quote from memory) are as follows: *Le Voyage Céleste à Chemin de Fer*, 3 tom., 1838. *Le nouveau Père Adam et la nouvelle Mère Eve*, 2 tom., 1839. *Roderic; ou le Serpent à l'estomac*, 2 tom., 1840. *Le Culte du Feu*, a folio volume of ponderous research into the religion and ritual of the old Persian Ghebers, published in 1841. *La Soirée du Château en Espagne*, 1 tom. 8vo, 1842; and *L'Artiste du Beau; ou le Papillon Mécanique*, 5 tom. 4to, 1843. Our somewhat wearisome perusal of this startling catalogue of volumes has left behind it a certain personal affection and sympathy, though by no means admiration, for M. de l'Aubépine; and we would fain do the little in our power towards introducing him favourably to the American public. The ensuing tale is a translation of his *Beatrice; ou la Belle Empoisonneuse*, recently published in *La Revue Anti-Aristocratique*.* This journal, edited by the Comte de Bearhaven, has for some years past led the defence of liberal principles and popular rights with a faithfulness and ability worthy of all praise.

A young man, named Giovanni Guasconti, came, very long ago, from the more southern region of Italy, to pursue his studies at the University of Padua.* Giovanni, who had but a scanty supply of gold ducats in his pocket, took lodgings in a high and gloomy chamber of an old edifice which looked not unworthy to have been the palace of a Paduan noble, and which, in fact, exhibited over its entrance the armorial bearings of a family long since extinct. The young stranger, who was not unstudied in the great poem* of his country, recollected that one of the ancestors of this family, and perhaps an occupant of this very mansion, had been pictured by Dante as a partaker of the immortal agonies of his Inferno. These reminiscences and associations, together with the tendency to heartbreak natural to a young man for the first time out of his native sphere, caused Giovanni to sigh heavily as he looked around the desolate and ill-furnished apartment.

'Holy Virgin, signor!' cried old Dame Lisabetta, who, won by the youth's remarkable beauty of person, was kindly endeavouring to give the chamber a habitable air, 'what a sigh was that to come out of a young man's heart! Do you find this old mansion gloomy? For the love of Heaven, then, put your head out of the window, and you will see as bright sunshine as you have left in Naples.'

Guasconti mechanically did as the old woman advised, but could not quite agree with her that the Paduan sunshine was as cheerful as that of Southern Italy. Such as it was, however, it fell upon a garden beneath the window and expended its fostering influences on a variety of plants, which seemed to have been cultivated with exceeding care.

'Does this garden belong to the house?' asked Giovanni.

'Heaven forbid, signor, unless it were fruitful of better potherbs than any that grow there now,' answered old Lisabetta. 'No; that garden is cultivated by the own hands of Signor Giacomo Rappaccini, the famous doctor, who, I warrant him, has been heard of as far as Naples. It is said that he distils these plants into medicines* that are as potent as a charm. Oftentimes you may see the signor doctor at work, and perchance the signora, his daughter, too, gathering the strange flowers that grow in the garden.'

The old woman had now done what she could for the aspect of the chamber; and, commending the young man to the protection of the saints, took her departure.

Giovanni still found no better occupation than to look down into the garden beneath his window. From its appearance, he judged it to be one of those botanic gardens which were of earlier date in Padua than elsewhere in Italy or in the world. Or, not improbably, it might once have been the pleasure-place of an opulent family; for there was the ruin of a marble fountain* in the centre, sculptured with rare art, but so wofully shattered that it was impossible to trace the original design from the chaos of remaining fragments. The water, however, continued to gush and sparkle into the sunbeams as cheerfully as ever. A little gurgling sound ascended to the young man's

window and made him feel as if the fountain were an immortal
spirit, that sung its song unceasingly and without heeding
the vicissitudes around it, while one century embodied it in
marble and another scattered the perishable garniture on the
soil. All about the pool into which the water subsided grew
various plants, that seemed to require a plentiful supply of
moisture for the nourishment of gigantic leaves, and, in some
instances, flowers gorgeously magnificent. There was one
shrub in particular, set in a marble vase in the midst of the
pool, that bore a profusion of purple blossoms, each of which
had the lustre and richness of a gem; and the whole together
made a show so resplendent, that it seemed enough to
illuminate the garden, even had there been no sunshine. Every
portion of the soil was peopled with plants and herbs, which,
if less beautiful, still bore tokens of assiduous care, as if all
had their individual virtues, known to the scientific mind
that fostered them. Some were placed in urns, rich with old
carving, and others in common garden pots; some crept
serpent-like along the ground or climbed on high, using
whatever means of ascent was offered them. One plant had
wreathed itself round a statue of Vertumnus,* which was thus
quite veiled and shrouded in a drapery of hanging foliage, so
happily arranged that it might have served a sculptor for a
study.

While Giovanni stood at the window he heard a rustling
behind a screen of leaves, and became aware that a person was
at work in the garden. His figure soon emerged into view, and
showed itself to be that of no common labourer, but a tall,
emaciated, sallow, and sickly-looking man, dressed in a
scholar's garb of black. He was beyond the middle term of life,
with grey hair, a thin, grey beard, and a face singularly
marked with intellect and cultivation, but which could never,
even in his more youthful days, have expressed much warmth
of heart.

Nothing could exceed the intentness with which this
scientific gardener examined every shrub which grew in his
path: it seemed as if he was looking into their inmost nature,
making observations in regard to their creative essence, and
discovering why one leaf grew in this shape and another in

that, and wherefore such and such flowers differed among themselves in hue and perfume. Nevertheless, in spite of this deep intelligence on his part, there was no approach to intimacy between himself and these vegetable existences. On the contrary, he avoided their actual touch or the direct inhaling of their odours with a caution that impressed Giovanni most disagreeably; for the man's demeanour was that of one walking among malignant influences, such as savage beasts, or deadly snakes, or evil spirits, which, should he allow them one moment of licence, would wreak upon him some terrible fatality. It was strangely frightful to the young man's imagination to see this air of insecurity in a person cultivating a garden, that most simple and innocent of human toils, and which had been alike the joy and labour of the unfallen parents of the race. Was this garden, then, the Eden of the present world? And this man, with such a perception of harm in what his own hands caused to grow,—was he the Adam?

The distrustful gardener, while plucking away the dead leaves or pruning the too luxuriant growth of the shrubs, defended his hands with a pair of thick gloves. Nor were these his only armour. When, in his walk through the garden, he came to the magnificent plant that hung its purple gems beside the marble fountain, he placed a kind of mask over his mouth and nostrils, as if all this beauty did but conceal a deadlier malice; but, finding his task still too dangerous, he drew back, removed the mask, and called loudly, but in the infirm voice of a person affected with inward disease,—

'Beatrice! Beatrice!'*

'Here am I, my father. What would you?' cried a rich and youthful voice from the window of the opposite house,—a voice as rich as a tropical sunset, and which made Giovanni, though he knew not why, think of deep hues of purple or crimson and of perfumes heavily delectable. 'Are you in the garden?'

'Yes, Beatrice,' answered the gardener; 'and I need your help.'

Soon there emerged from under a sculptured portal the figure of a young girl, arrayed with as much richness of taste

as the most splendid of the flowers, beautiful as the day, and
with a bloom so deep and vivid that one shade more would
have been too much. She looked redundant with life, health,
and energy; all of which attributes were bound down and
compressed, as it were, and girdled tensely, in their luxuriance, by her virgin zone. Yet Giovanni's fancy must have
grown morbid while he looked down into the garden; for the
impression which the fair stranger made upon him was as if
here were another flower, the human sister of those vegetable
ones, as beautiful as they, more beautiful than the richest
of them, but still to be touched only with a glove, nor to
be approached without a mask. As Beatrice came down the
garden path, it was observable that she handled and inhaled
the odour of several of the plants which her father had most
sedulously avoided.

'Here, Beatrice,' said the latter, 'see how many needful
offices require to be done to our chief treasure. Yet, shattered
as I am, my life might pay the penalty of approaching it so
closely as circumstances demand. Henceforth, I fear, this
plant must be consigned to your sole charge.'

'And gladly will I undertake it,' cried again the rich tones
of the young lady, as she bent towards the magnificent plant
and opened her arms as if to embrace it. 'Yes, my sister, my
splendour, it shall be Beatrice's task to nurse and serve thee;
and thou shalt reward her with thy kisses and perfumed
breath, which to her is as the breath of life.'

Then, with all the tenderness in her manner that was so
strikingly expressed in her words, she busied herself with such
attentions as the plant seemed to require; and Giovanni, at his
lofty window, rubbed his eyes, and almost doubted whether
it were a girl tending her favourite flower, or one sister
performing the duties of affection to another. The scene soon
terminated. Whether Dr. Rappaccini had finished his labours
in the garden, or that his watchful eye had caught the
stranger's face, he now took his daughter's arm and retired.
Night was already closing in; oppressive exhalations seemed
to proceed from the plants and steal upward past the open
window; and Giovanni, closing the lattice, went to his couch
and dreamed of a rich flower and beautiful girl. Flower and

maiden were different, and yet the same, and fraught with some strange peril in either shape.

But there is an influence in the light of morning that tends to rectify whatever errors of fancy, or even of judgement, we may have incurred during the sun's decline, or among the shadows of the night, or in the less wholesome glow of moonshine. Giovanni's first movement, on starting from sleep, was to throw open the window and gaze down into the garden which his dreams had made so fertile of mysteries. He was surprised, and a little ashamed, to find how real and matter-of-fact an affair it proved to be, in the first rays of the sun which gilded the dewdrops that hung upon leaf and blossom, and, while giving a brighter beauty to each rare flower, brought everything within the limits of ordinary experience. The young man rejoiced that, in the heart of the barren city, he had the privilege of overlooking this spot of lovely and luxuriant vegetation. It would serve, he said to himself, as a symbolic language to keep him in communion with nature. Neither the sickly and thought-worn Dr. Giacomo Rappaccini, it is true, nor his brilliant daughter, were now visible; so that Giovanni could not determine how much of the singularity which he attributed to both was due to their own qualities and how much to his wonder-working fancy; but he was inclined to take a most rational view of the whole matter.

In the course of the day he paid his respects to Signor Pietro Baglioni, professor of medicine in the university, a physician of eminent repute, to whom Giovanni had brought a letter of introduction. The professor was an elderly personage, apparently of genial nature and habits that might almost be called jovial. He kept the young man to dinner, and made himself very agreeable by the freedom and liveliness of his conversation, especially when warmed by a flask or two of Tuscan wine. Giovanni, conceiving that men of science, inhabitants of the same city, must needs be on familiar terms with one another, took an opportunity to mention the name of Dr. Rappaccini. But the professor did not respond with so much cordiality as he had anticipated.

'Ill would it become a teacher of the divine art of medicine,' said Professor Pietro Baglioni, in answer to a question of Giovanni, 'to withhold due and well-considered praise of a physician so eminently skilled as Rappaccini; but, on the other hand, I should answer it but scantily to my conscience were I to permit a worthy youth like yourself, Signor Giovanni, the son of an ancient friend, to imbibe erroneous ideas respecting a man who might hereafter chance to hold your life and death in his hands. The truth is, our worshipful Dr. Rappaccini has as much science as any member of the faculty—with perhaps one single exception—in Padua, or all Italy; but there are certain grave objections to his professional character.'

'And what are they?' asked the young man.

'Has my friend Giovanni any disease of body or heart, that he is so inquisitive about physicians?' said the professor, with a smile. 'But as for Rappaccini, it is said of him—and I, who know the man well, can answer for its truth—that he cares infinitely more for science than for mankind. His patients are interesting to him only as subjects for some new experiment. He would sacrifice human life, his own among the rest, or whatever else was dearest to him, for the sake of adding so much as a grain of mustard seed to the great heap of his accumulated knowledge.'

'Methinks he is an awful man indeed,' remarked Guasconti, mentally recalling the cold and purely intellectual aspect of Rappaccini. 'And yet, worshipful professor, is it not a noble spirit? Are there many men capable of so spiritual a love of science?

'God forbid,' answered the professor, somewhat testily; 'at least, unless they take sounder views of the healing art than those adopted by Rappaccini. It is his theory that all medicinal virtues are comprised within those substances which we term vegetable poisons. These he cultivates with his own hands, and is said even to have produced new varieties of poison more horribly deleterious than nature, without the assistance of this learned person, would ever have plagued the world withal. That the signor doctor does less mischief than might be expected with such dangerous substances is undeniable. Now and then, it must be owned, he has effected, or seemed to effect, a marvellous cure; but, to tell you my private mind, Signor Giovanni, he should receive little credit for such instances of success,—they being probably the work of chance,—but should be held strictly accountable for his failures, which might justly be considered his own work.'

The youth might have taken Baglioni's opinions with many grains of allowance had he known that there was a professional warfare of long continuance between him and Dr. Rappaccini, in which the latter was generally thought to have gained the advantage. If the reader be inclined to judge for himself, we refer him to certain black-letter tracts on both sides, preserved in the medical department of the University of Padua.

'I know not, most learned professor,' returned Giovanni, after musing on what had been said of Rappaccini's exclusive zeal for science,—'I know not how dearly this physician may love his art; but surely there is one object more dear to him. He has a daughter.'

'Aha!' cried the professor, with a laugh. 'So now our friend Giovanni's secret is out. You have heard of this daughter, whom all the young men in Padua are wild about, though not half a dozen have ever had the good hap to see her face. I know little of the Signora Beatrice save that Rappaccini is said to have instructed her deeply in his science, and that, young and beautiful as fame reports her, she is already qualified to fill a professor's chair. Perchance her father destines her for mine! Other absurd rumours there be, not worth talking about or listening to. So now, Signor Giovanni, drink off your glass of lachryma.'

Guasconti returned to his lodgings somewhat heated with the wine he had quaffed, and which caused his brain to swim with strange fantasies in reference to Dr. Rappaccini and the beautiful Beatrice. On his way, happening to pass by a florist's, he bought a fresh bouquet of flowers.

Ascending to his chamber, he seated himself near the window, but within the shadow thrown by the depth of the wall, so that he could look down into the garden with little risk of being discovered. All beneath his eye was a solitude. The strange plants were basking in the sunshine, and now and then nodding gently to one another, as if in acknowledgement

of sympathy and kindred. In the midst, by the shattered
fountain, grew the magnificent shrub, with its purple gems
clustering all over it; they glowed in the air, and gleamed back
again out of the depths of the pool, which thus seemed to
overflow with coloured radiance from the rich reflection that
was steeped in it. At first, as we have said, the garden was a
solitude. Soon, however,—as Giovanni had half hoped, half
feared, would be the case,—a figure appeared beneath the
antique sculptured portal, and came down between the rows
of plants, inhaling their various perfumes as if she were one
of those beings of old classic fable that lived upon sweet
odours. On again beholding Beatrice, the young man was even
startled to perceive how much her beauty exceeded his
recollection of it; so brilliant, so vivid, was its character, that
she glowed amid the sunlight and, as Giovanni whispered to
himself, positively illuminated the more shadowy intervals
of the garden path. Her face being now more revealed than
on the former occasion, he was struck by its expression of
simplicity and sweetness,—qualities that had not entered into
his idea of her character, and which made him ask anew what
manner of mortal she might be. Nor did he fail again to
observe, or imagine, an analogy between the beautiful girl and
the gorgeous shrub that hung its gem-like flowers over the
fountain,—a resemblance which Beatrice seemed to have
indulged a fantastic humour in heightening, both by the
arrangement of her dress and the selection of its hues.

Approaching the shrub, she threw open her arms, as with
a passionate ardour, and drew its branches into an intimate
embrace,—so intimate that her features were hidden in its
leafy bosom and her glistening ringlets all intermingled with
the flowers.

'Give me thy breath, my sister,' exclaimed Beatrice; 'for I
am faint with common air. And give me this flower of thine,
which I separate with gentlest fingers from the stem and place
it close beside my heart.'

With these words the beautiful daughter of Rappaccini
plucked one of the richest blossoms of the shrub, and was
about to fasten it in her bosom. But now, unless Giovanni's
draughts of wine had bewildered his senses, a singular

incident occurred. A small orange-coloured reptile, of the lizard or chameleon species, chanced to be creeping along the path, just at the feet of Beatrice. It appeared to Giovanni,— but, at the distance from which he gazed, he could scarcely have seen anything so minute,—it appeared to him, however, that a drop or two of moisture from the broken stem of the flower descended upon the lizard's head. For an instant the reptile contorted itself violently, and then lay motionless in the sunshine. Beatrice observed this remarkable phenomenon, and crossed herself, sadly, but without surprise; nor did she therefore hesitate to arrange the fatal flower in her bosom. There it blushed, and almost glimmered with the dazzling effect of a precious stone, adding to her dress and aspect the one appropriate charm which nothing else in the world could have supplied. But Giovanni, out of the shadow of his window, bent forward and shrank back, and murmured and trembled.

'Am I awake? Have I my senses?' said he to himself. 'What is this being? Beautiful shall I call her, or inexpressibly terrible?'

Beatrice now strayed carelessly through the garden, approaching closer beneath Giovanni's window, so that he was compelled to thrust his head quite out of its concealment in order to gratify the intense and painful curiosity which she excited. At this moment there came a beautiful insect over the garden wall: it had, perhaps, wandered through the city, and found no flowers or verdure among those antique haunts of men until the heavy perfumes of Dr. Rappaccini's shrubs had lured it from afar. Without alighting on the flowers, this winged brightness seemed to be attracted by Beatrice, and lingered in the air and fluttered about her head. Now, here it could not be but that Giovanni Guasconti's eyes deceived him. Be that as it might, he fancied that, while Beatrice was gazing at the insect with childish delight, it grew faint and fell at her feet; its bright wings shivered; it was dead,—from no cause that he could discern, unless it were the atmosphere of her breath. Again Beatrice crossed herself and sighed heavily as she bent over the dead insect.

An impulsive movement of Giovanni drew her eyes to the

window. There she beheld the beautiful head of the young man—rather a Grecian than an Italian head, with fair, regular features, and a glistening of gold among his ringlets—gazing down upon her like a being that hovered in mid-air. Scarcely knowing what he did, Giovanni threw down the bouquet which he had hitherto held in his hand.

'Signora,' said he, 'they are pure and healthful flowers. Wear them for the sake of Giovanni Guasconti.'

'Thanks, signor,' replied Beatrice, with her rich voice, that came forth as it were like a gush of music, and with a mirthful expression half childish and half woman-like. 'I accept your gift, and would fain recompense it with this precious purple flower; but, if I toss it into the air, it will not reach you. So Signor Guasconti must even content himself with my thanks.'

She lifted the bouquet from the ground, and then, as if inwardly ashamed at having stepped aside from her maidenly reserve to respond to a stranger's greeting, passed swiftly homeward through the garden. But, few as the moments were, it seemed to Giovanni, when she was on the point of vanishing beneath the sculptured portal, that his beautiful bouquet was already beginning to wither in her grasp. It was an idle thought; there could be no possibility of distinguishing a faded flower from a fresh one at so great a distance.

For many days after this incident the young man avoided the window that looked into Dr. Rappaccini's garden, as if something ugly and monstrous would have blasted his eyesight had he been betrayed into a glance. He felt conscious of having put himself, to a certain extent, within the influence of an unintelligible power by the communication which he had opened with Beatrice. The wisest course would have been, if his heart were in any real danger, to quit his lodgings and Padua itself at once; the next wiser, to have accustomed himself, as far as possible, to the familiar and daylight view of Beatrice,—thus bringing her rigidly and systematically within the limits of ordinary experience. Least of all, while avoiding her sight, ought Giovanni to have remained so near this extraordinary being that the proximity and possibility even of intercourse should give a kind of substance and reality to the wild vagaries which his imagination ran riot

continually in producing. Guasconti had not a deep heart,*—
or, at all events, its depths were not sounded now; but he
had a quick fancy, and an ardent Southern temperament,
which rose every instant to a higher fever pitch. Whether or
no Beatrice possessed those terrible attributes, that fatal
breath, the affinity with those so beautiful and deadly flowers,
which were indicated by what Giovanni had witnessed, she
had at least instilled a fierce and subtle poison into his system.
It was not love, although her rich beauty was a madness to
him; nor horror, even while he fancied her spirit to be imbued
with the same baneful essence that seemed to pervade her
physical frame; but a wild offspring of both love and horror
that had each parent in it, and burned like one and shivered
like the other. Giovanni knew not what to dread; still less did
he know what to hope; yet hope and dread kept a continual
warfare in his breast, alternately vanquishing one another and
starting up afresh to renew the contest. Blessed are all simple
emotions, be they dark or bright! It is the lurid intermixture
of the two that produces the illuminating blaze of the infernal
regions.

Sometimes he endeavoured to assuage the fever of his spirit
by a rapid walk through the streets of Padua or beyond its
gates: his footsteps kept time with the throbbings of his brain,
so that the walk was apt to accelerate itself to a race. One day
he found himself arrested; his arm was seized by a portly
personage, who had turned back on recognizing the young
man and expended much breath in overtaking him.

'Signor Giovanni! Stay, my young friend!' cried he. 'Have
you forgotten me? That might well be the case if I were as
much altered as yourself.'

It was Baglioni, whom Giovanni had avoided ever since
their first meeting, from a doubt that the professor's sagacity
would look too deeply into his secrets. Endeavouring to
recover himself, he stared forth wildly from his inner world
into the outer one and spoke like a man in a dream.

'Yes; I am Giovanni Guasconti. You are Professor Pietro
Baglioni. Now let me pass!'

'Not yet, not yet, Signor Giovanni Guasconti,' said the
professor, smiling, but at the same time scrutinizing the youth

with an earnest glance. 'What! did I grow up side by side with your father? and shall his son pass me like a stranger in these old streets of Padua? Stand still, Signor Giovanni; for we must have a word or two before we part.'

'Speedily, then, most worshipful professor, speedily,' said Giovanni, with feverish impatience. 'Does not your worship see that I am in haste?'

Now, while he was speaking there came a man in black along the street, stooping and moving feebly, like a person in inferior health. His face was all overspread with a most sickly and sallow hue, but yet so pervaded with an expression of piercing and active intellect that an observer might easily have overlooked the merely physical attributes and have seen only this wonderful energy. As he passed, this person exchanged a cold and distant salutation with Baglioni, but fixed his eyes upon Giovanni with an intentness that seemed to bring out whatever was within him worthy of notice. Nevertheless, there was a peculiar quietness in the look, as if taking merely a speculative, not a human, interest in the young man.

'It is Dr. Rappaccini!' whispered the professor when the stranger had passed. 'Has he ever seen your face before?'

'Not that I know,' answered Giovanni, starting at the name.

'He *has* seen you! he must have seen you!' said Baglioni, hastily. 'For some purpose or other, this man of science is making a study of you. I know that look of his! It is the same that coldly illuminates his face as he bends over a bird, a mouse, or a butterfly; which, in pursuance of some experiment, he has killed by the perfume of a flower; a look as deep as nature itself, but without nature's warmth of love. Signor Giovanni, I will stake my life upon it, you are the subject of one of Rappaccini's experiments!'

'Will you make a fool of me?' cried Giovanni, passionately. '*That*, signor professor, were an untoward experiment.'

'Patience! patience!' replied the imperturbable professor. 'I tell thee, my poor Giovanni, that Rappaccini has a scientific interest in thee. Thou hast fallen into fearful hands! And the Signora Beatrice,—what part does she act in this mystery?'

But Guasconti, finding Baglioni's pertinacity intolerable, here broke away, and was gone before the professor could again seize his arm. He looked after the young man intently and shook his head.

'This must not be,' said Baglioni to himself. 'The youth is the son of my old friend, and shall not come to any harm from which the arcana of medical science can preserve him. Besides, it is too insufferable an impertinence in Rappaccini thus to snatch the lad out of my own hands, as I may say, and make use of him for his infernal experiments. This daughter of his! It shall be looked to. Perchance, most learned Rappaccini, I may foil you where you little dream of it!'

Meanwhile Giovanni had pursued a circuitous route, and at length found himself at the door of his lodgings. As he crossed the threshold he was met by old Lisabetta, who smirked and smiled, and was evidently desirous to attract his attention; vainly, however, as the ebullition of his feelings had momentarily subsided into a cold and dull vacuity. He turned his eyes full upon the withered face that was puckering itself into a smile, but seemed to behold it not. The old dame, therefore, laid her grasp upon his cloak.

'Signor! signor!' whispered she, still with a smile over the whole breadth of her visage, so that it looked not unlike a grotesque carving in wood, darkened by centuries. 'Listen, signor! There is a private entrance into the garden!'

'What do you say?' exclaimed Giovanni, turning quickly about, as if an inanimate thing should start into feverish life. 'A private entrance into Dr. Rappaccini's garden?'

'Hush! hush! not so loud!' whispered Lisabetta, putting her hand over his mouth. 'Yes; into the worshipful doctor's garden, where you may see all his fine shrubbery. Many a young man in Padua would give gold to be admitted among those flowers.'

Giovanni put a piece of gold into her hand.

'Show me the way,' said he.

A surmise, probably excited by his conversation with Baglioni, crossed his mind, that this interposition of old Lisabetta might perchance be connected with the intrigue, whatever were its nature, in which the professor seemed to suppose that Dr. Rappaccini was involving him. But such a suspicion, though it disturbed Giovanni, was inadequate to restrain him. The instant that he was aware of the possibility of approaching Beatrice, it seemed an absolute necessity of his existence to do so. It mattered not whether she were angel or demon; he was irrevocably within her sphere, and must obey the law that whirled him onward, in ever-lessening circles, towards a result which he did not attempt to foreshadow; and yet, strange to say, there came across him a sudden doubt whether this intense interest on his part was not delusory; whether it were really of so deep and positive a nature as to justify him in now thrusting himself into an incalculable position; whether it were not merely the fantasy of a young man's brain, only slightly or not at all connected with his heart.

He paused, hesitated, turned half about, but again went on. His withered guide led him along several obscure passages, and finally undid a door, through which, as it was opened, there came the sight and sound of rustling leaves, with the broken sunshine glimmering among them. Giovanni stepped forth, and, forcing himself through the entanglement of a shrub that wreathed its tendrils over the hidden entrance, stood beneath his own window in the open area of Dr. Rappaccini's garden.

How often is it the case that, when impossibilities have come to pass, and dreams have condensed their misty substance into tangible realities, we find ourselves calm, and even coldly self-possessed, amid circumstances which it would have been a delirium of joy or agony to anticipate! Fate delights to thwart us thus. Passion will choose his own time to rush upon the scene, and lingers sluggishly behind when an appropriate adjustment of events would seem to summon his appearance. So was it now with Giovanni. Day after day his pulses had throbbed with feverish blood at the improbable idea of an interview with Beatrice, and of standing with her, face to face, in this very garden, basking in the Oriental sunshine of her beauty, and snatching from her full gaze the mystery which he deemed the riddle of his own existence. But now there was a singular and untimely equanimity within his breast. He threw a glance around the garden to discover if Beatrice or her father were present, and, perceiving that he was alone, began a critical observation of the plants.

The aspect of one and all of them dissatisfied him; their gorgeousness seemed fierce, passionate, and even unnatural. There was hardly an individual shrub which a wanderer, straying by himself through a forest, would not have been startled to find growing wild, as if an unearthly face had glared at him out of the thicket. Several also would have shocked a delicate instinct by an appearance of artificialness indicating that there had been such commixture, and, as it were, adultery* of various vegetable species, that the production was no longer of God's making, but the monstrous offspring of man's depraved fancy, glowing with only an evil mockery of beauty. They were probably the result of experiment, which in one or two cases had succeeded in mingling plants individually lovely into a compound possessing the questionable and ominous character that distinguished the whole growth of the garden. In fine, Giovanni recognized but two or three plants in the collection, and those of a kind that he well knew to be poisonous. While busy with these contemplations he heard the rustling of a silken garment, and, turning, beheld Beatrice emerging from beneath the sculptured portal.

Giovanni had not considered with himself what should be his deportment; whether he should apologize for his intrusion into the garden, or assume that he was there with the privity at least, if not by the desire, of Dr. Rappaccini or his daughter; but Beatrice's manner placed him at his ease, though leaving him still in doubt by what agency he had gained admittance. She came lightly along the path, and met him near the broken fountain. There was surprise in her face, but brightened by a simple and kind expression of pleasure.

'You are a connoisseur in flowers, signor,' said Beatrice, with a smile, alluding to the bouquet which he had flung her from the window. 'It is no marvel, therefore, if the sight of my father's rare collection has tempted you to take a nearer view. If he were here he could tell you many strange and interesting facts as to the nature and habits of these shrubs; for he has spent a lifetime in such studies, and this garden is his world.'

'And yourself, lady,' observed Giovanni, 'if fame says true, you likewise are deeply skilled in the virtues indicated by these rich blossoms and these spicy perfumes. Would you deign to be my instructress, I should prove an apter scholar than if taught by Signor Rappaccini himself.'

'Are there such idle rumours?' asked Beatrice, with the music of a pleasant laugh. 'Do people say that I am skilled in my father's science of plants? What a jest is there! No; though I have grown up among these flowers, I know no more of them than their hues and perfume; and sometimes methinks I would fain rid myself of even that small knowledge. There are many flowers here, and those not the least brilliant, that shock and offend me when they meet my eye. But pray, signor, do not believe these stories about my science. Believe nothing of me save what you see with your own eyes.'

'And must I believe all that I have seen with my own eyes?' asked Giovanni, pointedly, while the recollection of former scenes made him shrink. 'No, signora; you demand too little of me. Bid me believe nothing save what comes from your own lips.'

It would appear that Beatrice understood him. There came a deep flush to her cheek; but she looked full into Giovanni's eyes, and responded to his gaze of uneasy suspicion with a queen-like haughtiness.

'I do so bid you, signor,' she replied. 'Forget whatever you may have fancied in regard to me. If true to the outward senses, still it may be false in its essence; but the words of Beatrice Rappaccini's lips are true from the depths of the heart outward. Those you may believe.'

A fervour glowed in her whole aspect, and beamed upon Giovanni's consciousness like the light of truth itself; but while she spoke there was a fragrance in the atmosphere around her, rich and delightful, though evanescent, yet which the young man, from an indefinable reluctance, scarcely dared to draw into his lungs. It might be the odour of the flowers. Could it be Beatrice's breath which thus embalmed her words with a strange richness, as if by steeping them in her heart? A faintness passed like a shadow over Giovanni and flitted away; he seemed to gaze through the beautiful girl's eyes into her transparent soul, and felt no more doubt or fear.

The tinge of passion that had coloured Beatrice's manner

vanished; she became gay, and appeared to derive a pure delight from her communion with the youth not unlike what the maiden of a lonely island might have felt conversing with a voyager from the civilized world. Evidently her experience of life had been confined within the limits of that garden. She talked now about matters as simple as the daylight or summer clouds, and now asked questions in reference to the city, or Giovanni's distant home, his friends, his mother, and his sisters,—questions indicating such seclusion, and such lack of familiarity with modes and forms, that Giovanni responded as if to an infant. Her spirit gushed out before him like a fresh rill that was just catching its first glimpse of the sunlight and wondering at the reflections of earth and sky which were flung into its bosom. There came thoughts, too, from a deep source, and fantasies of a gem-like brilliancy, as if diamonds and rubies sparkled upward among the bubbles of the fountain. Ever and anon there gleamed across the young man's mind a sense of wonder that he should be walking side by side with the being who had so wrought upon his imagination, whom he had idealized in such hues of terror, in whom he had positively witnessed such manifestations of dreadful attributes,—that he should be conversing with Beatrice like a brother, and should find her so human and so maiden-like. But such reflections were only momentary; the effect of her character was too real not to make itself familiar at once.

In this free intercourse they had strayed through the garden, and now, after many turns among its avenues, were come to the shattered fountain, beside which grew the magnificent shrub, with its treasury of glowing blossoms. A fragrance was diffused from it which Giovanni recognized as identical with that which he had attributed to Beatrice's breath, but incomparably more powerful. As her eyes fell upon it, Giovanni beheld her press her hand to her bosom as if her heart were throbbing suddenly and painfully.

'For the first time in my life,' murmured she, addressing the shrub, 'I had forgotten thee.'

'I remember, signora,' said Giovanni, 'that you once promised to reward me with one of these living gems for the bouquet which I had the happy boldness to fling to your feet.

Permit me now to pluck it as a memorial of this interview.'

He made a step towards the shrub with extended hand; but Beatrice darted foward, uttering a shriek that went through his heart like a dagger. She caught his hand and drew it back with the whole force of her slender figure. Giovanni felt her touch thrilling through his fibres.

'Touch it not!' exclaimed she, in a voice of agony. Not for thy life! It is fatal!'

Then, hiding her face, she fled from him and vanished beneath the sculptured portal. As Giovanni followed her with his eyes, he beheld the emaciated figure and pale intelligence of Dr. Rappaccini, who had been watching the scene, he knew not how long, within the shadow of the entrance.

No sooner was Guasconti alone in his chamber than the image of Beatrice came back to his passionate musings, invested with all the witchery that had been gathering around it ever since his first glimpse of her, and now likewise imbued with a tender warmth of girlish womanhood. She was human; her nature was endowed with all gentle and feminine qualities; she was worthiest to be worshipped; she was capable, surely, on her part, of the height and heroism of love. Those tokens which he had hitherto considered as proofs of a frightful peculiarity in her physical and moral system were now either forgotten or by the subtle sophistry of passion transmuted into a golden crown of enchantment, rendering Beatrice the more admirable by so much as she was the more unique. Whatever had looked ugly was now beautiful; or, if incapable of such a change, it stole away and hid itself among those shapeless half-ideas which throng the dim region beyond the daylight of our perfect consciousness. Thus did he spend the night, nor fell asleep until the dawn had begun to awake the slumbering flowers in Dr. Rappaccini's garden, whither Giovanni's dreams doubtless led him. Up rose the sun in his due season, and, flinging his beams upon the young man's eyelids, awoke him to a sense of pain. When thoroughly aroused, he became sensible of a burning and tingling agony in his hand,—in his right hand,—the very hand which Beatrice had grasped in her own when he was on the point of plucking one of the gem-like flowers. On the back of that hand there was now a purple print like that of four small fingers, and the likeness of a slender thumb upon his wrist.

Oh, how stubbornly does love,—or even that cunning semblance of love which flourishes in the imagination, but strikes no depth of root into the heart,—how stubbornly does it hold its faith until the moment comes when it is doomed to vanish into thin mist! Giovanni wrapped a handkerchief about his hand and wondered what evil thing had stung him, and soon forgot his pain in a reverie of Beatrice.

After the first interview, a second was in the inevitable course of what we call fate. A third; a fourth; and a meeting with Beatrice in the garden was no longer an incident in Giovanni's daily life, but the whole space in which he might be said to live; or the anticipation and memory of that ecstatic hour made up the remainder. Nor was it otherwise with the daughter of Rappaccini. She watched for the youth's appearance and flew to his side with confidence as unreserved as if they had been playmates from early infancy,—as if they were such playmates still. If, by any unwonted chance, he failed to come at the appointed moment, she stood beneath the window and sent up the rich sweetness of her tones to float around him in his chamber and echo and reverberate throughout his heart: 'Giovanni! Giovanni! Why tarriest thou? Come down!' And down he hastened into that Eden of poisonous flowers.*

But, with all this intimate familiarity, there was still a reserve in Beatrice's demeanour, so rigidly and invariably sustained, that the idea of infringing it scarcely occurred to his imagination. By all appreciable signs, they loved; they had looked love with eyes that conveyed the holy secret from the depths of one soul into the depths of the other, as if it were too sacred to be whispered by the way; they had even spoken love in those gushes of passion when their spirits darted forth in articulated breath like tongues of long-hidden flame; and yet there had been no seal of lips, no clasp of hands, nor any slightest caress such as love claims and hallows. He had never touched one of the gleaming ringlets of her hair; her garment—so marked was the physical barrier between them— had never been waved against him by a breeze. On the few occasions when Giovanni had seemed tempted to overstep the limit, Beatrice grew so sad, so stern, and withal wore such a look of desolate separation, shuddering at itself, that not a spoken word was requisite to repel him. At such times he was startled at the horrible suspicions that rose, monster-like, out of the caverns of his heart and stared him in the face; his love grew thin and faint as the morning mist; his doubts alone had substance.But, when Beatrice's face brightened again after the momentary shadow, she was transformed at once from the mysterious, questionable being whom he had watched with so much awe and horror; she was now the beautiful and unsophisticated girl whom he felt that his spirit knew with a certainty beyond all other knowledge.

A considerable time had now passed since Giovanni's last meeting with Baglioni. One morning, however, he was disagreeably surprised by a visit from the professor, whom he had scarcely thought of for whole weeks, and would willingly have forgotten still longer. Given up as he had long been to a pervading excitement, he could tolerate no companions except upon condition of their perfect sympathy with his present state of feeling. Such sympathy was not to be expected from Professor Baglioni.

The visitor chatted carelessly for a few moments about the gossip of the city and the university, and then took up another topic.

'I have been reading an old classic author lately,' said he, 'and met with a story that strangely interested me. Possibly you may remember it. It is of an Indian prince, who sent a beautiful woman as a present to Alexander the Great. She was as lovely as the dawn and gorgeous as the sunset; but what especially distinguished her was a certain rich perfume in her breath,—richer than a garden of Persian roses. Alexander, as was natural to a youthful conqueror, fell in love at first sight with this magnificent stranger; but a certain sage physician, happening to be present, discovered a terrible secret in regard to her.'

'And what was that?' asked Giovanni, turning his eyes downward, to avoid those of the professor.

'That this lovely woman,' continued Baglioni, with

emphasis, 'had been nourished with poisons from her birth upward, until her whole nature was so imbued with them that she herself had become the deadliest poison in existence. Poison was her element of life. With that rich perfume of her breath she blasted the very air. Her love would have been poison,—her embrace death. Is not this a marvellous tale?'

'A childish fable,' answered Giovanni, nervously starting from his chair. 'I marvel how your worship finds time to read such nonsense among your graver studies.'

'By the by,' said the professor, looking uneasily about him, 'what singular fragrance is this in your apartment? Is it the perfume of your gloves? It is faint, but delicious; and yet, after all, by no means agreeable. Were I to breathe it long, methinks it would make me ill. It is like the breath of a flower; but I see no flowers in the chamber.'

'Nor are there any,' replied Giovanni, who had turned pale as the professor spoke; 'nor, I think, is there any fragrance, except in your worship's imagination. Odours, being a sort of element combined of the sensual and the spiritual, are apt to deceive us in this matter. The recollection of a perfume, the bare idea of it, may easily be mistaken for a present reality.'

'Ay; but my sober imagination does not often play such tricks,' said Baglioni; 'and, were I to fancy any kind of odour, it would be that of some vile apothecary drug, wherewith my fingers are likely enough to be imbued. Our worshipful friend Rappaccini, as I have heard, tinctures his medicaments with odours richer than those of Araby. Doubtless, likewise, the fair and learned Signora Beatrice would minister to her patients with draughts as sweet as a maiden's breath; but woe to him that sips them!'

Giovanni's face evinced many contending emotions. The tone in which the professor alluded to the pure and lovely daughter of Rappaccini was a torture to his soul; and yet the intimation of a view of her character, opposite to his own, gave instantaneous distinctness to a thousand dim suspicions, which now grinned at him like so many demons. But he strove hard to quell them and to respond to Baglioni with a true lover's perfect faith.

'Signor professor,' said he, 'you were my father's friend;

perchance, too, it is your purpose to act a friendly part to-wards his son. I would fain feel nothing towards you save respect and deference; but I pray you to observe, signor, that there is one subject on which we must not speak. You know not the Signora Beatrice. You cannot, therefore, estimate the wrong—the blasphemy, I may even say—that is offered to her character by a light or injurious word.'

'Giovanni! my poor Giovanni!' answered the professor, with a calm expression of pity, 'I know this wretched girl far better than yourself. You shall hear the truth in respect to the poisoner Rappaccini and his poisonous daughter; yes, poisonous as she is beautiful. Listen; for, even should you do violence to my grey hairs, it shall not silence me. That old fable of the Indian woman has become a truth by the deep and deadly science of Rappaccini and in the person of the lovely Beatrice.'

Giovanni groaned and hid his face.

'Her father,' continued Baglioni, 'was not restrained by natural affection from offering up his child in this horrible manner as the victim of his insane zeal for science; for, let us do him justice, he is as true a man of science as ever distilled his own heart in an alembic. What, then, will be your fate? Beyond a doubt you are selected as the material of some new experiment. Perhaps the result is to be death; perhaps a fate more awful still. Rappaccini, with what he calls the interest of science before his eyes, will hesitate at nothing.'

'It is a dream,' muttered Giovanni to himself; 'surely it is a dream.'

'But,' resumed the professor, 'be of good cheer, son of my friend. It is not yet too late for the rescue. Possibly we may even succeed in bringing back this miserable child within the limits of ordinary nature, from which her father's madness has estranged her. Behold this little silver vase! It was wrought by the hands of the renowned Benvenuto Cellini,* and is well worthy to be a love-gift to the fairest dame in Italy. But its contents are invaluable. One little sip of this antidote would have rendered the most virulent poisons of the Borgias innocuous. Doubt not that it will be as efficacious against those of Rappaccini. Bestow the vase, and the precious liquid within it, on your Beatrice, and hopefully await the result.'

Baglioni laid a small, exquisitely wrought silver vial on the table and withdrew, leaving what he had said to produce its effect upon the young man's mind.

'We will thwart Rappaccini yet,' thought he, chuckling to himself as he descended the stairs; 'but, let us confess the truth of him, he is a wonderful man,—a wonderful man indeed; a vile empiric, however, in his practice, and therefore not to be tolerated by those who respect the good old rules of the medical profession.'

Throughout Giovanni's whole acquaintance with Beatrice, he had occasionally, as we have said, been haunted by dark surmises as to her character; yet so thoroughly had she made herself felt by him as a simple, natural, most affectionate, and guileless creature, that the image now held up by Professor Baglioni looked as strange and incredible as if it were not in accordance with his own original conception. True, there were ugly recollections connected with his first glimpses of the beautiful girl; he could not quite forget the bouquet that withered in her grasp, and the insect that perished amid the sunny air, by no ostensible agency save the fragrance of her breath. These incidents, however, dissolving in the pure light of her character, had no longer the efficacy of facts, but were acknowledged as mistaken fantasies, by whatever testimony of the senses they might appear to be substantiated. There is something truer and more real than what we can see with the eyes and touch with the finger. On such better evidence had Giovanni founded his confidence in Beatrice, though rather by the necessary force of her high attributes than by any deep and generous faith on his part. But now his spirit was incapable of sustaining itself at the height to which the early enthusiasm of passion had exalted it; he fell down, grovelling* among earthly doubts, and defiled therewith the pure whiteness of Beatrice's image. Not that he gave her up; he did but distrust. He resolved to institute some decisive test that should satisfy him, once for all, whether there were those dreadful peculiarities in her physical nature which could not be supposed to exist without some corresponding monstrosity of soul. His eyes, gazing down afar, might have deceived him as to the lizard, the insect, and the flowers; but if he could witness, at the distance of a few paces, the sudden blight of one fresh and healthful flower in Beatrice's hand, there would be room for no further question. With this idea he hastened to the florist's and purchased a bouquet that was still gemmed with the morning dewdrops.

It was now the customary hour of his daily interview with Beatrice. Before descending into the garden, Giovanni failed not to look at his figure in the mirror,—a vanity to be expected in a beautiful young man, yet, as displaying itself at that troubled and feverish moment, the token of a certain shallowness of feeling and insincerity of character. He did gaze, however, and said to himself that his features had never before possessed so rich a grace, nor his eyes such vivacity, nor his cheeks so warm a hue of superabundant life.

'At least,' thought he, 'her poison has not yet insinuated itself into my system. I am no flower to perish in her grasp.'

With that thought he turned his eyes on the bouquet, which he had never once laid aside from his hand. A thrill of indefinable horror shot through his frame on perceiving that these dewy flowers were already beginning to droop; they wore the aspect of things that had been fresh and lovely yesterday. Giovanni grew white as marble, and stood motionless before the mirror, staring at his own reflection there as at the likeness of something frightful. He remembered Baglioni's remark about the fragrance that seemed to pervade the chamber. It must have been the poison in his breath! Then he shuddered,—shuddered at himself. Recovering from his stupor, he began to watch with curious eye a spider that was busily at work hanging its web from the antique cornice of the apartment, crossing and recrossing the artful system of interwoven lines,—as vigorous and active a spider as ever dangled from an old ceiling. Giovanni bent towards the insect, and emitted a deep, long breath. The spider suddenly ceased its toil; the web vibrated with a tremor originating in the body of the small artisan. Again Giovanni sent forth a breath, deeper, longer, and imbued with a venomous feeling out of his heart: he knew not whether he were wicked, or only desperate. The spider made a convulsive grip with his limbs and hung dead across the window.

'Accursed! accursed!' muttered Giovanni, addressing himself. 'Hast thou grown so poisonous that this deadly insect perishes by thy breath?'

At that moment a rich, sweet voice came floating up from the garden.

'Giovanni! Giovanni! It is past the hour! Why tarriest thou? Come down!'

'Yes,' muttered Giovanni again. 'She is the only being whom my breath may not slay! Would that it might!'

He rushed down, and in an instant was standing before the bright and loving eyes of Beatrice. A moment ago his wrath and despair had been so fierce that he could have desired nothing so much as to wither her by a glance; but with her actual presence there came influences which had too real an existence to be at once shaken off; recollections of the delicate and benign power of her feminine nature, which had so often enveloped him in a religious calm; recollections of many a holy and passionate outgush of her heart, when the pure fountain had been unsealed from its depths and made visible in its transparency to his mental eye; recollections which, had Giovanni known how to estimate them, would have assured him that all this ugly mystery was but an earthly illusion, and that, whatever mist of evil might seem to have gathered over her, the real Beatrice was a heavenly angel. Incapable as he was of such high faith, still her presence had not utterly lost its magic. Giovanni's rage was quelled into an aspect of sullen insensibility. Beatrice, with a quick spiritual sense, immediately felt that there was a gulf of blackness between them which neither he nor she could pass. They walked on together, sad and silent, and came thus to the marble fountain and to its pool of water on the ground, in the midst of which grew the shrub that bore gem-like blossoms. Giovanni was affrighted at the eager enjoyment—the appetite, as it were—with which he found himself inhaling the fragrance of the flowers.

'Beatrice,' asked he, abruptly, 'whence came this shrub?'

'My father created it,' answered she, with simplicity.

'Created it! created it!' repeated Giovanni. 'What mean you, Beatrice?'

'He is a man fearfully acquainted with the secrets of nature,' replied Beatrice; 'and, at the hour when I first drew breath, this plant sprang from the soil, the offspring of his science, of his intellect, while I was but his earthly child. Approach it not!' continued she, observing with terror that Giovanni was drawing nearer to the shrub. 'It has qualities that you little dream of. But I, dearest Giovanni,—I grew up and blossomed with the plant and was nourished with its breath. It was my sister, and I loved it with a human affection, for, alas!—hast thou not suspected it?—there was an awful doom.'

Here Giovanni frowned so darkly upon her that Beatrice paused and trembled. But her faith in his tenderness reassured her, and made her blush that she had doubted for an instant.

'There was an awful doom,' she continued, 'the effect of my father's fatal love of science, which estranged me from all society of my kind. Until Heaven sent thee, dearest Giovanni, oh, how lonely was thy poor Beatrice!'

'Was it a hard doom?' asked Giovanni, fixing his eyes upon her.

'Only of late have I known how hard it was,' answered she, tenderly. 'Oh yes; but my heart was torpid, and therefore quiet,'

Giovanni's rage broke forth from his sullen gloom like a lightning flash out of a dark cloud.

'Accursed one!' cried he, with venomous scorn* and anger. 'And, finding thy solitude wearisome, thou hast severed me likewise from all the warmth of life and enticed me into thy region of unspeakable horror!'

'Giovanni!' exclaimed Beatrice, turning her large bright eyes upon his face. The force of his words had not found its way into her mind; she was merely thunderstruck.

'Yes, poisonous thing!' repeated Giovanni, beside himself with passion. 'Thou hast done it! Thou hast blasted me! Thou hast filled my veins with poison! Thou hast made me as hateful, as ugly, as loathsome and deadly a creature as thyself,—a world's wonder of hideous monstrosity! Now, if our breath be happily as fatal to ourselves as to all others, let us join our lips in one kiss of unutterable hatred, and so die!'

'What has befallen me?' murmured Beatrice, with a low moan out of her heart. 'Holy Virgin, pity me, a poor heart-broken child!'

'Thou,—dost thou pray?' cried Giovanni, still with the same fiendish scorn. 'Thy very prayers, as they come from thy lips, taint the atmosphere with death. Yes, yes; let us pray! Let us to church and dip our fingers in the holy water at the portal! They that come after us will perish as by a pestilence! Let us sign crosses in the air! It will be scattering curses abroad in the likeness of holy symbols!'

'Giovanni,' said Beatrice, calmly, for her grief was beyond passion, 'why dost thou join thyself with me thus in those terrible words? I, it is true, am the horrible thing thou namest me. But thou,—what hast thou to do, save with one other shudder at my hideous misery to go forth out of the garden and mingle with thy race, and forget that there ever crawled on earth such a monster as poor Beatrice?'

'Dost thou pretend ignorance?' asked Giovanni, scowling upon her. 'Behold! this power have I gained from the pure daughter of Rappaccini.'

There was a swarm of summer insects flitting through the air in search of the food promised by the flower-odours of the fatal garden. They circled round Giovanni's head, and were evidently attracted towards him by the same influence which had drawn them for an instant within the sphere of several of the shrubs. He sent forth a breath among them, and smiled bitterly at Beatrice as at least a score of the insects fell dead upon the ground.

'I see it! I see it!' shrieked Beatrice. 'It is my father's fatal science! No, no, Giovanni; it was not I! Never! never! I dreamed only to love thee and be with thee a little time, and so to let thee pass away, leaving but thine image in mine heart; for, Giovanni, believe it, though my body be nourished with poison, my spirit is God's creature,* and craves love as its daily food. But my father,—he has united us in this fearful sympathy. Yes; spurn me, tread upon me, kill me! Oh, what is death after such words as thine? But it was not I. Not for a world of bliss would I have done it.'

Giovanni's passion had exhausted itself in its outburst from his lips. There now came across him a sense, mournful, and not without tenderness, of the intimate and peculiar relationship between Beatrice and himself. They stood, as it were, in an utter solitude, which would be made none the less solitary by the densest throng of human life. Ought not, then, the desert of humanity around them to press this insulated pair closer together? If they should be cruel to one another, who was there to be kind to them? Besides, thought Giovanni, might there not still be a hope of his returning within the limits of ordinary nature, and leading Beatrice, the redeemed Beatrice, by the hand? O weak and selfish and unworthy spirit, that could dream of an earthly union and earthly happiness as possible, after such deep love had been so bitterly wronged as was Beatrice's love by Giovanni's blighting words! No, no; there could be no such hope. She must pass heavily, with that broken heart, across the borders of Time; she must bathe her hurts in some fount of paradise, and forget her grief in the light of immortality, and *there* be well.

But Giovanni did not know it.

'Dear Beatrice,' said he, approaching her, while she shrank away as always at his approach, but now with a different impulse,—'dearest Beatrice, our fate is not yet so desperate. Behold! there is a medicine, potent, as a wise physician has assured me, and almost divine in its efficacy. It is composed of ingredients the most opposite to those by which thy awful father has brought this calamity upon thee and me. It is distilled of blessed herbs. Shall we not quaff it together, and thus be purified from evil?'

'Give it me!' said Beatrice, extending her hand to receive the little silver vial which Giovanni took from his bosom. She added, with a peculiar emphasis, 'I will drink; but do thou await the result.'

She put Baglioni's antidote to her lips; and, at the same moment, the figure of Rappaccini emerged from the portal and came slowly towards the marble fountain. As he drew near, the pale man of science seemed to gaze with a triumphant expression at the beautiful youth and maiden, as might an artist who should spend his life in achieving a picture or a group of statuary and finally be satisfied with his success. He paused; his bent form grew erect with conscious power; he spread out his hands over them in the attitude of a father imploring a blessing upon his children; but those were the same hands that had thrown poison into the stream of their lives. Giovanni trembled. Beatrice shuddered nervously, and pressed her hand upon her heart.

'My daughter, said Rappaccini, 'thou art no longer lonely in the world. Pluck one of those precious gems from thy sister shrub and bid thy bridegroom wear it in his bosom. It will not harm him now. My science and the sympathy between thee and him have so wrought within his system that he now stands apart from common men, as thou dost, daughter of my pride and triumph, from ordinary women. Pass on, then, through the world, most dear to one another and dreadful to all besides!'

'My father,' said Beatrice, feebly,—and still as she spoke she kept her hand upon her heart,—wherefore didst thou inflict this miserable doom upon thy child?'

'Miserable!' exclaimed Rappaccini. 'What mean you, foolish girl? Dost thou deem it misery to be endowed with marvellous gifts against which no power nor strength could avail an enemy,—misery, to be able to quell the mightiest with a breath,—misery, to be as terrible as thou art beautiful? Wouldst thou, then, have preferred the condition of a weak woman, exposed to all evil and capable of none?'

'I would fain have been loved, not feared,' murmured Beatrice, sinking down upon the ground. 'But now it matters not. I am going, father, where the evil which thou hast striven to mingle with my being will pass away like a dream,—like the fragrance of these poisonous flowers, which will no longer taint my breath among the flowers of Eden. Farewell, Giovanni! Thy words of hatred are like lead within my heart; but they, too, will fall away as I ascend. Oh, was there not, from the first, more poison in thy nature than in mine?'

To Beatrice,—so radically had her earthly part been wrought upon by Rappaccini's skill,—as poison had been life, so the powerful antidote was death; and thus the poor victim of man's ingenuity and of thwarted nature, and of the fatality that attends all such efforts of perverted wisdom, perished there, at the feet of her father and Giovanni. Just at that moment Professor Pietro Baglioni looked forth from the window, and called loudly, in a tone of triumph mixed with horror, to the thunder-stricken man of science,—

'Rappaccini! Rappaccini! and is *this* the upshot of your experiment?'

ETHAN BRAND

A Chapter from an Abortive Romance*

BARTRAM the lime-burner,* a rough, heavy-looking man, begrimed with charcoal, sat watching his kiln, at nightfall, while his little son played at building houses with the scattered fragments of marble, when, on the hillside below them, they heard a roar of laughter, not mirthful, but slow, and even solemn, like a wind shaking the boughs of the forest.

'Father, what is that?' asked the little boy, leaving his play, and pressing betwixt his father's knees.

'Oh, some drunken man, I suppose,' answered the lime-burner; 'some merry fellow from the bar-room in the village, who dared not laugh loud enough within doors lest he should blow the roof of the house off. So here he is, shaking his jolly sides at the foot of Graylock.'*

'But, father,' said the child, more sensitive than the obtuse, middle-aged clown, 'he does not laugh like a man that is glad. So the noise frightens me!'

'Don't be a fool, child!' cried his father, gruffly. 'You will never make a man, I do believe; there is too much of your mother in you. I have known the rustling of a leaf startle you. Hark! Here comes the merry fellow now. You shall see that there is no harm in him.'

Bartram and his little son, while they were talking thus, sat watching the same lime-kiln that had been the scene of Ethan Brand's* solitary and meditative life, before he began his search for the Unpardonable Sin. Many years, as we have seen, had now elapsed, since that portentous night when the IDEA was first developed. The kiln, however, on the mountain-side, stood unimpaired, and was in nothing changed since he had thrown his dark thoughts into the intense glow of its furnace, and melted them, as it were, into the one thought that took possession of his life. It was a rude, round, tower-like structure, about twenty feet high, heavily built of rough stones, and with a hillock of earth heaped about the larger part of its circumference; so that the blocks and fragments of marble might be drawn by cart-loads, and thrown in at the top. There was an opening at the bottom of the tower, like an oven-mouth, but large enough to admit a man in a stooping posture, and provided with a massive iron door. With the smoke and jets of flame issuing from the chinks and crevices of this door, which seemed to give admittance into the hillside, it resembled nothing so much as the private entrance to the infernal regions, which the shepherds of the Delectable Mountains* were accustomed to show to pilgrims.

There are many such lime-kilns in that tract of country, for the purpose of burning the white marble which composes a large part of the substance of the hills. Some of them, built years ago, and long deserted, with weeds growing in the vacant ground of the interior, which is open to the sky, and grass and wildflowers rooting themselves into the chinks of the stones, look already like relics of antiquity, and may yet be overspread with the lichens of centuries to come. Others, where the lime-burner still feeds his daily and night-long fire, afford points of interest to the wanderer among the hills, who seats himself on a log of wood or a fragment of marble, to hold a chat with the solitary man. It is a lonesome, and, when the character is inclined to thought, may be an intensely thoughtful occupation; as it proved in the case of Ethan Brand, who had mused to such strange purpose, in days gone by, while the fire in this very kiln was burning.

The man who now watched the fire was of a different order, and troubled himself with no thoughts save the very few that were requisite to his business. At frequent intervals, he flung back the clashing weight of the iron door, and, turning his face from the insufferable glare, thrust in huge logs of oak, or stirred the immense brands with a long pole. Within the furnace were seen the curling and riotous flames, and the burning marble, almost molten with the intensity of heat; while without, the reflection of the fire quivered on the dark intricacy of the surrounding forest, and showed in the foreground a bright and ruddy little picture of the hut, the spring beside its door, the athletic and coal-begrimed figure of the lime-burner, and the half-frightened child, shrinking into the protection of his father's shadow. And when again the iron door was closed, then reappeared the tender light of the half-full moon, which vainly strove to trace out the indistinct shapes of the neighbouring mountains; and, in the upper sky, there was a flitting congregation of clouds, still faintly tinged with the rosy sunset, though thus far down into the valley the sunshine had vanished long and long ago.

The little boy now crept still closer to his father, as footsteps were heard ascending the hillside, and a human form thrust aside the bushes that clustered beneath the trees.

'Halloo! who is it?' cried the lime-burner, vexed at his son's timidity, yet half infected by it. 'Come forward, and show yourself, like a man, or I'll fling this chunk of marble at your head!'

'You offer me a rough welcome,' said a gloomy voice, as the unknown man drew nigh. 'Yet I neither claim nor desire a kinder one, even at my own fireside.'

To obtain a distincter view, Bartram threw open the iron door of the kiln, whence immediately issued a gush of fierce light, that smote full upon the stranger's face and figure. To a careless eye there appeared nothing very remarkable in his aspect, which was that of a man in a coarse, brown, country-made suit of clothes, tall and thin, with the staff and heavy shoes of a wayfarer. As he advanced, he fixed his eyes—which were very bright—intently upon the brightness of the furnace, as if he beheld, or expected to behold, some object worthy of note within it.

'Good evening, stranger,' said the lime-burner; 'whence come you, so late in the day?'

'I come from my search,' answered the wayfarer; 'for, at last, it is finished.'

'Drunk!—or crazy!' muttered Bartram to himself. 'I shall have trouble with the fellow. The sooner I drive him away, the better.'

The little boy, all in a tremble, whispered to his father, and begged him to shut the door of the kiln, so that there might not be so much light; for that there was something in the man's face which he was afraid to look at, yet could not look away from. And indeed, even the lime-burner's dull and torpid sense began to be impressed by an indescribable something in that thin, rugged, thoughtful visage, with the grizzled hair* hanging wildly about it, and those deeply sunken eyes, which gleamed like fires within the entrance of a mysterious cavern. But, as he closed the door, the stranger turned towards him, and spoke in a quiet, familiar way, that made Bartram feel as if he were a sane and sensible man, after all.

'Your task draws to an end, I see,' said he. 'This marble has already been burning three days. A few hours more will convert the stone to lime.'

'Why, who are you?' exclaimed the lime-burner. 'You seem as well acquainted with my business as I am myself.'

'And well I may be,' said the stranger; 'for I followed the same craft many a long year, and here, too, on this very spot. But you are a newcomer in these parts. Did you never hear of Ethan Brand?'

'The man that went in search of the Unpardonable Sin?' asked Bartram, with a laugh.

'The same,' answered the stranger. 'He has found what he sought, and therefore he comes back again.'

'What! then you are Ethan Brand himself?' cried the lime-burner, in amazement. 'I am a new-comer here, as you say, and they call it eighteen years since you left the foot of Graylock. But, I can tell you, the good folks still talk about Ethan Brand, in the village yonder, and what a strange errand took him away from his lime-kiln. Well, and so you have found the Unpardonable Sin?'

'Even so!' said the stranger, calmly.

'If the question is a fair one,' proceeded Bartram, 'where might it be?'

Ethan Brand laid his finger on his own heart.

'Here!' replied he.

And then, without mirth in his countenance, but as if moved by an involuntary recognition of the infinite absurdity of seeking throughout the world for what was the closest of all things to himself, and looking into every heart, save his own, for what was hidden in no other breast, he broke into a laugh of scorn.* It was the same slow, heavy laugh, that had almost appalled the lime-burner when it heralded the wayfarer's approach.

The solitary mountain-side was made dismal by it. Laughter, when out of place, mistimed, or bursting forth from a disordered state of feeling, may be the most terrible modulation of the human voice. The laughter of one asleep, even if it be a little child,—the madman's laugh,—the wild, screaming laugh of a born idiot,—are sounds that we sometimes tremble to hear, and would always willingly forget. Poets have imagined no utterance of fiends or hobgoblins so fearfully appropriate as a laugh. And even the obtuse lime-burner felt his nerves shaken, as this strange man looked inward at his own heart, and burst into laughter that rolled away into the night, and was indistinctly reverberated among the hills.

'Joe,' said he to his little son, 'scamper down to the tavern in the village, and tell the jolly fellows there that Ethan Brand has come back, and that he has found the Unpardonable Sin!'

The boy darted away on his errand, to which Ethan Brand made no objection, nor seemed hardly to notice it. He sat on a log of wood, looking steadfastly at the iron door of the kiln. When the child was out of sight, and his swift and light footsteps ceased to be heard treading first on the fallen leaves and then on the rocky mountain-path, the lime-burner began to regret his departure. He felt that the little fellow's presence had been a barrier between his guest and himself, and that he must now deal, heart to heart, with a man who, on his own confession, had committed the one only crime for which Heaven could afford no mercy. That crime, in its indistinct blackness, seemed to overshadow him. The lime-burner's own sins rose up within him, and made his memory riotous with a throng of evil shapes that asserted their kindred with the Master Sin, whatever it might be, which it was within the scope of man's corrupted nature to conceive and cherish. They were all of one family; they went to and fro between his breast and Ethan Brand's, and carried dark greetings from one to the other.

Then Bartram remembered the stories which had grown traditionary in reference to this strange man, who had come upon him like a shadow of the night, and was making himself at home in his old place, after so long absence that the dead people, dead and buried for years, would have had more right to be at home, in any familiar spot, than he. Ethan Brand, it was said, had conversed with Satan himself in the lurid blaze of this very kiln. The legend had been matter of mirth heretofore, but looked grisly now. According to this tale, before Ethan Brand departed on his search, he had been accustomed to evoke a fiend from the hot furnace of the lime-kiln, night after night, in order to confer with him about the Unpardonable Sin; the man and the fiend each labouring to frame the image of some mode of guilt which could neither be atoned for nor forgiven. And, with the first gleam of light upon the mountain-top, the fiend crept in at the iron door, there to abide the intensest element of fire, until again summoned forth to share in the dreadful task of extending man's possible guilt beyond the scope of Heaven's else infinite mercy.

While the lime-burner was struggling with the horror of these thoughts, Ethan Brand rose from the log, and flung open the door of the kiln. The action was in such accordance with the idea in Bartram's mind, that he almost expected to see the Evil One issue forth, red-hot from the raging furnace.

'Hold! hold!' cried he, with a tremulous attempt to laugh; for he was ashamed of his fears, although they overmastered him. 'Don't, for mercy's sake, bring out your Devil now!'

'Man!' sternly replied Ethan Brand, 'what need have I of the Devil? I have left him behind me, on my track. It is with such half-way sinners as you that he busies himself. Fear not, because I open the door. I do but act by old custom, and am going to trim your fire, like a lime-burner, as I was once.'

He stirred the vast coals, thrust in more wood, and bent forward to gaze into the hollow prison-house of the fire, regardless of the fierce glow that reddened upon his face. The lime-burner sat watching him, and half suspected his strange guest of a purpose, if not to evoke a fiend, at least to plunge bodily into the flames, and thus vanish from the sight of man. Ethan Brand, however, drew quietly back, and closed the door of the kiln.

'I have looked,' said he, 'into many a human heart that was seven times hotter with sinful passions than yonder furnace is with fire. But I found not there what I sought. No, not the Unpardonable Sin!'

'What is the Unpardonable Sin?' asked the lime-burner; and then he shrank farther from his companion, trembling lest his question should be answered.

'It is a sin that grew within my own breast,' replied Ethan Brand, standing erect, with a pride* that distinguished all enthusiasts of his stamp. 'A sin that grew nowhere else! The sin of an intellect that triumphed over the sense of brotherhood with man and reverence for God, and sacrificed everything to its own mighty claims! The only sin that deserves a recompense of immortal agony! Freely, were it to do again, would I incur the guilt. Unshrinkingly I accept the retribution!'

'The man's head is turned,' muttered the lime-burner to himself. 'He may be a sinner, like the rest of us,—nothing more likely,—but, I'll be sworn, he is a madman too.'

Nevertheless, he felt uncomfortable at his situation, alone with Ethan Brand on the wild mountain-side, and was right glad to hear the rough murmur of tongues, and the footsteps of what seemed a pretty numerous party, stumbling over the stones and rustling through the underbrush. Soon appeared the whole lazy regiment that was wont to infest the village tavern, comprehending three or four individuals who had drunk flip beside the bar-room fire through all the winters, and smoked their pipes beneath the stoop through all the summers, since Ethan Brand's departure. Laughing boisterously, and mingling all their voices together in unceremonious talk, they now burst into the moonshine and narrow streaks of firelight that illuminated the open space before the lime-kiln. Bartram set the door ajar again, flooding the spot with light, that the whole company might get a fair view of Ethan Brand, and he of them.

There, among other old acquaintances, was a once ubiquitous man, now almost extinct, but whom we were formerly sure to encounter at the hotel of every thriving village throughout the country. It was the stage-agent. The present specimen of the genus was a wilted and smoke-dried man, wrinkled and red-nosed, in a smartly-cut, brown, bobtailed coat, with brass buttons, who, for a length of time unknown, had kept his desk and corner in the bar-room, and was still puffing what seemed to be the same cigar that he had lighted twenty years before. He had great fame as a dry joker, though, perhaps, less on account of any intrinsic humour than from a certain flavour of brandy-toddy and tobacco-smoke, which impregnated all his ideas and expressions, as well as his person. Another well-remembered though strangely altered face was that of Lawyer Giles, as people still called him in courtesy; an elderly ragamuffin, in his soiled shirt-sleeves and tow-cloth trousers. This poor fellow had been an attorney, in what he called his better days, a sharp practitioner, and in great vogue among the village litigants; but flip, and sling, and toddy,* and cocktails, imbibed at all hours, morning, noon, and night, had caused him to slide from intellectual to various kinds and degrees of bodily labour, till, at last, to adopt his own phrase, he slid into a soap-vat. In other words, Giles was now a soap-boiler, in a small way. He had come to be but the fragment of a human being, a part of one foot having been chopped off by an axe, and an entire hand torn away by the devilish grip of a steam-engine. Yet, though the corporeal hand was gone, a spiritual member remained; for, stretching forth the stump, Giles steadfastly averred that he felt an invisible thumb and fingers with as vivid a sensation as before the real ones were amputated. A maimed and miserable wretch he was; but one, nevertheless, whom the world could not trample on, and had no right to scorn, either in this or any previous stage of his misfortunes, since he had still kept up the courage and spirit of a man, asked nothing in charity, and with his one hand—and that the left one—fought a stern battle against want and hostile circumstances.

Among the throng, too, came another personage, who, with certain points of similarity to Lawyer Giles, had many more of difference. It was the village doctor; a man of some fifty years, whom, at an earlier period of his life, we introduced as paying a professional visit to Ethan Brand during the latter's supposed insanity. He was now a purple-visaged, rude, and brutal, yet half-gentlemanly figure, with something wild, ruined, and desperate in his talk, and in all the details of his gesture and manners. Brandy possessed this man like an evil spirit, and made him as surly and savage as a wild beast, and as miserable as a lost soul; but there was supposed to be in him such wonderful skill, such native gifts of healing, beyond any which medical science could impart, that society caught hold of him, and would not let him sink out of its reach. So, swaying to and fro upon his horse, and grumbling thick accents at the bedside, he visited all the sick-chambers for miles about among the mountain towns, and sometimes raised a dying man, as it were, by miracle, or quite as often, no doubt, sent his patient to a grave that was dug many a year too soon. The doctor had an everlasting pipe in his mouth, and, as somebody said, in allusion to his habit of swearing, it was always alight with hell-fire.

These three worthies pressed forward, and greeted Ethan Brand each after his own fashion, earnestly inviting him to partake of the contents of a certain black bottle, in which, as they averred, he would find something far better worth seeking for than the Unpardonable Sin. No mind, which has wrought itself by intense and solitary meditation into a high state of enthusiasm, can endure the kind of contact with low and vulgar modes of thought and feeling to which Ethan Brand was now subjected. It made him doubt—and, strange to say, it was a painful doubt—whether he had indeed found the Unpardonable Sin, and found it within himself. The whole question on which he had exhausted life, and more than life, looked like a delusion.

'Leave me,' he said bitterly, 'ye brute beasts, that have made yourselves so, shrivelling up your souls with fiery liquors! I have done with you. Years and years ago, I groped into your hearts, and found nothing there for my purpose. Get ye gone!'

'Why, you uncivil scoundrel,' cried the fierce doctor, 'is that the way you respond to the kindness of your best friends? Then let me tell you the truth. You have no more found the Unpardonable Sin than yonder boy Joe has. You are but a crazy fellow,—I told you so twenty years ago,—neither better nor worse than a crazy fellow, and the fit companion of old Humphrey, here!'

He pointed to an old man, shabbily dressed, with long white hair, thin visage, and unsteady eyes. For some years past this aged person had been wandering about among the hills, inquiring of all travellers whom he met for his daughter. The girl, it seemed, had gone off with a company of circus-performers; and occasionally tidings of her came to the village, and fine stories were told of her glittering appearance as she rode on horse-back in the ring, or performed marvellous feats on the tight-rope.

The white-haired father now approached Ethan Brand, and gazed unsteadily in his face.

'They tell me you have been all over the earth,' said he, wringing his hands with earnestness. 'You must have seen my daughter, for she makes a grand figure in the world, and everybody goes to see her. Did she send any word to her old father, or say when she was coming back?'

Ethan Brand's eye quailed beneath the old man's. That daughter, from whom he so earnestly desired a word of greeting, was the Esther of our tale, the very girl who, with such cold and remorseless purpose, Ethan Brand had made the subject of a psychological experiment, and wasted, absorbed, and perhaps annihilated her soul, in the process.

'Yes,' murmured he, turning away from the hoary wanderer; 'it is no delusion. There is an Unpardonable Sin!'

While these things were passing, a merry scene was going forward in the area of cheerful light, beside the spring and before the door of the hut. A number of the youth of the village, young men and girls, had hurried up the hillside, impelled by curiosity to see Ethan Brand, the hero of so many a legend familiar to their childhood. Finding nothing, however, very remarkable in his aspect,—nothing but a sunburnt wayfarer, in plain garb and dusty shoes, who sat looking into the fire, as if he fancied pictures among the coals,—these young people speedily grew tired of observing him. As it happened, there was other amusement at hand. An old German Jew,* travelling with a diorama* on his back, was passing down the mountain-road towards the village just as the party turned aside from it, and, in hopes of eking out the profits of the day, the showman had kept them company to the lime-kiln.

'Come, old Dutchman,' cried one of the young men, 'let us see your pictures, if you can swear they are worth looking at!'

'O yes, Captain,' answered the Jew,—whether as a matter of courtesy or craft, he styled everybody Captain,—'I shall show you, indeed, some very superb pictures!'

So, placing his box in a proper position, he invited the young men and girls to look through the glass orifices of the machine, and proceeded to exhibit a series of the most outrageous scratchings and daubings, as specimens of the fine arts, that ever an itinerant showman had the face to impose upon his circle of spectators. The pictures were worn out, moreover, tattered, full of cracks and wrinkles, dingy with tobacco-smoke, and otherwise in a most pitiable condition. Some purported to be cities, public edifices, and ruined castles in Europe; others represented Napoleon's battles and Nelson's sea-fights; and in the midst of these would be seen a gigantic, brown, hairy hand,—which might have been mistaken for the Hand of Destiny, though, in truth, it was only the showman's,—pointing its forefinger to various scenes of the conflict, while its owner gave historical illustrations. When, with much merriment at its abominable deficiency of merit, the exhibition was concluded, the German bade little Joe put his head into the box. Viewed through the magnifying-glasses, the boy's round, rosy visage assumed the strangest imaginable aspect of an immense Titanic child, the mouth grinning broadly, and the eyes and every other feature overflowing with fun at the joke. Suddenly, however, that merry face turned pale, and its expression changed to horror, for this easily impressed and excitable child had become sensible that the eye of Ethan Brand was fixed upon him through the glass.

'You make the little man to be afraid, Captain,' said the German Jew, turning up the dark and strong outline of his visage, from his stooping posture. 'But look again, and, by chance, I shall cause you to see somewhat that is very fine, upon my word!'

Ethan Brand gazed into the box for an instant, and then starting back, looked fixedly at the German. What had he seen? Nothing, apparently; for a curious youth, who had peeped in almost at the same moment, beheld only a vacant space of canvas.

'I remember you now,' muttered Ethan Brand to the showman.

'Ah, Captain,' whispered the Jew of Nuremburg, with a dark smile, 'I find it to be a heavy matter in my show-box,— this Unpardonable Sin! By my faith, Captain, it has wearied my shoulders, this long day, to carry it over the mountain.'

'Peace,' answered Ethan Brand, sternly, 'or get thee into the furnace yonder!'

The Jew's exhibition had scarcely concluded, when a great elderly dog—who seemed to be his own master, as no person in the company laid claim to him—saw fit to render himself the object of public notice. Hitherto, he had shown himself a very quiet, well-disposed old dog going round from one to another, and, by way of being sociable, offering his rough head to be patted by any kindly hand that would take so much trouble. But now, all of a sudden, this grave and venerable quadruped, of his own mere motion, and without the slightest suggestion from anybody else, began to run round after his tail, which, to heighten the absurdity of the proceeding was a great deal shorter than it should have been. Never was seen such headlong eagerness in pursuit of an object that could not possibly be attained; never was heard such a tremendous outbreak of growling, snarling, barking, and snapping—as if one end of the ridiculous brute's body were at deadly and most unforgivable enmity with the other. Faster and faster, round about went the cur; and faster and still faster fled the un-approachable brevity of his tail; and louder and fiercer grew his yells of rage and animosity; until, utterly exhausted, and as far from the goal as ever, the foolish old dog ceased his performance as suddenly as he had begun it. The next moment he was as mild, quiet, sensible, and respectable in his deportment, as when he first scraped acquaintance with the company.

As may be supposed, the exhibition was greeted with

universal laughter, clapping of hands, and shouts of encore, to which the canine performer responded by wagging all that there was to wag of his tail, but appeared totally unable to repeat his very successful effort to amuse the spectators.

Meanwhile, Ethan Brand had resumed his seat upon the log, and moved, it might be, by a perception of some remote analogy between his own case and that of this self-pursuing cur, he broke into the awful laugh, which, more than any other token, expressed the condition of his inward being. From that moment the merriment of the party was at an end; they stood aghast, dreading lest the inauspicious sound should be reverberated around the horizon, and that mountain would thunder it to mountain, and so the horror be prolonged upon their ears. Then, whispering one to another that it was late,—that the moon was almost down,—that the August night was growing chill,—they hurried homewards, leaving the lime-burner and little Joe to deal as they might with their un-welcome guest. Save for these three human beings, the open space on the hillside was a solitude, set in a vast gloom of forest. Beyond that darksome verge, the firelight glimmered on the stately trunks and almost black foliage of pines, intermixed with the lighter verdure of sapling oaks, maples, and poplars, while here and there lay the gigantic corpses of dead trees, decaying on the leaf-strewn soil. And it seemed to little Joe—a timorous and imaginative child—that the silent forest was holding its breath, until some fearful thing should happen.

Ethan Brand thrust more wood into the fire, and closed the door of the kiln; then looking over his shoulder at the lime-burner and his son, he bade, rather than advised, them to retire to rest.

'For myself, I cannot sleep,' said he. 'I have matters that it concerns me to meditate upon. I will watch the fire, as I used to do in the old time.'

'And call the Devil out of the furnace to keep you company, I suppose,' muttered Bartram, who had been making intimate acquaintance with the black bottle above mentioned. 'But watch, if you like, and call as many devils as you like! For my part, I shall be all the better for a snooze. Come, Joe!'

As the boy followed his father into the hut, he looked back at the wayfarer, and the tears came into his eyes, for his tender spirit had an intuition of the bleak and terrible loneliness in which this man had enveloped himself.

When they had gone, Ethan Brand sat listening to the crackling of the kindled wood, and looking at the little spirts of fire that issued through the chinks of the door. These trifles, however, once so familiar, had but the slightest hold of his attention, while deep within his mind he was reviewing the gradual but marvellous change that had been wrought upon him by the search to which he had devoted himself. He remembered how the night dew had fallen upon him,—how the dark forest had whispered to him,—how the stars had gleamed upon him,—a simple and loving man, watching his fire in the years gone by, and ever musing as it burned. He remembered with what tenderness, with what love and sympathy for mankind, and what pity for human guilt and woe, he had first begun to contemplate those ideas which afterwards became the inspiration of his life; with what reverence he had then looked into the heart of man, viewing it as a temple originally divine, and, however desecrated, still to be held sacred by a brother; with what awful fear he had deprecated the success of his pursuit, and prayed that the Unpardonable Sin might never be revealed to him. Then ensued that vast intellectual development, which, in its progress, disturbed the counterpoise between his mind and heart. The Idea that possessed his life had operated as a means of education; it had gone on cultivating his powers to the highest point of which they were susceptible; it had raised him from the level of an unlettered labourer to stand on a star-lit eminence, whither the philosophers of the earth, laden with the lore of universities, might vainly strive to clamber after him. So much for the intellect! But where was the heart? That, indeed, had withered,—had contracted,—had hardened,—had perished! It had ceased to partake of the universal throb. He had lost his hold of the magnetic chain of humanity. He was no longer a brother-man, opening the chambers or the dungeons of our common nature by the key of holy sympathy, which gave him a right to share in all its secrets; he was now a cold observer, looking on mankind as the subject of his experiment, and, at length, converting man and woman to be his puppets, and pulling the wires that moved them to such degrees of crime as were demanded for his study.

Thus Ethan Brand became a fiend. He began to be so from the moment that his moral nature had ceased to keep the pace of improvement with his intellect. And now, as his highest effort and inevitable development,—as the bright and gorgeous flower, and rich, delicious fruit of his life's labour,—he had produced the Unpardonable Sin!

'What more have I to seek? what more to achieve?' said Ethan Brand to himself. 'My task is done, and well done!'

Starting from the log with a certain alacrity in his gait and ascending the hillock of earth that was raised against the stone circumference of the lime-kiln, he thus reached the top of the structure. It was a space of perhaps ten feet across, from edge to edge, presenting a view of the upper surface of the immense mass of broken marble with which the kiln was heaped. All these innumerable blocks and fragments of marble were red-hot and vividly on fire, sending up great spouts of blue flame, which quivered aloft and danced madly, as within a magic circle, and sank and rose again, with continual and multitudinous activity. As the lonely man bent forward over this terrible body of fire, the blasting heat smote up against his person with a breath that, it might be supposed, would have scorched and shrivelled him up in a moment.

Ethan Brand stood erect, and raised his arms on high. The blue flames played upon his face, and imparted the wild and ghastly light which alone could have suited its expression; it was that of a fiend on the verge of plunging into his gulf of intensest torment.

'O Mother Earth,' cried he, 'who art no more my Mother, and into whose bosom this frame shall never be resolved! O mankind, whose brotherhood I have cast off, and trampled thy great heart beneath my feet! O stars of heaven, that shone on me of old, as if to light me onward and upward!—farewell all, and forever. Come, deadly element of Fire,—henceforth my familiar friend! Embrace me, as I do thee!'

That night the sound of a fearful peal of laughter rolled heavily through the sleep of the lime-burner and his little son; dim shapes of horror and anguish haunted their dreams, and seemed still present in the rude hovel, when they opened their eyes to the daylight.

'Up, boy, up!' cried the lime-burner, staring about him. 'Thank Heaven, the night is gone, at last; and rather than pass such another, I would watch my lime-kiln, wide awake, for a twelvemonth. This Ethan Brand, with his humbug of an Unpardonable Sin, had done me no such mighty favour, in taking my place!'

He issued from the hut, followed by little Joe, who kept fast hold of his father's hand. The early sunshine was already pouring its gold upon the mountain-tops; and though the valleys were still in shadow, they smiled cheerfully in the promise of the bright day that was hastening onward. The village, completely shut in by hills, which swelled away gently about it, looked as if it had rested peacefully in the hollow of the great hand of Providence. Every dwelling was distinctly visible; the little spires of the two churches pointed upwards, and caught a fore-glimmering of brightness from the sun-gilt skies upon their gilded weathercocks. The tavern was astir, and the figure of the old, smoke-dried stage-agent, cigar in mouth, was seen beneath the stoop. Old Graylock was glorified with a golden cloud upon his head. Scattered likewise over the breasts of the surrounding mountains, there were heaps of hoary mist, in fantastic shapes, some of them far down into the valley, others high up towards the summits, and still others, of the same family of mist or cloud, hovering in the gold radiance of the upper atmosphere. Stepping from one to another of the clouds that rested on the hills, and thence to the loftier brotherhood that sailed in air, it seemed almost as if a mortal man might thus ascend into the heavenly regions. Earth was so mingled with sky that it was a day-dream to look at it.

To supply that charm of the familiar and homely, which Nature so readily adopts into a scene like this, the stage-coach was rattling down the mountain-road, and the driver sounded his horn, while echo caught up the notes, and intertwined them into a rich and varied and elaborate harmony, of which the original performer could lay claim to little share. The great hills played a concert among themselves, each contributing a strain of airy sweetness.

Little Joe's face brightened at once.

'Dear father,' cried he, skipping cheerily to and fro, 'that strange man is gone, and the sky and the mountains all seem glad of it!'

'Yes,' growled the lime-burner, with an oath, 'but he has let the fire go down, and no thanks to him if five hundred bushels of lime are not spoiled. If I catch the fellow hereabouts again, I shall feel like tossing him into the furnace!'

With his long pole in his hand, he ascended to the top of the kiln. After a moment's pause, he called to his son.

'Come up here, Joe!' said he.

So little Joe ran up the hillock, and stood by his father's side. The marble was all burnt into perfect, snow-white lime. But on its surface, in the midst of the circle,— snow-white too, and thoroughly converted into lime,—lay a human skeleton, in the attitude of a person who, after long toil, lies down to long repose. Within the ribs—strange to say—was the shape of a human heart.

'Was the fellow's heart made of marble?' cried Bartram, in some perplexity at this phenomenon. 'At any rate, it is burnt into what looks like special good lime; and, taking all the bones together, my kiln is half a bushel the richer for him.'

So saying, the rude lime-burner lifted his pole, and, letting it fall upon the skeleton, the relics of Ethan Brand were crumbled into fragments.

EXPLANATORY NOTES

CE: *The Centenary Edition of the Works of Nathaniel Hawthorne*, ed. William Charvat, *et al.* (Columbus: Ohio State University Press, 1962–).

3 THE GENTLE BOY: *The Token* for 1832. *Twice-told Tales* (1837). Separate publication, with illustration by Sophia Peabody, 1839. *Twice-told Tales* (1842).

1656: the first Quakers to visit New England were Mary Fisher and Ann Austin, who arrived from Barbados in July.

pernicious: as Hawthorne knew from Baylies' *Historical Memoir* (see below, note to p. 5), John Winthrop and John Endicott had called the Quakers 'an accursed and pernicious sect of heretics' in a statement made in 1658.

pious forefathers: one of Hawthorne's ancestors, William Hathorne, had ordered the whipping of the Quaker Ann Coleman.

sectual: emended to 'sectarian' in the *Twice-told Tales* text, perhaps from a sense of delicacy, the original word being too suggestive. See Crowley (1974).

4 *martyrdom*: the first executions took place on 27 October 1659, when Marmaduke Stevenson and William Robinson were hanged. Mather, in his *Magnalia*, bk. VII, ch. vi (see below, note to p. 106) denied the Quakers this title: 'They died not like true martyrs of Jesus Christ . . . they were madmen, a sort of lunatics, demoniacs.'

That those who . . . virtue and religion: omitted in the *Twice-told Tales* text.

5 *head of the government*: John Endicott, or Endecott (*c*.1589–1665). For his fanaticism, see 'Endicott and the Red Cross'. For his 'iron' severity, see 'The Maypole of Merry Mount'. In 'Mrs Hutchinson' (1830) Hawthorne stated that Endicott 'would stand with his drawn sword at the gate of Heaven, and resist to the death all pilgrims thither, except they travelled his own path'. See *Tales and Sketches*, ed. Pearce.

historian of the sect: Hawthorne withdrew the 1774 edition of William Sewel's *History of the Rise, Increase, and Progress of the Christian People Called Quakers* (1722) from the Salem

Atheneum in January 1828 and October 1829. Other sources—
generally less favourable to the Quakers—include Cotton
Mather, *Magnalia Christi Americana* (1702); Daniel Neal,
History of New England (1720); Thomas Hutchinson, *History of
the Colony (Province) of Massachusetts Bay*, vol. i (1764); Francis
Baylies, *Historical Memoir of the Colony of New Plymouth* (1830).
For a study of Hawthorne's sources see Orians (1941).

rottenness: Sewel states that Endicott 'was visited with a loathsome Disease, insomuch that he stunk alive, and so died with
rottenness'.

house: changed to 'home' in the *Twice-told Tales* text, presumably to stress the value of domestic love and Ilbrahim's lack of
it. On the significance of this and Hawthorne's other revisions
in the *Twice-told Tales* version of the tale, see Gross (1954). On
the importance of the theme of the home in Hawthorne see Male
(1957).

 9 *The wife's eyes . . . husband apart*: omitted in *Twice-told Tales*.

10 *She drew near . . . little face*: omitted in *Twice-told Tales*.

11 *Pearson*: Hawthorne may have found the name in Hutchinson,
vol. i, p. 174, where a Pearson is mentioned as one of the Quaker
Wenlock Christison's friends. As Orians (1941) notes, there
were numerous examples in the histories of New England of
Puritans converted to the Quaker faith in reaction against the
cruelties of the persecution.

coronet ('cornet' in *Twice-told Tales* text): ensign, bearer of the
flag.

13 *in connection . . . armory*: omitted in *Twice-told Tales*.

On one side . . . otherwise employed: omitted in *Twice-told Tales*.

'Cobler of Agawam': Nathaniel Ward (1578–1652) was the author
of *The Simple Cobler of Aggawam in America* (1647), a satirical
attack on tolerance in New England and on the frivolity of
women and foppishness of men and women there. Aggawam is
the present Ipswich, Mass.

15 *yet not intellectual countenance*: omitted in *Twice-told Tales*.

Archbishop Laud: appointed Archbishop of Canterbury by
Charles I in 1633, Laud led the movement to suppress
Puritanism within the Church of England.

Into this discourse . . . stagnant pool: omitted in *Twice-told Tales*.

16 *Having thus . . . no title*: omitted in *Twice-told Tales*. For the

'sexist' implications of the Puritan attitude to the Quaker women's attempts to preach, see Pestana (1983).

sackcloth: Hawthorne had historical precedent for this incident in the behaviour of the Quaker Catherine Chatham. See Orians (1941).

17 *mistook for inspiration*: here, unequivocally, the narrator pronounces judgement on the 'inner voice' of the Quaker woman, yet when he talks of 'just indignation' and 'legitimate authority' he may merely be presenting the minister's views rather than endorsing them.

18 *the voice*: according to Sewel, *History*, p. 234, when Endicott asked Mary Dyer at her trial if she was a prophetess, she replied that she spoke the words that the Lord spoke in her.

frightful language: the historical incident involved Mary Prince, as Hawthorne knew from Hutchinson, vol. i. The Catharine of the tale is an amalgam of several actual Quaker women.

20 *rational piety*: at the heart of the tale, according to Colacurcio (1984), is Hawthorne's encounter with Jonathan Edwards' *Nature of True Virtue*, where parental love, like marital love, because it is not directed at Being-in-General and therefore—being *merely* human—falls short of general (or disinterested) benevolence, is seen as a possible source of evil.

21 *committed*: the sense requires 'uncommitted', which is the emendation found in *Twice-told Tales*.

22 *ate the bread*: changed to 'lay in the dungeons' in *Twice-told Tales*.

Turkey: Sewel tells of Mary Fisher's visit to Adrianople when Sultan Mahomet IV was encamped there. The Turks listened with attention and gravity to her when she claimed to have something to say to Mahomet 'from the Lord God'. In Hutchinson, i, p. 167 Hawthorne could have read that Mary 'fared better among the Turks than among christians'. Hawthorne has reversed the sequence of events. The historical Mary Fisher visited Turkey after her stay in New England.

23 *unappropriate*: the sense requires 'unappropriated', which is the emendation found in *Twice-told Tales*.

25 *devil of their fathers*: the phrase is obviously ambiguous and may suggest that their fathers created the devil they imagined. Certainly the Calvinist conception of the child's 'fallen' nature makes such diabolic behaviour unsurprising.

26 *in a tender part*: omitted in *Twice-told Tales*, presumably for reasons of delicacy. See Crowley (1974).

27 *At length . . . storm the walls*: omitted in *Twice-told Tales*.

28 *Such was . . . victory*: emended in *Twice-told Tales* to read: 'Such was his state of mind at the period of Ilbrahim's misfortune; and the emotions consequent upon that event completed the change, of which the child had been the original instrument.'

There was . . . was tender: omitted in *Twice-told Tales*.

. . . 'in his dominions': the words are quoted from Sewel, where they are attributed to Edward Burroughs.

was not prompt: Charles II's *mandamus*, a writ requiring that all Quakers imprisoned or condemned should be sent to England, was not signed in England till 9 September 1661.

exult in: emended to 'encounter' in *Twice-told Tales*.

29 *His features . . . attribute*: omitted in *Twice-told Tales*.

31 *on her dying bed*: this incident is not found in Hawthorne's sources, though Sewel records Stevenson's statement that he was called by the Lord to leave his wife and children.

32 *Catherine*: here, *et seq.*, the spelling is corrected to 'Catharine' in *Twice-told Tales*.

37 *My heart . . . close the tale*: omitted in *Twice-told Tales*.

MY KINSMAN, MAJOR MOLINEUX: *The Token* for 1832. *The Snow-Image* (1852).

colonial governors: in 1684 Charles II suspended the old charter of the Massachusetts Bay colony that had been brought over from England by John Winthrop in 1630 and gave to the colonists the right to elect their own governors. By the terms of the new charter, issued in October 1691, the governor and the lieutenant-governor were appointed by the crown.

annals of Massachusetts Bay: Hawthorne's major sources included Thomas Hutchinson, *The History of the Colony (Province) of Massachusetts Bay*, 3 vols (1764–1828) and Caleb H. Snow, *History of Boston* (1825). For detailed discussion of sources see Doubleday (1972); Grayson (1982); Colacurcio (1984). See also Marion Kesselring, *Hawthorne's Reading 1828–1850* (1949).

six governors: the two imprisoned were Sir Edmund Andros (1686–9) and Joseph Dudley (1702–15); the one driven from office by a musket ball was Samuel Shute (1716–28), who remained in England from 1723 on; William Burnet (1728–9) was driven to an early grave, worn out by the trials of office. The other two governors were Sir William Phipps (1692–4), the first royal governor of Massachusetts, and the Earl of Bellamont (1699–1700). See Doubleday (1972).

a hundred years ago: dating back from the publication of 'My Kinsman, Major Molineux' in *The Token* (1831, for 1832), this would obviously set the story in the early 1730s. However, the mob action that provides the climax to the tale is clearly based on the riot of 26 August 1765. On that day, according to Hutchinson, who was a victim as well as an historian of the violence, the whole town of Boston was in awe of the rioters, whose fury was directed against officials involved in administering (or considered sympathetic to) the hated Stamp Act.

inflammation of the popular mind: this judgement, together with the narrator's later comments on the 'frenzied' behaviour of the mob, is an implicit challenge to the tradition of celebratory rhetoric that dignified all the pre-Revolutionary challenges to British authority. See Pearce (1954), Julian Smith (1970), and Shaw (1976).

ferry: this would be the Charlestown ferry, which landed at Boston's North End. For Hawthorne's detailed knowledge of the geography of eighteenth-century Boston, see Grayson (1982).

39 *Major Molineux*: the name may have been taken, with ironic intention, from that of a leader of anti-loyalist mobs who was also a member of the Boston Revolutionary Committee of Correspondence. This William Molineux was said to have taken part in the Boston Tea Party. See Pearce (1954). Also possible is an allusion to the Molineux who posed to John Locke the problem of whether a blind man, who had learned by touch, could recognize a cube or a sphere by sight if his sight were restored to him. Hawthorne could have met the 'Molineux problem' in Thomas C. Upham's *Elements of Intellectual Philosophy* (1827). See Grayson (1982). Its relevance to a tale in which perception is a major theme cannot be doubted.

Ramillies wig: an elaborate wig that took its name from the town of Ramillies, Belgium.

authority: psychoanalytic interpretations of the tale (for example, Lesser, 1955) stress Robin's unconscious drive to achieve adulthood by avoiding, rather than submitting to, his surrogate father, Major Molineux. Recent commentary (for example, Smith, 1970) suggests that Robin merely rejects one form of authority to accept another—that of the *undemocratic* revolutionary leaders.

roar of laughter: the importance of laughter in the tale is stressed by Waggoner (1955). For the disruptive effects of laughter in several of the tales, see Dusenbery (1967).

shrewd youth: Robin's shrewdness—whatever the ironies with which the narrator endows it—becomes a leitmotiv of the tale. Hoffman (1961) cross-references to Brother Jonathan, who is nothing if not shrewd—in his own estimation. Robin, in Hoffman's phrase, is the Yankee Bumpkin.

40 *centre of business*: this would have been Dock Square, which was the site of Faneuil Hall and thus to become some ten years later (anachronistically, as far as 'My Kinsman, Major Molineux' is concerned) associated with events leading to the War of Independence. See Grayson (1982).

41 *Fast-day sermons*: in New England Fast Day was a day appointed every spring by the governor of the State for fasting.

caravansary: an inn with an inner court where caravans could rest.

45 *cunningly*: Robin's country innocence is quickly replaced by a sort of 'cunning' (knowingness) as he 'read in her eyes what he did not hear in her words'. He may be only 'half-willing', but the athletic youth is easily overcome by the young woman, who is obviously experienced. His return to 'shrewdness' and to the moral code appropriate to a clergyman's son may well have depended on the intervention of the nightwatchman.

. . . Thisbe: this direct allusion to *A Midsummer Night's Dream* reinforces the recurrent references to moonlight and dreams in the tale. Doubleday (1972) stresses the Shakespearian allusions, but believes that 'My Kinsman, Major Molineux' is a tale 'of lunacy, where the imagining is a nightmare', rather than a story of romance.

47 *infernal visage*: this figure has been identified as the mob leader of Revolutionary days who took the name of the regicide judge, Joyce Jr. He is named (and Molineux mentioned) in Hezekiah Niles's *Principle Acts of the Revolution* (1822), a work which

Hawthorne may have known. See Pearce (1954) and Shaw (1976).

48 *mansion*: possibly, as Smith (1970) argues, the Province House, residence of the governors from 1717 until the Revolution. But Colacurcio (1984) argues that the authoritarian old gentleman may represent the local 'Country Party' and may even be the speaker of the Massachusetts House of Representatives.

49 *shroud*: the concatenation of ideas that leads Robin from reflections on the possible death of Major Molineux to memories of his own father seems to Lesser (1955) to suggest that Robin's unconscious motive is the destruction of *both* authority figures.

50 *excluded*: contrary to Lesser's theory of Robin's drives, this would suggest that he feels the anguish of separation from father and home.

real kindness: this 'kindness' can be taken, apparently with the narrator's authority, to express 'non-inhibiting parental love' (Hoffman, 1961), but recent interpretations treat the 'kindness' as suspect: see, for example, Colacurcio (1984). The friendly gentleman may well have met the mob leader in the Province House, according to Smith (1970). One critic (Broes, 1964) goes as far as to treat the kindly gentleman as the devil's advocate. Such readings are, of course, incompatible with Seymour Gross's view (1957) that the story is essentially one of moral growth as Robin moves from naïvety and callow pride to adulthood.

52 *two complexions*: Robin's 'shrewdness' may have something to do with an ability to change his political complexion. If so, his personal story may throw an ironic light on the history of the young nation's growth towards independence. For a positive reading of the tale's implications in terms of the nation's growth towards maturity, see Leavis (1951).

56 *dead potentate . . . frenzied merriment*: Molineux, though only a junior official in the colonial government, is a scapegoat in what can be taken as a ritualistic sacrifice of the king, according to Hoffman (1961). If the victim is 'majestic' in his agony, the riotous mob and its politically astute leaders are hardly honourable. When he described the doings of 'the Hutchinson mob' in *The Liberty Tree* (1841), Hawthorne offered his juvenile readers only a qualified endorsement of the heroic view of the Revolution as a struggle for liberty and progress. Laurence, one of the young listeners to Grandfather's story, says indignantly,

'if the people acted in this manner, they were not worthy of even so much liberty as the king of England was willing to allow them' (*CE*, vi, 159). Grandfather, however, defends the cause, while deploring the behaviour of the mob.

ROGER MALVIN'S BURIAL: *The Token* for 1832. *United States Magazine and Democratic Review*, xiii (1843) (hereafter referred to as *Democratic Review*). *Mosses* (1846).

into the shade: among the circumstances it would be necessary to treat in this way if 'chivalry' were not to blush was the fact that Lovewell (or Lovell) and his party had collected bounties of one thousand pounds from the General Court for the scalps of ten Indians they had found asleep and killed on an expedition in the year before the Fight. When ambushed by chief Paugus and the Pigwacket Indians on the site of the present Fryeburg, Maine, in May 1725, Lovewell seems to have been on another scalping expedition. His chaplain, 'Gallant Frye', had killed and scalped a solitary Indian discovered before the ambush. Within weeks of the battle the 'heroism' of the whites was celebrated in sermon and ballad. Nineteenth-century glorification of the Fight—in particular the oratory of Fryeburg's 'Paugus Day' (19 May 1825)—is discussed in Bickford (1958) and in Stock (1964). Stock gives extracts from a celebratory account in the Boston *Columbian Centinel* on that day, with references to the 'chivalrous devotedness' of Lovewell's men.

Since Lovell's Pond is less than sixty miles from Brunswick, Maine, Hawthorne may have heard the legend in boyhood. He certainly knew the *Collections, Topographical, Historical, Biographical*, edited by John Farmer and J. B. Moore, which contained—in vol. i (1822)—the Revd T. Symmes's account of the battle, written and first published in the year it occurred. Symmes had also preached a sermon celebrating the heroic fight in 1725. Volume i of *Collections* also contained the story of the scalpings; vol. ii (1823) contained 'Indian Troubles at Dunstable', by 'J.B.H.' (Revd Joseph Bancroft Hill), an item from which Hawthorne took important details (see below). *Collections*, vol. iii (1824), contained 'Lovewell's Fight: a Ballad', which sentimentalized the death of chaplain Frye, who was said to have given Farwell a message to his parents as he was dying. On Hawthorne's sources see Orians (1938), Lovejoy (1954), Daly (1973).

58 *Reuben*: the biblical Reuben, as Stock points out, broke a promise to his father. See Genesis 27: 50.

howling wilderness: in doing battle with the Pigwacket Indians, Lovewell and his men were instrumental in pushing back the frontier, even if their motives were less than noble. See Bickford (1958).

60 *to wile him*: though Malvin's motive may be benevolent, Colacurcio (1984) points out that he in fact leads Reuben to temporize with truth and abuse his conscience.

61 *one coward*: in fact, the coward who fled from Lovewell's Fight spread such panic that the reserve garrison abandoned their post and failed to rescue the wounded left near the battlefield. See Lovejoy (1954).

hidden strength: the invitation to the reader to look for Reuben's unconscious motives had been taken up, most notably, by Crews (1964), who explores the latent hostility between Dorcas's lover and father in Freudian terms.

62 *topmost branch*: in J.B.H.'s 'Indian Troubles at Dunstable' Hawthorne read that when Eleazor Davis of Concord was obliged to leave his wounded companion Farwell in the forest he took Farwell's handkerchief 'and tied it to the top of a bush that it might afford a mark by which his remains could the more easily be found' (*Collections*, ii, 1823, 306).

63 *rites of sepulture*: classical antecedents are, of course, numerous. See Newman (1979).

towards home: this detail, which underlines the thematic contrast of home and wilderness and prepares ironic overtones for Reuben's dream of founding a frontier home, was not in Hawthorne's sources.

64 *blame . . . him?*: many readers have done precisely that, though the sacrifice he could have made would surely have been useless, as the narrator says. In any case, Reuben's guilt will be caused by the lie he subsequently tells to protect his pride, not by his 'desertion' of Roger Malvin. For the view that the tale is an allegory of the *nation's* repressed guilt, see Naples (1972).

67 *a murderer*: the Oedipal connotations of these words are discussed by Erlich (1984) in terms of the hostility the young Nathaniel may well have felt for his uncle Robert Manning, a surrogate father after the death of Nathaniel Hathorne in 1808.

audible only to himself: like the Quaker fanatics of 'The Gentle Boy', Reuben listens to an inner voice of doubtful authority.

71 *twelfth of May*: according to Jeremy Belknap's *History of New*

Hampshire (1784–92), a work with which Hawthorne was familiar, the battle actually took place on Sunday, 9 May. The Revd Symmes apparently changed the date because a battle on the Lord's day would seem impious. See Daly (1973).

73 *practised marksman*: in realistic terms it may well be unlikely (as Doubleday, 1972, argues) that an experienced hunter would fire so recklessly at an unidentified movement, but Hawthorne's key word 'instinct' surely suggests that Reuben's action comes from a layer of the self more profound than that of his activity as a hunter.

76 *sin was expiated*: the analogy to the biblical story of Abraham and Isaac had been enough to explain Reuben's involuntary action to most commentators. Doubleday, however, finds that 'explanation' unsatisfactory since the sacrifice of the son to assuage the guilt of the father seems not to make any real sense.

THE CANTERBURY PILGRIMS: *The Token* for 1833. *The Snow-Image* (1852).

PILGRIMS: Hawthorne's 'Ancient Pilgrims' article (see below, note to p. 101) shows his continuing interest in a theme that would provide him with the subject of one of his best satirical pieces, 'The Celestial Railroad' (1843). For the importance of the journey motif in Hawthorne's tales, see Weber (1973).

as the writer has: this personal reference was marked for deletion when Hawthorne revised a copy of the 1833 *Token* text for inclusion in the second volume of *Twice-told Tales*. The tale was not collected in the 1842 volume. When it was included in *The Snow-Image*, in 1851, the change was not observed. See *CE*, xi, 412–13.

Hawthorne visited the Shaker village at Canterbury, New Hampshire in 1831. His account of the Shakers in a letter to his sister Louisa on 17 August—though mixed—is more favourable than his tales (this one and 'The Shaker Bridal' in *The Token* for 1838) would lead one to expect. 'On the whole, they lead a good and comfortable life, and if it were not for their ridiculous ceremonies, a man could not do a wiser thing than to join them.' (*CE*, xv, 213). Hawthorne went on to say (perhaps with ironic intent) that he had spoken to them about becoming a member of the society. Gollin (1978) argues that Hawthorne took the Shaker alternative seriously, in spite of any ridicule in his letters on the subject. Gross (1958) suggests that Hawthorne's opinion was influenced unfavourably by his subsequent reading of Thomas Brown's *An Account of the People Called Shakers* (1812), which treats them as fanatics.

77 *'Thee and I'*: the Shaker idiom was as distinctive as their dress.

78 *little charity*: the clear implication here—as in 'The Man of Adamant'—is that without 'charity' for the flesh the seeker after virtue may well become 'a very awful man to speak with'. In 'The Shaker Bridal' Ephraim is 'awful' in his fanatical virtue.

81 *vague revery*: clearly a disparaging comment, though 'revery' can be considered a distinctive feature of Hawthorne's own art. For the view that Hawthorne is himself the artist as 'conscious dreamer' see Pattison (1967).

Castalia: a fountain on Mount Parnassus, sacred to Apollo and the Muses, and a source of inspiration to those who drank at it.

82 *rich establishment*: Shaker communities were among the most economically successful of the numerous communitarian experiments of the 1830s and 1840s. See Alice Felt Tyler, *Freedom's Ferment* (1944), ch. 7, 'The Shaker Communities'.

84 *the Oregon expedition*: in 1832 Nathaniel Wyeth, an ice-dealer in Cambridge, Massachusetts, set out with a party of twenty-four to cross the continent and set up trading posts on the Columbia River. His Oregon Colonization Society was a failure. See Bernard de Voto, *Across the Wide Missouri* (1947).

86 *would be sundered*: celibacy was the rule in Shaker communities. Existing marriages were dissolved when new members joined.

THE SEVEN VAGABONDS: *The Token* for 1833. *Twice-told Tales* (1842)

to Canada: in a letter to John Franklin Pierce dated 28 June 1832, Hawthorne mentioned that his plans for a trip to Canada—by way of Albany and Niagara—had been cancelled because of an outbreak of cholera. He went on to say that he wanted to take the journey 'on account of a book . . . which I cannot commence writing till I have visited Canada' (*CE*, xv, 224). The projected book—which was to be called 'The Story Teller'—was never published, but parts of it appeared in the *New-England Magazine* in November and December 1834. Under the heading 'Passages from a Relinquished Work' these pieces were reprinted in the 1854 edition of *Mosses*. In 'At Home', part of 'The Story Teller, No. 1' (November 1834), the narrator explains that he got the idea of becoming a wandering story-teller 'by an encounter with several merry vagabonds in a showman's wagon, where they and I had sheltered ourselves during a summer shower'. Adkins (1945) believes that 'The Seven Vagabonds' might well have been the original introduction to the projected 'Story Teller' volume. He also suggests that Hawthorne's interest in the idea of travel-sketches as links between tales might have been stimulated by Washington Irving's *Sketch-book* and *Tales of a Traveller*. Weber (1973) treats this story as Hawthorne's first attempt to develop a frame narrative for a cycle of tales. He relates Hawthorne's fiction to the tradition of the *voyage imaginaire*.

Stamford: Hawthorne had visited Stamford, Connecticut, with his uncle Samuel Manning in 1829.

87 *Merry-Andrew*: in Strutt's *Sports and Pastimes* (see below, note to p. 133) Hawthorne could have read that in the England of James II this figure was an inseparable companion of the mountebank (a seller of medicines) and acted as his fool, engaging him in dialogue.

88 *Don Quixote*: for Hawthorne's knowledge of Cervantes' works, see below, note to p. 115.

toper: an habitual drunkard.

89 *Scottish Chiefs:* Hawthorne's own early enthusiasm for the novels of Sir Walter Scott is recorded in a letter to his sister Elizabeth dated 31 October 1820 (*CE*, xv, 132).

Primer: the earliest known edition of this work, which combined traditional hornbook material (alphabet and syllabarium) with traditional primer material (Lord's Prayer, Creed, Decalogue, and catechism) came from the press of Benjamin Harris of Boston in 1690. It used couplets as learning aids, among them: 'In Adam's Fall / We sinned all.' The *Primer* sold in immense quantities and was frequently revised and reprinted. It included 'The Dutiful Child's Promises': 'I will . . . honor my Father and Mother . . . I will learn my catechism'. As Duban (1979) points out, a *Primer* entry under 'Youth' is particularly relevant to this story. In it the devil tempts man to his doom through 'sports and plays of art'.

Life of Franklin: *The Life of Benjamin Franklin, written by himself* was first published in the United States in 1794, having been published in England in 1793. An incomplete version of the *Autobiography* was published in 1818. Franklin's self-advertised pragmatism and shrewdness would not appeal to the narrator of this tale.

Webster's Spelling-Book: Noah Webster (1758–1843), biographer and lexicographer, published the first part of *A Grammatical Institute of the English Language* (1783–5) with the aim of standardizing American spellings and differentiating them from English usage.

92 *born in it*: in *The Token* there followed a passage which Hawthorne had omitted when the tale was collected, possibly in deference to the taste of his larger reading public:

> I hardly know how to hint, that, as the brevity
> of her gown displayed rather more than her ancles,
> I could not help wishing that I had stood at a little
> distance without, when she stept up the ladder
> into the wagon. (*CE*, ix, 630.)

commencements: in American universities, these are degree-giving ceremonies at the end of the academic year.

93 *old song*: the song is quoted by William Pryce in his *Archaeologia Cornu-Brittanica* (1790).

camp-meeting: outdoor religious meetings which drew participants from a wide area and which often lasted for several days were a feature of the eighteenth-century evangelical revivals. By the early nineteenth century they had extended throughout the country.

94 *Suffolk Bank*: in *The Token* this read 'U.S. Bank'. Hawthorne's emendation may have been intended to strengthen the local references of the tale by referring to a Boston bank. In the *American Magazine of Useful and Entertaining Knowledge* in August 1836, Hawthorne described the elegant new building erected in 1834. See Turner, *Hawthorne as Editor* (1941).

specie: coin. Bank scrip was commonly *not* better than specie and was often discounted.

96 *bibliopolist*: dealer in rare books.

97 *'wandering up and down . . .'*: Job 1: 7. The Lord said to Satan, 'Whence have you come?' Satan answered the Lord 'From going to and fro on the earth, and from walking up and down on it.'

98 *Penobscot tribe*: one of the tribes of the Algonquian confederacy that gave its name to the river in central Maine. If Weber (1973) is right in taking the theme of this tale to be the freedom of the

artist-entertainer, then the inclusion of an Indian among the crew is highly appropriate, since 'the Indian' was a symbol of wild freedom in antebellum American thought. Fussell (1965) takes the Indian in this tale to represent *the* American writer, but this is to overstate his significance.

100 *Oriental travellers*: Hawthorne's interest in oriental traditions of story-telling has already been noticed in 'The Gentle Boy'. Doubleday (1972) suggests that the idea of the peripatetic story-teller may have been suggested by Moore's *Lalla Rookh* (1817).

L'Allegro: the Miltonic debate between Mirth (*L'Allegro*) and Melancholy (*Il Penseroso*) is a structural principle of Hawthorne's tale, in which 'sad thought' is opposed to merriment. For a fuller—and a more searching—treatment of the themes, see 'The Maypole of Merry Mount'.

101 *pilgrimage*: in his 'Ancient Pilgrims' article in the *American Magazine of Useful and Entertaining Knowledge*, April 1836, Hawthorne wrote that 'generally, a pilgrimage . . . must have been a very pleasant interlude in a man's life'. See Turner (1941).

102 *travelling preacher*: at this period, Methodist ministers commonly took part in camp-meetings. The 'iron gravity' of this preacher links him with the 'iron' Puritans of 'The Maypole'. On the significance of this 'eighth vagabond's' presence in the tale, see Colacurcio (1984).

103 THE GREY CHAMPION: *New-England Magazine*, viii (January 1835); *Twice-told Tales* (1837).

annulled the charters: see above, p. 37. James II succeeded to the throne in February 1685 and ruled until December 1688 when he was deposed by William of Orange. News of William's landing in England provoked the insurrection in Boston.

Andros: Sir Edmund Andros (1637–1714) was appointed Vice-Regent by James when the Northern colonies were consolidated as the Dominion of New England in 1686. He was soon regarded as a tyrant by the colonists. In *Grandfather's Chair* Hawthorne's narrator explains that there was no liberty and scarcely any law in the colonies over which Andros ruled. Resentment reached its climax in the insurrection that began on 18 April 1689. Andros was imprisoned and subsequently sent to England for trial. Patriotic American historians (such as George Bancroft) described the revolt as the expression of a unanimous love of liberty, ignoring the factionalism of New England politics of the 1680s and the split between town and country parties in Massachusetts. Hawthorne's narrator gives a similar impression of unity among the colonists and their descendants. See Doubleday (1972) and McWilliams (1984).

Prince of Orange: William of Orange ascended to the throne in 1689 and ruled with Mary until her death in 1694, after which he ruled alone until 1702.

104 *King Street*: to be the site of the Boston Massacre, on 5 March 1770, when three citizens were killed and eight wounded (two mortally) by troops of the British garrison. The name was later changed to State Street.

more than sixty years: though the Pilgrims had settled at Plymouth, Massachusetts in 1620, the Great Migration that brought thousands of Englishmen to New England took place in the years 1628–40.

righteous cause: though the phrase seems to suggest that the narrator endorses the Puritans' sense of divine favour, it may merely report it.

King Philip's war: in 1675, Metacomet (King Philip), son of Massasoit, the chief of the Wampanoag Indians who had aided the Pilgrims, attacked Swansea, Massachusetts, to avenge the wrongs he believed the settlers had committed against his tribe. As Hawthorne knew from the histories—for example Thomas Hutchinson's (see above, note to p. 37)—on 18 December 1675, the Narragansett Indians were slaughtered in their fortress in the Great Swamp, Rhode Island, when the Puritans put five to six hundred wigwams to the torch, burning old men, women, and children.

105 *Smithfield fire*: the market-place at Smithfield, London, was the scene of many executions of Protestants in the reign of Queen Mary (1553–8).

John Rogers: John Rogers (?1500–55) was an orthodox Catholic priest until converted to Protestantism by William Tindall in 1538. He was burned alive as a heretic in February 1555.

Primer: see above, p. 89.

St Bartholomew: the massacre of French Protestants on St Bartholomew's day in 1572 fuelled fears of Roman Catholic cruelty and fanaticism for a very long time.

to be massacred: these rumours are mentioned in Daniel Neal, *History of New England* (1720).

Bradstreet: Simon Bradstreet (1603–97) was governor of Massachusetts from 1679 to 1686 and from 1689 to 1692, and was secretary to the governor until his death. According to Joseph Felt, in his *History of Salem* (one of Hawthorne's major historical sources) Bradstreet advised Andros to surrender to the people to avoid bloodshed.

106 *Edward Randolph*: Randolph came to Massachusetts in 1676 to report for the king. His report led to action against the colony for violations of trade regulations. The hatred he inspired is the subject of Hawthorne's 'Edward Randolph's Portrait' (1838), collected in *Twice-Told Tales* (1842), where he is described as the 'arch enemy of New England' and held responsible for the repeal of the old charter.

Cotton Mather: (1663–1727) son of Increase Mather, whose colleague at the North Church, Boston, he became in 1685, succeeding to his father in 1723. Hawthorne knew intimately Mather's *Magnalia Christi Americana* (1702), a learned and encyclopaedic history of New England, which was one of Hawthorne's major sources, though he did not endorse Mather's Puritan bias. See above, notes to pp. 4, 5.

Bullivant: Hawthorne's sketch 'Dr Bullivant' (1831) is an essay on the secularization that had occurred in New England society in the sixty or seventy years since the arrival of the first settlers. Bullivant, the jolly apothecary, represents the new worldliness as well as royalist sympathies. See *Tales and Sketches*, ed. Pearce, pp. 34–41.

Dudley: Joseph (1647–1720), son of Governor Thomas Dudley, served as President of the Dominion of New England in 1686 until the arrival of Andros and was governor of Massachusetts from 1702 to 1715.

King's Chapel: established in 1754, this was the first Episcopalian church in New England. To nineteenth-century historians, the Episcopalians (in contrast to the Puritans) were associated with Toryism and tradition.

107 *Champion*: Brumm (1976) argues that Hawthorne's tale is related to the legend of the 'King of the Mountain', the leader who sleeps in a cave until called to save his people from danger. The legend of Emperor Frederick Barbarossa was still current in Germany in the early nineteenth century.

Winthrop: John Winthrop (1588–1649) sailed to the New World on the *Arbella* in 1630, bringing the charter with him. He became the first governor of Massachusetts on arrival and was re-elected in 1631, 1632, and 1633.

109 *Old Noll*: nickname for Oliver Cromwell.

stayed the march of a king: the statement leaves no doubt that this champion is the regicide judge William Goffe, who, together with Edmund Whalley, had fled to America on the accession of Charles II and had been obliged to go into hiding to avoid the King's agents. They had lived incognito in Hadley, Massachusetts. In 1675, when the town was surprised by Indians, a mysterious figure dressed in outlandish costume is supposed to have appeared to organize the defences of the panic-stricken townspeople. When the Indians were repulsed, the figure disappeared. The Legend of 'The Angel of Hadley' was told in Hutchinson's *History*, vol. 1, and in Timothy Dwight's *Travels in New England and New York*, vol. 1 (1821). Walter Scott took the story from Dwight to use it in *Peveril of the Peak* (1822), ch. 14. See Orians (1932).

110 *eighty years had passed*: which would take us to 1769, or even 1770, when the blood of the victims of the Boston Massacre flowed in King Street.

Lexington: the skirmish at Lexington on 19 April 1775 marked the beginning of the War of Independence and was, of course, regularly celebrated by historians and public speakers in Hawthorne's day.

Bunker's Hill: the battle of Bunker Hill, 17 June 1775, was celebrated in the new nation as a triumph of American arms and an example of the heroism of the Revolutionaries, although the British actually won the field. British losses were so severe that their victory—if such it was—could only be Pyrrhic.

111 YOUNG GOODMAN BROWN: *New-England Magazine*, 8 (April 1835), 'By the Author of "The Gray Champion" '. *Mosses* (1846).

Goodman: in the opinion of some separatist ministers, as Cotton Mather reported in his *Magnalia*, it was unlawful to call an unregenerate man 'Goodman', but Governor Winthrop insisted that this was a civil British custom, the title being used when juries were called over. Thus, as Levin (1962) notes, the term could mean 'good enough to serve on a jury'. When we are told that Brown 'could have sworn' that he recognized the voices he heard in the forest, the legal implications of 'Goodman' became sinister. On the more general irony of the title 'Goodman' in a tale that vividly realizes a sense of human evil, see Robinson (1963).

Salem village: not the town of Salem, where Hawthorne grew up, but the nearby village, now named Danvers, which was the centre of the witchcraft hysteria in 1692. In *Famous Old People* (1841), Hawthorne's narrator describes this episode as 'the saddest and most humiliating passage in our history' (*CE*, vi, 79). As Levin (1962) demonstrated, the events of 1692, which culminated in the hanging of twenty supposed witches, provide an historical reference for the tale without which its metaphorical or psychological meaning cannot be understood.

all nights in the year: clearly this must be 31 October, Halloween, as Hoffman (1961) insists.

112 *Old South*: the Old South Meeting House in Boston was first built in 1669.

fifteen minutes: since the distance from Boston to Danvers is almost twenty miles, the speed of travel is obviously supernatural.

King William's court: as William of Orange ruled from 1689 to 1702, the allusion means that we are close to the fatal year 1692. The implied dating also means that Brown must be a third-generation New England Puritan who has grown up in a condition of presumptive, but not yet professed, sainthood, under the Half-way covenant. See Colacurcio (1984) for the implications of Brown's historical situation.

113 *grandfather, the constable*: in this grandfather we can recognize Major William Hathorne (1607–81), the first of the family to settle in New England. His warrant led to the almost fatal whipping of Ann Coleman. See above, note to p. 3. For a detailed account of Hathorne's career, see Loggins (1951). Hawthorne returned to this incident in 'Main Street' (1849) where he also retold the story of the witchcraft trials, making particular mention of the fate of Martha Carrier and the Revd Mr Burroughs. See *CE*, xi, 70–7.

Indian village: Captain William Hathorne (1645–78), a son of Major William, took part in the campaign against the Narragansett Indians and participated in the burning of the village fort on 18 December 1675. See Clark (1975).

114 *'Can this be so?'*: Brown's response is a feeble defence against the devil's insinuations. He quickly falls into the trap against which Increase Mather warned—belatedly—in his *Cases of Conscience Concerning Evil Spirits Personating Man* (1693). To make his lies acceptable, the devil tells some truths. (See Levin, 1967.) The burning of the Indian village was historical fact.

Deacon Gookin: the name derives from Cotton Mather's *Magnalia*, as Turner (1936) notes.

Goody Cloyse: the historical Goodwife Sarah Cloyse (or Cloyce) lived in Salem Village, was accused of witchcraft and imprisoned, but was not condemned and was freed when the hysteria died down and opinion swung against the judges in 1693. The devil points to her 'figure'. In assuming that she then *is* in the forest, Brown is acting as witnesses at the trial did. As one contemporary noted at the height of the proceedings, witnesses 'positively swear that (for example) G. Proctor did afflict them' when they meant 'only the appearance and shape of such an one'. See Levin (1962).

115 *gossip*: a gossip is a person spiritually related to another (god-sib), as—for example—a sponsor in baptism, but Hoffman (1961) sees an implication that grandfather Brown has had carnal knowledge of Goody Cory.

Goody Cory: Goodwife Martha Cory (or Corey) was examined by Colonel John Hathorne (1641–1717), fourth son of Major William Hathorne, on 24 March 1692, in a pre-trial hearing (Hathorne was not a trial judge in 1692, though Hawthorne refers to him as 'the witch-judge' in his notebook—*CE*, viii, 172). Colonel Hathorne asked Martha Cory the sort of leading question that typified the proceedings when he asked 'Why she afflicted those children'—that is, the girls who claimed to be victims of witchcraft. Cory was committed, subsequently tried, found guilty, and hanged on 22 September 1692. Clark (1975) believes that Hawthorne may have read the manuscript account of the examination of Martha Cory in the archives of the Essex Institute, Salem. In any case, Judge Hathorne's question was recorded in Robert Calef's scathing attack on Cotton Mather's account of the witchcraft episode, *Wonders of the Invisible World* (1693). Calef's *More Wonders of the Invisible World* (1700) was also available to Hawthorne.

anointed: in the July 1836 issue of the *American Magazine of Useful and Entertaining Knowledge* Hawthorne had included an article on witches' ointment and mentioned a tale of Cervantes in which the ointment was said to have put witches into a trance, enabling them to dream of intercourse with Satan. The editorial comment—'If so, witchcraft differs little from a nightmare'—is obviously relevant to this tale. The Cervantes story has been identified as 'El Coloquio de los Perros'. See Cherry (1934).

smallage, and cinquefoil, and wolf's—bane: plants associated with witchcraft: wild celery; a type of rose with five-lobed leaves; an aconite with medicinal properties.

Egyptian magi: the magi had copied Aaron in demonstrating their magic power by turning their rods into serpents, at Pharaoh's command. See Exodus 7: 11–13.

117 *Falmouth*: a town on Cape Cod, some seventy miles from Salem Village.

pow-wows: medicine men or priests, from the Algonquian *pauwaw*—literally, he dreams.

119 *on he flew*: the innocuous metaphor is given dangerous possibilities by one of Hawthorne's sources. In the appendix to Deodat Lawson's *Christ's Fidelity* (1704), a work dedicated to Judge John Hathorne, there was material on the bodily transportation of witches to their meetings with the devil. See Cohen (1968).

an altar or a pulpit: witches' sabbaths such as the one at which Brown finds himself, or imagines that he does, were described in Hawthorne's sources, among them Mather's *Wonders*. Orians (1930) defines such a sabbath as 'a kind of cursed sacrament, an infernal service profaning that of the church, with diabolical hymns and orgiastic rites and blasphemous sermons by the Black Man'.

120 *the lady of the governor*: in *Famous Old People*, Grandfather states that 'the lady of Sir William Phipps was accused of being a witch, and of flying through the air to attend witch meetings' (*CE*, vi, 79).

121 *figure*: in the *New-England Magazine* and 1846 *Mosses* texts the word was 'apparition'. Levin (1962) considers that Hawthorne's emendation in the 1854 *Mosses* is in the direction of a 'superbly appropriate vagueness'.

grave divine: one of the actual victims of the witchcraft hysteria was George Burroughs, who had been pastor of Salem Village from 1680 to 1683 and was minister of Wells in Maine when he was accused. He was condemned and hanged, as Hawthorne would note in *Famous Old People* and in 'Main Street' (1849). The story of his trial is told in Mather's *Wonders*.

queen of hell: Martha Carrier, who lived in Andover, was tried and condemned in August 1692. In *Wonders*, Mather recorded that 'This Rampant Hag, Martha Carrier, was the Person, of whom the Confessions of the Witches, and of her own Children among the rest, agreed, That the Devil had promised her, she should be Queen of Hell'. See George L. Burr (ed.), *Narratives of the Witchcraft Cases, 1648–1706* (New York, 1914; 1959), p. 244.

124 WAKEFIELD: *New-England Magazine*, viii (1835). *Twice-told Tales*, 1837.

newspaper: Hawthorne's actual source was Dr William King's *Political and Literary Anecdotes of His Own Times* (1818), as Warren (1934) first noted.

125 *till death*: in King's *Anecdotes* the errant husband (Mr Howe) is absent seventeen years. On his return, he and his wife 'lived together in great harmony from that time to the day of his death'. This Mr Howe deserts his wife and home in Jermyn Street, St James, and takes up lodgings in Westminster.

cold but not depraved: coldness of heart is a recurrent theme in Hawthorne's writings. Compare, for example, 'The Christmas Banquet' in this volume. His own 'coldness' seemed to him to be a curse from which only his love for Sophia (and hers for him) was able to save him. In a letter to Sophia dated 4 October 1840, Hawthorne said of the years he spent in isolation after leaving college: 'sometimes (for I had no wife then to keep my heart warm) it seemed as if I were already in the grave, with only life enough to be chilled and benumbed' (*CE*, xv, 494). Chibka (1982) argues that in imagining Wakefield, the narrator risks becoming a version of him. He goes on to treat Wakefield as an image of Hawthorne himself.

128 *morbid vanity*: in his *Anecdotes*, King states that Mr Howe never confessed the cause of his 'singular conduct' and adds 'apparently there was none'.

129 *buying a new wig*: this detail is taken from King's *Anecdotes*.

130 *yonder church*: Mr Howe spies on his wife in church. He also becomes a friend of a corn-chandler who lives opposite his wife's new home and is thus able to spy on her in her own dining room when he dines (twice a week) with his new friend. As Perry (1978) points out, Hawthorne omits most of the voyeurism in Mr Howe's story.

131 *busy and selfish London*: although Hawthorne had not visited London when he wrote this tale, as Gatta (1977) points out, the city was already seen by Americans as the representative urban

colossus. In *Anecdotes*, though the story of Mr Howe is set at the beginning of the eighteenth century, King remarks that London is *the* place in Europe where a man can remain unknown for years.

132 *wet and shivering*: Hawthorne has heightened the drama of the return and stressed the element of whim. In *Anecdotes* Mr Howe's return is premeditated; he sends an anonymous billet to his wife inviting her to meet him.

133 *Outcast of the Universe*: though all commentators have noted the centrality of this theme in Hawthorne's works, not all of them have considered this tale successful. Waggoner (1955) considers the framework too slight for the burden of thought. Doubleday (1972) believes that the tale becomes 'more than a stunt', but he grants it only qualified success. Crowley (1971) gives this tale importance by treating it as a story of how to tell a story, with the central drama being the narrative itself. Swann (1978) interestingly relates its moral to Oberon's perception of his situation in 'Fragments from the Journal of a Solitary Man'.

THE MAYPOLE OF MERRY MOUNT: *The Token* for 1836. *Twice-told Tales* 1837.

Mount Wollaston: Mount Wollaston was named for Captain Wollaston, who set up a trading post at Passonagessit (now Quincy, Massachusetts) in 1623. When Wollaston left for Virginia, in 1625, Thomas Morton usurped his authority and turned the settlement into a morally dissolute community, though it remained an effective commercial enterprise. Morton named it Maremount, because of its sea view, then Merry Mount. The behaviour of the Merrymounters gave offence to the other settlers in that part of Massachusetts, and the sense of outrage reached a climax with the 1627 May Day ceremonies when—according to William Bradford's *History*—Indian squaws were included in the drinking and general licentiousness. In 1628 Miles Standish, and military officer at Plymouth, was hired to arrest Morton and send him to England for trial. This was done, but no action was taken against Morton in England. He returned to cause more trouble in 1629 and was deported once more. Endicott's visit to Merrymount took place in Morton's absence in 1628: it could not have occurred in May since Endicott did not arrive in Naumkeag (now Salem) until September of that year. Hawthorne has obviously adapted the history (which he knew well) to stress thematic contrasts between hedonist and Puritan. He has also made the clash of values a purely moral one, though—as he knew—the determination to restrain Morton was the result of the physical, as well as the moral, threat posed by the Merrymounters: they were trading in firearms with the Indians.

New England annalists: though Bradford's *History of Plymouth Plantation* was not available to Hawthorne (it was first published in 1865), he was familiar with the works of several historians who drew on Bradford's manuscript. These included: Nathaniel Morton, *New England's Memorial* (1669), Thomas Prince, *A Chronological History of New England in the Form of Annals* (1736), Francis Baylies, *Historical Memoir of the Colony of New Plymouth* (1830), Joseph Felt, *Annals of Salem* (1827). For discussion of the sources, see Orians (1938) and Doubleday (1972). The history of the Merry Mount settlement is told succinctly in Sterne (1970).

Sports and Pastimes: published in 1801, this work incorporated sixteenth-century Puritan denunciations of May Day ceremonies, as well as providing a wealth of information about traditional English games.

ribbons: Strutt quotes Philip Stubbes' *Anatomie of Abuses* (1583). The villagers, says Stubbes, treat 'their stinking idol'—the Maypole—with 'great veneration' when it has been 'covered all over with flowers and hearbes, bound round with stringes from the top to the bottom . . . with handkerchieves and flages'. The passage leaves no doubt that the ceremonies were licentious: 'of fourtie, threescore, or an hundred maids going to the wood there have scarcely the third part of them returned home again as they went'. The last phrase is Strutt's euphemism; Stubbes wrote 'returned home again undefiled'.

134 *Golden Age*: Hoffman (1961) argues that Hawthorne's awareness of the literary tradition of the Golden Age was strengthened by reading William Hone's *The Every Day Book* (1826), with its accounts of the pagan festival of Flora. Hone included Thomas Hall's *Funebria Flora. The Downfall of the May Games* (1661), in which the association of May and poetry, as well as the conflict between Puritan fanaticism and the spirit of jollity, could be found. However, as Doubleday (1972) points out, Hawthorne first borrowed *The Every Day Book* from the Atheneum in September 1835 and it is possible that 'Maypole' was written as early as 1828.

likeness of a bear: when weary travellers accept the liquor offered to them by Comus in Milton's masque:

> Soon as the potion works, their human countenance,
> The express resemblance of the gods, is changed
> Into some brutish form of wolf, or bear,
> Or ounce, or tiger, hog, or bearded goat.
>
> *Comus* (1634), ll. 68–72

Salvage Man: 'salvage', the archaic form of 'savage', reveals its etymology, from the Latin *silva*, woods.

wampum: beads made of shells, often made into necklaces or belts, used as currency by the North American Indians.

135 *airiest forms*: Hawthorne's description of the Lord and Lady of the May derives from Strutt, whose source was the Beaumont and Fletcher play *The Knight of the Burning Pestle*: 'With gilded staff and crossed scarf the May/Lord here I stand.' See Doubleday (1972).

clerk: since the Reformation, a lay officer of the Church; in pre-Reformation times, a man ordained to the ministry.

136 *cithern*: guitar.

pensive glance: compare 'The Seven Vagabonds', where acceptance into Mirth's 'crew' means banishing 'sad thought'.

137 *Two hundred years ago, and more*: see above, note to p. 104.

minstrels: the association between minstrels and the maypole ceremonies is stressed in Stubbes's *Anatomie*.

mirth-makers of every sort: though the narrator links them with 'triflers', the mirth-makers are, in their various ways, artists. As in 'Seven Vagabonds', the province of Mirth includes art.

138 *Lord of Misrule*: Strutt, *Sports and Pastimes*, pp. 267–9, describes the Lord of Misrule as a mock-prince whose rule extended through the greater part of the Christmas holidays in former times. Holinshed, says Strutt, calls him a court officer, but his rule was not restricted to the court, for such 'masters of merry disport' were appointed in all strata of society. Strutt quotes Stubbes's attack on the 'heathenage, devilrie, whoredom, dronkenness, pride and whatnot' of 'these hell-hounds' (the Lords of Misrule and their followers). In his *History*, Bradford says that Morton became the Lord of Misrule at Merry Mount.

eve of Saint John: Midsummer's eve.

140 *Baal*: a fertility god whose prophets were put to death at Elijah's command. See 1 Kings 18.

Blackstone: Orians (1938) identifies Blackstone as the Revd William Blackstone, an Anglican who resided at Wessagusset for a year or more, but far from assisting at the maypole rites contributed to the cost of Miles Standish's expedition against Morton. Hawthorne could have found references to this Blackstone in Snow's *History of Boston*, where he is described as an eccentric who rejected the rule of the 'Lord Brethren' of Massachusetts, considering that as pernicious as the rule of the 'Lord Bishops' had been in England. In the first published text of the story, in *The Token*, the name was Claxton and may have alluded to the Revd Lawrence Claxton, an Anabaptist who tolerated maypoles but did not live in New England. See Martin (1983). Hawthorne's emendation of the name has been interpreted by M. D. Bell (1971) as a means of stressing the link between the sensuality of the Merrymounters and the Anglican Church. The effect of such a plan would, of course, depend on the reader's prior knowledge of an extremely obscure detail of New England history. Hawthorne's footnote has a deviousness worthy of Poe in *The Narrative of Arthur Gordon Pym*, since he (not Endicott) named the minister.

141 *assaulted the hallowed Maypole*: the historical Endicott did nothing so impractical as to attack a forty-foot-tall pine-tree trunk with a sword. Nathaniel Morton's *New England's Memorial* (1699) told the story clearly: 'That worthy gentleman, Mr John Endicott . . . caused the maypole to be cut down, and rebuked them for their profaneness, and admonished them that they walked better.' Morton was quoting from William Bradford's 'History of Plymouth Plantation'. See Orians (1938).

only Maypole: the statement is quoted from Prince's *Annals*. See Orians (1938).

Peter Palfrey, the Ancient: Palfrey was actually a member of Roger Conant's settlement of Naumkeag (later Salem) in 1626. He is mentioned in 'Main Street' (1849). See Taylor (1965). An 'ancient' was a flag-bearer, or ensign.

142 *General Court*: the legislative body of Massachusetts.

143 *our Israel*: seventeenth-century Puritans regarded the Old Testament Israel, with its Chosen People, as the type of New England. On typological thinking, see note to p. 169 below.

144 *They went heavenward*: compare *Paradise Lost*, Book XII, 648–9: 'They hand in hand with wand'ring steps and slow,/ Through Eden took their solitary way.'

THE MINISTER'S BLACK VEIL: *The Token* for 1836. *Twice-told Tales*, 1837.

Relevant passages from the *Notebooks*:

'An essay on the misery of being always under a mask. A veil may be needful, but never a mask.' *CE*, viii, 23 (between 25 October 1836 and 5 July 1837).

'A Father Confessor—his reflections on character, and the contrast of the inward man with the outward, as he looks round on his congregation—all whose secret sins are known to him.' *CE*, viii, 235 (between 1 June 1842 and 27 July 1844).

A Parable: according to Stibitz (1962), the 'parable' tells us that man tends to hide or rationalize his guilt, but at another level it says that to exalt one idea—even a valid one—to the level of absolute truth is prideful.

Milford: Milford, Connecticut.

Spruce bachelors: this opening account of the congregation suggests, as Altschuler (1974) points out, that there has been a 'declension of piety'. For the evidence that the tale is set at the time of the Great Awakening, see below, note to p. 147.

Mr Joseph Moody: the story of the Revd Joseph Moody (1700–53) was told in volume one of Dr William Sprague's *Annals of the American Pulpit*; Benjamin Trumbull's *History of Connecticut* (1818), vol. ii, tells of a Mr Ruggles of Guilford, Connecticut, a good man though an uninspiring preacher, who had 'a great talent for hiding his real sentiments'.

145 *Westbury*: Westbury, Long Island. Exchange of pulpits was common practice in the eighteenth and nineteenth centuries.

something awful: the words are precise, since Hooper inspires that mixture of terror and reverence that constituted 'awe'—the emotion appropriate to the Sublime—in Burke's *Philosophical Enquiry* (1757). To Burke, the mystery and power of the deity was the ultimate source of sublime emotion.

147 *lighter spirits*: the effect of Mr Hooper's sermon on the congregation is here described in the language of enthusiastic response, according to Altschuler (1974), and thus belongs to the enthusiasm of the Great Awakening of the 1740s.

148 *fearful of her glance*: this phrase led Edgar Allan Poe, in his review of *Twice-told Tales* in *Graham's Magazine* in 1842, to suppose that Hooper was guilty of a sexual sin connected with this woman (see Poe's *Complete Works* (1902), xi, 111). Thus Poe was among the first to fall into the trap laid for the reader by the narrator's false leads. According to Carnochan (1969), the veil is not merely an object that conceals but also a sign of concealment. Being its own symbol, it is beyond interpretation; that is to say, beyond explanation in referential terms.

149 *wedding knell*: Hawthorne's story 'The Wedding Knell' was also first published in *The Token* for 1836 and collected in *Twice-told Tales*, 1837.

151 *melancholy smile*: Hooper's smile is not merely sad, it is diabolical in its condescension and self-satisfaction, according to Canaday (1967).

general synod: the ecclesiastical council.

152 *do the same*: Hooper's account of the symbolic meaning of the veil paraphrases Thomas Shepherd's *Sincere Convert* (1641): 'no unregenerate man . . . but . . . lives in some one sin or other, secret or open, little or great'. His sermon has an affective impact similar to Jonathan Edwards' 'Sinners in the Hands of an Angry God', which was preached at the height of the Great Awakening. See Morsberger (1973). Colacurcio (1984) argues that though, by Edwardsean standards, Hooper's spiritual life is lacking (because it shows no advance beyond the preparatory stage), the reader must get beyond the evangelical bias of the narrator and allow for the seriousness and psychological power of Hooper's way of salvation. In this view, to come up to Hawthorne's own standard of judgement, we must imagine that Hooper may really *know* something and the Puritans may actually *have seen* something which their liberal historians do not see.

154 *Governor Belcher*: the dates of Belcher's governorship, 1730–41, lend support to the theory that the tale is set at the time of the Great Awakening.

158 DR HEIDEGGER'S EXPERIMENT: *Knickerbocker*, ix (January 1837), under the title 'The Fountain of Youth'. *Twice-told Tales*, 1837.

experiments: like other 'scientists' in Hawthorne's fictions (most notably Dr Rappaccini and Roger Chillingworth) Dr Heidegger enters into an exploitative 'I'–'It' relationship with the human subjects of his enquiry and thus robs himself to some extent of his own humanity. For an illuminating application to Hawthorne's works of Martin Buber's theory of the failure of 'I'–'Thou' relationships see Waggoner (1979).

159 *Hippocrates*: born 460 BC, this Greek philosopher and writer was the first to base the practice of medicine on principles of induction rather than superstition. He therefore became known as the Father of medicine.

book of magic: as in 'The Birthmark', alchemy provides the link between science and magic. On the relationship between magic and art in Hawthorne, see Millicent Bell (1962).

161 *Ponce de Leon*: in 1514 Juan Ponce de Leon (1460–1521) at the age of fifty-three secured a patent from the King of Spain to colonize the Isle of Florida, where he is supposed to have sought the fountain of youth. He was mortally wounded by the Seminole Indians as he attempted to land in Charlotte Harbour.

bloom of youth: Hawthorne's interest in the related theme of the elixir of life is evidenced by his incomplete works *Septimius Felton* and *The Dolliver Romance*. For a survey of that theme in Hawthorne, see Hull (1972). In an article in the *American Magazine of Useful and Entertaining Knowledge* (August 1836) with the title 'Incurable Diseases', Hawthorne had noted that men have often sought for a medicine that would restore youth and stated that God has 'absolutely debarred mankind' from such inventions and discoveries. See Turner (1941).

165 *merry youngsters*: compare Cotton Mather, *Ornaments for the Daughters of Zion*: 'The aged show themselves to be twice children, and not put away childish things.' Homan (1966) notes Hawthorne's use of the Mather quotation in 'The Wedding Knell'.

167 *English Review*: this was the *Universal Review*, III (June 1860), which carried an unsigned article accusing Hawthorne of plagiarizing Dumas' *Mémoires d'un médecin*. The review is included in Crowley, ed., *The Critical Heritage*.

168 ENDICOTT AND THE RED CROSS: *The Token*, for 1838, with no attribution. *Twice-told Tales* (1842).

two centuries ago: the incident on which this story is based took place in 1634. It was recorded in John Winthrop's journal, published as *The History of New England from 1630 to 1649* (Boston, 1825–6), which Hawthorne borrowed from the Salem Atheneum in 1828. It was also recounted in Hutchinson's

History of Massachusetts, vol. I, and in Felt's *Annals of Salem*. Doubleday (1972) stresses the borrowings from Felt; Colacurcio (1984) argues that the tale depends on Winthrop's journal. On the sources, see also Gallagher (1968).

Laud: see above, note to p. 15. Many of the minsters who emigrated to Massachusetts had been 'silenced' by Laud in England.

King's right arm: in his journal, Winthrop makes it clear that King's threat to the patent of the colony was itself a threat to the religious freedom of the colonists.

169 *breastplate*: in the Old Testament the breastplate was the emblem of the theocratic state of Israel (see Leviticus 8: 8–15). To the Hebrews, the breastplate mirrored the Chosen People, protected by their Covenant with God, and resolute to win their Promised Land. To the New England Puritans, not only was the Old Testament the 'type' of the New, so that events in the New Testament were read 'typologically' as the fulfilments of Old Testament prophesy, but also their own history was understood in terms of biblical 'types'. Thus Endicott's breastplate could be read as an emblem of New England theocracy. See Bercovitch (1967).

health to the King: the implication that any sign of loyalty to the throne would bring retribution from the colonial authorities at this time is unhistorical.

Wanton Gospeller: this is perhaps the historical John Clark, who was whipped at Endicott's order. See Bercovitch (1967).

170 *punishment*: the list of Puritan punishments is derived from Felt's *Annals*.

letter A on the breast of her gown: in Felt, Hawthorne could have read that the law which imposed this punishment dated from 1694. In his notebook, at some time between 1841 and 1845, Hawthorne mentioned the old colony law that prescribed such treatment, but the old colony was New Plymouth, where the law was introduced in 1636. See *CE*, viii, 254 and the note at *CE*, viii, 618. Both the tale and notebook, of course, anticipated Hawthorne's development of this theme in *The Scarlet Letter*.

171 *Roger Williams*: (?1604–83) arrived in New England in 1631. From the beginning of his career as a minister in Massachusetts, Williams offended the general council, and the majority of Puritans, by asserting that the civil powers should have no authority over men's consciences. Williams fled to Narragansett

Indian territory in 1636 to avoid being sent back to England. There he named his new settlement Providence. Hawthorne's tale makes a contrast between Endicott's bigotry and Williams's moderation, but historically Endicott's action was inspired by Williams's teaching. Hawthorne kept closer to historical facts when he retold the story in *True Stories*, where Williams is shown to be in agreement with Endicott on the subject of the Red Cross.

172 *Black tidings*: the Governor's letter presumably contains news of the threat posed by the Privy Council to the patents of the colonies. This crisis is described in Winthrop's *Journal*. The colonists, he says, were prepared to resist any attempt to force them to receive a new governor (appointed by the Crown) and the discipline of the Church of England.

my own best judgement: in fact, Endicott's intemperate act of defiance brought censure from the colonial authorities. Winthrop notes that Endicott was censured at a meeting of the general court in January 1635 and was barred from public office for one year, partly for 'giving occasion to the State of England to think ill of us'.

hollow square: Newberry (1977) sees this as a diabolical ritual rather than a drill movement and takes Endicott to be the antithesis of the Red Cross Knight in Spenser's *Faerie Queene*, Bk II, Canto i, stanza 23.

173 *liberty of conscience*: to the original Puritan settlers who founded Massachusetts, liberty of conscience was not an ideal to be extended to all. Their colony was to be a theocracy (under the rule of the godly) from which dissidents would be banished, lest they corrupted the model community.

Scotch tyrant: James I, who had been James VI of Scotland before ascending to the throne of England.

175 *for ever honoured*: Hawthorne certainly did not always honour Endicott. See note to p. 5 above.

THE BIRTHMARK: *The Pioneer* (March 1843). *Mosses* (1846). Written between 13 January and 1 February, 1843. See McDonald (1972).

Relevant passages from the *Notebooks*:

'Those who are very difficult in choosing wives seem as if they would take none of Nature's ready-made works, but want a woman manufactured particularly to their order.' *CE*, viii, 20 (between 25 October 1836 and 5 July 1837).

'A person to be in the possession of something as perfect as mortal man has a right to demand; he tries to make it better, and ruins it entirely.'

'A person to spend all his life and splendid talents in trying to achieve something naturally impossible,—as to make a conquest over Nature.' CE, viii, 165 (between 16 October and 6 December 1837).

'A person to be the death of his beloved in trying to raise her to more than mortal perfection, yet this should be a comfort to him for having aimed so highly and holily.' CE, viii, 184 (between 4 January and 7 February 1839).

'The case quoted in Combe's *Physiology* [Andrew Combe, *Principles of Physiology*, 1842] from Pinel, of a young man of great talents and profound knowledge of chemistry, who had in view some new discovery of importance . . . he shut himself up, for several successive days, and used various methods of excitement . . . he was seized with a fit of frenzy, which terminated in mania.' *CE*, viii, 236 (between 1 June 1842 and 27 July 1844).

last century: though this comment links Aylmer with late eighteenth-century science, there are important parallels with the seventeenth-century scientific and alchemical experiments of Sir Kenelm Digby. See Reid (1966) and Van Leer (1976).

higher intellect: Stoehr (1978) gives a further relevant quotation from Combe's *Principles*: 'Men of exalted intellect perish by their brains, such is the noble end of those whose genius procures for them that immortality which many so ardently desire.'

creative force: possibly, like the protagonist in Mary Shelley's novel *Frankenstein* (1828), Aylmer wants to usurp the divine function by creating life.

love of science: this 'passion' is the *libido sciendi* that features in many of Hawthorne's fictions (see, for example, 'Rappaccini's Daughter' and 'Dr Heidegger's Experiment').

176 *stain upon the snow*: 'snow' in nineteenth-century usage frequently stood for feminine purity. The fact that the 'mark' vanishes when the blood rushes to Georgiana's cheek clearly links it with her passionate nature and with her sexuality. Digby's *Private Memoirs* (ed. Harris, 1827) tells of the promiscuous Lady Venetia Digby whose sensuality is suggested by her rosy cheek. Lady Venetia died in 1633, poisoned, as rumour had it, by her husband. See Reid (1966).

177 *Eve of Powers*: Hiram Powers (1805–73), the American sculptor, who worked in Florence from 1837 until his death, was famed for his *Eve before the Fall* and for his *The Greek Slave*. His treatment of the female form was considered so 'pure' that it made nudity into 'high' art.

fatal flaw of humanity: the mark is, then, the sign of birth into postlapsarian Nature.

178 *deeper one*: the narrator's suggestion that the life of dreams may be deeper than waking reality is consistent which many of Hawthorne's observations concerning dreams. See Gollin (1979).

179 *Pygmalion*: compare 'Drowne's Wooden Image' for a variation on this myth. See below, note to p. 277.

181 *Aminadab*: an anagram for bad-in-man, or bad anima. Reid (1966) proposes that Aminadab has some of the characteristics of Digby.

183 *polished plate of metal*: Aylmer's unsuccessful invention almost anticipates the daguerreotype, which was actually invented in the 1830s. As Franklin (1966; 1978) points out, Aylmer impresses his wife with discoveries that would have been new in the 1840s, when 'The Birthmark' was first published. These were, in addition to the daguerreotype, the diorama (1822) and the stereoscope (1832).

alchemists: as Reid (1966) has noted, Digby was one of those who sought the golden principle in base metals. Burns (1979) argues that Aylmer's quest is a perversion of the true alchemical goal of freeing the spirit by achieving a new, unified, androgynous personality. Van Leer (1976) offers a more persuasive account of Aylmer's alchemical activities.

elixir vitae: see above, note to p. 161.

185 *philosophers of the Middle Ages*: as Van Leer (1976) points out, all the writers in Aylmer's library took part in the search for a material source of spiritual ills. Cornelius Agrippa attempted to overturn Ficino's orthodox reconciliation of Hermetic and Neoplatonic traditions with Christianity, positing a world of demons between the divine and the human. Paracelsus placed matter immediately below God in the cosmic hierarchy, thus incurring the risk that spirit and matter would become identified with each other. Albertus Magnus was at the centre of the debate on spiritual, or demonic, influences. For Hawthorne's interest in Magnus's automaton, see below, p. 263.

Transactions of the Royal Society: Like the fictional Aylmer, the historical Sir Kenelm Digby was a member of the Royal Society, at a time when science and magic were not always differentiated. His library contained the works of Roger Bacon and Albertus Magnus. See Reid (1966) and Van Leer (1976).

187 *poured out the liquid music*: in Digby's *Private Memoirs*, Theagenes has the virtuous Stelliana sing to him when she refuses to gratify his lust.

189 *pure and lofty*: rejecting the notion that Aylmer is a noble idealist (Elmer), Fetterley (1978) offers a cogently feminist reading in which his attitude to Georgiana's body is a sign of his sickness (Ailmore). The fact that Georgiana identifies with her husband's attitude to her own body reveals the consequences for the woman of male dominance. For the positive view of Aylmer's science, see Heilman (1949).

geranium: one of Digby's experiments was to restore living verdure to a dying geranium. See Reid (1966).

192 THE CELESTIAL RAILROAD: *Democratic Review*, xii (1843); *Mosses* (1846). Written between 1 and 20 March, 1843. See McDonald (1972).

Relevant passages from the *Notebooks*:

'What were the contents of the burden of Christian, in the Pilgrim's Progress? He must have been taken for a pedler, travelling with his pack.' *Hawthorne's Lost Notebook, 1835–1841*, p. 34.

'An Auction (perhaps in Vanity Fair) of offices, honors, and all sorts of things considered desirable by mankind; together with things eternally valuable, which shall be considered by most people as worthless lumber.' *CE*, viii, 238 (between 1 June 1842 and 27 July 1844).

gate of dreams: compare Bunyan's *Pilgrim's Progress*, 'I dreamed, and behold, I saw a man clothed with rags . . . a book in his hand, and a great burden upon his back.' On Hawthorne's use of the method of the dream as he found it in Bunyan, see Johnson (1951). On the importance of Bunyan to Hawthorne, see Stanton (1956).

City of Destruction: 'You dwell, said he [Evangelist] in the City of Destruction . . . and dying there, sooner or later, you will sink lower than the grave, into a place that burns with fire and brimstone.'

liberal curiosity: since the Unitarians were known as the 'liberal

Christians' in nineteenth-century New England, the word may not be innocent here. In 'The Old Manse' sketch (*CE*, x, 19–20), the narrator characterizes the volumes of the *Liberal Preacher* and the *Christian Examiner* (the Unitarian periodical) as 'frigid'. Doubleday (1942) points out that the American Sunday School Union—not famous for liberal views in religion—republished Hawthorne's tale as a tract.

Smooth-it-away: the actual model for this character may have been the prominent Unitarian minister Mr Waterston, to whom—Hawthorne supposed—his story might have given offence. 'If so,' as he wrote to Sophia, 14 April 1844, 'I shall feel as if Providence had sufficiently rewarded me for that pious labor' (*CE*, xvi, 30). Colacurcio (1984) finds the model for this figure in Timothy Dwight's *Triumph of Infidelity* (1788), which he regards as a major source. It tells of the 'smooth Divine, unus'd to wound/The Sinner's heart'.

enterprise: 'enterprise'—in the sense of capitalistic initiative—was a popular slogan of the 1840s, the decade of immense development of the railroads. As early as 1836, in his 'Ancient Pilgrims' article in the *American Magazine of Useful and Entertaining Knowledge*, Hawthorne had contrasted the pilgrim of Chaucer's day with the modern pilgrim who 'would simply put down his name at the coach office, or get on board a steamboat . . . or, perchance, would do his pilgrimage in a rail-road car.' Such a man 'would be graver than the ancient pilgrims, but with earthly cares, not heavenly meditations'. See Turner (1941), p. 105.

193 *Slough of Despond*: Christian began to sink into this quagmire 'because of the burden that was on his back'.

wicket-gate: Evangelist told Christian to knock at that gate at which 'it shall be told thee what thou shalt do'. Bunyan's allusion is to Matthew 7: 13 'Enter by the narrow gate; for the gate is wide and the way is easy, that leads to destruction.' Liberal minds apparently go with broad stomachs and the consequent need to avoid such narrow gates.

194 *an imposture*: Matthew 7: 15, 'Beware of false prophets, who come to you in sheep's clothing but inwardly are ravenous wolves.' On the parchment Evangelist gave to Christian was written 'Fly from the wrath to come'. A railroad ticket might be more 'convenient,' but the narrator is clearly well advised to doubt its efficacy at the gate of the Celestial City.

tastefully into the background: our narrator, then, has too much taste to be pious in the Puritan sense. Smith (1966) takes him to be Ignorance, Christian's erstwhile travelling companion, who believes that Christ's atonement has rendered a sense of one's own depravity unnecessary for salvation. He may also suggest Mr Worldly Wiseman, who promises Christian all 'without the dangers that thou in this way wilt run thyself into'.

Beelzebub: Lord of the Flies, a Philistine deity. In *Paradise Lost*, second in rank to Satan.

195 *Mr Greatheart*: the servant of the Interpreter, he conducts Christiana and her companions to the House called Beautiful, protecting them from the lions and Giant Grim.

196 *Apollyon*: when Christian encountered him in the Valley of Humiliation, Apollyon was a monster 'hideous to behold . . . clothed with scales . . . he had wings like a dragon . . . and out of his belly came fire and smoke'.

modern improvements: this phrase, commonly used for technological advances in the period, rings particularly hollow when applied to the conscience.

197 *Interpreter's House*: here Christian received illumination and instruction that would help him on his journey. He learned of the work of grace in the heart.

Hill Difficulty: Christian found that, though were two other ways, 'the narrow way lay right up the hill'.

198 *Shadow of Death*: Christian 'must needs go through it, because the way to the Celestial City lay through the midst of it'.

199 *Tophet*: hell; in the Old Testament, a place near Jerusalem where children were said to be sacrificed to Moloch.

201 *Pope and Pagan*: in Bunyan, two giants 'by whose power and tyranny' men were 'cruelly put to death'.

Giant Transcendentalist: the difficulty of defining Transcendentalism was something of a national joke, shared by Charles Dickens in his *American Notes* (1842). Emerson defined it, in an 1841 lecture, as Idealism, and defined that in neo-Kantian terms as belief in a class of ideas not derived from sense experience (as in the Lockean empirical tradition) but directly intuited. Hawthorne's narrator takes a popular line in ridiculing the 'German' obscurantism of the Transcendentalist, but Hawthorne showed considerable respect for Emerson in his 'Old Manse' sketch in *Mosses*.

202 *Vanity Fair*: in *Pilgrim's Progress*, Beelzebub, Apollyon, and

Legion set up a fair 'wherein should be sold all sorts of vanity . . . as houses, lands, trades, places, honours . . . pleasures and delights of all sorts'.

206 *Demas*: Bunyan's Demas promises Christian riches for little effort, but he is 'an enemy to the right ways of the Lord' and deserves to be hanged as a traitor like his father Judas.

207 *Delectable Mountains*: these are Immanuel's Land, as the Shepherds tell Pilgrim, and they are within sight of the Celestial City.

byway to hell: through which, according to Bunyan's Shepherds, hypocrites, traitors to God, and liars pass.

land of Beulah: in Bunyan, the land of rest where pilgrims abide till death. In Isaiah 62: 4 the land of Israel.

208 *ferry-boat*: the Salem to Boston railroad, opened in 1838, terminated across the harbour, so that passengers had to complete their journey by ferry. See Cronkhite (1951), who suggests that Hawthorne parodies the glib phrasing of contemporary railroad prospectuses and travel books at a time when journeys by rail were still hazardous and derailments were common.

209 THE CHRISTMAS BANQUET: *Democratic Review*, xiv (January 1844). *Mosses* 1846. Written between 16 November and 12 December 1843. See McDonald (1972).

Relevant passages from the *Notebooks*:

'A Thanksgiving Dinner—all the miserable on earth are to be invited—as, the drunkard, the prostitute, the bereaved parent, the ruined merchant, the broken-hearted lover, the poor widow . . . But who must be the giver of the feast . . .? A man who has never found out what he is fit for, who has no settled aim or object in life, and whose mind gnaws him.' *Lost Notebook*, p. 27 (1836–7).

'A man tries to be happy in love; he cannot sincerely give his heart, and the affair seems like a dream;—in domestic life, the same . . . all seems like a theatre.' *Lost Notebook*, p. 40 (1837).

Relevant passage from the *Letters*:

'We are but shadows—we are not endowed with real life, and all that seems most real about us is but the thinnest substance of a dream—till the heart is touched.' *CE*, xv, 495.

Allegories of the Heart: for Hawthorne's continuing interest in the possibility of a series of linked stories see McDonald (1974).

Roderick: in 'Egotism; or the Bosom-Serpent', which appeared in the *Democratic Review* in March 1843 and was collected in *Mosses* (1846), Roderick's 'sad experience' was his subjection to an egotism so consuming that it isolated him from other human beings. Only Rosina's love was able to save him from his isolation.

210 *dark cavern*: compare *Notebooks* (1 June 1842): 'The human Heart to be allegorized as a cavern; at the entrance there is sunshine, and flowers growing . . . You step within . . . and begin to find yourself surrounded with a terrible gloom . . . [However, at the deepest levels there is] eternal beauty.' *CE*, viii, 237.

214 *wandering up and down*: see above, note to p. 97.

215 *apples of Sodom*: Deuteronomy 32: 32, 'their grapes [from the vine of Sodom] are grapes of poison,/their clusters are bitter.'

216 *woful man of Uz*: Job 1: 1 'There was a man in the land of Uz, whose name was Job.'

222 *Aaron Burr*: Burr (1756–1836) is thought by many historians to have planned the separation of the West from the Union, in order to form a new nation west of the Alleghenies. Though acquitted of treason in 1807, his 'period of ruin' lasted at least until 1812, when he returned from exile to practise law in New York.

Stephen Girard: Girard (1750–1831) was a merchant, financier, and philanthropist whose religion was work, according to E. D. Duyckinck's *National Portrait Gallery of Eminent Americans* (1862). His married life was known to be unhappy.

225 *Father Miller*: William Miller (1782–1849) was a Baptist preacher who announced that Christ would come again in 1843 and held revivalist meetings across the nation to prepare for the coming. After the first non-event, the date was postponed until the spring equinox 1844, but the repeated failure of the prophesy calmed the excitement Miller had caused.

Pandemonium: literally, the place of all demons.

228 EARTH'S HOLOCAUST: *Graham's Magazine*, xxv (May 1844). *Mosses* (1846). Written between 22 December 1843 and 9 January 1844. See McDonald (1972).

Relevant passages from the *Notebooks*:

'Curious to imagine what murmurings and discontent would be excited, if any of the great so-called calamities of human beings were to be abolished,—as, for instance, death.' *CE*, viii, 23 (between 25 October 1836 and 5 July 1837).

'A bonfire to be made of the gallows and of all symbols of evil.' *CE*, viii, 185 (1840).

'When the reformation of the world is complete, a fire shall be made of the gallows; and the Hangman shall come and sit down by it, in solitude and despair. To him shall come the Last Thief, the Last Prostitute, the Last Drunkard, and other representatives of past crimes and vice; and they shall hold a dismal merrymaking, quaffing the contents of the Drunkard's last Brandy Bottle.' *CE*, viii, 237 (between 1 June 1842 and 27 July 1844).

prairies of the West: Hawthorne's choice of a site for this ritualistic rejection of the burden of the human past is an appropriate one since, by the 1840s, a decade of vast territorial expansion for the United States, the West seemed to offer the prospect of new possibilities for man in America.

229 *Society of Cincinnati*: formed in 1783, this society of officers in the Continental Army was designed to maintain contacts and to raise funds for windows and orphans of fallen officers. Washington, the American Cincinnatus, was the first president of the society. It aroused hostility among republicans who suspected it of aristocratic tendencies.

230 *privileged orders*: the appeal of the Democratic Party, which had swept to power when Andrew Jackson became President in 1829, was partly due to its attack on 'privilege'.

231 *mouldy bones of his ancestors*: compare Emerson's *Nature* (1836), which begins: 'Our age is retrospective. It builds the sepulchres of the fathers . . . Why should we grope among the dry bones of the past?'

emperors and kings: the sketch anticipates by only four years the Year of Revolutions in Europe (1848).

Drury Lane Theatre: Drury Lane was then, as now, the centre of the London theatre district.

232 *Washingtonians*: the Washingtonian temperance movement—characterized by the use of parades, children's groups, and eye-catching publicity—was founded in April 1840. There were estimated to be 23,000 members in New York, New Jersey, and Pennsylvania by the end of 1841.

Father Mathew: (1790–1856), an Irish Capuchin priest and temperance leader who came to the United States in the 1840s.

His inspiration led to the formation of a number of Catholic temperance societies.

233 *Tokay*: a wine named from a town in Hungary where the grape is grown.

234 *Revd Sidney Smith*: (1771–1845) helped found the *Edinburgh Review* and contributed to it. In 1843 he petitioned Congress, complaining that the state of Pennsylvania had suspended payment of interest on its bond. His petition attracted wide publicity.

235 *assume the garb*: among the numerous manifestations of the reform impulse in the 1840s was an interest in more practical clothing for women. This cause, which was adopted in some of the utopian communes that flourished in the decade, culminated in the fashion for bloomers (named after Mrs Amelia Bloomer) among women of advanced views in the early 1850s.

munitions of war: the American Peace Society had been formed in 1828, when various earlier peace societies had merged. Though its numbers were never large, the Society's cause was vigorously advocated by Elihu Burritt, who edited the *Advocate of Peace* from 1846.

239 *property*: few of the reformers of the 1840s went so far as to challenge the sacred institution of private property, though some of the communitarian experiments (in particular, the Fourierist communes) offered alternatives to private ownership.

240 *progress*: this was one of the slogans of the antebellum period. The Romantic historians, in particular George Bancroft, interpreted the history of their country as an illustration of the law of progress, from colony or province to an independent statehood embodying the principles of liberty.

French tomes: having examined the record of his borrowings from the Salem Atheneum library for the years 1829 to 1831, Kesselring (1949) decided that Hawthorne planned a course of reading in French authors such as Corneille, Racine, Montaigne, and—most of all—Voltaire, from whose *Œuvres complètes* he borrowed on over fifty separate occasions.

241 *German stories*: several anthologies of translated German stories, many dealing with witches, elves, and goblins, had been published in the 1820s. See Donald A. Ringe, *American Gothic* (1982).

Mother Goose's Melodies: Mother Goose was first associated with nursery rhymes in *Mother Goose's Melody: or Sonnets for the Cradle*, edited by John Newbery in the 1760s.

242 *Lord Byron*: in contrast to Shelley, Byron was a *risqué* author in Victorian America. Earlier, in Britain, the first cantos of *Don Juan* had been denounced as filthy and impious in *Blackwood's* in 1819 and Byron's body was refused interment in Westminster Abbey.

Tom Moore: Thomas Moore (1779–1852) had built up a reputation as a national bard with his *Irish Melodies*, which he produced from 1801 to 1834. For Hawthorne's possible response to his *Lalla Rookh*, see above note to p. 100.

Ellery Channing: William Ellery Channing II (1818–1901) was the nephew of the famous Unitarian minister William Ellery Channing I (1780–1842). A poet and vaguely Transcendentalist admirer of Emerson, he went to live in Concord in 1843, when his *Poems* were published, some having already appeared in the *Dial* magazine. He accompanied his friend Thoreau on excursions and wrote the first biography of him—*Thoreau, the Poet Naturalist* (1873).

243 *Cadmus*: founder of Thebes, Cadmus introduced the Phoenician alphabet to Greece.

carry reform to any farther point: for a vivid account of the contemporary zealots for reform, see Emerson's 'The Charndon Street Convention', *Dial*, July 1842, in *Works* (1902), x. For Emerson's profound, and sympathetic, appraisals of the reform impulse see his 'Man the Reformer' (1841), in *Works*, i, and his 'New England Reformers' (1844) in *Works*, iii.

247 *that foul cavern*: for Hawthorne's Notebook entry on the heart as a cavern, see above, note to p. 210.

248 THE ARTIST OF THE BEAUTIFUL: *Democratic Review*, xiv (June 1844). *Mosses*, 1846. Written between 12 March and 3 May 1844. See McDonald (1972).

Relevant passages from the *Notebooks*:

'A person to spend all his life and splendid talents in trying to achieve something naturally impossible—as to make a conquest over nature.' *Lost Notebook*, p. 56 (between 16 October and 6 December 1837).

'To represent a man as spending life in the intensest labor, in the accomplishment of some mechanical trifle—as in making a miniature coach to be drawn by fleas, or a dinner service to be put into a cherry stone.' *Lost Notebook*, p. 2 (1841).

best watches: the cluster of values associated with Hovenden include—as adjuncts of his essentially Philistine utilitarianism—a high regard for regularity and realism. His realism is the sort on which Industry depends. Exact time-keeping had achieved a new importance with the development of the railroad system in the 1830s and 1840s and the growth of the factory system in New England (particularly the textile factories) from the 1830s on.

249 *reality*: in making iron the symbol of the real, Hovenden is the true heir to the 'iron' Puritans of 'The Maypole of Merry Mount'.

250 *movements of nature*: in one of the most elaborate—if not the most convincing—defences of Owen as the exemplary or ideal artist, Bassil (1984) claims that he fuses the mechanical with the mythological. Supposedly, the phases of Owen's growth resemble those of the butterfly, emblem of the cult of Eros from the fifth century BC. Owen is said, improbably, to assume the attributes of Eros. Among the many other apologists for Owen Warland are: Millicent Bell (1962), who argues that the butterfly in the story is not mechanical but an organism embodying Coleridgean theories of the imagination; and Fogle (1952) who regards Owen as the Romantic idealist.

steam-engine: Thomas Carlyle's influential essay 'Signs of the Times' (1829) took the steam-engine to be *the* symbol of life in the nineteenth century, when—he argued—the whole of existence had become mechanized. For the importance of this essay, see Leo Marx, *The Machine in the Garden* (1964).

252 *trifled with*: as in 'The Maypole of Merry Mount', an association between the aesthetic and the trifling is insinuated. Here the utilitarian Hovenden has replaced (or is the inheritor of) the iron Puritans and their contempt for art and entertainment.

253 *cotton-machine*: the cotton-machine, that was to transform New England life, was set up at Pawtucket, Rhode Island, by Samuel Slater in 1793. Slater, who emigrated from England in 1789, copied Arkwright's machinery.

254 *leaden weights*: in alchemical terms, lead is the base metal to be transformed into gold; in metaphorical terms, time measured only for practical, utilitarian purposes is time unredeemed by the artist's imagination.

256 *witchcraft in these little chains*: there will be 'witchcraft', also, in the art by which the carver Drowne brings the material to life. See below, p. 283.

261 *narrowness and dullness*: a letter in the *Gentleman's Magazine*, ci (December 1831) discussed the contempt ignorant men show for genius and for anything tending to enlighten the mind. In the dark ages, so the writer argued, any genius able to rise above the ignorance of the time was likely to be labelled a magician. See Curran (1966).

263 *Albertus Magnus . . . Friar Bacon*: the story of the Brass Man which took thirty years to make, could move and talk before it was smashed by Thomas Aquinas, was told in the letter in the *Gentleman's Magazine* mentioned above. So, too, was the Brazen Head of Friar Roger Bacon. It had magic powers that would have benefited mankind had its words been attended to, but they went unheeded by Bacon's servant.

little coach and horses: David Brewster's *Letters on Natural Magic Addressed to Sir Walter Scott* (1832) tells of a mechanical coach and horses which drove around a table made for Louis XIV by M. Camus. According to Curran (1966), Hawthorne, who had borrowed Brewster's book from the Salem Atheneum in 1837, changed the recipient to the Dauphin to stress the childishness of the wonder. However, Brewster makes it clear that the ingenious toy was made for Louis as a child.

living fly: Brewster describes an iron fly which flew from the hand of its master and returned to it. This was the work of John Muller.

mechanical apparition of a duck: M. Vaucanson's mechanical duck that moved, ate and drank like a real one is described by Brewster as the most wonderful piece of mechanism ever made. West (1975) suggests that Hawthorne's source for the story of the duck and of the Man of Brass might have been Isaac D'Israeli's *Curiosities of Literature* (1791), since he borrowed four of the five volumes of the 1821 edition in 1833. D'Israeli treats Aquinas's destruction of the Man of Brass as an example of the persecution of the learned.

265 *Allston*: Washington Allston (1779–1843) began work on *Belshazzar's Feast* in 1817. He lost interest in it, since paintings of miraculous biblical stories went out of vogue in Boston, the city to which he returned after successes in Europe, and left it incomplete at his death. In his *Notebooks*, Hawthorne mentioned the picture, referring to the advantages or otherwise of having life assured to us to complete important tasks (*CE*, viii, 242).

272 DROWNE'S WOODEN IMAGE: *Godeys Magazine and Lady's Book*, xxix (July 1844). *Mosses* 1846. Written between 16 February and 11 March 1844. See McDonald (1972).

Drowne: Hawthorne took the name from Deacon Shem Drowne (1684–1744), a coppersmith and prominent Bostonian, who made the copper weathervane on Faneuil Hall. See Doubleday (1972).

Fayal: an island of the central Azores.

273 *Admiral Vernon*: Edward Vernon (1684–1757) had distinguished himself at the capture of Porto Bello, Jamaica, in 1739.

273-4 *the Parian or the Carrara*: marble mined at the Greek island of Paros or at the city of Carrara in central Italy. Emerson's poem 'The Snow-Storm', first published in the *Dial* magazine— the Transcendentalist periodical—in January 1841, tells of the 'Parian wreaths' hung by the snow on such humble buildings as kennels and hencoops. Since the theme of that poem is the 'fierce artificer' (the snow) that creates wonders of beauty though it cares nothing for 'number or proportion', it seems likely that Hawthorne's story was stimulated by Emerson's verse. The title story of Hawthorne's *The Snow-Image*, another variation on the theme of snow-sculpture, was first published in *The Memorial* (1851).

274 *Galen or Hippocrates*: Galen (AD 130–200) the great Graeco-Roman medical scientist who served the emperor Marcus Aurelius, was known as the prince of physicians. Hippocrates: see above, note to p. 159.

276 *Copley*: John Singleton Copley (1738–1815), a professional portrait-painter whose reputation was such that he painted the foremost personages of New England, established his reputation with *Boy with a Squirrel* (1765). His great talent was for capturing character as well as the physical form. Copley took up residence in England in 1774 (which sets the action of the tale before then) and was elected to the British Academy for his *Watson and the Shark* (1778).

General Wolfe: Wolfe's great victory over the French at Quebec took place in 1759, so he would be a popular subject for figureheads in the following decades.

277 *Pygmalion*: in seeking to embrace the statue, Drowne is acting as Pygmalion had done. In Ovid's *Metamorphoses*, x, Hawthorne could have read that the artist kissed his statue and imagined that it kissed him back, that he spoke to it and embraced it.

However, Pygmalion's attitude to women is antithetical to Drowne's for he creates the perfect image of a woman from dissatisfaction with all real women.

278 *spoiled by artistic rules*: Davis (1981) argues that Hawthorne may have been influenced by Margaret Fuller's article on Canova in the *Dial*, 3 (April 1843), which he praised in a notebook entry dated 9 April (*CE*, viii, 374). To Fuller, Canova was a craftsman rather than an artist as a sculptor. He was a neo-classicist in his theoretical views, but—like Drowne—he was prepared to ignore the rules to achieve effect.

ideal as an antique statue: Copley's statement relates to the account of Pygmalion's art in Ovid, *Metamorphoses*, x, 247–51. See Doubleday (1972).

280 *a Yankee*: by the 1840s Yankees (the inhabitants of New England) were famous for their enterprise, their energy, and their shrewdness in money matters.

bigots of the day: since the story is set in the 1760s or early 1770s, the bigots cannot harm Drowne or the beautiful form he has created. In the 1690s, however, such rumours could have had fatal consequences for both, as the reference to 'witch times' on p. 283 makes clear. Millicent Bell (1962) notes that Hawthorne frequently quotes views that his narrators categorize as superstitious when he wishes to present anti-romantic attitudes.

282 *sold himself to the Devil*: compare 'The Artist of the Beautiful', where the Philistine attitude to art associates it with Faustian pacts.

image, or . . . apparition: compare 'Young Goodman Brown' and the doubtful status of the shapes that appeared to the young Puritan in the dark forest.

285 RAPPACCINI'S DAUGHTER: *Democratic Review*, xv (December 1844) as 'Writings of Aubépine', with the interior title 'Rappaccini's Daughter'. *Mosses* (1846). Written between 16 October and 13 November 1844. See McDonald (1972).

Relevant passages from the *Notebooks*:
'A story there passeth of an Indian King, that sent unto Alexander a fair woman, fed with aconites and other poisons, with this intent, either by converse or copulation complexionally to destroy him.' Sir Thomas Browne [*Pseudodoxia Epidemica*, Bk 7, Ch. 17]; *Lost Notebook*, p. 85 (4 January 1839). The phrase 'either by converse or by copulation' was omitted from early

published versions of the notebooks, having been censored by Sophia. See Waggoner (1979), p. 102.

'Madame Calderon de la B (in Life in Mexico) speaks of persons who have been innoculated with the venom of rattlesnakes . . . Their own bite becomes poisonous . . . part of the serpent's nature appears to be transfused into them.' *CE*, viii, 238 (between 1 June 1842 and 27 July 1844). Madame de la Barca's *Life in Mexico* was published in 1843.

'Ladislaus, King of Naples, besieging the city of Florence, agreed to show mercy, provided the inhabitants would deliver to him a certain virgin of famous beauty, the daughter of a physician of the city . . . her father gave her a perfumed handkerchief . . . poisoned with his utmost art . . . in their first embrace . . . they presently died in one another's arms.' *CE*, viii, 241–2 (between 1 June 1842 and 27 July 1844).

Writings of Aubépine: this introduction was omitted when the tale was collected in *Mosses* (1846) but restored in 1854. Hawthorne's name was 'frenchified' to Aubépine by a M. Schaeffer, from whom he took French lessons in 1837. See Turner (1980).

Transcendentalists: see above, note to p. 201. Hawthorne had found himself at the hub of New England Transcendentalism in his years at Concord. In his 'Old Manse' sketch in *Mosses*, he wrote admiringly of Emerson and Thoreau, but ridiculed some of Emerson's followers.

inveterate love of allegory: Poe's strictures on Hawthorne's fondness for allegory appeared in his 'Tale Writing—Nathaniel Hawthorne', in *Godey's Magazine and Lady's Book*, xxxv (November 1847), three years *after* this self-disparagement.

286 *Eugene Sue*: pseudonym of Marie Joseph Sue (1804–57), author of *The Mysteries of Paris* and *The Wandering Jew*.

long series: *Twice-Told Tales* were hardly that! The collection had grown from its one-volume form (1837) to two volumes in 1842. All the French titles refer to actual sketches or tales (though their length is magnified) except for *La Soirée du Château en Espagne*.

La Revue Anti-Aristocratique: the *Democratic Review* of course, whose editor, John L. O'Sullivan, had an ancestor who was given the title Earl of Bearhaven by Philip III of Spain (see *CE*, xv, 702). Between 1837 and 1840, Hawthorne had ten pieces in the *Democratic Review*. In March 1842 he had visited O'Sullivan in New York, seeking his patronage for a projected book. From 1843 to 1845, thirteen new Hawthorne pieces appeared in the review. See Crowley 1974, p. 501.

Padua: from the fourteenth to the sixteenth centuries, Padua was the centre of fideism, the doctrine that makes faith the ultimate test of religious truth and minimizes reason. At Padua it was opposed by the rationalist Pomponazzi, who denied that the soul could perceive independently of the body, and who believed that all knowledge originated in sense perception. See Daly (1973). In Hawthorne's day a parallel to this was the debate between the orthodox Unitarians, who maintained that revelation had occurred in biblical times and that, since then, men had been limited to knowledge gained through experience (i.e. who accepted a Lockean epistemology) and the Transcendentalists, who believed that men could have direct intuition of ultimate truths and could thus transcend the limits of experience.

great poem: *The Divine Comedy*, of which *The Inferno* is one part. Dante's Beatrice—unlike Giovanni's—redeems him; she is the activating agent of the grace without which he could not get out of the dark wood.

287 *plants into medicines*: Uroff (1972) takes Rappaccini to be a practitioner of homoeopathic medicine (treatment of illness by afflicting the system of the sick person with similar diseases to stimulate the vital principle), whereas Baglioni practises allopathy (the use of massive doses of medicine). In New England in the 1840s the two medical philosophies were in conflict.

ruin of a marble fountain: to many commentators, a symbol of the spiritual life after the Fall. See, for example, Waggoner (1955) and Male (1957).

288 *Vertumnus*: in Ovid's *Metamorphoses*, xiv, Vertumnus enters the garden of Pomona in disguise to win her from her chaste devotion to her garden. Milton, *Paradise Lost*, ix, 393-5, compares Eve to Pomona: 'To Pales, or Pomona thus adorned/ Likest she seemed, Pomona when she fled/Vertumnus'.

287 *Beatrice*: Rahv (1941) regards Beatrice as the first of Hawthorne's 'dark ladies' (Hester Prynne, Zenobia, Miriam being the others) who are physically interchangeable and who share the exotic appeal of luxuriant sexuality. Finding a 'mystic

sensuality' in the tale's 'hallucinating atmosphere', Rahv believes that *Hawthorne* cannot forgive Beatrice for her beauty.

297 *had not a deep heart*: Fryer (1976) suggests that the name Giovanni is intended to link him with Don Juan and thus with the sexual insecurity of the male's need to possess women.

301 *commixture, and, as it were, adultery*: a reference, Boewe (1958) believes, to the widespread belief—derived from Leviticus 19: 19—that plant hybridization was immoral.

305 *Eden of poisonous flowers*: an oxymoron that may suggest the paradox of the fortunate fall (as Male has argued). Crews (1964) believes that the 'poison' is Beatrice's sexuality, as Giovanni understands (or fears) it.

308 *Benvenuto Cellini*: Cellini made silver vases for a surgeon whose wisdom did not prevent him from sending his patients to early graves.

309 *grovelling*: Giovanni 'grovels' under the influence of Baglioni's rationalism, although—according to Colacurcio (1969)—he already has the only evidence of a spirituality that can be valid.

312 *venomous scorn*: whatever the ultimate meaning and reality of Beatrice's poison, there is no doubt that Giovanni's 'venom' is real in its human consequences. The metaphor carries the emotional reality of the relationship between the two lovers.

313 *my spirit is God's creature*: Hawthorne read the incomplete story to Sophia. When she asked how it was to end and whether Beatrice was to be a demon or an angel, he replied, with emotion, 'I have no idea'. See Julian Hawthorne, *Nathaniel Hawthorne and his Wife* (1884), i, 36. Colacurcio (1969) maintains that Hawthorne's Beatrice embodies the presence of the Word in the flesh; she is a genuine incarnation of divine truth and goodness.

316 ETHAN BRAND: *Boston Weekly Museum*, ii (5 January 1850). *Dollar Magazine*, vii (May, 1851). *The Snow-Image* (1852).
Relevant passages from the *Notebooks*:

'The search of an investigator for the Unpardonable Sin;—he at last finds it in his own heart and practice . . . The Unpardonable Sin might consist in a want of love and reverence for the Human Soul; in consequence of which, the investigator pried into its dark depths . . . from a cold philosophical curiosity.' *CE*, viii, 251 (between 27 July and 13 October 1844).

The real-life originals of the minor characters in the tale are described in notes Hawthorne took while staying at North Adams, Massachusetts, July to September 1838. See *CE*, viii, 86–151.

Abortive Romance: in the *Boston Weekly Museum* the tale was headed 'The Unpardonable Sin. From an Unpublished Work'. The story of Hawthorne's plans for a work that would include 'Ethan Brand' is told in the 'Historical Commentary' to *The Snow-Image*, *CE* xi, 383 ff. In January 1850, Hawthorne's proposed title was 'Old Time Legends, Together with Sketches, Experimental and Ideal'.

lime-burner: the original for this figure was 'dark, black-bearded' and seemed glad of visitors 'to vary his solitary night-watch' (*CE*, viii, 144–5).

Graylock: Mount Graylock, in the Berkshire Hills, is the highest point in Massachusetts.

Ethan Brand: in Hawthorne's day annotated bibles commonly linked Genesis 4: 13–15 (in which Cain is condemned to be a fugitive and a wanderer, with the Lord's mark on him) and Matthew 12: 31–2 ('whoever speaks against the Holy Spirit will not be forgiven'). Thomas Stockhouse's *New History of the Bible* (1752), a work borrowed by Hawthorne in 1832, pronounced Cain's crime 'unpardonable'. See Stock (1965).

317 *Delectable Mountains*: see above note to p. 207.

319 *grizzled hair*: the description is close to that of Cain in Pierre Bayle's *Dictionary*. See Stock (1965).

320 *laugh of scorn*: on the psychological significance of laughter here, and generally in Hawthorne's works, see Dusenbery (1967).

322 *standing erect, with a pride*: McCullen (1960) argues that Brand's pride is evidence of a wilful impenitence that damns him, and quotes from Jeremy Taylor's 'Doctrine and Practice of Repentance', *Works* (1822), ix, 202, to the effect that only impenitence is finally unpardonable.

323 *flip, and sling, and toddy*: drinks made by mixing spirits or other liquor with sugar, lemon, spices and hot water.

325 *old German Jew*: for Hawthorne's account of the original of this figure, his diorama and his dog, see *CE*, viii, 130 (31 August 1838). A further notebook entry for 9 August 1845 (*CE*, viii, 271) discusses the Wandering Jew. Anderson (1965) shows that the legend derived from Genesis 4: 1–15. He also points out that Schubart's *Der ewige Jude* (1783) had been translated

into English in 1802, after Coleridge used it in *The Ancient Mariner*.

diorama: a three-dimensional exhibition, with solid objects in front of a backdrop of transparent material through which lights shine to produce changed impressions.

SELECT BIBLIOGRAPHY

AL   *American Literature*

AQ   *American Quarterly*

ATQ   *American Transcendental Quarterly*

ESQ   *Emerson Society Quarterly*

EIHC   *Essex Institute Historical Collections*

ELH   *Journal of English Literary History*

NHJ   *Nathaniel Hawthorne Journal*

NEQ   *New England Quarterly*

NCF   *Nineteenth-Century Fiction*

PMLA   *Publications of the Modern Language Association*

SIR   *Studies in Romanticism*

SSF   *Studies in Short Fiction*

TSLL   *Texas Studies in Literature and Language*

Adams, Richard P., 'Hawthorne's Provincial Tales', NEQ, 30 (1957), 39–57.

Adams, Timothy D., ' "To Prepare a Face to Meet the Faces that You Meet": Autobiographical Rhetoric in Hawthorne's Prefaces', ESQ, 23 (1977), 89–98.

Adkins, Nelson F., 'The Early Projected Works of Nathaniel Hawthorne', *Papers of the Bibliographical Society of America*, 39 (1945), 119–55.

Allison, Alexander W., 'The Literary Contexts of "My Kinsman, Major Molineux" ', NCF, 23 (1968), 304–11.

Alsen, Eberhard, 'The Ambitious Experiment of Dr Rappaccini', AL, 43 (1971), 430–1.

Altschuler, Glenn C., 'The Puritan Dilemma in "The Minister's Black Veil" ', ATQ, 24, suppl. 1 (1974), 25–7.

Anderson, George K., *The Legend of the Wandering Jew* (Providence, RI, 1965).

Askew, Melvin W., 'Hawthorne, the Fall, and the Psychology of Maturity', AL, 34 (1962), 335–43.

Bales, Kent, 'Sexual Exploitation and the Fall from Natural Virtue in Rappaccini's Garden', ESQ, 24 (1978), 133–44.

Bassil, Veronica, 'Eros and Psyche in "The Artist of the Beautiful" ', ESQ, 30, no. 1 (1984), 1–21.

Baym, Nina, 'The Head, the Heart, and the Unpardonable Sin', NEQ, 40 (1967), 31–47.

——, 'Hawthorne's Women: the Tyranny of Social Myths', *Centennial Review*, 15 (1971), 250–72.

——, *The Shape of Hawthorne's Career* (Ithaca, NY, 1976).

Becker, John E., *Hawthorne's Historical Allegory. An Examination of the American Conscience* (Port Washington, New York, and London, 1971).

Bell, Michael D., *Hawthorne and the Historical Romance of New England* (Princeton, NJ, 1971).

——, *The American Romance: The Sacrifice of Relation* (Chicago and London, 1980).

Bell, Millicent, *Hawthorne's View of the Artist* (New York, 1962).

Bercovitch, Sacvan, 'Diabolus in Salem', ELH, 6 (1969), 280–5.

——, 'Endicott's Breastplate: Symbolism and Typology in "Endicott and the Red Cross" ', SSF, 4 (1967), 289–99.

Bickford, Gail H., 'Lovewell's Fight, 1725–1958', AQ, 10 (1958), 358–66.

Boewe, Charles, 'Rappaccini's Garden', AL, 30 (1958), 37–49.

Brenzo, Richard, 'Beatrice Rappaccini: A Victim of Male Love and Horror', AL, 48 (1976), 152–64.

Broes, Arthur T., 'Journey into Moral Darkness: "My Kinsman, Major Molineux" as Allegory', NCF, 19 (1964), 171–84.

Brumm, Ursula, 'A Regicide Judge as "Champion" of American Independence', *Amerikastudien*, 21 (1976), 177–86.

Burns, Shannon, 'Alchemy and "The Birth-mark" ', ATQ, 42. (1979), 147–58.

Canaday, Nicholas J. Jr., 'Hawthorne's Minister and the Veiling Deceptions of Self', SSF, 4 (1967), 135–42.

Carnochan, W. B., ' "The Minister's Black Veil": Symbol, Meaning, and the Context of Hawthorne's Art', NCF, 24 (1969), 182–92.

Cherry, Fannye N., 'The Sources of Hawthorne's "Young Goodman Brown" ', AL, 5 (1934), 342–48.

Chibka, Robert L., 'Hawthorne's Tale Told Twice: A Reading of "Wakefield" ', ESQ, vol. 28, no. 4 (1982), 220–32.

Clark, James W. Jr., 'Hawthorne's Use of Evidence in "Young Goodman Brown" ', EIHC, 111 (1975), 12–34.

Cohen, B. Bernard, 'Deodat Lawson's *Christ's Fidelity* and Hawthorne's "Young Goodman Brown"', EIHC, 104 (1968), 349–70.

Colacurcio, Michael J., 'A Better Mode of Evidence—the Transcendental Problem of Faith and Spirit', ESQ, 54 (1969), 12–22.

——, 'Visible Sanctity and Specter Evidence: The Moral World

of Hawthorne's "Young Goodman Brown" ', EIHC, 110 (1974), 259–99.

—, *The Province of Piety: Moral History in Hawthorne's Early Tales* (Cambridge, Mass. and London, 1984).

Connolly, Thomas E., Introduction to *Nathaniel Hawthorne: 'Young Goodman Brown'* (Columbus, Ohio, 1968).

—, Introduction to *The Scarlet Letter and Selected Tales* (Harmondsworth: Penguin Books, 1970).

Cook, Reginald, 'The Forest of Goodman Brown's Night: A Reading of Hawthorne's "Young Goodman Brown" ', NEQ, 43 (1970), 473–81.

Cox, James M., 'Emerson and Hawthorne: Trust and Doubt', *Virginia Quarterly Review* 45 (1969), 88–107.

Crews, Frederick, 'Giovanni's Garden', AQ, 16 (1964), 402–18.

—, 'The Logic of Compulsion in "Roger Malvin's Burial" ', PMLA, 79 (1964), 457–65.

—, *The Sins of the Fathers: Hawthorne's Psychological Themes* (New York, 1966).

Cronkhite, G. Ferris, 'The Transcendental Railroad', NEQ, 24 (1951), 306–28.

Crowley, J. Donald, 'The Artist as Mediator: The Rationale of Hawthorne's Large-Scale Revisions in his Collected Tales and Sketches', in Henry A. Murray and others, *Melville and Hawthorne in the Berkshires* (1968).

—, 'Introduction' to *Hawthorne: The Critical Heritage*, ed. Crowley (London, 1970).

—, *Nathaniel Hawthorne* (Profiles in Literature Series: London, 1971).

—, 'The Unity of Hawthorne's "Twice-told Tales" ', *Studies in American Fiction* 1 (1973), 35–61.

—, 'Historical Commentary', *Twice-told Tales, Works*, Centenary edition, vol. 9 (1974), 485–533.

—, 'Historical Commentary', *Mosses from an Old Manse, Works*, Centenary edition, vol. 10 (1974), 499–536.

Curran, Ronald T., 'Irony: Another Thematic Dimension to "The Artist of the Beautiful" ', SIR, 6 (1966), 34–45.

Daly, Robert J., 'Fideism and the Allusive Mode in "Rappaccini's Daughter" ', NCF, 28 (1973), 25–37.

—, 'History and Chivalric Myth in "Roger Malvin's Burial"', EIHC, 109 (1973), 99–115.

Dauber, Kenneth, *Rediscovering Hawthorne* (Princeton, NJ, 1977).

Davis, Richard B., 'Hawthorne, Fanny Kemble, and "The Artist of the Beautiful" ', *Modern Language Notes*, 70 (1955), 589–92.

Davis, Sarah I., 'Margaret Fuller's "Canova" and Hawthorne's "Drowne's Wooden Image" ', ATQ, 49 (1981), 73–8.

Dawson, Edward, *Hawthorne's Use and Knowledge of New England History: A Study of Sources* (Nashville, Tennessee, 1939).

Donohue, Agnes McN., ' "The Fruit of that Forbidden Tree": A Reading of "The Gentle Boy" ', in *A Casebook on the Hawthorne Question*, ed. Agnes McN. Donohue (New York, 1971).

Doubleday, Neal F., 'Hawthorne's Satirical Allegory', *College English*, 3 (1942), 325–37.

—, *Hawthorne's Early Tales, A Critical Study* (Durham, NC, 1972).

Dreher, Diane E., 'Hawthorne and Melancholy: A New Source for "Rappaccini's Daughter" ', ATQ, 52 (1981), 255–8.

Dryden, Edgar A., *Nathaniel Hawthorne: The Poetics of Enchantment* (Ithaca and London, 1977).

Duban, James, 'The Triumph of Infidelity in Hawthorne's "The Story Teller" ', *Studies in American Fiction*, 7 (1979), 49–60.

Dusenbery, Robert, 'Hawthorne's Merry Company. The Anatomy of Laughter in the Tales and Short Stories', PMLA, 82 (1967), 285–8.

Eisinger, Chester E., 'Hawthorne as Champion of the Middle Way', NEQ, 27 (1954), 27–52.

Erlich, Gloria, 'Guilt and Expiation in "Roger Malvin's Burial" ', NCF, 26 (1972), 377–89.

—, *Family Themes and Hawthorne's Fictions: The Tenacious Web* (New Brunswick, 1984).

Fetterley, Judith, *The Resisting Reader: A Feminist Approach to American Literature* (Bloomington, Indiana and London, 1978).

Fick, Leonard J., *The Light Beyond: A Study of Hawthorne's Theology* (Westminister, Maryland, 1955).

Fiedler, Leslie, *Love and Death in the American Novel* (NY, 1960; revised edition, 1966).

Fogle, Richard H., *Hawthorne's Fiction: The Light and the Dark* (Norman, Oklahoma, 1952).

Fossum, Robert H., *Hawthorne's Inviolable Circle: The Problem of Time* (Deland, Florida, 1972).

Franklin, H. Bruce, *Future Perfect: American Science Fiction of the Nineteenth Century* (London, Oxford, New York, 1966; revised edition, 1978).

Fryer, Judith, *The Faces of Eve: Woman in the Nineteenth-century American Novel* (New York, 1976).

Fussell, Edwin, *Frontier: American Literature and the American West* (Princeton, NJ, 1965).

Gallagher, Edward J., 'History in "Endicott and the Red Cross" ', ESQ, 50 suppl. (1968), 62–5.

Gargano, James W., 'Hawthorne's "The Artist of the Beautiful" ', AL, 35 (1963), 225–30.

Gatta, John Jr., ' "Busy and Selfish London": The Urban Figure in Hawthorne's "Wakefield" ', ESQ, 23 (1977), 164–72.

Gilmore, Michael T., *American Romanticism and the Marketplace* (Chicago and London, 1985).

Gollin, Rita K., 'Hawthorne: the Writer as Dreamer', *Studies in The American Renaissance 1977*, ed. Myerson, Boston, 1978.

—, 'Hawthorne Contemplates the Shakers: 1831–1851', NHJ, 8 (1978) 57–65.

—, *Nathaniel Hawthorne and the Truth of Dreams* (Baton Rouge and London, 1979).

Grayson, Robert, 'The New England Sources of "My Kinsman, Major Molineux" ', AL, 54 (1982), 545–59.

Gross, Seymour L., 'Hawthorne's Revision of "The Gentle Boy" ', AL, 26 (1954), 196–208.

—, 'Hawthorne's "My Kinsman, Major Molineux": History as Moral Adventure', NCF, 12 (1957), 97–109.

—, 'Hawthorne and the Shakers', AL, 29 (1958), 457–63.

—, ' "Rappaccini's Daughter" and the Nineteenth-century Physicians', in Thompson and Lokke, eds., *Ruined Eden of the Present*.

Gupta, R. K., 'Hawthorne's Treatment of the Artist', NEQ, 45 (1972) 65–80.

Hallissy, Margaret, 'Hawthorne's Venomous Beatrice', SSF, 19 (1982), 231–40.

Heilman, Robert B., 'Hawthorne's "The Birth-mark": Science as Religion', *South Atlantic Quarterly*, 48 (1949), 573–83. Reprinted in Donohue, ed., *A Casebook on the Hawthorne Question*.

Herndon, Jerry A., 'Hawthorne's Dream Imagery', AL, 46 (1975), 538–45.

Hoeltje, Hubert H., 'Hawthorne, Melville, and Blackness', AL, 37 (1966), 41–5.

—, *Inward Sky. The Mind and Heart of Nathaniel Hawthorne* (Durham, NC, 1962).

Hoffman, Daniel G., *Form and Fable in American Fiction* (New York, 1961).

—, 'Myth, Romance, and the Childhood of Man', in Pearce, ed., *Hawthorne Centenary Essays*.

Homan, John Jr., 'Hawthorne's "Wedding Knell" and Cotton Mather', ESQ, 43 (1966), 66–7.

Hull, Raymona, 'Hawthorne and the Magic Elixir of Life. The Failure of a Gothic Theme', ESQ, 67 (1972), 97–107.

Janssen, James, 'Hawthorne's Seventh Vagabond: The Outsetting Bard', ESQ, 62 (1971), 22–8.

Johnson, Claudia D., *The Productive Tension of Hawthorne's Art* (University of Alabama, 1981).

Johnson, W. Stacey, 'Hawthorne and *The Pilgrim's Progress*', *Journal of English and Germanic Philology*, 50 (1951), 156–66.

Kaul, A.N. (ed.), *Hawthorne: A Collection of Critical Essays* (Englewood Cliffs, NJ, 1966).

Kesselring, Marion L., *Hawthorne's Reading, 1828–1850* (New York, 1949).

Kloeckner, Alfred J., 'The Flower and the Fountain: Hawthorne's Chief Symbols in "Rappaccini's Daughter" ', AL, 38 (1966), 323–36.

Leavis, Q. D., 'Hawthorne as Poet', *Sewanee Review*, 59 (1951), 179–205, and 426–58. Reprinted in Kaul, ed., *Hawthorne: A Collection of Critical Essays*.

Lee, A. Robert (ed.), *Nathaniel Hawthorne: New Critical Essays* (Totowa, NJ and London, 1982).

Leibowitz, Herbert A., 'Hawthorne and Spenser: Two Sources', AL, 30 (1959), 459–66.

Lesser, Simon O., 'The Image of the Father: A Reading of "My Kinsman, Major Molineux" and "I Want to Know Why" ', *Partisan Review*, 22 (1955), 372–90.

Levin, David, 'Shadows of Doubt: Specter Evidence in Hawthorne's "Young Goodman Brown" ', AL, 34 (1962), 344–52.

——, *In Defense of Historical Literature* (New York, 1967).

Levy, Leo B., 'Hawthorne's Middle Ground', SSF, 2 (1964), 56–60.

Liebman, Sheldon W., 'The Reader in "Young Goodman Brown" ', NHJ, 5 (1975), 156–67.

Loggins, Vernon, *The Hawthornes: The Story of Seven Generations of an American Family* (New York, 1951, reprinted 1968).

Lovejoy, David S., 'Lovewell's Fight and Hawthorne's "Roger Malvin's Burial" ', NEQ, 27 (1954), 527–30.

McCullen, Joseph, 'The Unpardonable Sin in Hawthorne. A Re-Examination', NCF, 15 (1960), 221–37.

McDonald, John J., 'The Old Manse Period Canon', NHJ, 2 (1972), 13–40.

——, 'The Old Manse and Its Mosses: The Inception and Development of *Mosses from an Old Manse*', TSLL, xvi (Spring 1974), 77–108.

——, 'A Guide to the Primary Source Materials for the Study of Hawthorne's Old Manse Period', *Studies in the American Renaissance, 1977* (1978), 261–312.

McKeithan, D. M., 'Hawthorne's "Young Goodman Brown": An Interpretation', *Modern Language Notes*, 67 (1952), 93–6.

McPherson, Hugo, *Hawthorne as Mythmaker: A Study in Imagination* (Toronto, 1969).

McWilliams, John P., *Hawthorne, Melville and the American Character: A Looking-Glass Business* (Cambridge, 1984).

Mailloux, Steven, *Interpretive Conventions. The Reader in the Study of American Fiction* (Ithaca and London, 1982).

Male, Roy R., *Hawthorne's Tragic Vision* (Austin, Texas, 1957).

——, 'Hawthorne's Literal Figures', in Thompson and Lokke (eds.), *Ruined Eden of the Present* (1981).

Marks, Barry, 'The Origin of Original Sin in Hawthorne's Fiction', NCF, 14 (1960), 359–62.

Martin, Terence, 'The Method of Hawthorne's Tales', in Pearce (ed.), *Hawthorne Centenary Essays*.

——, *Nathaniel Hawthorne* (revised edition, Boston, 1983).

Marx, Leo, *The Machine in the Garden* (New York, 1964).

Mathews, James W., 'Antinomianism in "Young Goodman Brown" ', SSF, 3 (1965), 73–5.

Matthiessen, F. O., *American Renaissance: Art and Expression in the Age of Emerson and Whitman* (New York, 1941).

Mellow, James R., *Nathaniel Hawthorne in His Times* (Boston, 1980).

Miller, Harold P., 'Hawthorne Surveys His Contemporaries', AL, 12 (1940), 228–35.

Mills, Barriss, 'Hawthorne and Puritanism', NEQ, 21 (1948), 78–102.

Morsberger, Robert E., ' "The Minister's Black Veil": Shrouded in Blackness Ten Times Black', NEQ, 46 (1973), 454–63.

Murray, Henry A. (ed.), *Melville and Hawthorne in the Berkshires: a Symposium* (Kent, Ohio, 1968).

Naples, Diane C., ' "Roger Malvin's Burial": A Parable for Historians', ATQ, 13 (1972), 45–9.

Newberry, Fred, ' "The Gray Champion": Hawthorne's Ironic Criticism of the Puritan Rebellion', SSF, 13 (1976), 363–70.

——, 'The Demonic in "Endicott and the Red Cross" ', *Papers on Language and Literature*, 13 (1977), 251–9.

Newman, Lea B. V., *A Reader's Guide to the Short Stories of Nathaniel Hawthorne* (Boston, 1979).

Nissenbaum, Stephen, and Boyer, Paul, *Salem Possessed* (Cambridge, Mass., 1974).

Norford, N. Parry, 'Rappaccini's Garden of Allegory', AL, 50 (1978), 161–86.

Orians, G. Harrison, 'New England Witchcraft in Fiction', AL, 2 (1930), 54–71.

—, 'The Angel of Hadley in Fiction: A Study of the Source of Hawthorne's "The Gray Champion" ', AL, 4 (1932), 257–69.

—, 'Hawthorne and "The Maypole of Merry Mount" ', *Modern Language Notes*, 53 (1938), 159–67.

—, 'The Source of Hawthorne's "Roger Malvin's Burial" ', AL, 10 (1938), 313–18.

—, 'The Sources and Themes of Hawthorne's "The Gentle Boy" ', NEQ, 14 (1941), 664–78.

Pattison, Joseph C., 'Point of View in Hawthorne', PMLA, 82 (1967), 363–9.

Pearce, Roy H., 'Hawthorne and the Sense of the Past', ELH, 21 (1954), 327–49.

—, 'Robin Molineux on the Analyst's Couch: A Note on the Limits of Psychoanalytic Criticism', *Criticism*, 1 (1959), 83–90.

—, 'Romance and the Study of History' in *Hawthorne Centenary Essays*, ed. Pearce (Columbus, Ohio, 1964).

—, *Historicism Once More: Problems and Occasions for the American Scholar* (Princeton, 1969).

Perry, Ruth, 'The Solitude of Hawthorne's "Wakefield" ', AL, 49 (1977–8), 613–19.

Pestana, Carla G., 'City upon a Hill under Siege: The Puritan Perception of the Quaker Threat', NEQ, 56 (1983), 323–53.

Porte, Joel, *The Romance in America: Studies in Cooper, Poe, Hawthorne, Melville and James* (Middletown, Conn., 1969).

Rahv, Philip, 'The Dark Lady of Salem', *Partisan Review*, 8 (1941), 362–81.

Reid, Alfred S., 'Hawthorne's Humanism: "The Birthmark" and Sir Kenelm Digby', AL, 38 (1966), 337–51.

Robinson, E. Arthur, 'The Vision of Goodman Brown: A Source and Interpretation', AL, 35 (1963), 218–25.

Ross, Morton L., 'What Happens in "Rappaccini's Daughter" ', AL, 43 (1971), 336–45.

Sanders, Charles, 'A Note on Metamorphosis in Hawthorne's "Artist of the Beautiful" ', SSF, 4 (1966), 82–3.

Schiller, Andrew, 'The Moment and the Endless Voyage: A Study of Hawthorne's "Wakefield" ' in *A Casebook on the Hawthorne Question*, ed. Donohue.

Schriber, Mary S., 'Emerson, Hawthorne, and "The Artist of the Beautiful" ', SSF, 8 (1971), 607–16.

Schurr, William H., 'Eve's Bower. Hawthorne's Transition from Public Doctrine to Private Truth', in *Ruined Eden of the Present*, ed. Thompson and Lokke.

Schwartz, Joseph, 'Three Aspects of Hawthorne's Puritanism',

NEQ, 36 (1963), 192–208.

Shaw, Peter, 'Fathers, Sons, and the Ambiguities of Revolution in "My Kinsman, Major Molineux" ', NEQ, 49 (1976), 55–76.

—, 'Hawthorne's Ritual Typology of the American Revolution', *Prospects*, 3 (1977), 483–98.

Smith, David E., 'Bunyan and Hawthorne', in *John Bunyan in America* (Bloomington, Indiana, 1966).

Smith, Julian, 'Historical Ambiguity in "My Kinsman, Major Molineux" ', *English Language Notes*, 8 (1970), 115–20.

Stanton, Robert, 'Hawthorne, Bunyan and the American Romances', PMLA, 71 (1956), 155–65.

Stein, William B., *Hawthorne's Faust: A Study of the Devil Archetype* (Gainesville, Florida, 1953).

—, 'The Parable of the AntiChrist in "The Minister's Black Veil" ', AL, 267 (1955), 386–92.

Sterne, Richard C., 'Puritans at Merry Mount: Variations on a Theme', AQ, 22 (1970), 846–58.

Stibitz, E. Earle, 'Ironic Unity in Hawthorne's "The Minister's Black Veil" ', AL, 34 (1962), 182–90.

Stock, Ely, 'History and the Bible in Hawthorne's "Roger Malvin's Burial" ', EIHC, 100 (1964), 279–96.

—, 'The Biblical Context of "Ethan Brand" ', AL, 37 (1965), 115–34.

Stoehr, Taylor, ' "Young Goodman Brown" and Hawthorne's Theory of Mimesis', NCF, 23 (1969), 393–412.

—, *Hawthorne's Mad Scientists: Pseudoscience and Social Science in Nineteenth-Century Life and Letters* (Hamden, Conn., 1978).

Strandberg, Victor, 'The Artist's Black Veil', NEQ, 41 (1968), 567–74.

Swann, Charles, ' "Alice Doane's Appeal": Or, How to Tell a Story', *Literature and History*, 5 (1977), 9–25.

—, 'The Practice and Theory of Storytelling: Nathaniel Hawthorne and Walter Benjamin', *Journal of American Studies*, 12, no. 2 (1978), 185–202.

Taylor, J. Golden, *Hawthorne's Ambivalence Towards Puritanism*, Logan, Utah, Utah State U.P. Monograph Series, xii, no. 1 (July 1965).

Thompson, G. W., and Lokke, Virgil L. (eds.), *Ruined Eden of the Present: Hawthorne, Melville, and Poe* (West Lafayette, Indiana, 1981).

Trilling, Lionel, 'Our Hawthorne', in *Hawthorne Centenary Essays*, ed. Pearce.

Turner, Arlin, 'Hawthorne's Literary Borrowings', PMLA, 51 (1936), 543–62.

—, *Hawthorne as Editor: Selections from his Writings in the American Magazine of Useful and Entertaining Knowledge* (Baton Rouge, La., 1941).

—, *Nathaniel Hawthorne: An Introduction and Interpretation* (New York, 1961).

—, *Nathaniel Hawthorne: A Biography* (New York, 1980).

Uroff, M. D., 'The Doctors in "Rappaccini's Daughter" ', NCF, 27 (1972), 61–70.

Van Leer, David, 'Aylmer's Library: Transcendental Alchemy in Hawthorne's "The Birthmark", ESQ, 22 (1976), 211–21.

Von Abele, Rudolph, *The Death of the Artist: A Study of Hawthorne's Disintegration* (The Hague, 1955).

Waggoner, Hyatt, 'Art and Belief', in *Hawthorne Centenary Essays*, ed. Pearce.

—, *Hawthorne: A Critical Study* (Cambridge, Mass., 1955; reprinted and revised 1963).

—, 'Grace in the Thought of Emerson, Thoreau, and Hawthorne', ESQ, 54 (1969), 68–72.

—, *The Presence of Hawthorne* (Baton Rouge and London, 1979).

Walsh, Thomas F. Jr., 'The Bedevilling of Young Goodman Brown', *Modern Language Quarterly*, 19 (1958), 331–6.

—, 'Hawthorne: Mr Hooper's "Affable Weakness" ', *Modern Language Notes*, 74 (1959), 401–6.

—, ' "Wakefield" and Hawthorne's Illustrated Ideas: A Study in Form', ESQ, 25 (1961), 29–35.

Warren, Austin, *Nathaniel Hawthorne: Representative Selections* (New York, 1934).

Way, Brian, 'Art and the Spirit of Anarchy: A Reading of Hawthorne's Short Stories', in *Nathaniel Hawthorne: New Critical Essays*, ed. Lee (1982).

Weber, Alfred, *Die Entwicklung der Rahmenerzählungen Nathaniel Hawthornes: "The Story Teller" und andere frühe Werke (1825–1835)* (Berlin, 1973).

West, Harry C., 'The Sources for Hawthorne's "The Artist of the Beautiful" ', NCF, 30 (1975), 105–11.

—, 'Hawthorne's Magic Circle. The Artist as Magician', *Criticism*, 16 (1974), 311–25.

Winters, Ivor, *In Defense of Reason* (New York, 1937; reprinted 1947).

Yoder, R. A., 'Hawthorne and His Artist', SIR, 7 (1968), 193–206.

Ziff, Larzer, 'The Artist and Puritanism', in *Hawthorne Centenary Essays*, ed. Pearce.

TEXTUAL NOTES

ABBREVIATIONS

BW: *Boston Weekly Museum*
CE: *Centenary Edition of the Works of Nathaniel Hawthorne*
DR: *Democratic Review (United States Magazine and Democratic Review)*
GL: *Godey's Magazine and Lady's Book*
K: *Knickerbocker, or New-York Monthly Magazine*
MM46: *Mosses from an Old Manse*, 1846
MM54: *Mosses from an Old Manse*, 1854
NEM: *New-England Magazine*
P: *The Pioneer*
SI: *The Snow-Image*, 1852
T: *The Token*
TT37: *Twice-told Tales*, 1837
TT42: *Twice-told Tales*, 1842

THE GENTLE BOY   *The Token* for 1832; *Twice-told Tales* (1837)

3, 17   ¶ The   *TT37*
4, 1   abstractly] abstractedly   *TT37*
5, 34   house] home   *TT37*
6, 22   continued] walked   *TT37*
7, 17   spirited] spiritual   *TT37*
8, 30   to day] today   *TT37*
11, 22   coronet]   *TT37*
12, 11   ¶ Their   *TT37*
15, 6   them] then   *TT37*
15, 19   bent] lent   *TT37*
15, 39   that thy] that even thy   *TT37*
21, 33   committed] uncommitted   *TT37* (cf. explanatory notes)
22, 6   ate the bread] lay in the dungeons   *TT37*
22, 36   precious views] rich treasures   *TT37*
22, 38   treasure] gold   *TT37*
23, 37   unappropriate] unappropriated   *TT37* (cf. explanatory notes)
26, 3   ¶ The   *TT37*
26, 6   Having watched] After watching   *TT37*
28, 2   warfare] mind   *TT37*

28, 4   enlisted . . . victory] completed the change, of which the
          child had been the original instrument
28, 20–1 exult in the midst of] encounter   *TT37* (cf. explanatory notes)
29, 3   ¶ He   *TT37*
30, 36   might] mightst   *TT37*
31, 31   thou] Thou   *TT37*
32, 5   imaging] imagining   *TT37*
32, 20 *et seq.*   Catherine] Catharine   *TT37* (cf. explanatory notes)
34, 9   Favourite sister] Sister   *TT37*

MY KINSMAN, MAJOR MOLINEUX   *The Token* for 1832; *The Snow-Image*
(1852)

37, 16   their] the   *T*
37, 31   as a preface] as preface   *T*
38, 8–9   fitted tight] sat tight   *T*
38, 10   work] handiwork   *T*
39, 7   above] about   *T*
39, 16   tell] to tell   *T*
39, 30   show for your] show your   *T*
40, 27   sit at] sit down at   *T*
40, 31   the fumes] fumes   *T*
41, 1   West India] great West India   *T*
41, 3   appearance] aspect   *T*
41, 8   Fast-day] the Fast-day   *T*
41, 21   on] in   *T*
41, 32   circumstances] circumstance   *T*
41, 35   Beg leave to] Beg to   *T*
42, 9   confidence] consequence   *T*
42, 9   My   *T*
42, 12   when I] I   *T*
42, 14   my way] the way   *T*
42, 26   whosoever] whoever   *T*
42, 26   jail of] jail in   *T*
43, 1   those] these   *T*
43, 8   the numerous] numerous   *T*
43, 39   now was] was now   *T*
45, 18–17 leather small-clothes. But] leather—But   *T*
45, 21   the touch] though the touch   *T*
46, 32   that] which   *T*
47, 13   his face] his own face   *T*
47, 23   an intense] of an intense   *T*
47, 29–30 party-coloured] parti-colored   *T*
47, 33   kinsman] kinsman's appearance.   *T*

47, 35   species of man] species of the *genus homo* *T*
47, 37   his amusement] amusement *T*
48, 1–2   creating . . . objects] 'creating . . . objects' *T*
48, 7   snow-white] milk-white *T*
48, 10   the walls] the plastered walls *T*
48, 35   around] round *T*
48, 36   open] opened *T*
48, 38   built] builded *T*
49, 10   dimly passing] passing dimly *T*
49, 27   fell] shone *T*
49, 37   the younger] his younger *T*
50, 13   into] in *T*
51, 15   seemed] had seemed *T*
51, 23   drawing] raising *T*
51, 28   dark] dusk *T*
52, 22–4 went up to make] went to make up *T*
52, 24   a man] one man *T*
52, 38   we step] we just step *T*
53, 16   onwards] onward *T*
53, 19   kinsman, if] kinsman, Robin, if *T*
53, 36   that] which *T*
54, 3   sidewalk] sidewalks *T*
54, 7   an uncomfortable] uncomfortable *T*
54, 15   ears] ear *T*
54, 19   and then held] then held *T*
54, 21   allied] nearly allied *T*
54, 27   found means] found the means *T*
54, 36   head grown] head that had grown *T*
55, 23   hanging about] hanging down about *T*
56, 1   around] round *T*
56, 10   as] while *T*
56, 12   as lively as] so lively as *T*
56, 23   wish it] continue to wish it *T*

ROGER MALVIN'S BURIAL *The Token* for 1832; *Democratic Review* (1843); *Mosses* (1846)

56, 35   judicially] judiciously *T*
58, 8   in his dreaming] to his dreaming *T*
61, 39   your friends] our friends *T*
62, 35   bid her to have] bid her have *T*
66, 23–4 a few months] two years *T*
69, 32   after long years] after long, long years *T*
70, 37   backwards] backward *T*

72, 11   dies . . . lies] die . . . lie *T*
74, 5   shadows] shades *T*
75, 5   report had] report of the gun had *T*

THE CANTERBURY PILGRIMS *The Token* for 1833; *The Snow-Image* (1852)

76, 34   toiling, as the writer has] toiling *CE*. Hawthorne's marked copy of *The Token*, though his suggested emendation was not followed in *SI*, is the authority for the *CE* deletion.
83, 31   about your] about of your *SI*
86, 13   mortal] moral *T;* human *CE*. Authority for the *CE* text is Hawthorne's marked copy of *The Token*.

SEVEN VAGABONDS *The Token* for 1833; *Twice-told Tales* (1842)

86, 32   Brobdignags] Brobdingnags *CE*
88, 12   somersaults] somersets *T*
88, 17   mask] masque *T*
94, 38   Suffolk Bank] United States Bank *T* (cf. explanatory notes)
100, 5   Oriental] Eastern *T*

THE GREY CHAMPION *New-England Magazine*, viii (1835); *Twice-told Tales* (1837)

104, 26 There were] There was *CE*

YOUNG GOODMAN BROWN *New-England Magazine*, viii (1835); *Mosses* (1846)

121, 14 figure] apparition *NEM* and *MM46* (The emendation to 'figure' occurs in the *MM54*).

WAKEFIELD *New-England Magazine*, viii (1835); *Twice-told Tales* (1837)

125, 8   generous] general *NEM*
130, 26 and moves] but moves *CE*
131, 17 himself] itself *NEM*

THE MAYPOLE OF MERRY MOUNT *The Token* for 1836; *Twice-told Tales* (1837)

140, 33 Blackstone] Claxton *T*

THE MINISTER'S BLACK VEIL *The Token* for 1836; *Twice-told Tales* (1837)

144, 14 busily] lustily *T*

DR HEIDEGGER'S EXPERIMENT *Knickerbocker*, ix (1837), with the title 'The Fountain of Youth'; *Twice-told Tales* (1837)

161, 23 Floridan] Floridian *K*
164, 29 brimful] brim full *K*
167, 11 chilliness] chillness *K*

THE BIRTHMARK *The Pioneer*, i (1843); *Mosses* (1846)

177, 1 *et seq.* bloody hand] Bloody Hand *P*
177, 24 *et seq.* crimson hand] Crimson Hand *P*
178, 22 dream of it?] dream of it, *P*
186, 1 its original] with its original *P*
188, 39 rapt] wrapt *P* and *MM54*. See *CE*, x, 585 on the authority of the *Pioneer* text.
191, 8 lightest] slightest *P*
191, 32 the earth] that earth *P*. See *CE* x, 585 for a justification of the *Pioneer*'s 'that earth' (planet earth) as distinct from 'the earth' (mere dirt).

THE CELESTIAL RAILROAD Manuscript; *Democratic Review*, xii (1843); *Mosses* (1846)

195, 17 *et seq.* conductor] engineer *CE*
200, 2 themselves] itself MS; *DR*; *CE*. See *CE*, x, 590 for justification of the *CE* text.
205, 30 bound to] bound for MS; *CE*
Note: the World's Classics lower case for the *Democratic Review*'s 'Wicket-House', 'Enchanted Ground', 'Conscience' etc. is consistent with the editorial policy of modernizing (as well as anglicizing) the text.

THE CHRISTMAS BANQUET *Democratic Review*, xiv (1844), 'From the Unpublished "Allegories of the Heart" '; *Mosses* (1846)

218, 25 has] had *DR*
219, 23 hunter] haunter *DR*
221, 5 mysteries] mystery *DR*
223, 12 magnificent] munificent *DR*
223, 13 happiness] domestic happiness *DR*
227, 17 joy] joys *DR*

EARTH'S HOLOCAUST Manuscript; *Graham's Magazine*, xxv (1844); *Mosses* (1846)

228, 35 of the evening] of evening MS; *CE*
229, 30 armfulls] armsfull MS; *CE*

230, 2   instruments] instrument MS; *CE*
230, 3   brand-new] bran-new MS; *CE*
231, 30   time] times MS; *CE*
232, 10   around] round MS; *CE*
233, 11   overheard] had overheard MS; *CE*
234, 21   ribbons] ribbon MS; *CE*
236, 33   seared] scarred MS; *CE*
237, 2   cannon-founders] cannon-founderies MS; *CE*
237, 38   legend] legends MS; *CE*
238, 21   Heaven-ordained] heaven-oriented MS; *CE*
239, 9   attained the] attained to the MS; *CE*
239, 21   opened] open MS; *CE*
245, 17   utterance] utterances MS; *CE*
245, 25   assurances] assurance MS; *CE*
246, 28   would] will MS; *CE*

THE ARTIST OF THE BEAUTIFUL *Democratic Review*, xiv (1844);
Mosses (1846)

253, 4   than all you] than all that you *DR*
255, 27   ever] never *DR*
256, 32   one] ones *DR*
257, 32   progress] process *DR*
259, 33   him that] him, that *DR*
260, 25   or conjecture] nor conjecture *DR*
261, 18   had] has *DR*
262, 34   creature] creation *DR*
264, 24   passed] past *DR*
266, 38   looking] was looking *DR*
268, 6   over-reached] overarched *DR*
270, 24   a sneer] the sneer *DR*

DROWNE'S WOODEN IMAGE *Godey's Magazine and Lady's Book*, xxix
(1844); *Mosses* (1846)

273, 9–10 do you prefer] would you prefer *GL*
273, 11   and scarlet] and a scarlet *GL*
275, 14   moment] morning *GL*
276, 8   of professional] of any professional *GL*
279, 12   them?'] them'. *GL*
279, 31   be?] be. *GL*
280, 5   perplexing] perplexed *GL*
280, 30   astounded] to be astonished *GL*
280, 30   in astonishment] with astonishment *GL*
281, 9   Who do you] what do you *GL*

RAPPACCINI'S DAUGHTER *Democratic Review*, xv (1844); *Mosses* (1846)

287, 11   Paduan] Lombard   *DR*
295, 27   or verdure] nor verdure   *DR*
298, 20   Dr Rappaccini] Doctor Rappaccini   *DR*

ETHAN BRAND *Boston Weekly Museum*, ii (1850); *Dollar Magazine*, vii (1851); *Snow-Image* (1852)

317, 3   the blocks] blocks   *BW*
317, 23–4 hold a chat] hold chat   *BW*
317, 35   were seen] was seen   *BW*
319, 15   as I am myself] as I myself   *BW*
320, 30   the one only] the only   *BW*
323, 37   many more] more   *BW*
323, 39   introduced] should have introduced   *BW*
327, 8   Nuremburg] Nuremberg   *CE*
327, 22   motion] notion   *BW*
329, 2   at] to   *BW*
329, 30   star-lit] star-light   *BW*
331, 20   upwards] upward   *BW*

A SELECTION OF   **OXFORD WORLD'S CLASSICS**

WASHINGTON IRVING   **The Sketch-Book of Geoffrey Crayon, Gent.**

HENRY JAMES   **The Ambassadors**
The Aspern Papers and Other Stories
The Awkward Age
The Bostonians
Daisy Miller and Other Stories
The Europeans
The Golden Bowl
The Portrait of a Lady
Roderick Hudson
The Spoils of Poynton
The Turn of the Screw and Other Stories
Washington Square
What Maisie Knew
The Wings of the Dove

SARAH ORNE JEWETT   **The Country of the Pointed Firs and Other Fiction**

JACK LONDON   **The Call of the Wild**
White Fang and Other Stories
John Barleycorn
The Sea-Wolf
The Son of the Wolf

HERMAN MELVILLE   **Billy Budd, Sailor and Selected Tales**
The Confidence-Man
Moby-Dick
Typee
White-Jacket

FRANK NORRIS   **McTeague**

FRANCIS PARKMAN   **The Oregon Trail**

EDGAR ALLAN POE   **The Narrative of Arthur Gordon Pym of Nantucket and Related Tales**
Selected Tales

HARRIET BEECHER STOWE   **Uncle Tom's Cabin**

A SELECTION OF   **OXFORD WORLD'S CLASSICS**

HENRY DAVID THOREAU	**Walden**
MARK TWAIN	**The Adventures of Tom Sawyer** **A Connecticut Yankee in King Arthur's Court** **Life on the Mississippi** **The Prince and the Pauper** **Pudd'nhead Wilson**
LEW WALLACE	**Ben-Hur**
BOOKER T. WASHINGTON	**Up from Slavery**
EDITH WHARTON	**The Custom of the Country** **Ethan Frome** **The House of Mirth** **The Reef**
WALT WHITMAN	**Leaves of Grass**
OWEN WISTER	**The Virginian**

A SELECTION OF **OXFORD WORLD'S CLASSICS**

JANE AUSTEN
**Catharine and Other Writings
Emma
Mansfield Park
Northanger Abbey, Lady Susan, The
  Watsons, and Sanditon
Persuasion
Pride and Prejudice
Sense and Sensibility**

ANNE BRONTË
**Agnes Grey
The Tenant of Wildfell Hall**

CHARLOTTE BRONTË
**Jane Eyre
The Professor
Shirley
Villette**

EMILY BRONTË
Wuthering Heights

WILKIE COLLINS
**The Moonstone
No Name
The Woman in White**

CHARLES DARWIN
The Origin of Species

CHARLES DICKENS
**The Adventures of Oliver Twist
Bleak House
David Copperfield
Great Expectations
Hard Times
Little Dorrit
Martin Chuzzlewit
Nicholas Nickleby
The Old Curiosity Shop
Our Mutual Friend
The Pickwick Papers
A Tale of Two Cities**

A SELECTION OF **OXFORD WORLD'S CLASSICS**

GEORGE ELIOT
Adam Bede
Daniel Deronda
Middlemarch
The Mill on the Floss
Silas Marner

ELIZABETH GASKELL
Cranford
The Life of Charlotte Brontë
Mary Barton
North and South
Wives and Daughters

THOMAS HARDY
Far from the Madding Crowd
Jude the Obscure
The Mayor of Casterbridge
A Pair of Blue Eyes
The Return of the Native
Tess of the d'Urbervilles
The Woodlanders

WALTER SCOTT
Ivanhoe
Rob Roy
Waverley

MARY SHELLEY
Frankenstein
The Last Man

ROBERT LOUIS STEVENSON
Kidnapped and Catriona
The Strange Case of Dr Jekyll and Mr Hyde and Weir of Hermiston
Treasure Island

BRAM STOKER
Dracula

WILLIAM MAKEPEACE THACKERAY
Barry Lyndon
Vanity Fair

OSCAR WILDE
Complete Shorter Fiction
The Picture of Dorian Gray

A SELECTION OF   OXFORD WORLD'S CLASSICS

APOLLINAIRE,
ALFRED JARRY, and
MAURICE MAETERLINCK — **Three Pre-Surrealist Plays**

HONORÉ DE BALZAC — **Cousin Bette**
Eugénie Grandet
Père Goriot

CHARLES BAUDELAIRE — **The Flowers of Evil**
The Prose Poems and **Fanfarlo**

DENIS DIDEROT — **This is Not a Story and Other Stories**

ALEXANDRE DUMAS (PÈRE) — **The Black Tulip**
The Count of Monte Cristo
Louise de la Vallière
The Man in the Iron Mask
La Reine Margot
The Three Musketeers
Twenty Years After

ALEXANDRE DUMAS (FILS) — **La Dame aux Camélias**

GUSTAVE FLAUBERT — **Madame Bovary**
A Sentimental Education
Three Tales

VICTOR HUGO — **The Last Day of a Condemned Man and
Other Prison Writings**
Notre-Dame de Paris

J.-K. HUYSMANS — **Against Nature**

JEAN DE LA FONTAINE — **Selected Fables**

PIERRE CHODERLOS
DE LACLOS — **Les Liaisons dangereuses**

MME DE LAFAYETTE — **The Princesse de Clèves**

GUY DE MAUPASSANT — **A Day in the Country and Other Stories**
Mademoiselle Fifi

PROSPER MÉRIMÉE — **Carmen and Other Stories**

A SELECTION OF   OXFORD WORLD'S CLASSICS

BLAISE PASCAL   Pensées and Other Writings

JEAN RACINE   Britannicus, Phaedra, and Athaliah

EDMOND ROSTAND   Cyrano de Bergerac

MARQUIS DE SADE   The Misfortunes of Virtue and Other Early
                       Tales

GEORGE SAND   Indiana
                     The Master Pipers
                     Mauprat
                     The Miller of Angibault

STENDHAL   The Red and the Black
                     The Charterhouse of Parma

JULES VERNE   Around the World in Eighty Days
                     Journey to the Centre of the Earth
                     Twenty Thousand Leagues under the Seas

VOLTAIRE   Candide and Other Stories
                     Letters concerning the English Nation

ÉMILE ZOLA   L'Assommoir
                     The Attack on the Mill
                     La Bête humaine
                     Germinal
                     The Ladies' Paradise
                     The Masterpiece
                     Nana
                     Thérèse Raquin

A SELECTION OF   **OXFORD WORLD'S CLASSICS**

SERGEI AKSAKOV   **A Russian Gentleman**

ANTON CHEKHOV   **Early Stories**
Five Plays
The Princess and Other Stories
The Russian Master and Other Stories
The Steppe and Other Stories
Twelve Plays
Ward Number Six and Other Stories
A Woman's Kingdom and Other Stories

FYODOR DOSTOEVSKY   **An Accidental Family**
Crime and Punishment
Devils
A Gentle Creature and Other Stories
The Idiot
The Karamazov Brothers
Memoirs from the House of the Dead
**Notes from the Underground and
    The Gambler**

NIKOLAI GOGOL   **Village Evenings Near Dikanka and
    Mirgorod**
Plays and Petersburg

ALEXANDER HERZEN   **Childhood, Youth, and Exile**

MIKHAIL LERMONTOV   **A Hero of our Time**

ALEXANDER PUSHKIN   **Eugene Onegin**
The Queen of Spades and Other Stories

LEO TOLSTOY   **Anna Karenina**
The Kreutzer Sonata and Other Stories
The Raid and Other Stories
Resurrection
War and Peace

IVAN TURGENEV   **Fathers and Sons**
First Love and Other Stories
A Month in the Country

ANTHONY TROLLOPE

An Autobiography

Ayala's Angel

Barchester Towers

The Belton Estate

The Bertrams

Can You Forgive Her?

The Claverings

Cousin Henry

Doctor Thorne

Doctor Wortle's School

The Duke's Children

Early Short Stories

The Eustace Diamonds

An Eye for an Eye

Framley Parsonage

He Knew He Was Right

Lady Anna

The Last Chronicle of Barset

Later Short Stories

Miss Mackenzie

Mr Scarborough's Family

Orley Farm

Phineas Finn

Phineas Redux

The Prime Minister

Rachel Ray

The Small House at Allington

La Vendée

The Warden

The Way We Live Now

A SELECTION OF   **OXFORD WORLD'S CLASSICS**

THOMAS AQUINAS	Selected Philosophical Writings
GEORGE BERKELEY	Principles of Human Knowledge and Three Dialogues
EDMUND BURKE	A Philosophical Enquiry into the Origin of Our Ideas of the Sublime and Beautiful Reflections on the Revolution in France
THOMAS CARLYLE	The French Revolution
CONFUCIUS	The Analects
FRIEDRICH ENGELS	The Condition of the Working Class in England
JAMES GEORGE FRAZER	The Golden Bough
THOMAS HOBBES	Human Nature and De Corpore Politico Leviathan
JOHN HUME	Dialogues Concerning Natural Religion and The Natural History of Religion Selected Essays
THOMAS MALTHUS	An Essay on the Principle of Population
KARL MARX	Capital The Communist Manifesto
J. S. MILL	On Liberty and Other Essays Principles of Economy and Chapters on Socialism
FRIEDRICH NIETZSCHE	On the Genealogy of Morals Twilight of the Idols
THOMAS PAINE	Rights of Man, Common Sense, and Other Political Writings
JEAN-JACQUES ROUSSEAU	Discourse on Political Economy and The Social Contract Discourse on the Origin of Inequality
SIMA QIAN	Historical Records
ADAM SMITH	An Inquiry into the Nature and Causes of the Wealth of Nations
MARY WOLLSTONECRAFT	Political Writings

A SELECTION OF   **OXFORD WORLD'S CLASSICS**

HANS CHRISTIAN ANDERSEN	Fairy Tales
J. M. BARRIE	Peter Pan in Kensington Gardens and Peter and Wendy
L. FRANK BAUM	The Wonderful Wizard of Oz
FRANCES HODGSON BURNETT	The Secret Garden
LEWIS CARROLL	Alice's Adventures in Wonderland and Through the Looking-Glass
CARLO COLLODI	The Adventures of Pinocchio
KENNETH GRAHAME	The Wind in the Willows
THOMAS HUGHES	Tom Brown's Schooldays
CHARLES KINGSLEY	The Water-Babies
GEORGE MACDONALD	The Princess and the Goblin and The Princess and Curdie
EDITH NESBIT	Five Children and It The Railway Children
ANNA SEWELL	Black Beauty
JOHANN DAVID WYSS	The Swiss Family Robinson

The Oxford World's Classics Website

www.worldsclassics.co.uk

- Information about new titles
- Explore the full range of Oxford World's Classics
- Links to other literary sites and the main OUP webpage
- Imaginative competitions, with bookish prizes
- Peruse *Compass*, the Oxford World's Classics magazine
- Articles by editors
- Extracts from Introductions
- A forum for discussion and feedback on the series
- Special information for teachers and lecturers

www.worldsclassics.co.uk

American Literature

British and Irish Literature

Children's Literature

Classics and Ancient Literature

Colonial Literature

Eastern Literature

European Literature

History

Medieval Literature

Oxford English Drama

Poetry

Philosophy

Politics

Religion

The Oxford Shakespeare